Raj faced his men, hands clenched behind his back.

"Fellow soldiers," he began. A long surf-wave of noise rose from the packed ranks, like a wave over deep ocean. The impact was stunning in the confined space. So was the response when he raised a hand; suddenly he could hear the blood beating in his own ears.

"Fellow soldiers, those of you who've campaigned with me before, in the desert, at Sandoral where we crushed Jamal's armies, in the Southern Territories where we broke a kingdom in one campaign — you and I, we know each other."

This time the sound was white noise, so loud as to be physically painful. He raised his hand again and felt it cease, like his wardog answering to the rein. The raw intoxication of it struck him for a moment; *this* was power. Not the ability to compel, but thousands of armed men who would follow wherever he chose to lead them — because he could *lead*.

remember, you are human, Center's voice whispered. They would follow; and many would die. Duty was heavier than mountains.

"You know what's demanded of you now," he went on.

"For those of you who haven't been in the field with me before, only this: obey your orders, stand by your comrades and your salt. Treat the peasants kindly; we're fighting to give them right governance, not to oppress them. Treat captive foes according to the terms of their surrender, for my honor and yours and the sake of good faith between fighting men.

"And never, never be afraid to engage anyone who stands before you. Because nowhere in this world will you meet troops who are your equal. The Spirit of Man marches with us!"

The shouting started with the former *Squadrones*, the 1st and 2nd Cruisers.

"Hail! Hail! Hail!"

Their deep-chested bellows crashed into the moment of silence after Raj finished speaking. The 5th Descott and the 7th, the Slashers — one by one they rose to their feet, helmets on the muzzles of their rifles.

"RAJ! RAJ! RAJ!"

THE ANVIL

Book III of THE GENERAL

S.M. STIRLING
DAVID DRAKE

BAEN

The General, Vol . III: THE ANVIL

This is a work of fiction. All the characters and events portrayed in this book are fictional, and any resemblance to real people or incidents is purely coincidental.

A Baen Books Original

Baen Publishing Enterprises
P.O. Box 1403
Riverdale, NY 10471

ISBN: 0-671-72171-2

Cover art by Paul Alexander

Maps by Eleanor Kostyk, from sketches by the author

First Printing, June 1993

Distributed by Simon & Schuster
1230 Avenue of the Americas
New York, NY 10020

Printed in the United States of America

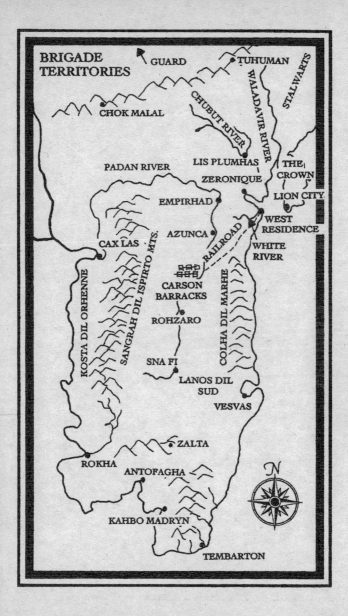

BRIGADE TERRITORIES

GUARD
TUHUMAN
CHOK MALAL
CHUBUT RIVER
WALADAVIR RIVER
STALWARTS
PADAN RIVER
LIS PLUMHAS
ZERONIQUE
THE CROWN
LION CITY
EMPIRHAD
WEST RESIDENCE
AZUNCA
RAILROAD
WHITE RIVER
CAX LAS
KOSTA DIL ORHENNE
SANGRAH DIL ISPIRTO MTS.
CARSON BARRACKS
COLHA DIL MARHE
ROHZARO
SNA FI
LANOS DIL SUD
VESVAS
ZALTA
ROKHA
ANTOFAGHA
KAHBO MADRYN
TEMBARTON

N

CHAPTER ONE

"Raj!" Thom Poplanich blurted.

Raj Whitehall's mouth quirked. "You sound more shocked this time," he said.

The way you look, I am *more shocked*, Thom thought, blinking and stretching a little. There was no physical need; his muscles didn't stiffen while Center held him in stasis. But the psychological satisfaction of movement was real enough, in its own way.

The silvered globe in which they stood didn't look different, and the reflection showed Thom himself unchanged — down to the shaving nick in his chin and the tear in his tweed trousers. A slight, olive-skinned young man in gentleman's hunting clothes, looking a little younger than his twenty-five years. He'd cut his chin before they set out to explore the vast tunnel-catacombs beneath the Governor's Palace in East Residence. The trousers had been torn by a ricocheting pistol-bullet, when the globe closed around them and Raj tried to shoot his way out. Everything was just as it had been when Raj and he first stumbled into the centrum of the being that called itself Sector Command and Control Unit AZ12-b14-c000 Mk. XIV.

That had been years ago, now.

Raj was the one who'd changed, living in the outer — the real — world. That had been obvious on the first visit, two years after their parting. It was much more noticeable this time. They were of an age, but someone meeting them together for the first time would have thought Raj a decade older.

"How long?" Thom said. He was half-afraid of the answer.

"Another year and a half."

Thom's surprise was visible. *He's aged that much in so little time?* he thought. His friend was a tall man, 190 centimeters, broad-shouldered and narrow-hipped, with a swordsman's thick wrists. There were a few silver hairs in the bowl-cut black curls now, and his gray eyes held no youth at all.

"Well, I've seen the titanosauroid, since," Raj went on.

"Governor Barholm did send you to the Southern Territories?"

Raj nodded; they'd discussed that on the first visit. After Raj's victories against the Colony in the east, he was the natural choice.

"A hard campaign, from the way you look."

"No," Raj said, moistening his lips. "A little nerve-racking sometimes, but I wouldn't call it *hard*, exactly."

observe, the computer said. The walls around them shivered. The perfect reflection dissolved in smoke, which scudded away —

— and returned as a ragged white pall spurting from the muzzles of volleying rifles. From behind a court-yard wall, Raj Whitehall and troopers wearing the red and orange neckscarves of the 5th Descott shot down an alleyway toward the docks of Port Murchison. Each pair of hands worked rhythmically on the lever, *ting*, and the spent brass shot backward, *click*, as they thumbed a new round into the breech and brought the lever back up, *crack* as they fired.

There were already windrows of bodies on the pavement: Squadron warriors killed before they knew they were at risk. Survivors crouched behind the corpses of their fellows and fired back desperately. Their clumsy flintlocks were slow to load, inaccurate even at this range; they had to expose themselves to reload, fumbling with powder horns and ramrods, falling back dead more often than not as the Descotter marksmen fired. A few threw the firearms aside with screams of frustrated rage, charging with their long single-edged swords whirling. By some freak one got as far as the wall, and a bayonet punched through his belly. The man fell backward off the steel, his mouth and eyes perfect O's of surprise.

A ball ricocheted from one of the pillars and grazed Raj's buttock before slapping into the small of the back of the officer beside him in the firing line. The stricken man dropped his revolver and pawed blindly at his wound, legs giving their final twitch. Raj shot carefully, standing in the regulation pistol-range position with one hand behind the back and letting the muzzle fall back before putting another round through the center of mass.

"Marcy!" the barbarians called in their Namerique dialect. *Mercy!* They threw down their weapons and began raising their hands. *"Marcy, migo!"* *Mercy, friend!*

Both men blinked as the vision faded — Raj to force memory away, Thom in surprise.

"You brought the Southern Territories back?" Thom said, slight awe in his voice. The *Squadrones* — the Squadron, under its Admiral — had ruled the Territories ever since they came roaring down out of the Base Area a century and a half ago and cut a swath across the Midworld Sea. The only previous Civil Government attempt to reconquer them had been a spectacular disaster.

Raj shrugged, then nodded: "I was in command of the Expeditionary Force, yes. But I couldn't have achieved anything without good troops — and the Spirit."

"Center isn't the Spirit of Man of the Stars, Raj. It's a Central Command and Control Unit from before the Collapse — the Fall, we call it now."

Neither of them needed another set of Center's holographic scenarios to remember what they had been shown. Earth — Bellevue, the computer always insisted — from the holy realm of Orbit, swinging like a blue-and-white shield against the stars. Points of thermonuclear fire expanding across cities . . . and the descent into savagery that followed. Which must have followed everywhere in the vast stellar realm the Federation once ruled, or men from the stars would have returned.

Raj shivered involuntarily. He had been terrified as a child, when the household priest told of the Fall. It was even more unnerving to see it played out before the mind's eye. Worse yet was the knowledge that Center had given him. The Fall was *still* happening. If Center's plan failed, it would go on until there was nothing left on Bellevue — anywhere in the human universe — but flint-knapping cannibal savages. Fifteen thousand years would pass before civilization rose again.

Thom went on: "Center's just a computer."

Raj nodded. Computers were holy, the agents of the Spirit, but Thom's stress on the word meant something different now. Different since he'd been locked in stasis down here, being shown everything Center knew. Nearly four years of continuous education.

"You know what you know, Thom," Raj said gently. "But I know what I know." He shook his head. "We slaughtered the whole Squadron," he went on. *Literally*. "Made them attack us, then shot the shit out of them."

"And how did Governor Barholm react?" Thom asked dryly. By rights, Thom Poplanich should have been Seated on the Chair; his grandfather had been. Barholm Clerett's uncle had been Commander of Residence Area Forces when the last Governor died, however, which had turned out to be much more important.

"Well, he was certainly pleased to get the Southern

Territories back," Raj said, looking aside. That was hard to do inside the perfectly reflective sphere. "The expedition more than paid for itself, too — and that's not counting the tax revenues."

observe, Center said.

— and men in the black uniforms of the Gubernatorial Guard were marching Raj away, while the leveled rifles of more kept Suzette Whitehall and Raj's men stock-still —

— and Raj stood in a prisoner's breechclout and chains before a tribunal of three judges in ceremonial jumpsuits and bubble helmets —

— and he sat bound to an iron chair, as the glowing rods came closer and closer to his eyes —

Raj sighed. "That *might* have happened, yes. According to Center, and I don't doubt it myself. I *was* a little . . . apprehensive . . . about something like that. I'm not any more, the Army grapevine has been pretty conclusive. In fact, when the Levee is held this afternoon, I'm confident of getting another major command."

"The Western Territories?"

"How did you guess?"

"Even Barholm isn't crazy enough to try conquering the Colony. Yet."

"Yes." Raj nodded and ran a hand through his hair. "The problem is, he's probably too suspicious to give me enough men to actually do it."

Thom blinked again. *Raj has changed*, he thought. The young man he had known had been ambitious — dreaming of beating back a major raid from the Colony, say, out on the eastern frontier. This weathered young-old commander was casually confident of overrunning the second most powerful realm on the Middle Sea, given adequate backing. The Brigade had held the Western Territories for nearly six hundred years. They were almost civilized . . . for barbarians. Odd to think that they were descendants of Federation troops stranded in the Base Area after the Fall.

"Barholm," Raj went on with clinical detachment — sounding almost like Center, for a moment — "thinks that either I'll fail —"

observe, Center said.

Dead men gaped around a smashed cannon. The Starburst banner of the Civil Government of Holy Federation draped over some of the bodies, mercifully. Raj crawled forward, the stump of his left arm tattered and red, still dribbling blood despite the improvised tourniquet. His right just touched the grip of his revolver as the Brigade warrior reined in his riding dog and stood in the stirrups to jam the lance downward into his back. Again, and again . . .

"— or I'll succeed, and he can deal with me then."

observe, Center said.

Raj Whitehall stood by the punchbowl at a reception; Thom Poplanich recognized the Upper Promenade of the palace by the tall windows and the checkerboard pavement of the terrace beyond. Brilliant gaslight shone on couples swirling below the chandeliers in the formal patters of court dance; on bright uniforms and decorations, on the ladies' gowns and jewelry. He could almost smell the scents of perfume and pomade and sweat. Off to one side the orchestra played, the soft rhythm of the steel drums cutting through the mellow brass of trumpets and the rattle of *marachaz*. Silence spread like a ripple through the crowd as the Gubernatorial Guard troopers clanked into the room. Their black-and-silver uniforms and nickel-plated breastplates shone, but the rifles in their hands were very functional. The officer leading them bowed stiffly before Raj.

"General Whitehall —" he began, holding up a letter sealed with the purple-and-gold of a Governor's Warrant.

"Barholm doesn't *deserve* to have a man like you serving him," Thom burst out.

"Oh, I agree," Raj said. For a moment his rueful grin made him seem boyish again, all but the eyes.

"Then stay here," Thom urged. "Center could hold you in stasis, like me, until long after Barholm is dust. And while we wait, we can be learning *everything*. All the knowledge in the human universe. Center's been teaching me things . . . things you couldn't imagine."

"The problem is, Thom, I'm serving the Spirit of Man of the Stars. Whose Viceregent on Earth —"

bellevue, Center said.

"— Viceregent on Bellevue happens to be Barholm Clerett. Besides the fact that my wife and friends are waiting for me; and frankly, I wouldn't want my troops in anyone else's hands right now, either." He sighed. "Most of all . . . well, you always were a scholar, Thom. I'm a soldier; and the Spirit has called me to serve as a soldier. If I die, that goes with the profession. And all men die, in the end."

essentially correct, Center noted, its machine-voice more somber than usual. **restoring interstellar civilization on bellevue and to humanity in general is an aim worth more than any single life.** A pause. **more than any million lives.**

Raj nodded. "And besides . . . in a year, I may die. Or Barholm may die. Or the dog may learn how to sing."

They made the *embrhazo* of close friends, touching each cheek. Thom froze again; Raj swallowed and looked away. He had seen many men die. Too many to count, over the last few years, and he saw them again in his dreams far more often than he wished. This frozen un-death disturbed him in a way the windrows of corpses after a battle did not. No breath, no heartbeat, the chill of a corpse — yet Thom lived. Lived, and did not age.

He stepped out of the doorway that appeared silently in the mirrored sphere, into the tunnel with its carpet of bones — the bones of those Center had rejected over the years as it waited for the man who would be its sword in the world.

Then again, he thought, *stasis isn't so bad, when you consider the alternatives.*

"Bloody hell," Major Ehwardo Poplanich said, sotto voce. "How long is this going to take? If I'd wanted to sit on my butt and be bored, I would have stayed home on the estate." He ran a hand over his thinning brown hair.

He was part of the reason that Raj Whitehall and his dozen Companions had plenty of space to themselves on the padded sofa-bench that ran down the side of the anteroom. Nobody at Court wanted to stand *too* close to a close relation of the last Poplanich Governor. Quite a few wondered why Poplanich was with Raj; Thom Poplanich had disappeared in Raj's company years before, and Thom's brother Des had died when Raj put down a bungled coup attempt against Governor Barholm.

Another part of the reason the courtiers avoided them was doubt about exactly how Raj stood with the Chair, of course.

The rest of it was the other Companions, the dozen or so close followers Raj had collected in his first campaign on the eastern frontier or in the Southern Territories. Many of the courtiers had spent their adult lives in the Palace, waiting in corridors like this. The Companions seemed part of the scene at first, in dress or walking-out uniforms like many of the men not in Court robes or religious vestments. Until you came closer and saw the scars, and the eyes.

"We'll wait as long as His Supremacy wants us to,

Ehwardo," Colonel Gerrin Staenbridge said, swinging one elegantly booted foot over his knee. He looked to be exactly what he was: a stylish, handsome professional soldier from a noble family of moderate wealth, a man of wit and learning, and a merciless killer. "Consider yourself lucky to have an estate in a county that's boring; back home in Descott County —"

"— bandits come down the chimney once a week on Starday," Ehwardo finished. "Isn't that right, M'lewis?"

"I wouldna know, ser," the rat-faced little man said virtuously.

The Companions were unarmed, despite their dress uniforms — the Life Guard troopers at the doors and intervals along the corridor were fully equipped — but Raj suspected that the captain of the 5th Descott's Scout Troop had something up his sleeve.

Probably a wire garotte, he thought. M'lewis had enlisted one step ahead of the noose, having made Bufford Parish — the most lawless part of not-very-lawful Descott County — too hot for comfort. Raj had found his talents useful enough to warrant promotion to commissioned rank, after nearly flogging the man himself at their first meeting — a matter of a farmer's pig lifted as the troops went past. The Scout Troop was full of M'lewis's friends, relatives and neighbors; it was also known to the rest of the 5th as the Forty Thieves, not without reason.

Captain Bartin Foley looked up from sharpening the inner curve of the hook that had replaced his left hand. His face had been boyishly pretty when Raj first saw him, four years before. Officially he'd been an aide to Gerrin Staenbridge, unofficially a boyfriend-in-residence. He'd had both hands, then, too.

"Why don't you?" he asked M'lewis. "Know about bandits coming down the chimney, that is."

Snaggled yellow teeth showed in a grin. "Ain't no sheep nor yet any cattle inna chimbley, ser," M'lewis answered in the rasping nasal accent of Descott. "An'

ridin' dogs, mostly they're inna stable. No use comin'
down t'chimbly then, is there?"

The other Companions chuckled, then rose in a
body. The crowd surged away from them, and split as
Suzette Whitehall swept through.

*Messa Suzette Emmenalle Forstin Hogor Wenqui
Whitehall,* Raj thought. *Lady of Hillchapel. My wife.*

Even now that thought brought a slight lurch of
incredulous happiness below his breastbone. She was a
small woman, barely up to his shoulder, but the force
of the personality behind the slanted hazel-green eyes
was like a jump into cool water on a hot day. Seventeen
generations of East Residence nobility gave her slim
body a greyhound grace, the tilt of her fine-featured
olive face an unconscious arrogance. Over her own
short black hair she was wearing a long blond court wig
covered in a net of platinum and diamonds. More
jewels sparkled on her bodice, on her fingers, on the
gold-chain belt. Leggings of embroidered torofib silk
made from the cocoons of burrowing insects in far-off
Azania flashed enticingly through a fashionable split
skirt of Kelden lace.

Raj took her hand and raised it to his lips; they stood
for a moment looking at each other.

A metal-shod staff thumped the floor, and the tall
bronze panels of the Audience Hall swung open. The
gorgeously robed figure of the Janitor — the Court
Usher — bowed and held out his staff, topped by the
star symbol of the Civil Government.

Suzette took Raj's arm. The Companions fell in
behind him, unconsciously forming a column of twos.
The functionary's voice boomed out with trained
precision through the gold-and-niello speaking trumpet:

"General the Honorable Messer Raj Ammenda
Halgern da Luis Whitehall, Whitehall of Hillchapel,
Hereditary Supervisor of Smythe Parish, Descott
County! His Lady, Suzette Emmenalle —"

Raj ignored the noise, ignored the brilliantly-decked crowds who waited on either side of the carpeted central aisle, the smells of polished metal, sweet incense and sweat. As always, he felt a trace of annoyance at the constriction of the formal-dress uniform, the skin-tight crimson pants and gilt codpiece, the floor-length indigo tails of the coat and high epaulets and plumed silvered helmet. . . .

The Audience Hall was two hundred meters long and fifty high, its arched ceiling a mosaic showing the wheeling galaxy with the Spirit of Man rising head and shoulders behind it. The huge dark eyes were full of stars themselves, staring down into your soul.

Along the walls were automatons, dressed in the tight uniforms worn by Terran Federation soldiers twelve hundred years before. They whirred and clanked to attention, powered by hidden compressed-air conduits, bringing their archaic and quite nonfunctional battle lasers to salute. The Guard troopers along the aisle brought their entirely functional rifles up in the same gesture. They ignored the automatons, but some of the crowd who hadn't been long at Court flinched from the awesome technology and started uneasily when the arclights popped into blue-white radiance above each pointed stained-glass window.

The far end of the audience chamber was a hemisphere plated with burnished gold, lit via mirrors from hidden arcs. It glowed with a blinding aura, strobing slightly. The Chair itself stood four meters in the air on a pillar of fretted silver, the focus of light and mirrors and every eye in the giant room. The man enchaired upon it sat with hieratic stiffness, light breaking in metallized splendor from his robes, the bejeweled Keyboard and Stylus in his hands. From somewhere out of sight a chorus of voices chanted a hymn, inhumanly high and sweet, *castrati* belling out the chorus and young girls on the descant:

"He intercedes for us —
    Viceregent of the Spirit of Man of the Stars!
By Him are we boosted to the Orbit of Fulfillment —
    Supreme! Most Mighty Sovereign Lord!
In His hands is the power of Holy Federation Church —
    Ruler without equal! Sole rightful Autocrat!
He wields the Sword of Law and the Flail of Justice —
    Most excellent of Excellencies! Father of the State!
Download His words and execute the Program, ye People —
    Endfile! Endfile! Ennd . . . fiille."

On either side of the arch framing the Chair were golden trees ten times taller than a man, with leaves so faithfully wrought that their edges curled and quivered in the slight breeze. Wisps of white-colored incense drifted through them from the censers swinging in the hands of attendant priests in stark white jumpsuit vestments, their shaven heads glittering with circuit diagrams. The branches of the trees glittered also, as birds carved from tourmaline and amethyst and lapis lazuli piped and sang. Their song rose to a high trilling as the pillar that supported the Chair sank toward the white marble steps; at the rear of the enclosure two full-scale statues of gorgosauroids rose to their three-meter height and roared as the seat of the Governor of the Civil Government sank home with a slight sigh of hydraulics. The semicircle of high ministers came out from behind their desks — each had a ceremonial viewscreen of strictly graded size — and sank down in the full prostration, linking their hands behind their heads. So did everyone in the Hall, except for the armed guards.

The Companions had stopped a few meters back. Now Raj felt Suzette's hand leave his; she sank down with a courtier's elegance, making the gesture of reverence seem a dance. He walked three more steps to the edge of the carpet and went to one knee, bowing his head deeply and putting a hand to his breast — the privilege of his rank, as a general and as one of Barholm's chosen Guards. It *might* have done him some good to have made the three prostrations of a supplicant; on the other hand, that could be taken as an admission of guilt.

You never know, with Barholm, Raj thought. *You never know. Center?*

effect too uncertain to usefully calculate, the passionless inner voice said. After a pause: **with barholm even chaos theory is becoming of limited predictive ability.**

Raj blinked. There were times he *thought* Center was developing a sense of humor. That was obscurely disturbing in its own right. Dark take it, he'd never been much good at pleading anyway. Flickers of holographic projection crossed his vision; Barholm calling the curse of the Spirit down on his head, Barholm pinning a high decoration to Raj's chest —

Cloth-of-gold robes sewn with emeralds and sapphires swirled into Raj's view. The toes of equally lavish slippers showed from under them. A tense silence filled the Hall; Raj could feel the eyes on his back, hundreds of them. *Like a pack of carnosauroids waiting for a cow to stumble,* he thought. Then:

"Rise, Raj Whitehall!"

Barholm's voice was a precision instrument, deep and mellow. With the superb acoustics of the hall behind it, the words rolled out more clearly than the Janitor's had through the megaphone. Behind them a long rustling sigh marked the release of tension.

Raj came to his feet, bending slightly for the ceremonial embrace and touch of cheeks. He was several centimeters taller than the Governor, although they were both Descotters. Barholm had the brick build and dark heavy features common there, but Raj's father had married a noblewoman from the far northwest, Kelden County. Folk there were nearly as

tall and fair as the Namerique-speaking barbarians of
the Military Governments.

The two men turned, the tall soldier and the stocky
autocrat. Barholm's hand rested on his general's
shoulder, a mark of high favor. Behind them the
hidden chorus sang a high wordless note.

"Nobles and clerics of the Civil Government —
behold the man who We call *Savior of the State!*
Behold the *Sword of the Spirit of Man!*" The orator's
voice rolled out again. The chorus came crashing in on
the heels of it:

"Praise him! Praise him! Praise him!"

Raj watched the throng come to their feet, putting
one palm to their ears and raising the other hand to the
sky — invoking the Spirit of Man of the Stars as they
shouted, "Glory, glory!" and "You conquer, Barholm!"

Every one of them would have cheered his summary
execution with equal enthusiasm — or greater.

Suzette's shining eyes met his.

not quite all, Center reminded him. Behind
Suzette the Companions were grinning as they
cheered. **far less than all.**

The cheering died as Barholm raised a hand. "On
Starday next shall be held a great day of rejoicing in the
Temple and throughout the city. For three days
thereafter East Residence shall hold festival in honor
of General Whitehall and the brave men he led to
victory over the barbarians of the Squadron; wine
barrels shall stand at every crossroads, and the government storehouses will dispense to the people. On the
third day, the spoils and prisoners will be exhibited in
the Canidrome, to be followed by races and games in
honor of the Savior of the State."

This time the cheers were deafening; if there was
one thing everyone in East Residence loved, it was a
spectacle. The chorus was barely audible, and the
sound rose to a new peak as Barholm embraced Raj
once more.

"There'll be a staff meeting right after all this play-acting," he said into Raj's ear, his voice flat. "There's the campaign in the Western Territories to plan."

He turned, and everyone bowed low as he withdrew through the private entrance behind the Chair.

So passes the glory of this world, Raj thought. *Death or victory, and if victory —*

observe, Center said. Holographic vision shimmered before his eyes, invisible to any but himself:

It took a moment for Raj to recognize the naked man: it was himself, his face contorted and slick with the burnt fluid of his own eyeballs, after the irons had had their way with them. Thick leather straps held his wrists and ankles splayed out in an X.

The hooded executioners were just fastening each limb to the pull-chain of a yoke of oxen. The crowd beyond murmured, held back by a line of leveled bayonets.

CHAPTER TWO

Governor Barholm stood while the servants stripped off his heavy robes. The Negrin Room dated to the reign of Negrin III, three centuries before; the walls were pale stone, traced over with delicate murals of reeds and flying dactosauroids and waterfowl; there was only one small Star, a token obeisance to religion as had been common in that impious age. The heads of the Ministries were there, and Mihwel Berg as Administrator of the newly-conquered Southern Territories and representative of the Administrative Service; Chancellor Tzetzas, of course; General Klostermann, Master of Soldiers, Bernardinho Rivadavia, the Minister of Barbarians, and Lady Anne Clerett as well, the Governor's wife. She gave Raj a sincere smile as they waited for the Governor to finish disrobing.

There's one real friend at court, he thought. Suzette's friend, actually.

Barholm sat, and the others bowed and joined him.

"Well, messers," he said abruptly, opening the file an aide placed before him. "It's time to deal with the Western Territories and the barbarians of the Brigade who impiously hold the Old Residence, original seat of the Civil Government of Holy Federation — since we've reduced the Southern Territories quite satisfactorily, thanks to the aid of the Spirit of Man of the Stars, and Its Sword, General Whitehall."

There was a murmur of applause, and Raj looked down at his hands. "I had good troops and officers," he said.

"Your Supremacy," Tzetzas said. "We all give praise

to the Spirit" — there was a mass touching of amulets, most of them genuine ancient computer components, in this assembly — "and to our General Whitehall, and to your wise policy, that the barbarian heretics were defeated so easily. Yet I would be remiss in my duties if I failed to point out that the Civil Government is still reeling from the expense of the southern campaign — completed less than a year ago. Which has, in fact, so far served to enrich only the officers involved in the operation."

observe, Center said:

Muzzaf Kerpatik was on the docks in Port Murchison, capital of the reconquered Southern Territories. He was a small dark man from Komar, near the Colonial border; once a merchant and agent of Chancellor Tzetzas, until the latter's schemes had grown too much for even his elastic conscience. Since then he'd proven himself useful to Raj in a number of ways . . . although Raj hadn't known about this one, precisely. He was overseeing the loading of a ship, a medium-sized three-masted merchantman. Bolts of silk were going aboard, and burlap sacks filled with crystals of raw saltpeter, bales of rosauroid hides, and slatted wooden boxes stuffed with what looked like gold and silver tableware. A coffle of women chained neck-and-neck waited to board later: all young and good-looking, some stunningly so, and in the remnants of rich clothing in the gaudy style of the Squadron nobility — families of those barbarian nobles who'd refused to yield to the Spirit of Man of the Stars or missed the amnesty after the surrender, headed for Civil Government slave markets.

Raj thought he could place the time: about a month after the final battle on the docks. It had taken that long, and repeated scrubbings, before the rotting blood stopped drawing crawling mats of flies.

I'd heard about streets running with blood, he

reminded himself. *Never seen it until then.* Vice-Admiral Curtis Auburn had landed ten thousand Squadron warriors on those docks, unaware that the main Squadron host was defeated and Raj in control of the city. Curtis had been lucky enough to be captured almost immediately, but less than one in ten of his men had survived the day.

The vision couldn't be much more than a month after that, because Suzette was riding up and leaning down to examine the checklist in Kerpatik's hand, and both Whitehalls had sailed home when Raj was recalled in quasi-disgrace.

"Should we not pause and recoup our resources?" the Chancellor concluded. "Especially when our internal situation is so delicate."

Due in no small measure to Your Most Blatant Corruptibility, Raj thought ironically. There was a popular East Residence legend that a poisonous fangmouth had once bitten Tzetzas at a garden party; the unfortunate reptile was believed to have died in horrible convulsions within minutes. The Chancellor had raised enormous sums for Barholm's wars and public works projects, and a good deal of it had stuck to his own beautifully manicured fingers.

Raj's expression was blandly respectful and attentive. On the expedition to the Southern Territories, Tzetzas had seen that Raj sailed with weevily hardtack and bunker coal that was half shale; Raj had returned the favor in his last stop in Civil Government territory by exchanging the goods for replacements from Tzetzas's own estates and mines, at full book price.

observe, Center said.

Sesar Chayvez stood before his patron. The plump little man was sweating as Tzetzas sat leafing through the documents in the file before him.

"And here, my dear Sesar, we come to your

signature, right next to that of then-Brigadier White-hall and Mihwel Berg of the Administrative Service, on the bottom of this requisition order. Authorizing the exchange of worthless trash for goods from my estates in Kolobassa District."

His voice was light, even slightly amused. "An exchange which, since the hardtack in question was useful only for pig feed and the coal unsalable in an exporting center like Hayapalco, cost me approximately fourteen thousand gold FedCreds. Not to mention the expenses for repairing estates ruined when Whitehall quartered Skinner mercenaries on them to . . . shall we say, motivate the staff to cooperation."

"Your Most Excellent Honorability," Chayvez said, twining his fingers together.

His eyes flicked around the room, on the cabinets of well-thumbed books, the curios, the restrained elegance of the mosaic floor. Oddly, that was mostly covered with a square of waxed canvas on this visit. He swallowed and forced himself to continue:

"The . . . the hill-bandit of a Descotter occupied my headquarters with troops loyal only to him!" he burst out. "One of his thugs started to *strangle* me with a wire noose until I signed. What could I do?"

"Oh, I can understand your fears," Tzetzas said, waving a deprecatory hand. Chayvez began to relax. "In fact, it isn't the first time that Whitehall and those ruffian Companions of his have caused me substantial trouble. They brutalized a number of my placemen and employees in Komar, when stationed there. Brutalized them so thoroughly — I believe they began to *skin* one of them — that they revealed far, far too much, and I was forced to turn over all my investments in the province to the Chair to avoid serious disfavor."

Barholm had been quite annoyed. The scheme had involved holding up the landgrants usually given to infantry garrison troops, and then pocketing the revenues from the State farms. It might have gone unnoticed if Raj Whitehall hadn't been sent to bolster that particular frontier against the Colony.

Chayvez nodded enthusiastically. "The man is a menace to peace and orderly government, Your Most Excellent Honorability," he said.

"True. You will understand, then."

"Ah . . ." The plump provincial governor hesitated. "Understand, Your —"

"Yes, yes. That I *cannot* have my servants more afraid of Whitehall than of me. I believe his tame thug *began* to strangle you?"

A shadow moved from a corner of the darkened room. It grew into a man, a black man in a long dark robe. Not from one of the highly civilized city-states of Zanj; his tribal scars showed him to be from much farther south and west, from the savannahs of Majinga. The slave was nearly two meters tall, with shoulders like a bull moving beneath the cloth of his *kanzu*. His tongueless mouth gobbled in thick joy as he closed his fingers around the little man's neck and lifted him clear of the floor. Chayvez's arms and legs thrashed for a moment, beating at the boulder-solid form of the black and then twitching helplessly. The massive hands clamped tighter and tighter, closing by increments. When the neck snapped at last the bureaucrat had been still for several minutes. Urine and other fluids dripped to the waxed canvas on the floor.

"Wrap the body, and drop it in an alley," Tzetzas said, in a language quite unlike the Sponglish of civilization. The mute bowed silently and bent to his task as the Chancellor turned up the coal-oil lamp and took another file from the sauroid-ivory holder on his desk.

Raj met Tzetzas's eyes and inclined his head. The Chancellor matched the gesture with one almost as imperceptible and far more graceful.

Barholm explained to Raj: "There's been another outbreak of the anti-hardcopyist heresy down in Cerest. It's nothing serious; just a boil. When you've got a boil on your bum, you lance it and ignore it."

There were shocked murmurs; Raj touched his own amulet, a gold-chased chipboard fragment blessed by Saint Wu herself. "Wasn't that heresy anathematized two centuries ago?" he said.

"Yes, but it's like black plague, always breaking out again," the Governor said. "This time they're taking a new tack; calling circuit diagrams themselves 'false schematics' and corrupted data, not just denouncing allegorical representations. We can't afford trouble in Cerest —"

Raj nodded; a good deal of the capital's grain was shipped from there, and the Tarr Valley was the trade route to the rich tropical lands of the Zanj city-states. Or at least the only route that didn't run through the hostile Colony.

"— so I'm sending a brigade and a Viral Cleanser Sysup to purge their subroutines of heresy for good and all." He shook his square-jawed head; there was more silver in the black hair than Raj remembered. Being Governor was a high-stress occupation too.

observe, Center said.

Blinding sunlight in the main square of Cerest, a prosperous-looking provincial capital. A domed Star Temple, with the many-rayed symbol atop it; the square bulk of a regional Prefect's palace across from it, fountains and arcades all about. A crowd filled most of the open paved space. It moaned as men — and a few women — were led out to a long row of iron posts set deep in the pavement. They shook their heads and refused the offered Headsets, symbolic connection to the Terminals of confession; two spat at the officiating priests. The soldiers hustled them on, supporting as much as forcing. Most of the prisoners' bare feet showed oozing sores where their toenails should have been.

The iron posts were joined in a complete loop by thick copper cables; the ends of the cables disappeared into a wagon-mounted box with an external flywheel belt-driven by the power take-off of a steam haulage engine. As the steel chains bound them to the posts, the prisoners began to sing, a hymn in some thick local dialect Raj couldn't follow. Out in the crowd others took it up, men in the rough brown robes of desert monks, women in the archaic jumpsuits and tunics of Renunciate Sisters, then the ragged *dezpohblado* crowd of town laborers. An officer barked an order and the troops blocking off the execution ground formed, the first rank dropping to one knee, both leveling their rifles.

The belt drive to the generator whined, and a hooded executioner put his hand on a scissor-switch. The Sysup in his gold-embroidered overrobe stood in the attitude of prayer — one hand over his ear, the other stretched up with its fingers making keying motions — and then swept it down. The man in the leather hood matched his gesture with a showman's timing, and blue sparks popped from the dangling cables. The prisoners stopped singing, but they could not scream with the DC current running through their bodies, only convulse against the iron poles.

A rock arched through the air and took one of the soldiers in the mouth. He collapsed backward limply; there was no motion from the others besides a ripple of movement as they closed ranks. They were Regulars, dragoons. . . .

More rocks flew. Raj could see the officer's lips move silently, in a prayer or curse. Then he shouted an order:

"Volley fire!" An endless line of white puffs, and the crowd recoiled, all but those smashed off their feet by the heavy bullets. The soldiers worked the levers of their rifles, reloaded. Another order, and they began to advance in a serried line, bayonets advanced.

Raj blinked. As always, the holographic vision lasted far less time than it seemed. Chancellor Tzetzas was steepling his fingers:

". . . necessary measures, true. Cerest Province is far too valuable to risk."

Especially with what our dear Chancellor makes from the chocolate, torofib and kave monopolies, Raj thought ironically. *And I'll bet he fiddles on the share the fisc is supposed to get.*

probability 97% +/-2%, Center said. **however, total receipts to the fisc have increased while he holds the monopolies, due to volume growth.**

"Still, undertaking another campaign at this time — when, as I mentioned, we have yet to recoup the expenses of the last, well . . ." There was a spare gesture of the long hand.

Mihwel Berg, now Administrator of the Southern Territories, sniffed; he was a mousy little man, and watching him defy Tzetzas was like seeing a sheep turn on a carnosauroid. "Your Excellency, I might point out that all out-of-pocket expenses for the Expeditionary Force have already been recouped, with plunder, sale of prisoners, and other cash receipts alone leaving a surplus of no less than seven hundred fifty-four thousand FedCreds to the fisc. Gold."

Barholm sat straighter, casting a sidelong glance at his Chancellor. That was a considerable sum even by the Civil Government's standards. The Governor might be obsessed with reclaiming the territories lost to the Military Governments centuries ago, but he was keenly aware of financial matters.

"Furthermore, and even without the *invaluable* services which Your Excellency's tax-farming syndicates provide to the fisc, the first six months' revenues from the Southern Territories under Administrative

Services control, annualized, are tenth out of the twenty-two Counties and Territories currently under effective Civil Government control.

"And," Berg went on, warming to his topic, "that does *not* include the revenues from estates confiscated from deceased or captured members of the Squadron — which amount to nearly half of the arable land in the district, if we include the one-third confiscation of Squadron nobles who surrendered before the collapse and, of course, the Admiral's own lands. Ex-Admiral, that is. That revenue alone will double the overall receipts from the Territories, and this is after we deduct lands to be deeded to peasant militia, infantry garrison plots, and estates to support the Church. Furthermore, the Territories have much untapped potential neglected under the Admirals. If our Sovereign Mighty Lord will examine the proposals —"

He slid a package of documents across the table; Barholm untied the ribbon and began riffling through them with interest. Tzetzas's fingers crooked like talons. The Chancellor usually had a say in what reached the Governor's desk, and he valued that power. Governor Barholm was a hard-working administrator, and an enthusiast for useful public works.

"— a railway to the saltpeter mines alone would increase the total yield of the Territories by fifteen percent" — saltpeter was a Chair monopoly, and the deposits south of Port Murchison were the richest in the known world — "besides making economical the copper and zinc deposits there, closed for three generations. There are also irrigation works to be brought back into operation, road repairs . . . Your Supremacy, launching the Expeditionary Force was the most lucrative stroke of policy any Governor has made in two hundred years."

Klosterman pulled at his muttonchop whiskers. "Still, even if the Colony is quiet, I'd not like to take too many troops away from the border," he said. The

Master of Soldiers' last regional field command had been of Eastern Forces. "Ali's no fool, but he's vain, and he's vicious as a starving carnosauroid to boot."

Barholm shrugged. "He may have killed his brother Akbar, but they'll take a while to recover from their civil war."

Good fortune had given the Civil Government four strong Governors in a row, with no usurpations or civil conflicts — the primary reason for its current strength and unprecedented prosperity — but disputed successions were a problem both the Civil Government and the Colony were thoroughly familiar with.

observe, Center said.

A one-eyed man stood among burned-out ruins. Raj recognized him instantly: Tewfik bin-Jamal, son of the late Settler of the Colony, and commander of all his armies. Raj had lost one minor battle to him, and won a major one by a thin margin; and every day in his prayers the general thanked the Spirit of Man for the Colonist superstition that made Tewfik ineligible for the Settler's throne because he lacked an eye.

The stocky, muscular body filled the regulation crimson djellaba with a solid authority, and the Seal of Solomon marked his eyepatch. Officers of the Colonial regulars and black-robed personal mamelukes followed the Muslim general as he stalked through the shattered building. He kicked at a frame of cindered boards; they slid away in ash that drifted ghostly under the bright sun, revealing the warped brass and iron shape of a lathe. Other machines stood amid the ruins, as did the cast-iron poles that had carried the drive shaft from a steam engine.

Tewfik's face was impassive beneath his spired spike-topped helmet, but the grip of his left hand on the plain wired brass hilt of his scimitar was white-knuckled with the effort of controlling his rage. The Colony armed its forces with lever-operated repeating

carbines, and the machine shops that turned them out
were a rare and precious asset. Now there was one less.

He turned; the viewpoint turned with him, staying
behind his left shoulder. Beyond the fallen door-arch
of the factory were more ruins, then intact buildings,
and a long slope down to a great river. Flat roofs and
minarets, smokestacks, towers glinting with colored
tile, narrow twisting streets and irregular plazas around
splashing fountains: Al-Kebir, the capital of the Colony
and the oldest city on Bellevue. Half a dozen huge
bridges crossed the river, and the water was thronged
with lateen-sailed dhows and sambuks, with barges and
rafts and steamboats. Across the river was a burst of
greenery, palms and jacaranda trees, and a great
interlinked pile of low, ornately carved marble buildings taking up scores of hectares before the sprawl of
the city resumed. An endless low rumble carried
through the air, the sound of a million human beings
and their doings, pierced through with the high wailing
call of a muezzin.

The robed men sank to their knees in prayer; Tewfik
waited an instant as his attendants spread a prayer rug
before he bent his head towards the distant holy city of
Sinnar, where the first ships to reach Bellevue had
carried a fragment of the Kaaba from burning Mecca.

When he rose he turned to the man in a civilian
outfit of baggy pantaloons, sash, turban and curl-toed
slippers. At his finger's motion two of the mameluke
slave-soldiers — one blond, one black, both huge men
moving as lightly as cats — stood behind the civilian.
The heavy curved swords in their hands rested lightly
on his shoulders.

"Sa'id —" the man began.

Prince. That much Raj would have known, but as
always Center somehow provided the knowledge that
made the Arabic as understandable as his native
Sponglish.

"Prince," the man went on, "what could we do? Your

brother Akbar's followers came and demanded the finished arms; then the household troops of your brother Ali attacked them. We are not fighting men here."

Tewfik nodded, his hand stroking his beard. "*Kismet*," he said: fate. "When the *kaphar*, the infidels of the Civil Government, slew our father, it was Akbar's fate to reach for power and fail" — and leave his head on a pole before the Grand Mosque — "and yours to repair the damage as quickly as may be. If I thought you truly responsible, I would not threaten."

The manager nodded unconsciously; if Tewfik thought that the staff were dragging their feet, there would have been another set of heads on a pole some time ago.

"How long?" Tewfik asked, his voice like millstones of patience that would grind results out of time and fate by sheer force of will.

"If the Settler Ali, upon whom may Allah shower His blessings, advances the necessary funds, we will be turning out carbines again in six months," he said.

Tewfik's right hand rested on the butt of his revolver. One index finger gestured, and the mamelukes pressed the factory manager to his knees with the blunt back edges of their scimitars. The blades crossed before his neck, ready to scissor through it like a gardener's shears through the stem of a tulip.

"Six months!" the man cried; he ripped open his jacket to bare his breast in token of his willingness to die. "Prince Tewfik, we are adepts of the mechanic arts here, not dervishes or magicians! Machine tools cannot be flogged into obedience — six months and no more, but no less. May I be boiled alive and my children's flesh eaten by wild dogs if I lie!"

"That can be arranged . . . if you lie," Tewfik said somberly. The man met his eyes, ignoring the blades so near his flesh. The Colonist general sighed and signed the swordsmen back.

"There is no God but God, and all things are accomplished according to the will of God. In the name of the Merciful, the Lovingkind, I shall not make you bear the weight of an anger earned elsewhere. Come, my friend; rise, and we will speak of details over sherbert with my staff. Soon the Dar 'as-Salaam will need the weapons. There is a great stirring in the House of War."

Raj nodded. "Ali will wait; a year, maybe two if he has enough sense to listen to Tewfik.

"Still," he went on, "the Brigade's a more serious proposition than the Squadron was. They've been in contact with civilization longer, and they do have a standing army of sorts; plus they've some recent combat experience."

Mostly against the Stalwarts in the north; those were savages, but numerous, vicious and treacherous to a fault.

"Also the Western Territories are bigger — not just in raw area, the population. Not so much desert. I'd say for a really thorough pacification . . . forty thousand troops. Fifteen thousand cavalry."

There were outraged screams around the table. "Out of the question!" Tzetzas barked, startled out of his usual suavity, and Barholm was looking narrow-eyed.

"That *would* be a little large," he said carefully. "Particularly as we're hoping that General Forker won't fight."

"Sovereign Mighty Lord, Forker may not fight but I doubt the Brigade will roll over that easily," Raj said.

"Fifteen thousand is about as much as we could spare," Barholm said, tapping a knuckle against the table to show that the question was closed. "That proved ample for the Squadron. Another battalion or two of cavalry, perhaps more guns."

The ruler leaned back. "Besides that," he went on,

"General Forker —" the Brigade's ruler kept the ancient title, although in the Western Territories it had come to mean *king* rather than a military rank "— is by no means necessarily hostile to the Civil Government. He spent better than a year negotiating for help while he was maneuvering to replace the late General Welf."

"He managed to do that *without* our aid, though, didn't he, Sovereign Mighty Lord?"

The Minister of Barbarians shuffled through his notes. "Yes, General Whitehall. In fact, he showed an almost, well, almost *civilized* subtlety during the negotiations. Then he married Charlotte Welf, the late General's widow. That made his election to the General's position inevitable. We were, I confess, surprised."

"Not as surprised as she was when he murdered her as soon as he was firmly in power," Barholm said, grinning; there was a polite chuckle.

observe, Center said. A brief flicker this time; a woman in her bath. Handsome in a big-boned way, with grey in her long blond hair. She looked up angrily when the maidservant scrubbing her back fled, then tried to stand herself as she saw the big bearded men who had forced their way through the door. They wore bandanas over their lower faces, but the short fringed leather jackets marked them as Brigade nobles. Water fountained over the marble tiles of the bathroom as they gripped her head and held it under the surface. Her feet kicked free, thrashing at the water for a moment until the body slumped. Then there were only the warriors' arms, rigid bars down through the floating soapsuds. . . .

Chancellor Tzetzas raised an index finger in stylized horror. "Quite a gothic tale," he said. "Barbarians."

Raj nodded. "We can certainly spare seventeen or eighteen thousand men," he went on. "The Southern Territories are fairly quiet, all they need is garrison forces to keep the desert nomads in order. The military

captives sent here will more than replace any draw-
down. We could ship a substantial force into Stern
Island —" that was directly north of the reconquered
Southern Territories, and the easternmost Brigade
possession "— and . . . hmm. Don't we have some
claim to it, being heirs to the Admirals? It would make
a first-rate base for an advance to the west."

The Minister of Barbarians leaned forward.
"Indeed," he said, pushing up his glasses. "The former
Admiral of the Squadron — ex-Admiral Auburn's
predecessor's father — married Mindy-Sue Grakker, a
daughter of the then General of the Brigade, and
acquired extensive estates on Stern Island as her
dower. The Brigade commander there has refused to
turn over their administration to the envoys I sent."

"Excellent," Barholm said, leaning back and steepling his fingers. He might be of Descotter descent,
but his fine-honed love of a good, legally sound swindle
was that of a native-born East Residencer. "From
there, we can exploit opportunity as it offers."

"Your Supremacy," Raj said in agreement. "We
could move most of the troops up from the Southern
Territories? They're surplus to requirements, closer,
and I know what they can do. It's going on for summer
already, so there's a time factor here."

"Ah," Barholm said, giving him a long, considering
look. "Well, General, I'll certainly withdraw some of
those forces . . . but it wouldn't be wise to make it
appear that you have some sort of private army of your
own. People might misunderstand. . . ."

Raj smiled politely. "Quite true, Your Supremacy,"
he said.

*Everyone understands that it's the Army that
disposes of the Chair, in the end.* Three generations
without a *coup* would be something of a record — if
you didn't count Barholm's own uncle Vernier Clerett.
He hadn't shot his way onto the Chair, strictly
speaking, but he *had* been Commander of East

Residence Forces when the last Poplanich Governor died of natural causes.

Probably natural causes.

"We certainly don't want people to think *that*," Raj went on. "Half the cavalry battalions from the Southern Territories, then?" Barholm nodded.

"And the infantry?"

"By all means," the Governor said, slightly surprised Raj would mention the subject. Infantry were second-line troops, and Barholm saw little difference between one battalion of them and another.

You haven't seen what Jorg Menyez and I can do with them, Raj thought. "I'll draw the other cavalry battalions and artillery from the Residence Area Forces Group, then?"

Barholm signed assent. "I'll be sending along my nephew Cabot Clerett, as well," the Governor said. "He's been promoted to Major, in command of the 1st Residence Battalion." A Life Guards unit; they rarely left East Residence, but many of the men were veterans from other outfits. Of late, most had been from the Clerett family's estates. "It's time Cabot got some military experience."

Raj spread his hands. "At your command, Your Supremacy. I've met him; he seems an intelligent young officer, and doubtless brave as well." A subtle reminder: *don't blame me if he stops a bullet somewhere.*

"Indeed. Although I hope he won't be seeing *too* much action." An equally subtle hint: *he's my heir.* Barholm was nearly forty, and he and Lady Anne hadn't produced a child in fifteen years of marriage. The Governor smiled like a shark at the exchange. It was worth the risk, since he had other nephews. A Governor didn't *have* to be a general, but he did need enough field experience for fighting men to respect him. He continued:

"In fact — this doesn't go beyond these walls — we

are, in fact, negotiating with General Forker right now. The, ah, death of Charlotte Welf . . . Charlotte Forker . . . aroused considerable animosity among some of the Brigade nobles. Particularly since Forker's main claim to membership in the Amalson family was through her. General Forker has expressed interest in our offer of a substantial annuity and an estate near East Residence in return for his abdication in favor of the Civil Government."

"He may abdicate, Sovereign Mighty Lord, but I doubt his nobles would all go along with it. The Brigade monarchy is elective within the House of Theodore Amalson. The Military Council includes all the adult males, and they can depose him and put someone else in his place."

"That," Barholm said dryly, "is why we're sending an army."

Raj nodded. "I'll get right on to it, then, Your Supremacy, as soon as the Gubernatorial Receipt —" a general-purpose authorizing order "— comes through. It'll take a month or so to coordinate . . . by your leave, Sovereign Mighty Lord?"

CHAPTER THREE

How utterly foolish of him, Suzette Whitehall thought, looking at the petitioner.

Lady Anne leaned her head on one hand, her elbow on the satinwood arm of her chair. Her levees were much simpler than the Governor's, as befitted a Consort. Apart from the Life Guard troopers by the door, only a few of her ladies-in-waiting were present, and the room was lavish but not very large. A pleasant scent of flowers came through the open windows, and the sound of a *gitar* being strummed. The cool spring breeze fluttered the dappled silk hangings.

Despite that, the Illustrious Deyago Rihvera was sweating. He was a plump little man whose stomach strained at the limits of his embroidered vest and high-collared tailcoat, and his hand kept coming up to fiddle with the emerald stickpin in his lace cravat.

Suzette reflected that he probably just did not connect the glorious Lady Anne Clerett with Supple Annie, the child-acrobat, actress and courtesan. He'd only been a client of hers once or twice, from what Suzette had heard — even then, Anne had been choosey when she could. But since then Rihvera had been an associate of Tzetzas, and *everyone* knew how much the Consort hated the Chancellor. To be sure, the men who owed Rihvera the money he needed so desperately — to pay for his artistic pretensions — were under Anne's patronage. Not much use persuing the claims in ordinary court while she protected them.

" . . . and so you see, most glorious Lady, I petition only for simple justice," he concluded, mopping his face.

"Illustrious Rihvera —" Anne began.

A chorus broke in from behind the silk curtains. They were softer-voiced, but otherwise an eerie reproduction of the Audience Hall singers, castrati and young girls:

> *"Thou art flatulent, Oh Illustrious Deyago*
> *   Pot-bellied, too:*
> *Oh incessantly farting, pot-bellied one!"*

Silver hand-bells rang a sweet counterpoint. Anne sat up straighter and looked around.

"Did you hear anything?" she murmured.

Suzette cleared her throat. "Not a thing, glorious Lady. There's an unpleasant smell, though."

"Send for incense," the Consort said. Turning back to Rihvera, her expression serious. "Now, Illustrious —"

> *"You have a toad's mouth, Oh Illustrious Deyago —*
> *   Bug eyes, too:*
> *Oh toad-mouthed, bug-eyed one!"*

This time the silver bells were accompanied by several realistic croaking sounds.

I wonder how long he can take it? Suzette thought, slowly waving her fan.

His hands were trembling as he began again.

"Are you well, my dear?" Suzette asked anxiously, when the petitioners and attendants were gone.

"It's nothing," Anne Clerett said briskly. "A bit of a grippe."

The Governor's lady looked a little thinner than usual, and worn now that the amusement had died away from her face. She was a tall woman, who wore her own long dark-red hair wound with pearls in defiance of Court fashion and protocol. For the rest she wore the tiara and jewelled bodice, flounced silk split skirt, leggings and slippers as if she had been born to them. Instead of working her way up from acrobat and child-whore down by the Carnidrome and the Circus . . .

Suzette took off her own blond wig and let the spring breeze through the tall doors riffle her sweat-dampened black hair. It carried scents of greenery and flowers from the courtyard and the Palace gardens, with an undertaste of smoke from the city beyond.

"Thank you," she said to Anne. There was no need to specify, between them.

Anne Clerett shrugged. "It's nothing," she said. "I advise Barholm for his own good — and putting Raj in charge *is* the best move." She hesitated: "I realize my husband can be . . . difficult, at times."

He can be hysterical, Suzette thought coldly as she smiled and patted Anne's hand. In a raving funk back during the Victory Riots, when the city factions tried to throw out the Cleretts, Anne had told him to run if he wanted to, that she'd stay and burn the Palace around her rather than go back to the docks. That had put some backbone into him, that and Raj taking command of the Guards and putting down the riots with volley-fire and grapeshot and bayonet charges to clear the barricades.

He can also be a paranoid menace. Barholm was the finest administrator to sit the Chair in generations, and a demon for work — but he suspected everyone except Anne. Nor had he ever been much of a fighting man, and his jealousy of Raj was poisoning what was left of his good sense on the subject. A Governor was theoretically quasi-divine, with power of life and death over his subjects. In practice he held that power until he used it too often on too many influential subjects, enough to frighten the rest into killing him despite the dangerous uncertainty that always followed a coup. Barholm hadn't come anywhere near that.

Yet.

"Besides," Anne went on, "I stand by my friends."

Which was true. When Anne was merely the tart old Governor Vernier Clerett's nephew had unaccountably married, the other Messas of the Palace had barely noticed her. Except in the way they might have scraped something nasty off their shoes. Suzette had had better sense than those more conventional gentlewomen. *Or perhaps just less snobbery*, she thought. Her family was as ancient as any in the City; they had been nobles when the Cleretts and Whitehalls were minor bandit chiefs in the Descott hills. They had also been quite thoroughly poor by the time she came of age, years before she met Raj. The last few farms had been mortgaged to buy the gowns and jewels she needed to appear at Court.

"You'll be accompanying Raj again?" Anne asked.

"Always," Suzette replied.

Anne nodded. "We both," she said, "have able husbands. But even the most able of men —"

"— needs help," Suzette replied. The Governor's Lady raised a fingertip and servants appeared with cigarettes in holders of carved sauroid ivory.

"*I* may need help with young Cabot," Suzette said. "He hasn't been much at Court?"

"Mostly back in Descott," Anne said. "Keeping the Barholm name warm on the ancestral estates."

Which were meagre things in themselves. Descott was remote, a month's journey on dogback east and north of the capital, a poor upland County of volcanic plateaus and badlands. Mostly grazing country, with few products beyond wool, riding dogs and ornamental stone. Its other export was fighting men, proud poor backland squires and their followings of tough *vakaros* and yeoman-tenant ranchers, men born to the rifle and saddle, to the hunt and the blood feud. Utterly unlike the tax-broken peons of the central provinces. Only a fraction of the Civil Government's people lived there, but one in five of the elite mounted dragoons were Descotters. Most of the rest came from similar frontier areas, or were mercenaries from the *barbaricum*.

It was no accident that Descotters had held the Chair so often of late, nor that the Cleretts were anxious to keep first-hand ties with the clannish County gentry.

"Seriously, my dear," Anne went on, "you should look after young Clerett. He's . . . well, he's been champing at the bridle of late. Twenty, and a head full of romantic yeast and old stories. Quite likely to get himself killed — which would be a *disaster*. Barholm, ah, is quite attached to him."

The two women exchanged a look; both childless, both without illusion. It said a great deal for Anne that Barholm had not put her aside for not giving him an heir of his body, which was sufficient cause for divorce under Civil Government law.

"I'll try to see he comes back, Anne," Suzette said. *If possible*, she added to herself with clinical detachment. Romantic, ambitious young noblemen were not difficult to control; she had found that out long before her marriage. They could also be trouble when serious business was in question, such as the welfare of one's husband.

"I'm sure you can handle Cabot," Anne said. That sort of manipulation was skill they shared, in their somewhat different contexts.

"Poplanich needn't come back," Anne went on.

She smiled; Suzette looked away with a well-concealed shudder. A strayed ox might have noticed an expression like that on the last carnosauroid it ever saw.

Anne clapped her hands. "Thom Poplanich, Des Poplanich — Ehwardo would make a beautiful matched set, don't you think?" And it would leave the Poplanich *gens* without an adult male of note. Thom's grandsire had been a well-loved Governor.

"Des was a rebel," Suzette said carefully. "I've never known what happened to Thom. Ehwardo is a loyal officer."

"Of course, of course," Anne said, chuckling and giving Suzette's hand a squeeze.

Raj's wife chuckled herself. *There's irony for you*, she thought: *I really don't know what happened to Thom.*

Raj simply refused to discuss it, and he had been *different* ever since he came back from the tunnels they'd gone exploring in; the ground under East Residence was honeycombed with them. Suzette might have advised quietly braining Thom Poplanich and leaving him in the catacombs, as a career move and personal insurance — except that she knew that Raj would never have considered it. He had changed, but not like that.

You are too good for this Fallen world, my angel, she thought toward the absent Raj. *It is not made for so honorable a knight.*

Then Lady Clerett's mouth twisted; she covered it with her palms and coughed rackingly.

"*Anne!*" Suzette cried, rising.

"It's nothing," she said, biting her lip. "Go on; you'll have a lot to do. Just a cough, it'll pass off with the spring. I'll deal with it."

There was blood on her fingers, hidden imperfectly by their fierce clench. Suzette made the minimal bow and withdrew.

"*At the narrow passage there is no brother, no friend,*" she quoted softly to herself. And no allies against some enemies.

"So, what do we get?" Colonel Grammeck Dinnalsyn said; the artillery specialist had seen to his beloved 75mm field-guns, and was ready to take an interest in the less technical side of the next Expeditionary Force.

Raj and the other officers were riding side-by-side down the Main Street of the training base, in the peninsula foothills west of East Residence.

"5th Descott Guards, 7th Descott Rangers, 1st Rogor Slashers, 18th Komar Borderers, 21st Novy Haifa Dragoons, and Poplanich's Own from the cavalry in the Southern Territories. And all the infantry and guns."

"Jorg will be glad to get out of the Territories. Spirit

knows I went and Entered my thanks when I got the movement orders for home. Not much happening there now, except that idiot they sent to replace you giving damn-fool orders."

"*I'm* glad we're getting Jorg. Nobody else I know can handle infantry like Menyez."

Most commanders didn't even try; infantry were used mainly for line-of-communication and garrison work in the Civil Government's army. Jorg had had his own 17th Kelden Foot and the 24th Valencia under his eye since Sandoral, nearly four years ago. Raj and he had done a fair bit with the other infantry battalions during the Southern Territories campaign, and Menyez had been working them hard in the year since.

"Then for the rest of the cavalry, the 1st and 2nd Residence Battalions, the Maximilliano Dragoons, and the the 1st and 2nd Mounted Cruisers from here." The artillery specialist raised an eyebrow at the last two units.

"Yes, they're *Squadrones* — but coming along nicely. Full of fight, too — for some reason they don't seem to resent our beating the *scramento* out of them. Quite the contrary, if anything. Eager to learn from us."

observe, Center said:

"Right, ye horrible buggers," the sergeant said. "Who's next?"

He spun the rifle in his hands into a blurring circle; the bayonet was fixed, but with the sheath wired on to the blade. The three big men lying wheezing or moaning on the ground before the stocky Descotter had been holding similar weapons. The company behind them were standing at ease in double line with their rifles sloped. None of them looked very enthusiastic about serving as an object lesson. . . .

"Ten-'hut!" the sergeant said. The men were stripped to their baggy maroon pants, web-belts and boots; he was wearing in addition the blue sash,

sleeveless grey cotton shirt and the orange-black
checked neckerchief of the 5th Descott. "Now, we'uns
will *learn* how to *use* the fukkin' baynit, *won't we?*"

"YES SERGEANT!" they screamed.

"Right. Now, yer feints to the eyes loik *this*, then
gits 'em in t'belly loik *this*. Baynit forrard! An' *one* an'
two —"

"Eager to learn from *you*, sir, actually," the artilleryman said. He was a slim man of medium height, with
cropped black hair and black eyes and pale skin, and a
clipped East Residence accent.

"It soothes their pride," he went on. "They call you
an Avatar of the Spirit. And what man needs to be
ashamed of yielding to the Spirit Incarnate? Not that
I'd dispute you the title myself."

Raj frowned, touching his amulet. Dinnalsyn's casual
blasphemy was natural enough for a man born in the
City, but Raj had been raised in the old style back
home on Hillchapel. A soldier of the Civil Government
was also a warrior of the Spirit.

**the ex-squadron personnel are undergoing
transference**, Center said. **a common psychological phenomenon. and technically, you are an
avatar.**

"Speak of the Starless," Dinnalsyn noted.

He and Raj turned their dogs aside as a battalion
came down the camp street toward them. First the
standard-bearer, the long pole socketed to a ring in his
right stirrup; the colors were furled in a tubular leather
casing. Then the trumpeters and drummers, four of
them. The battalion commander and his aides in a
clump with the Senior Sergeant of the unit; then the
six hundred and fifty men in column-of-fours, each
man an exact three meters from the stirrups of his
squadmates on either side, half a length from the dog
before and behind. Triple gaps between companies,
the company pennant, signaler and commander in

each. An Armory rifle in a scabbard before each right knee, and a long slightly-curved saber strapped to the saddle on the other side.

The men wore round bowl-helmets with neckguards of chainmail-covered leather, dark-blue swallowtail coats, baggy maroon pants tucked into knee boots. Their mounts were farmbreds, Alsatians and Ridgebacks for the most part, running to a thousand pounds weight and fifteen hands at the shoulder. Everything regulation and by the handbooks, all the more startling because the men wearing the Civil Government uniforms were *not* the usual sort. The predominant physical type near East Residence was short, slight, olive to light-brown of skin, with dark hair and eyes. There were regional variations; Descotters tended to be darker than the norm, square-faced and built with barrel-chested solidity, while men from Kelden County were taller and fairer. The troops riding toward Raj and his companion were something else again. Big men, most near Raj's own 190 centimeters, and bearded in contrast to local custom; fair-skinned despite their weathered tans, many with blond or light-brown hair.

The massed thudding of paws and the occasional whine or growl was the only sound until a sharp order rang out:

"2nd Mounted Cruisers — eyes *right*. General salute!"

A long rippling snap followed, each man's head turning sharply and fist coming to breast as they passed Raj. Raj returned the gesture. It was still something of a shock to see the barbarian faces in Army uniform. Even more shocking to remember the Squadron host as it tumbled toward the line of Civil Government troops; individual champions running out ahead to roar defiance, shapeless clots around the standards of the nobles, dust and movement and a vast, shambling chaos . . .

The ones who couldn't learn mostly died, he thought.

The battalion commander fell out and reined in beside them as the column passed in a pounding of pads on gravel and a jingle of harness.

"Bwenya dai, seyhor!" Ludwig Bellamy said.

He's changed too, Raj thought, offering his hand after the salute. Karl Bellamy had surrendered early to the Expeditionary Force, to preserve his estates and because he hated the Auburns who'd usurped rule of the Squadron. His eldest son had gone considerably further; the chin was bare, and his yellow hair was cut bowl-fashion in the manner of Descotter officers. His Sponglish had always been good in a classical East Residence way — tutors in childhood — but now it had caught just a hint of County rasp, the way a man of the Messer class from Descott would speak. Much like Raj's own, in fact. The lower part of the Squadron noble's face was still untanned, making him look a little younger than his twenty-three years.

"Movement orders?" he said eagerly. "I'm taking them out —" he tossed his head in the direction of his troops "— on a field problem, but we could —"

"*No es so hurai*," Raj said, fighting back a grin: *not so fast*. He had been a young, eager battalion commander himself, once. "But yes, we're moving. Stern Isle, first. You'll get a chance to show your men can remember their lessons in action."

"They will," Bellamy said flatly. Some of the animation died out of his face. "They remember — they know courage alone isn't enough."

They should, Raj thought.

Their families had been settled by military tenure on State lands as well, which meant their homes were here too.

"And they're eager to prove themselves."

Raj nodded; they would be. Back in the Southern Territories, they'd been members of the ruling classes, the descendants of conquerors. Proud men, anxious to earn back their pride as warriors.

I just hope they remember they're soldiers, *now,* Raj thought. Putting a *Squadrone* noble in command had been something of a risk; he'd transferred a Companion named Tejan M'Brust from the 5th Descott to command the 1st Cruisers. So far the gamble with the 2nd seemed to be paying off.

Aloud: "Speaking of education, Ludwig, I've got a little job for you, to occupy the munificent spare time a battalion commander enjoys. We'll be having a young man by the name of Cabot along."

The fair brows rose in silent enquiry.

"Cabot Clerett. I'd like —"

CHAPTER FOUR

The longboat's keel grounded on the beach, grating through the coarse sand. Sailors leaped overside into water waist-deep, heaving their shoulders against the planks of its hull. Raj vaulted to the sand, ignoring the water that seethed around his ankles, and swept his wife up in his arms to carry her beyond the high-tide mark. Miniluna and Maxiluna were both up, leaving a ghostly gloaming almost bright enough to read by even as the sun slipped below the horizon.

Offshore on a sea colored dark purple with sunset the fleet raised spars and sails tinted crimson by the dying light. Three-masted merchantmen for the most part, with a squadron of six paddle-wheel steam warships patrolling offshore like low-slung wolves. Not that there was much to fear; unlike the Squadron, who had been notable pirates, the Brigade didn't have much of a navy. Some of the smaller transports had been beached to unload their cargo; the rest were offloading into skiffs and rowboats. Except for the dogs. The half-ton animals were simply being pushed off the sides, usually with a muzzle on and fifteen or twenty men doing the pushing. Mournful howls rang across the water; once they were in, the intelligent beasts followed their masters' boats to shore. A few who'd been on the expedition against the Squadron jumped in on their own.

As Horace did; the big black hound shook himself, spattering Raj and Suzette equally, flopped down on the sand, put his head on his paws and went to sleep. Raj laughed; so did Suzette, close to his ear. He jumped when she ran her tongue into it briefly.

"When you start ignoring me even when I'm in your arms, my sweet . . ." she said playfully.

He walked a few steps further and set her down. In linen riding clothes, with a Colonial-made repeating carbine across her back, Suzette Whitehall did not look much like a Court lady of East Residence. But she looked very good to Raj, very good indeed.

"To work," he said.

The camp was already fully set up, a square half a kilometer on a side and ringed with ditch and earth embankment, and a palisaded firing-step on top. Within was a regular network of dirt lanes, flanked by the leather tents of the eight-man squads which were the basic unit of the Civil Government's armies. Broader lanes separated battalions, each with its Officer's Row and shrine-tent for the unit standards. The two main north-south and east-west roadways met in the center at a broad open plaza, and in the center of *that* was a local landowner's house that would be the commander's quarters. Dog-lines to the east, thunderous with barking as the evening mash was served; artillery park to the west; stores piled up mountainously under tarpaulins . . .

"Nicely done," he said. *And exactly where we camped the last time*, he thought, with a complex of emotions.

A tall rangy man with a moustache pulled up — on a riding steer, an unusual choice of mount. Especially for a man with a Colonel's eighteen-rayed gold and silver star on his helmet and shoulder-patches. The inflamed rims around his eyes told why; he was violently allergic to dogs. A misfortune for a nobleman, disastrous for a nobleman set on a military career. Unless one was willing to settle for the despised infantry, of course. Probably a source of anguish to the man, but extremely convenient to Raj Whitehall. Usually the infantry got the dregs of the officer corps, men without either the connections or the ability to make a career in the mounted units.

"Nicely done, Jorg," Raj repeated, as the man swung down.

Jorg Menyez shrugged. "We've had three days, and I haven't wasted the time we spent stuck down there around Port Murchison," he said. They saluted and exchanged the *embhrazo*. "Spirit of *Man* but I'm glad to be out of the Territories! Nineteen battalions of infantry, five of cavalry, thirty guns, reporting as ordered, *seyhor!* And campgrounds, food, fodder and firewood for five more battalions of mounted troops." He bowed over Suzette's hand. "Enchanted, Messa."

"Excellent," Raj said again. It was *damned* good to have subordinates you could rely on to get their job done without hand-holding. That had taken years.

indeed, Center said.

"All the old *kompaydres* together again, eh?" Jorg went on, as Gerrin Staenbridge came up. His eyes widened slightly as Ludwig Bellamy joined them, dripping.

"Sinkhole," the ex-member of the Squadron said, and sneezed.

"Make that sixty field guns, now," Grammek Dinnalsyn noted. "We brought another thirty, and some mortars. They may be useful."

"Staff meeting at dinner," Raj said. He toed Horace in the flank. "Up, you son of a bitch."

The hound sighed, yawned and stretched before rising.

"To fallen comrades," Bartin Foley said, rising and offering the toast as junior officer present. The remainder were battalion commanders and up, two dozen men who would form the core of the Western Territories Expeditionary Force from this day on. Plus the Honored Messer Fidal Historiomo, the head of the Administrative Department team who would handle civil control, but he had been notably quiet.

"Fallen comrades," the others replied, raising their

wineglasses as the servants cleared away the desserts
which had followed the roast suckling pig and vegetables.

Raj rose in his turn. "Messers, the Governor!"

"The Governor!" Then they all stood. "To victory!"
At that the wineglasses went cascading out the tall glass
doors which stood open around three sides of the
commandeered villa's dining room. A mild curse from
one of the sentries followed the tinkle and crash of
shattering crystal. A louder one followed, from his
NCO.

The ladies withdrew in a flutter of fans and
lace-draped headdresses; ladies by courtesy, for the
most part, of course. Except Suzette, and she stayed.
Nobody looked surprised at that, except possibly Cabot
Clerett, and *he* had been looking at her with a
sandbagged expression all evening as she teased him
gently out of shyness. The servants set out liqueurs and
kave, and withdrew.

Raj rose and walked to a map-board on an easel that
had probably served the local squire's daughter when she
dabbled in watercolors, before the Civil Government
armada landed. Now it held a tacked map of Stern Isle, a
blunt wedge shape of about thirty thousand square
kilometers. The bottom of the wedge pointed south, and
the Expeditionary Force was encamped on the northern
coast. It was an excellent map; the Civil Government's
cartographic service was one of its major advantages over
its barbarian opponents. Center could give him more
data, in any form it pleased . . . although some of it was a
thousand years old, the time-lag since Bellevue's
surveillance satellites had died.

Silence fell as he took up a pointer. "All right,
messers," he said quietly. "Most of you have campaigned with me before; those who haven't, know my
reputation."

Which was why there had been a flurry of resigna-
tions and shifts of posting among the commands of
units assigned to him. The first time he'd led an army

in the field he'd broken one in six officers out of the service before the campaign even started. This time there had been plenty of officers volunteering for the slots opened; in fact, there had been duels and massive bribery to get *into* the Expeditionary Force. That had not happened the first time, out on the eastern frontier. The type who *wanted* to join a field force under Raj Whitehall's command presented their own problems, of course.

Better to be forced to restrain the fiery war-dog than prod the reluctant ox, he thought, and went on:

"Let me sketch out the general situation. We have eleven thousand Regular infantry, about seven thousand Regular cavalry, since some of the battalions are overstrength, and about a thousand tribal auxiliaries. Mostly mounted. Including six hundred Skinners, who will be useful while there's fighting and a *cursed* nuisance the rest of the time." There were a few chuckles at that. "The Skinners will join us when and if we move to the mainland — leaving them on this island for any length of time would wreck it.

"The Brigade territories have a total population of about thirty million." Less than a third what the Civil Government did, but still a vast number for thirty-one battalions to attack. "Of those, the overwhelming majority are civilians."

Worshippers of the Spirit of Man of the Stars, and closely related to the population of the Civil Government proper. In theory, they — more importantly, the landowners, priests and merchants among them — would be on the invaders' side.

"One and a half million are *Brigaderos*. Unlike the late unlamented Squadron, the Brigade has a regular army, besides the private retainers of noblemen — some of whom have whole regiments, by the way. Fifty thousand of the General's troops are under arms at any one time; they have a system of compulsory service. Another two hundred thousand can be called out at need, not counting mercenaries — and all of them will have *some* military experience. The Brigade has strong enemy tribes on its northern frontiers, and most of their standing army has seen action.

"Furthermore," he went on, "also unlike the Squadron, the Brigade troops are *not* armed with flintlock smoothbores." Raj nodded to the orderlies standing in the back of the room. The men laid half-a-dozen long muskets on the table among the kave-cups.

"An external percussion cap fits under the hammer," he said, as the officers examined the enemy weapons. "It's loaded with a paper cartridge and a hollow-base pointed bullet, from the muzzle. Two rounds a minute, but the extreme range is up to a thousand meters. Note the adjustable sights. At anything under six hundred meters, it's man-killing accurate against individual targets. The *Brigaderos* are landed men, mostly, even those who aren't full-time soldiers. They like to hunt, and most of them are crack shots."

Which was more than could be said of the Civil Government force, especially the infantry, even after more than a year under Jorg Menyez' training.

Cabot Clerret stirred. Like his uncle, he was a square-faced, barrel-chested man. Unlike him he had the weathered look of an outdoorsman despite being in his twenties.

"The Armory rifle fires at better than six rounds a minute," he said. "Twelve, in an emergency."

"I'm aware of that, Major Clerett," Raj replied dryly. A flush spread under the natural olive brown of the younger man's skin. Suzette leaned close to whisper in his ear, and he relaxed again.

"However, it means we're not going to be able to stand in full sight and shoot them down outside the effective range of their weapons, the way we did with the *Squadrones*. Nor can we count on them simply rushing at us head-on, like a bull at a gate. They're barbarians and will fight like barbarians —"

They'd better, he added to himself, *or Center or not we're fucking doomed*

"— but they won't be *that* stupid."

observe, Center said.

Rat-tat-tat beat the drum. The line of blue-coated Civil Government infantry stretched across the fields, wading through the waist-high wheat and leaving trampled desolation behind them. The battalion colors waved proudly ahead of the serried double rank of bayonets; officers strode before their units, sabers sloped over their shoulders. Sun glinted on edged steel, hot and bright. Shells went by overhead with a tearing-canvas sound, to burst in puffs of dirty-white smoke and plumes of black earth at the edge of the treeline ahead. Apart from the shelling and the crunching, rustling sound of the riflemen's passage, the battlefield was silent.

Then malignant red fireflies winked in the shadow of the trees. Thousands of them, through the offwhite smoke of black powder rifles. Men staggered and fell down the Civil Government line, silent or screaming and twisting. The Armory rifles jerked up in unison in response to shouted orders and volley-fire crashed out; then the bayonets leveled and the men charged forward with the colors slanting down ahead of them. More muzzle flashes from the treeline and the snake-rail fence that edged it, again and again, winking through the growing cloud of powder smoke and tearing gaps in the advancing line. It wavered, hesitated — trapping itself in the killing zone, caught between courage and fear.

Raj blinked. The audience was still attentive; it had only been a few seconds, and men were used to Raj Whitehall's peculiar moments of introspection. Night had fallen, and glittering six-winged insects flew in through the opened windows to batter themselves against the coal-oil lanterns along the pillastered wall.

"— so we have two problems, tactical and operational." *I get the strategic worries.*

"Tactically, we're going to have to make use of our strong points. Artillery, and we've twice the guns a force this size usually does. The Armory rifle's higher rate of fire and, even more important, the fact that it can be loaded lying down. Field entrenchments wherever possible; you'll note the number of shovels which have been issued. You'll also note that the cavalry have been ordered to hang their sabers from the saddle, not their belts. The cult of cold steel is strictly for the barbs, messers — I want nobody to forget that.

"Our true advantage is our discipline and maneuverability; and that applies to tactics *and* operations. I intend to move fast, keep the enemy off balance, and never fight except at a time *and* place of my own choosing. I need to know — *must* know that my orders will be obeyed with speed and precision *and* common sense, at all times. Against an enemy with respectable weapons and reasonable organization who outnumbers us eight or more to one, we cannot afford to lose a battle, we cannot afford to lose even a major *skirmish* . . . and since we can't possibly win a war of attrition, we can't be excessively cautious, either. Is that clear?"

Nods, and a few uncomfortably thoughtful faces. "Good." *Because it's all right if the* men *think I'm invincible, but the* Spirit *help us if you do.*

With Center whispering in his mind's ear, he was unlikely to fall victim to that illusion himself. Occasional doubts about his own sanity were another matter. Night sweats when he thought about the Spirit having a direct link to his own grimy soul were part of it, too — although come to think of it, *everyone* had a Personal Computer, according to orthodox doctrine.

"Which brings us," he went on, balancing the pointer with an end in each palm, "to Stern Isle. I regard this as

in the nature of a training exercise — assuming that the
negotiations with the Brigade leaders fail and we have to
conquer the mainland. Because, gentlemen, if we can't
take this island from the Brigade with dispatch, then
we'd cursed well better blow our own brains out and
send the troops home before we do *real* damage to the
Civil Government.

"According to the Ministry of Barbarians' files and
Colonel Menyez' scouting reports" — collated and
interpreted by Center — "there are about twelve
thousand *Brigaderos* males of military age on the
island. No more than three thousand are actual
professional fighting men, including those in the
service of individual nobles. We'll snap the rural nobles
and their retainers up with mobile columns. I want you
messers to pay particular attention to perfecting
movement from battalion to company columns and
from column into line-of-battle in any particular
direction. The enemy are fairly slow at that, and we'll
need any advantage we can get.

"We'll then move the main body of the army south"
— he traced the route across the center of the island
— "to the provincial capital at Wager Bay. The city
itself shouldn't be much of a problem; the enemy
doesn't have enough men to hold the walls."

He flipped the map, revealing another of Wager Bay
itself. Over it Center painted a holographic diagram,
rotating it to show different angles. Raj blinked back to
the flat paper his officers would see. The city was a C
with the open end pointing south at the ocean, around
a harbor that was three-quarters of a circle.

"Wager Bay; most of the island's trade goes through
here. About forty thousand people, virtually none of
them *Brigaderos*. So, no problem . . . except for the
fortress."

His pointer tapped the irregular polygon which
topped the hill closing the east flank of the harbor. Raj
had memorized schematic drawings of all the major

fortresses within the Civil Government, and quite a few without. Center amplified that knowledge with three-dimensional precision. Deep stone-lined moats all around and a steep drop to the shingled beaches on the water side where an arc of cliffs fronted the sea. Low-set modern walls of thick stone and earthwork behind the moats, built to withstand siege guns. They mounted scores of heavy built-up smoothbore guns, able to sweep the bay. Bastions and ravelins, outworks giving murderous crossfire all along the landward side, a smooth sloping approach with neither cover nor dead ground.

"We're certainly not going to take *that* with a rush. But take it we must, and soon."

observe, Center said.

— and ships sailed into Wager Bay, their blunt wooden bows casting back plumes of white spray from blue ocean; whitecaps glittered across the broad reach of the harbor. There was a stiff breeze, enough to belly out the brown canvas of the sails and snap the double lightning flash flag of the Brigade from every masthead. The decks were black with troops, dozens of ships, thousands of men.

A Civil Government steam ram came butting through the waves, water flinging back in wings from the steel beak just below the surface at its bows, frothing away from the midships paddle-boxes. Black coal smoke streamed from its funnel, and five more rams followed behind. Behind them the city rose from the waterside in whitewashed and pastel-colored tiers, its tile roofs glowing in the sun. The fortress on its headland was built of dun-colored rock, squatting like a coiled dragon on the heights. No cannon fired from the water could reach that high, and the walls were broad and squat and sunken behind their ditch, built to resist fire from guns far heavier than the converted fieldpieces the rams carried on their decks.

Guns as heavy as the ones mounted in the fort's casements. The first of them boomed like distant thunder, a long rolling sound that echoed from the cliffs and the facing buildings across the bay. The sound of the shell passing was like thick sailcloth ripping, tearing the sky. A long plume of smoke with a red spark at its heart blossomed from the bay-side wall of the fortification. The forty-kilogram cast-iron cannonball was a trace of blurr in the air, and then a fountain of spray near one of the rams. The ships ignored the shot — the ranging shot, it must be — and kept on toward the Brigade transports a kilometer away. Their formation began to open out, as each steamship picked a target and fell out of line behind the leading vessel. A whistle screeched a signal, and the flat huff*chuff* of their engines blatted louder as they went to ramming speed.

Staccato thunder rolled across Wager Bay. *BOOM-BOOM-BOOM-BOOM* as the cannon fired one after another at two-second intervals, then *bambambam-bambambambmmmm* — as the echoes slapped back and forth across the water. The whistling shriek of the projectiles was a dimuendo under the coarser sounds of the discharge. Suddenly the warships were moving amid a forest of waterspouts, dozens of them . . . except for the two ships that were struck.

The heavy cannonballs had been fired from mounts over a hundred meters above sea level. They were plunging almost vertically downward when they struck the plank decks of the ships. They went through the inch-thick decking without slowing perceptibly, sending lethal foot-long splinters of wood spinning like shrapnel accross both flush decks.

One ship was struck near the stern. Some of the splinters flicked through the vision slit of the sheet-iron binnacle that was raised and bolted about the wheel and slashed the face off the steersman there. His convulsing body spun the wheel, but the ship was already turning so rapidly that it heeled one paddle almost out of the water; the cannonball had snapped and jammed the underdeck chains that connected wheel to rudder. The captain clinging to the bridge that crossed the hull between the paddle boxes could only watch in horrified fascination as the vessel's ram drove at full speed into the hull of the warship next to it — aimed with an accuracy no deliberate skill could have equalled. He was flung high by the impact, an instant before the steel tip of the ram gashed open the steamer's boiler. Beams, bodies and pieces of machinery fountained skyward.

The other ship hit by plunging fire had been struck amidships; its paddles froze in their boxes as the boiler rang and flexed and cracked along a rivet-line. Superheated steam flooded the tween-decks spaces, scalding men like lobsters in a pot. Water from the boiler shell cascaded down onto the glowing-hot coal fires in the brick furnaces beneath. It exploded into steam. That and the sudden flexing as ceramic shed heat into the water ripped the iron frames of the firebrick ovens apart like the bursting charge of a howitzer shell, sending them into the backs of the screaming black gang as they ran for the ladders. It also ripped ten meters of hull planking loose from the composite teak-and-iron frame of the warship; the vessel stopped dead in the water, heeled, and began to sink level as seawater gurgled into the engine room.

The cannon began to fire again, more slowly this time, and a little raggedly with the different reloading speeds of their crews. Another ship was struck, this time twice by rounds that crashed straight through the decking and deflected off major timbers to punch out through the hull below the waterline.

One of the warships turned back; the captain reversed one paddle-wheel and kept the other at full ahead, and the vessel spun about in almost its own length. The lead ram plunged forward into the midst of the Brigade ships. They were backing their sails to try and steer clear of it, but the Civil Government warship pirouetted with the same swift-turning grace that its sister had shown in fleeing. Cannon spoke from the bow as it lunged for the flank of a transport, and cannister chopped the *Brigaderos* warriors along the near rail into a thrashing chaos. Then the whole transport surged away as the steel beak slammed home below the waterline.

Just before it struck, the Civil Government ram had backed its paddles, trying to pull the beak free. This time the heavy sailing transport rocked back down too quickly, and its weight gripped the steel of the underwater ram, pushing the warship's bow down until water swirled across its decks. Brigade marksmen picked themselves up and crowded to the rail, or swarmed into the rigging to sweep the steamer's decks.

Beyond, the rest of the relief force sailed forward to anchor under the fort's walls, protected by its guns, and men and supplies began to swarm ashore.

observe, Center said, and the scene changed:

— to night. Dark, with both moons down and only the stars lighting the advancing men. They moved silently up the long slope toward the landward defences of Fort Wager, carrying dozens of long scaling ladders and knotted ropes with iron grapnel hooks. Silent save for the click of equipment and breathing, and the crunch of hobnailed boots on the coarse gravel soil beneath them.

Arc lights lit along the parapet with a popping crackle and showers of sparks. Mirrors behind them reflected the light into stabbing blue-white beams that paralyzed the thousands of advancing troops as thoroughly as the carbide lanterns hunters might use to jacklight a hadrosauroid. Less than a second later, nearly a hundred cannon fired at once, from the main fort wall, from the bastions at the angles and from the triangular ravelins flung out before the works. Many of the guns were of eight-inch bore, and they were firing case-shot, thin tin sheets full of lead musket balls. Multiple overlapping bursts covered every centimeter of the approaches, and most of the Civil Government troops vanished like hay struck by a scythe-blade. . . .

"We'll deal with the fortress when we come to it," Raj concluded. Acid churned in his stomach. "In the meantime, it's an early day tomorrow. Gerrin, you'll take half the 5th Descott and the 2nd Cruisers —"

"You think too much, my darling," Suzette whispered in the dark.

"Well, Starless Dark take it, *somebody* has to," he mumbled, with an arm thrown over his eyes. The bedroom was dark anyway, and the arm could not block out the visions Center sent; nor the images his own mind manufactured.

They've got artesian water and supplies for a year in there, he thought. *How —*

"I can't tell you how to take the fort," Suzette said. "But you'll think of a way, my heart. Right now you need your sleep, and you can't sleep until you stop thinking for a while," Suzette's voice said, her voice warm and husky in the darkness, her fingers cool and unbearably delicate, like lacivious butterflies. "That I *can* do."

And for a while, thought ceased.

CHAPTER FIVE

"Surely 'tis brave to be a king, And ride in triumph through Persepolis," Bartin Foley quoted to himself.

"Ser?" his Master Sergeant said.

"Nothing," the young officer replied; it was unlikely that the NCO would be interested in classical Old Namerique drama.

He bowed left and right and waved to the cheering citizens of Perino. Sprays of orange-blossom and roses flew through the air, making the dogs of the 5th Descott troopers behind him bridle and curvette; two hundred men and a pair of field-guns followed at his heels, less those fanning out to secure the gates and the warehouses. Perino was a pleasant little town of flat-roofed pastel-colored houses sloping down to a small but snug harbor behind a breakwater, and backed by lush vineyards and sulphur-mines in the hills. The walls were old-fashioned, high narrow stone curtains, but the inhabitants hadn't shown any particular desire to hold them against the Civil Government anyway — even the few resident *Brigaderos* had mostly been incoherent with joy when they realized the terms allowed them to retain their lives, personal liberty, and some of their property.

The town councilors had been waiting at the open gates, barefoot and with ceremonial rope nooses around their necks in symbol of surrender. The clergy had been out in force, too, spraying holy water and incense — orthodox clergy, of course, not the Spirit of Man of This Earth priests of the heretical Brigade cult, who were staying prudently out of sight — and a chorus of children of prominent families singing a hymn of welcome. One of them was riding on his saddlebow at the moment, in point of fact, held by the crook of his left arm. She was about eight, flushed with joy and waving energetically to friends and relatives; the wreath of flowers in her hair had come awry.

"Stop wriggling," he mock-growled under his breath. "That's an order, soldier."

The girl giggled, then looked at his hook. "Can I touch it?" she said.

"Careful, it's sharp," he warned.

Children weren't so bad, after all. For that matter, he was the father of two himself, or at least had a fifty-fifty chance of being their father. It wasn't something he had expected so soon, not being a man much given to women. He grinned to himself; you couldn't exactly say he'd saved Fatima from a bunch of troopers bent on gang-rape and revenge for a foot in the testicles and an eye nearly gouged out, back at the sack of El Djem. More in the nature of the Arab girl insisting on being rescued, when she came running out ahead of the soldiers and swung him around bodily by the equipment-belt. It had been Gerrin who talked the blood-mad trooper with the bayonet in his hand into going elsewhere, with the aid of a couple of bottles of *slyowtz*; he'd wanted Bartin to get used to women, since he'd have to marry and beget for the family honor, someday.

Somehow the girl had kept up with them during the nightmare retreat from El Djem after Tewfik mousetrapped the 5th Descott and wiped out the other battalion with them; and she helped him nurse the wounded Staenbridge back to health in winter-quarters outside Sandoral. She'd been pregnant, and Gerrin — whose wife back home in Descott was still childless, despite twice-yearly duty-inspired visits — had freed her and adopted the child. Both children, now.

"Did you kill him with your sword?" the awestruck child went on with bloodthirsty enthusiasm, after touching the hook with one finger. They were nearly to the town plaza. "The one who cut off your hand."

"Possibly," Bartin said severely.

Actually, it had been a pom-pom shell, one of the last the enemy fired in the battle outside Sandoral. That had been right after he led the counterattack out of the command bunker, past the burning Colonist armored cars. Probably the enemy gun-crew had been slaughtered as they tried to get back to the pontoon bridge across the Drangosh.

Who can tell? he thought. There had been so many bodies that day; dead ragheads, all sizes and shapes, all dead; dead Civil Government soldiers too, piled in the trenches. Bartin Foley had been on a stretcher travelling back to the aid station in town.

"Right, we'll —" he began to the NCO beside him.

Crack. The bullet went overhead, far too close. *Crack. Crack. Crack.* More shots from the building to his left — the heretic Brigaderos church, it must be fanatics, holdouts.

Someone was screaming; a lot of people were, as the crowd scattered back into the arcades. The child whimpered and grabbed at him. Foley kicked his left leg over the saddle and vaulted to the ground.

"Take cover!" he shouted. "Return fire! Lieutenant Torridez, around and take them from the rear."

Armory rifles crackled, their sounds crisper than the Brigaderos' muskets. Foley dashed to the arcade opposite, his dog following in well-trained obedience; the officer shoved the girl into the arms of a matron with a lace mantilla who was standing quietly behind a pillar — unlike most of the civilians, who were running and shrieking and exposing themselves to the ricochets that whined off the cobblestones and the stucco of the buildings around the square. Without pausing he ran around the other side of the pillar and back into the square, pulling free the cut-down shotgun he wore in a holster over his right shoulder.

"Stay!" he ordered the animal. Then: "Follow me, dog-brothers!" A fat lead slug from an enemy musket plucked at the sleeve of his jacket as he ran, opening it as neatly as a tailor's scissors, and then he was in the shadow of the church portico.

A dozen troopers and an NCO were close behind him; the rest of the detachment were circling 'round behind the building, or returning fire on the roof and upper story from behind watering-troughs, treetrunks, overturned carts or their own crouching dogs. Bullets spanged and sparked off the stone overhead, and sulfur-smelling gunsmoke drifted down the street past the trampled flowers and discarded hats that the crowds had been waving a moment before.

Idiots, he thought. Sniping from a bell-tower; downward shots were difficult at best, and stood no chance of hitting another man *behind* your target.

"One, two, *three!*" he said.

Two of the troopers blasted the lock; metal whined across the colored tile of the portico, and someone shouted with pain. Foley ignored him, ignored everything but the tight focus that pulled everything into crystalline clarity in a tunnel ahead of him. They smashed through the tall olivewood doors of the barbarian church. He'd closed his eyes for just a second, and the gloom inside didn't blind him. A long room with wooden benches and a central aisle, leading up to an altar with the blue-and-white globe that the heretics substituted for the rayed Star of the true faith. Reliquaries along the walls under small high windows, holding the bones of saints or holy computer equipment from before the Fall.

And men coming down the stairs at either far corner of the room; evidently somebody had had a rush of intelligence to the head, a few minutes too late. Ten men, the leader in the blue jumpsuit and ear-to-ear tonsure of the Earth Spiritist clergy.

Foley took stance with his left arm tucked into the

small of his back and the coach gun leveled like a huge pistol. *Whump*, and the hate-filled face of the Brigadero priest disappeared backward in a blur of red that spattered over the whitewashed walls. Buckshot shattered glass and peened off silver and gold around the altar; the Earth-Sphere tumbled in fragments to the floor. The massive recoil jarred at his leather-strapped wrist, and he let it carry the weapon high before gravity dropped it back on target. Two of the enemy returned the fire, the only ones with loaded muskets; one had been reloading, and his shot sent the iron ramrod he'd forgotten to remove spearing across the church to lance into a bench like a giant arrow. Neither hit anything, not surprising since they were snapshooting in a darkened room. The bullet thudded into wood.

Another man leaping over the dead priest, charging down the aisle with clubbed musket. *Careful*, a corner of Foley's mind thought. *Long musket, big man. Three-meter swing*. He waited, you were never too close to miss, and fired the left barrel of the coach gun into his belly. *Whump* again, and the man folded backward a meter, sprawling in a puddle of thrashing limbs and blood and intestines that spilled out through the hole the buckshot ripped. A swordsman leaped forward with his long single-edged broadsword raised; Foley threw the coach gun between his feet, and the man tripped — as much on the body fluids that coated the slick marble floor as the weapon. His blade clanged off the young officer's hook; then he spasmed and died as he tried to rise, the point of the hook going *thock* into the back of his skull.

Muzzle flashes strobed from around Foley, the troopers with him firing aimed rounds toward the stairwells. The last Brigadero tumbled, the revolvers falling from his hands before he could shoot.

Foley put a boot on the shoulder of the dead man before him and freed his hook with a grunt of effort. Overhead, on the second floor, came another crash of

Armory rifles; screams, a spatter of individual rounds, then Torridez' shout:

"Second story and tower clear, sir!"

Foley took a long breath, and another; a band seemed to be locked around his chest. His throat was raw, but he knew from experience that taking a drink from his canteen would make him nauseous if he did it before his muscles stopped their subliminal quivering. The air stank of violent death, shit and the seaweed smell of blood and wet chopped meat, all underlain by decades of incense and beeswax from the church. It was a peculiarly repulsive variation on the usual battlefield stench.

Join the Army and see the world; then burn it down and blow it up, he thought with weary disgust. His aide picked up the coach gun and wiped it clean with his bandana.

"Cease fire!" Foley called out the door as he flicked the weapon open and reloaded from the shells in his jacket pocket; that was a knack, but you learned knacks for doing things if you lost a hand. "Cease fire!"

Soldiering wasn't a safe profession, but he didn't intend to die from a Civil Government bullet fired by accident. The plaza had the empty, tumbled look of a place abandoned in a hurry — although, incredibly, some civilians were drifting back already, even with the last whiffs of powder smoke still rising from the gun muzzles.

"Torridez?"

"Sir," the voice called down from overhead. "I've got men on the roofs, the whole area's under observation. Looks like it was only these barbs . . . their families are in the back rooms up here. Couple of men prisoner."

"Keep them under guard, Lieutenant," Foley called back. "Post lookouts at vantage points from here to the town wall. Sergeant, get me the *halcalde* and town councilors back here, and —"

A man came running down the arcade before the

town hall, with several others chasing him. He was a Brigadero by the beard and short jacket; the pursuers looked like prosperous townsmen, in sashes and ruffled shirts and knee-breeches with buckled shoes. All of them had probably been standing side by side to greet him fifteen minutes ago.

"You! You there!" he called sharply, and signed to a squad seeing to their dogs.

The would-be lynch mob skidded to a halt on the slick brown tiles of the covered sidewalk as crossed rifles swung down in their path and the dogs growled like millstones deep in their chests; the Brigadero halted panting behind them. He blanched a little as Foley came up, and the young man holstered his coach gun over his shoulder and began dabbing at his blood-speckled face with his handkerchief.

"You've nothing to fear," he said, cutting off the man's terrified gabble. "Corporal," he went on, "my compliments to Senior Lieutenant Morrsyn at the gate, and I want redoubled guards on all Brigadero houses; they're to fire warning shots if mobs approach, and to kill if they persist."

He glanced around; the woman he'd handed off the child to was still pressed tightly into the reverse of her pillar, standing with the girl between her and the stone to protect the child from both sides.

Sensible, Foley thought. "You know her family?" he said.

"My cousins," the woman said quietly.

Foley followed her well enough, the Spanjol of the western provinces was closely related to his native Sponglish, unlike the Namerique of the barbarians . . . although he spoke that as well, and Old Namerique and fair Arabic.

"Take her home. You, trooper — escort these Messas." He stepped over the back of his crouching dog, and the animal rose beneath him. "Now, where the *Dark* are those —

The *halcalde* — Mayor, the word was *alcalle* in Spanjol — and the councilors came walking gingerly back into the plaza a few minutes later, as if it were unfamiliar territory. They shied from the bodies laid out before the Brigade church, and the huddle of prisoners.

As they watched, troopers of the 5th were shaking loose the lariats most of them carried at their saddle-bows and tossing them over limbs of the trees that fringed the plaza. Others pushed the adult males among the prisoners under the nooses; most of them were silent, one or two weeping. One youngster in his mid-teens began to scream as the braided leather touched his neck. Foley chopped his hand downward. The troopers snubbed their lariats to their saddlehorns and backed their dogs; the men rose into the air jerking and kicking. Nobody had bothered to tie their hands. One managed to get a grip on the rawhide rope that was strangling him, until two of the soldiers grabbed his ankles and pulled. Others tied off the ropes to hitching-posts.

Foley waited until the bodies had twitched into stillness before turning his eyes on the town notables. His dog bared its teeth, nervous from the smell of blood and taking its cue from its rider's scent; he ran a soothing hand down its neck. An irritable snap from a beast with half-meter jaws was no joke, and war-dogs were bred for aggression.

"Messers," he said. "You realize that by the laws of war I'd be justified in turning this town over to my troops to sack? I have a man dead and four badly wounded, after you yielded on terms."

The *halcalde* was still wearing the noose around his neck; he touched it, a brave man's act when a dozen men swung with bulging eyes and protruding tongues not a dozen meters from where he stood.

"The responsibility is mine, *seynor*," he said, in the lisping western tongue. "I did not think even Karl

Makermine would be so foolish . . . but let my life alone answer for it."

Foley nodded with chill respect. "My prisoners —" he began; a long scream echoed from the church, as if on cue. "My prisoners tell me this was the work of the heretic priest and his closest followers. Accordingly, I'm inclined to be merciful. Their property is forfeit, of course, along with their lives, and their families will be sold. The rest of you, civilian and Brigaderos, will have the same terms as before — *except* that I now require hostages from every one of the fifty most prominent families, *and* the Brigaderos of Perino are to pay a fine of one thousand gold FedCreds within twenty-four hours. On pain of forfeiture of all landed property."

Some of the heretics winced, but the swinging bodies were a powerful argument; so were the Descotter troopers sitting their dogs with their rifles in the crook of their arms, or standing on the rooftops around the square.

"Furthermore, I'm in a hurry, messers. The supplies I specified —" to be paid for with chits drawn on the Civil Government, and you could decide for yourself how much they were really worth "— had better be loaded and ready to go in six hours, or I won't answer for the consequences. *Is that clear?*"

He watched them walk away before he rinsed out his mouth and then drank, the water tart with the vinegar he'd added. Another old soldier's trick.

"I should have gone into the theatre," he muttered.

"Tum-ta-*dum*," Antin M'lewis hummed to himself, raising the binoculars again. The air was hot and smelled of dust and rock, coating his mouth. He spat brownly and squinted; with the wind in their favor, there wasn't much chance of being scented by the enemy's dogs.

There wasn't much ground cover here, in the center of the island. The orchards and vineyards that clothed the narrow coastal plain to the north, the olive groves further inland, had given way to a high rolling plateau. In the distant past it had probably been thinly forested with native trees; a few Terran cork-oaks were scattered here and there, each an event for the eyes in the endless bleakness. Most of it was benchlands where thin crops of barley and wheat were already heading out, interspersed with erosion-gullies. There were no permanent watercourses, and the riverbeds were strings of pools now that the winter rains were over.

The manor houses which dotted the coastlands were absent too; nobody lived here except the peon serfs huddled into big villages around the infrequent springs and wells. Like the grain, the profits would be hauled out down the roads to the port towns, to support pleasant lives in pleasant places far away from here. Flowing downhill, like the water and topsoil and hope.

Pleasant places like Wager Bay, which was where the long column ahead of him was heading, southeast down the road and spilling over onto the fields on either side in milling confusion. Dust smoked up from it, from the hooves of oxen and the feet of dogs and servants, and from the wheels of wagons and carriages.

"There goes t' barb gentry," M'lewis muttered to himself, adjusting the focusing screw.

Images sprang out at him; the heraldic crest on the door of a carriage drawn by six pedigree wolfhounds, household goods heaped high on an ox-wagon. Armed men on good dogs, in liveries that were variations on a basic gray-green jacket and black trousers; some were armored lancers, others with no protection save lobster-tail helmets, and all were armed to the teeth. He saw one with rifle-musket, sword, mace, lance and two cap-and-ball revolvers on his belt, two more thrust into his high boots, and another pair on the saddle. He made an estimate, scribbled notes — he had been a literate watch-stander even before he met Raj Whitehall and managed to hitch his fortunes to that ascending star.

Behind him, a man whispered. One of the Forty Thieves, a new recruit from back home.

"D'ye think we'll git a chanst at t'women?"

A soft chuckle answered him. "Chanst at t'gold an' siller, loik."

M'lewis leopard-crawled backward, careful not to let the morning sun catch the lenses of his binoculars. The metalwork on the rifle slung across his elbows had been browned long ago and kept that way.

"Ye'll git me boot upside yer head iff'n ye spook's 'em," he said with quiet menace.

"Ser," the man whispered, and shut up.

M'lewis' snaggled, tobacco-stained teeth showed; he might not be messer-born, but by the *Spirit* he could make this collection of gallows-bait obey. Not least because the veterans had spent the voyage vividly describing all the booze, cooze and plunder they'd gotten in the last campaign to the recruits. He looked along the northeast-trending ridge that hid most of his command. The dogs hidden in the gully behind him were difficult to spot amid the tangled scrub, even knowing where to look. Most of the men were invisible even to him, spread out with nearly a hundred meters between each pair. He slid down to the brown dusty pebbles of the gully bottom; a little water glinted as his feet touched.

"Cut-nose, Talker," he called, very softly. There was a trick to pitching your voice so it carried just so far and no further. One of the many skills his father had lessoned him in, with a heavy belt for encouragement.

Two other men crawled backward out of a thicket, then stepped down from rock to rock, raising no dust. Cut-nose had lost most of his to a knife when he tried to sell a saddle-dog back to the man he stole it from, which was an example of the unwisdom of drinking in bad company; he was a second cousin of M'lewis, and looked enough like him to be a brother. Talker was huge, taller than a *Squadrone* and broad with it. A bit touched, perhaps — he'd pass up lifting a skirt or a purse to kill — but he knew his business.

And he was devoted to Raj, in his way. Where Messer Raj led, death followed.

"Here. Git thisshere t' the Messer, an' tell him. Quiet an' fast."

"Is this report completely reliable, sir?" Ludwig Bellamy asked.

Raj and Gerrin Staenbridge looked at him, blinking with almost identical expressions of surprise. Raj held out a hand to stop Gerrin from speaking, asking himself:

"Why would you doubt it?"

"Ahh —" Bellamy cleared his throat. "Well, this man M'lewis, he *was* a bandit. A man like that — how can we be sure he didn't take the easy way out and go nowhere near the enemy? Men steal because it's easier than working, after all."

Both the older men grinned, not unkindly. Raj gripped him companionably on the shoulder for an instant; Gerrin forbore, since he'd noticed his touch made the ex-*Squadrone* nervous.

"Oh, M'lewis was a bandit, all right — it's virtually hereditary, where he comes from," Raj explained. "It's just . . . well, he was a bandit in my home County."

Gerrin chuckled. "And if you think stealing sheep from Descotters is an easy living, Major . . . let's put it this way, I don't know any better preparation for hostile-country reconnaissance."

Bellamy smiled back. "If you say so, sir." He turned his attention to the map. "What are your plans, General?"

Raj looked up. Four companies of the 5th Descott, only half the unit since it was at nearly double strength, the whole of the 2nd Cruisers, and four guns; the dogs were crouched resting, and the men mostly squatting beside them. A few were watering their animals, drinking from their own canteens, or enjoying a cigarette. There was little shelter on this scorched plain, none at the dusty crossroads where they had halted. Nearly a thousand men, more than enough . . .

"Let me hear your plan, Major Bellamy," he said formally.

The younger man halted in mid-swallow, lowering the canteen and looking up sharply. Raj met his gaze with bland impassiveness, and Ludwig nodded once.

"Sir." He traced the line of the road with his finger. "Two thousand fighting men, according to the report. Say six thousand people in all, proceeding at foot pace. Hmmm . . . we don't summon them to surrender?"

Raj shook his head. Most of these were from the western end of the island, around the towns of Perino and Sala. He'd sent out flying columns to round up those willing to give in without a fight, promising to spare the lives, personal liberty and one-third of the landed wealth of anyone on the Brigade rolls who'd swear allegiance to the Civil Government. These Brigaderos ahead had heard the terms and decided to make for Wager Bay and the illusory security of its walls instead. Showing too much mercy was as bad as too little; he didn't need Center to show him the endless revolts he would face behind his lines, if men thought they could defy him and get amnesty for it. He had seventeen thousand troops to conquer a country of half a million square kilometers, full of fortified cities and warlike men. Best to begin as he meant to go on.

"They've had their chance," he said.

"Well, then," Bellamy nodded. "We don't want any of the men to get away even as scattered individuals; they might make it to Wager Bay. That column has to go *here*. They're not going to get wheeled vehicles across this ravine without using the bridge. We could —"

Henrik Carstens looked back over his shoulder. The

dust-clouds were growing larger, three of them — one to either side of the road, one on it. *About four, maybe five clicks*, he decided, and a couple of hundred mounted men each at least. Distances were deceptive in these bare uplands, what with the dry air and heat-shimmer. Coming up fast, too; they were going to reach the column of refugees well before they crossed the bridge. Nothing it could be but enemy cavalry. He cursed tiredly and blinked against the grit in his bloodshot blue eyes, fanning himself with his floppy leather hat. Sweat cooled for a second in the thinning reddish hair of his scalp, then the sun burned at his skin and he put it back on. The helmet could wait for a moment, he needed his brains functioning and not in a stewpot.

It was a pity. The bridge would have made a perfect spot for a rearguard to hold them off while the families and transport reached Wager Bay, or at least got within supporting distance of the patrols operating out of the city.

Of course, Captain of Dragoons Henrik Carstens would have ended up holding that rearguard anyway. He hawked and spat dust into the roadway. A man lived as long as he lived, and not a day more. Forty-five was old for someone who'd been in harm's way as often as he had, anyway. His battered pug-nosed face set, jaw jutting out under a clipped beard that was mostly gray.

The problem was that now he couldn't just hold a defensive line. The open wheatfields were no barrier to men on dogback, or even to field guns, not anywhere short of the bridge over the Trabawat. He'd have to maneuver to hold the enemy off the refugees long enough for them to get over the bridge.

And damn-all to maneuver with, he thought.

A hundred of the fan Morton family retainers, whom he'd managed to lick into some sort of shape since he signed on here. He'd expected a Stern Isle noble's household to be a good place for a nice quiet retirement, Stardemons eat his soul for a *fool*. The rest were fairly numerous, but they were odds-and-sods, household troopers more like guards and overseers than soldiers. Pinchpenny garrisons from here and there thrown in. *None* of them were worth the powder to blow them away! Carstens was from the northwest part of the Brigade territories, where many of the folk were pure-bred Brigade and only serfs spoke Spanjol. Hereabouts, some so-called unit brothers barely knew enough Namerique for formal occasions. To his way of thinking, even the Brigade members on the Isle were little better than natives.

His employer included. Fortunately Jeric fan Morton was in Wager Bay on business when the alert came, and his wife was worth two of him for guts and brains. Between them, she and Carstens had gotten most of the household out before the *grisuh* cavalry arrived, and the neighbors too.

"Gee-up, Jo," he said; the brindled Airedale bitch he rode took her cues from balance and voice, spinning and loping back down the column of fleeing Brigade members. The gait was easy, but the small of his back still hurt and the sun had turned his breastplate into a bake-oven, parboiling his torso in his own sweat.

Grisuh, he thought. Civvies, natives. Nobody in the Military Governments had taken them very seriously; hadn't their ancestors overrun the whole western half of the Civil Government without much trouble? Natives were fit only for farming, trading and paying taxes to their betters. The Civil Government made fine weapons, but they'd as soon pay tribute as fight. Heretic bastards besides. Carstens had fought the Squadron — not too difficult, they had more balls than brains — and the Guard, who had started out as a fragment of the Brigade who stayed in the north instead of migrating into the Midworld Sea lands generations ago. And the Stalwarts, who'd moved south from the Base Area in his grandfather's time; so primitive they were still heathen and fought on foot with shotguns and throwing axes, but terrifyingly numerous, fierce and treacherous. This would be the first time he'd walked the walk with civvie troops.

From what the bewildered Squadron refugees had been saying over the past year, counting out the *grisuh* was a thing of the past. Especially under their new war-leader, Raj Whitehall. Come to think of it, Whitehall had a Namerique sound to it. . . .

He pulled up beside the fan Morton carriage. Lady fan Morton was in there with her teen-age daughter and the other children. She shielded her eyes against the sun with her fan and leaned out to him, still dressed in the filmy morning gown she had worn when the courier had come into the manor on a dog collapsing from exhaustion.

"Captain?" she said.

"They're coming up on us fast, ma'am. We've got to get moving, and I'd appreciate it kindly if you'd talk to the other *brazaz* —" officer-class families "— because I need some men to slow them up."

Sylvie fan Morton's nostrils flared; she was still a fine-looking woman at thirty-eight, and Carstens had thought wistfully more than once that it would be nice if her husband fell off his dog and broke his neck. Which wasn't unlikely, as often as he went hunting drunk. She would make a very marriageable widow.

"I don't like the thought of running from *natives*, Captain," she said.

"Neither do I, ma'am," Carstens said sincerely. "But believe me, we don't have much time."

In the event, it took nearly half an hour to muster a thousand men, all mounted and armed — more or less armed, since some of the landowners skimped by equipping their hired fighters with shotguns instead of decent rifles. Good enough for keeping peons in order, but now they were going to pay in spades for their economizing. Or rather their men would pay, which was usually the way of it. That left a thousand or so to shepherd the convoy on.

"Spread out, spread out!" he screamed, waving his sword. The fan Morton men did, lancers to the rear and dragoons forward. For the others it was a matter of yelling, pushing and occasionally whacking men and dogs into position with the flat of his sword and the fists of his under-officers. Only the manifest presence of the enemy saved him from a dozen death-duels, and that barely. Two young noblemen *did* promise to call him out, when he had to pistol their dogs after the beasts lost their heads and started fighting. In the end, the Brigade men were deployed north-south. That gave him more than a kilometer of front at right-angles to the road, but it was thin, men stretched like a string of dark or steel-shining beads across the rolling cropland. He had no confidence in their ability to change front, and the worrisome clouds of dust to his right and left could still curl in behind him and strike for the refugees.

For the moment he had only the dust-cloud coming straight up the road. They ought to reach him first; if he could see them off for a while, he might be able to turn and counterpunch one of the side-columns before they could coordinate.

A man had to hope.

"Here they come," his second-in-command grunted beside him, pulling at his grizzled beard. "Still say we should have signed on for another go at the Stalwarts, boss."

"Shut up." Carstens raised his brass telescope, squinting through the bubbled, imperfect lenses. "Damn, they've got a cannon." Rolling along behind a six-dog hitch, with men riding several of the draught-dogs, on the carriage, and beside it. The rest of them in their odd-looking round helmets with the neck-flaps, riding in a column of fours. "No more'n a hundred. Must be their vanguard."

He licked his lips, tasting salty sweat and dust; Jo was panting like a bellows between his knees, and the day was hot. A brief vivid flash of nostalgia for the rolling green hills and oakwoods and apple-orchards of his youth siezed him; he pushed it away with an effort of will and swung his own helmet on. The felt-and-cork lining settled around his head, the forehead band slipping into the groove it had worn over the years, and he pulled the V-shaped wire visor down and fastened the cheek-flaps. Those and the lobster-tail neckguard muffled sound and sight, but he was used to that. It would come to handstrokes before the day was over. He took a moment to check his pistols and carbine and glance back. With men prodding the oxen with sword-points, the convoy had gotten up some speed at the cost of shedding bits of load and stragglers.

An enemy trumpet-call, faint and brassy, answered by the whirring roar of his own kettledrums. Ahead the Civil Government column split; a moment later there were four smaller units coming at him, holding to a slow canter. Another movement, and the platoon columns swung open like the back of a fan. Less than two minutes, and he was facing a long line. Another trumpet, and the enemy stopped stock-still, the dogs crouched beneath the riders, and the men stepped forward with their rifles at the port. Muffled with distance, the actions went click*clack* as the troopers worked the levers and reached to their bandoliers for a round. *Clack* in unison as they thumbed a round home and loaded, marching without breaking stride. Tiny as dolls with distance, like toy soldiers arranged with impossible neatness.

"Shit," Carstens mumbled into his beard. That was as smooth as the General's Life Guards on the parade-ground in Carson Barracks. Faster, too — Brigade troops would have stopped and counter-marched to get into position. Aloud, he shouted:

"Dragoons, dismount to firing line!" The fan Morton

men did, swinging out of the saddle and forming up two deep, one rank kneeling and one standing. Few of the others did anything but watch.

"Martyred Avatars bleeding *wounds*!" he screamed, riding out in front of the straggling line. "Everyone with a fucking rifle, get ready to shoot!"

He sheathed his sword and pulled out his own carbine, thumbing back the hammer. He also heeled his dog behind the firing line; no way was he going to have his ass out in front of *this* lot when they pulled their triggers.

"Wait for the word of command. Set your sights, set your sights!"

A rifle could kill at a thousand meters, but only if you estimated the range right — the natural trajectory of the bullet was above head-height past about three hundred, so you had to elevate the muzzle and *drop* the bullet down on your target. That was why some commanders preferred to wait until two-fifty meters or less; Carstens did himself, unless he were facing one of the huge densely-packed Stalwart columns where a bullet that missed one man would hit another. Here —

Shots banged out along the line. "Hold your fucking *fire*," he screamed again. At nine hundred meters distance the Civil Government line was utterly undamaged. A shouted order, and the enemy all went to ground, first to one knee and then prone. Carstens felt his testicles drawing up. He'd been in this position before from the other side, facing Stalwart warbands with greater numbers but no distance weapons. The enemy rifles could be loaded while a man was flat on his belly, while his rifle-muskets had to have the shot rammed down their muzzles.

As if to punctuate his thought, a volley crashed out from the enemy, *BAM-BAM-BAM-BAM* as the platoons fired in unison. Greasy off-white smoke curled up from their positions, then drifted away in the scudding breeze. Something went whirrr-*brack* past his ear. Dogs and men screamed in pain and shock, mostly among those still mounted, but a few in the firing-line as well.

"Fire!"

An unnecessary order, and a ragged stutter sent demon-scented fog back into his face. His men had barely grounded their muskets and reached for a paper cartridge when the next enemy volley came. Another after they'd bitten open the cartridges and poured powder and minnie bullet down the barrels; a third as the pulled out their ramrods. Just then a dull *POUMPF* came from the enemy field-gun, fifteen hundred meters back and well out of small-arms range. A tearing whistle and a *crack* of dirty smoke in mid-air, not twenty meters ahead of his riflemen; half a dozen were scythed down by the shrapnel. Then the Brigade warriors were capping their weapons and firing again — he ground his teeth as he saw a few ramrods go flying out toward the enemy — and beginning the cumbersome task of loading once more. Three more enemy volleys cut into his makeshift command; he could see men looking nervously backward out of the corners of his eyes.

He wasn't particularly worried about that, though. Raw courage was not the quality in short supply here today, and he'd also loudly ordered his lancers to ride down any man who fled without permission.

"Remember it's your families we protect," he called, keeping his voice calm. "One more volley and we'll —"

POUMPF. This time the tearing-canvas sound went right overhead, and the shell went *crack* sixty meters behind him. Dogs reared, then whimpered as their riders sawed on reins that connected to levers on the bridles, pressing steel bars against the animals' heads.

One under, one over, and I know what comes next, Carstens thought. His head whipped from side to side; the dust-columns weren't closing in as fast as he'd feared, and neither was the one behind the enemy vanguard. That heartened him, since it was the first mistake the civvies had made.

"— one more volley and we'll give them the steel."

He touched toes to Jo's forelegs, signaling her to stock-stillness, and fired his own rifled carbine. More as a gesture than anything else, but it made him feel better. A little.

"Everybody mount up," he called, riding out in front again. Enemy bullets pocked the earth around him.

POUMPF-*crack*. This time the shell burst right over the position he'd been in a few minutes before. Shrapnel skeened off body armor and tore into flesh; pistol-shots followed as injured dogs were put down. The wounded men probably wished they rated the same mercy, but needs must. Jo hunched her back slightly and laid her ears down at the sounds of pain.

"Easy, girl, easy," he said. He drew a revolver in one hand and his basket-hilted broadsword in the other. No sense in getting too subtle, just get out in front and wave them forward. "*Charge!*" he shouted, and the ancient Brigade warcry: "*Upyarz!*"

His legs clamped on the barrel of his dog. Jo howled and leaped forward off her hindquarters, building to a flexing gallop. From the chorus of shrieks behind him, human and canine, most of the scratch force were following. The *grisuh* dragoons rose and fired a volley standing; then half of them turned and trotted back to their dogs. Another volley, and they were all mounted and wheeling away. Behind them the gunners were adjusting their weapon, and a shell raced by to throw up a poplar-tall column of black dirt with a spark at the center. Men and dogs and parts of both pinwheeled away from it. The gun crew fired a final round of cannister that cut a wedge out of the Brigade line as cleanly as a knife. The Civil Government troops were trotting to the rear now, heeling their mounts into a canter and then a gallop with the same fluid unison that had disturbed him before. The gunners snatched up the trail of their fieldpiece as it recoiled, running it back onto the caisson and jumping aboard as the team-master switched his mount into motion.

"Shit," Carstens said again. Lanceheads were bristling down on either side of him, but the enemy had had plenty of warning, and their dogs were fresher and less heavily burdened. The distance closed to a hundred meters, still beyond mounted pistol shot — and several of the blue-coated, dark-faced troopers turned in their saddles to pump fists at the Brigade troops with an unmistakable single finger raised. Then the gap began to grow again, with increasing speed. The fieldgun was a little slower, but it had had an extra half-kilometer of distance to start with.

He looked left and right, standing in the stirrups. *Yes.* Those tell-tale dust-clouds *were* closing in, moving fast past him on either side. He could catch the first winks of sunlight on metal from both directions. Plus the men he was chasing were retreating toward a force of unknown size.

"Halt, *halt!*" he shouted. The fan Morton house-troopers halted as the family pennant did, beside Carstens . . . but big chunks of the motley host kept right on pursuing.

"Tommins, Smut, Villard," Carstens snapped to his under-officers. "Stop 'em, and *fast.*"

He spurred his dog out ahead of the closest pack, curving in front of them and waving his sword in their faces. That made some of them pull up, at least.

"*Ni, ni!*" a Squadron refugee-mercenary shouted in their thick guttural dialect of Namerique. "No! The cowards flee!"

The man was literally frothing into his beard; Carstens wasted no time. The point of his broadsword punched into the man's stomach through the stiff leather and doubled him over with an *ooff* of surprise. His dog started to snap in defense of its master, but Jo already had her jaws around its muzzle; it whined and licked hers in surrender as the *Squadrone* fell to the ground vomiting blood.

Carstens felt no regret; you had to stop a rout before it got started, and a rout forward was just as bad as one going to the rear. *No wonder they lost*, he thought of the Squadron. Although the mindset was not unknown among the Brigade, either. He'd just had too much experience to keep up that sort of illusion.

"How many have we?" he asked his second-in-command, when they had the band mostly turned around and trotting to the rear.

"Seven hundred, maybe fifty more," the man said. "Fifty dead 'r down, and two hundred kept after the civvies."

Carstens grunted, grunted again when rifle fire broke out anew over the rise a kilometer to their rear where the pursuit had gone. What the incurably reckless had thought was a pursuit, at least. More rifle fire than before, much more, twice as many guns. "We won't be seeing them again," he said.

"Nohow," the other man agreed. "But the civvies will be up our ass again in half an hour."

Carsten pushed back his visor and looked northeast and southwest. Then he blinked dust out of his eyes and unlimbered the telescope again, on one flanking force and then the other.

"Suckered, by the Spirit!" he said.

At a soundless question, he went on: "Fucking *grisuh* were dragging bush to make more dust — look, there's troops there, but not anything like what they seemed. *Eh bi gawdammit!* Now they've dropped it and they're making speed, see the difference in the dust-plume? I *thought* they were co-ordinating too slow."

The Civil Government company had been dangled out like a chunk of meat in front of a carnosauroid, and now a much bigger set of jaws were closing on the outstretched head. On his whole force, if he hadn't pulled back.

"We still delayed them," his second said.

Faint thunder rolled from a clear sky. Coming from the southeast, down the road toward the bridge. Field guns; Carstens' trained ear counted the tubes, separating the sound from the echoes.

"Four guns," he said hollowly. Men were shouting and calling questions to each other all along the rough column. The alarm turned to panic as a burbling joined the deeper sound of the cannon. Massed rifles volleying.

"Bastards are ahead of us," the second-in-command said. His voice was calm, the information had sunk in but not the impact. "At the bridge, waiting at the bridge."

"Hang on, Sylvie!"

The Brigade warriors rocked into a gallop behind him.

"Well done, Major Bellamy," Raj Whitehall said, clapping him on the back. He raised his voice slightly. "Very well done, you and your men."

The headquarters company of the 2nd Cruisers raised a roaring shout at that, Bellamy's name and Raj's own, crying them hail.

"And you too, Gerrin," Raj went on, as the three senior officers and their bannermen turned to ride down the length of the refugee column.

One or two of the wagons were burning — that always seemed to happen, somehow — but most were in place, looking slightly forlorn with their former owners sitting beside them with their hands clasped behind their necks under guard. Or off digging hasty mass graves for the tumbled bodies, stacking captured weapons, the usual after-battle chores. The smoke smelled of things that should not burn, singed hair and cloth.

"It was young Bellamy's plan," Gerrin said. "And a damned sound one, too." He nodded to where a priest-doctor and his assistants were setting up, with a row of stretchers beside them. As they watched, the first trooper was lifted to the folding operating table. "Not many for the butcher's block, this time."

Ludwig flushed with pleasure and grinned. "The 5th carried off the difficult part, drawing away their rearguard," he said. "My boys just had to stand in the gully and shoot over the edge when they tried to rush the bridge."

A dispatch rider pulled up in a spray of gravel, his dog's tongue hanging loose. He wore the checkered neckcloth of the 5th Descott over his mouth as a shield against the dust. When he pulled it down the lower part of his face was light-brown to the caked yellow-brown of his forehead.

"Ser!" he saluted.

Staenbridge took the papers, opened them at Raj's nod. "Ah, good," he said. "From Bartin. Perino and Sala are secured. A few minor skirmishes; terms of surrender, hostages, supplies on the way — the usual."

He flipped to the other papers. "And the same from Ehwardo, Peydro and Hadolfo," he said, listing the other flying-column commanders. "The cities of Ronauk and Fontein opened their gates and tried to throw a party for the troops. Jorg back at base reports civilian and Brigaderos landowners coming in by the dozens to offer submission."

They were coming up to the head of the refugee column; the smell of powdersmoke still hung here, and of death. Flies swarmed in black mats, drawn by the rotting blood and meat already giving the hot day a sickly odor; hissing packs of waist-high bipedal scavenger sauroids waited at the edge of sight for living men to depart, their motions darting and impatient. Leathery wings soared overhead, spiralling up the thermals, and the ravens were perched on wagons. An occasional *crack* came as riflemen finished off wounded dogs, or Brigade warriors too badly hurt to be worth the slave-traders' while. Nearly to the front of the column was a huge tangle of dead men and mounts, with lances and broken weapons jutting up from the pile. Near the center was a man in three-quarter armor, lying with his sword in hand and his drying eyes peering up at the noonday sun. Lead had splashed across his breastplate, and blood from the three ragged holes that finally punched through the steel.

That armor really did seem to offer some protection, at extreme range and against glancing shots. Raj reflected it was just as well he'd ordered brass-tipped hardpoint rounds for this campaign as well as the usual hollowpoint expanding bullets. Generally those were sauroid-hunting ammunition, but they'd serve very well.

"They died fairly hard, here," he said. "What's your appraisal, messers?"

Bellamy shrugged. "Up at the bridge they charged us and we shot them," he said. "When they ran away, we chased them and shot them." He waved a hand at the scattered clumps of Brigaderos dead out over the fields. The ones away from the convoy were already seething with winged and scaled feasters.

Gerrin ran a thoughtful finger over his lips. "Rather better at my end," he said. "Those rifle-muskets of theirs do carry. And their unit articulation was much better than the *Squadrones* — particularly considering this was a thrown-together job lot of landowners' household troops. Some of the individual units worked quite well; they all stood fire, and *some* of them even managed a retreat when it seemed called for. Which is why I didn't get the whole of their rearguard."

He paused. "That was this fellow, I think," he said, nodding at the armored corpse and the banner that lay across his legs. "From the way they acted, I'd say their usual tactic was to push their dragoons forward to pin you with fire and hit you in the flank with the cuirassiers. I wouldn't like to take a charge of those lancers while I was in the saddle, my oath, no. The damned things are three meters long. *And* that heavy cavalry would be a nasty piece of work in a melee. They didn't have enough drilled troops to do it here, but I doubt we'll have as easy a time in the west."

Raj nodded. "That's about what I thought," he said. "Remember the old saying: *a charging Brigadero would knock down the walls of Al-Kebir.*" A little of the animation died out of Bellamy's face.

"Still, a good day's work," Raj said judiciously. "Ludwig, I'm leaving you this sector; push some patrols down the road, and find out how much of a perimeter whoever-it-is in Port Wager is trying to hold. I doubt he'll even try to hold the city. We've taken the island in less than four days; these here were the only ones we'd have had to worry about, and they make a good negative example to contrast with those who surrendered in time."

Some of the Scout Troop were living up to their informal name; the loot in the bulk of the column was being tallied for later distribution, but several of the Forty Thieves were slitting pouches and pulling rings off fingers — or cutting off the fingers, and ears with rings in them — as they moved among the enemy dead. Men riding to what they think is sanctuary will take all their ready cash with them. One big Scout was ignoring the dead. Every time he came to a man still breathing he took him by the chin and the back of the head and twisted sharply. The sound was a tooth-grating *crunch*.

Several other troopers surrounded a carriage at the very front of the column; beyond it was only the drift of enemy dead where they'd charged for the stone-built bridge, and gunners policing up their shell casings. Those around the coach were a mixed group from the 5th Descott and the 2nd Cruisers. Dead wolfhounds lay in the traces, and a cavalryman was sitting at some distance having a gunshot wound in one shoulder bandaged. Another jumped up to the running board and ripped open the door, then tumbled backward with a yell as the pointed ferrule of a parasol nearly gouged out his eye.

"*Scramento*," the man yelled, clapping a hand to the bleeding trough in his face.

His comrades laughed and hooted. "*Hole* for the pihkador, Halfonz!" one of them cried, slapping his thigh. "Lucky fer ye t'hoor didn't hev anither derringer."

A huge 2nd Cruiser trooper batted the parasol aside with one hand and reached in with the other to pitch the wielder out; she was a tall buxom woman in her thirties, richly dressed in layers of filmy silk. A teenager followed her, shrieking like a rabbit as the big soldier's strength tore loose her frantic grip on the carriage and set it rocking.

He looked inside, holding the girl three-quarters off the ground despite her thrashing. "*Ni mor cunne*," he grunted in Namerique. "*Kinner iz*."

"*Ci*, just kids," a Descotter said, and slammed the door shut again.

The older woman was hammering at the Cruiser with two-handed strokes of her umbrella. The man she had nearly blinded came up behind her and ripped her gown down to the waist, pinning her arms and exposing her breasts, then kicked her feet from under her.

"Hold 'er legs, ye dickheads," he said irritably. Two did, spreading them wide and back as he tossed up her skirts and ripped off the linen underdrawers. Blood from his face wound spattered her breasts as he knelt, but she did not begin to scream until her daughter was thrown down beside her.

Raj heeled Horace to one side with a slight grimace of distaste. War was war, and soldiers soldiers. He'd had men hung for murder and rape in friendly territory, or towards enemies who'd surrendered on

terms — crucified men for plundering a farm on Civil
Government territory, once. Very bad for discipline to
let anything like that go by. The sullen resentment he'd
meet if he tried to deprive men of their customary
privileges towards those who *hadn't* surrendered on
terms would be even worse for order and morale.
Besides which, of course, all the prisoners in this
convoy were going to the slave markets — to domestic
service or a textile mill if they were very lucky, more
probably to die in the mines or building Governor
Barholm's grandiose new temples, dams, railroads and
irrigation canals.

"Shall I send everything back to base, then?"
Staenbridge said, waving a hand toward the convoy.

"No," Raj said. "We'll be moving to someplace with
a harbor soon. Just take them back a village or two,
somewhere with good water; we'll pass you by and pick
you up with the baggage train. And it'll be a good
object lesson for the district."

"Ci," Ludwig Bellamy said. "When Messer Raj
offers you terms, you take them. Or get your lungs
ripped out your nose. Sure as fate; sure as death."
Gerrin nodded somberly.

Raj looked up. *Perfect sincerity,* he thought. Center
confirmed it wordlessly with a scan of face-tempera-
ture, bloodflow, voice-tension and pupil dilation.

It bewildered him sometimes, that such men would
move so willingly into his orbit and live for his
purposes. He could understand why someone like
M'lewis followed him, more-or-less. But Ludwig Bellamy could have gone home to the Territories and lived
like a minor king on his estates, and Staenbridge had
more than enough in the way of charm and connections to get a posting in East Residence, not too far
from the bullfights, the opera and the better restau-
rants. Raj knew why he did what he did; he would
always do what he thought of as his duty to the Civil
Government of Holy Federation and the civilization it

protected. He also knew that that degree of obsession was rare.

i know the reason, raj whitehall, Center said. **but although you know what you do, you will never understand all the effect it has on others. and while I can analyze it, i cannot duplicate it. for this, as much as any other factor, i chose you and trained you to be what you are.**

Raj neck-reined Horace about. The escort platoon fell in behind him. The day was getting on for half-done, with a mountain of work yet to do, he should look in on the wounded, they liked that, poor bastards — and Suzette was waiting for him back at base-camp.

"Ah, general," Bellamy said. Raj leaned back in the saddle and Horace halted with a resentful wuffle. He tried to sit, too, until Raj gave him a warning heel. The blond officer's voice dropped, even though nobody else was within normal hearing.

"You remember you told me to strike up an acquaintance with young Cabot?"

Who is fully three years your junior, Raj thought. "Yes?" he said.

"I did. A very . . . energetic young man. Intelligent, I'd say. Brave, certainly."

"And?"

"And . . . we were drinking one night on the voyage. He commiserated with me, saying he knew how it was, to be forced to serve an enemy of one's family."

"Ah," Raj said. "Thank you again, Ludwig."

"I'll probably hoist a few with him again, sometime, Messer." A shrug. "He knows some remarkably good filthy drinking songs, too."

CHAPTER SIX

"Thank you, thank you," Suzette said. Her servants bore out the glittering heap of gifts. "You have nothing to fear, messas, nothing at all. The proclaimed terms are open for *everybody*."

The crowd of women looked at her desperately, willing themselves to believe. Most of them were civilian landowners' wives, with a fair sprinkling of *Brigaderos* magnates' spouses; they came in a clump, for mutual protection. She smiled at them, willing gracious reassurance. They seemed to take some comfort that the fearsome Raj Whitehall had brought an actual wedded wife along with him; it made him seem less of the ogre who had slashed the neighboring Squadron into oblivion in one summer's campaign.

"But," she went on, "your husbands really will have to come in themselves. Or I can't answer for what will happen to you and your families. And that *is* the final word."

Suzette sighed and sank back on her chair as the whispering clump left the room; it was an upper chamber of the little manor house. She fanned herself against the mingled odor of perfume and fear, until the sea-breeze dispelled it and left only a hint of camp-stink in its place. This was the second time the Whitehalls had stayed here. The jumping-off camp for the Southern Territories campaign had been on this spot, although the Brigade had been neutral in that war. Those memories were far from uniformly happy.

At her feet, Fatima cor Staenbridge strummed her *sitar*. The *cor* meant that she had been legally freed from chattel-slave status; it was followed by her patron's name, because that relationship carried a number of obligations.

"Strange," she said, in Sponglish that now carried only a trace of throaty Arabic accent. "They come to plead for their men, yes?"

"Yes," Suzette said. "It's a tradition, rather out of date, but the customs here on Stern Isle are like the clothes, a generation behind East Residence. I take it they wouldn't have done so back in the Colony?"

Fatima laughed. She was dressed in the long pleated skirt, embroidered jacket and lace mantilla of an East Residence matron of the middle classes, but she had the oval face and plump prettiness of Border Arab stock from the desert oases south of Komar. After two children, only her consistent practice of her people's dancing — what outlanders called belly-dancing — kept her opulence within bounds.

"Muslim general throw them to his men as abandoned women," she said. "Muslim man cut off his wife's nose rather than take life from her hands after she see enemy with face uncovered."

"Interesting," Suzette said.

And rather appalling. Our own men are bad enough, most of them, sometimes.

One of the few men she knew who had little or no false pride of that sort was Gerrin Staenbridge — which was understandable, all things considered. It made him disconcertingly hard to fool, more so even than Raj, and Raj had grown disturbingly, delightfully insightful over the past four years. She glanced down at Fatima; the Arab girl had had an interesting life so far as well. The rather bizarre menage a trois she'd fallen into seemed to suit all parties, though. Gerrin got the children he'd wanted, and which a nobleman needed; he and Bartin both got a willing woman at the very, very occasional times they desired one — Bartin more often than Gerrin, but then he was much younger; and

Fatima acquired the legal status of an acknowledged mistress and mother of acknowledged heirs to a wealthy nobleman.

Certainly better than what the other women of El Djem were undergoing now; most of them were probably dead. If Fatima ever desired something more passionate than the avuncular/brotherly relationship she had with Gerrin and Bartin, she never showed it. *Of course, she was harem-raised.* And the despised daughter of a minor concubine at that.

"I have a problem," she said. "With young Cabot."

Fatima sat erect, bright-eyed. Suzette and Raj had stood Starparents to her children, a close bond, and had sponsored her into the Church. "Anything I can do, my lady. I poison his food?"

"No, no," Suzette laughed. *Actually, my dear, when I need poisons I have Ndella or Abdullah.* "I need *advice* about him. He grovels at my feet, but he talks to you, occasionally; you're more nearly his age, and you aren't born Messa."

"He want you, and he hate Raj," Fatima said. "His uncle would send Raj the bowstring —" she fell back into Arabic for that phrase "— if he did not need him so much."

Suzette nodded. The Arab girl continued more slowly: "His uncle hate and fear Raj. Cabot, he hate and envy Raj. Envy his victory in war, envy that the soldiers love and fear Raj as he were All—, ah, as he were the Spirit of Man." She frowned. "He would not be bad young man, if he not an enemy."

The East Residence patrician chuckled: "My dear girl, you've lived among us of the Civil Government for years and not noticed that the *definition* of a bad man is someone who belongs to the other faction?"

"Oh," Fatima said, with her urchin grin, "Arab think that way too." More seriously, she continued: "The *Sultan al'Residance*, he would kill Raj for spite. Young Cabot, he would *be* Raj if he could. Want his fame, want his glory, his followers. Want his woman — not just open her legs, but have her love. He want all. That why he must think bad of Raj, but can't be away from him either; he think to learn from him, then take all that is his. But maybe in deepest heart, he love Raj like other soldiers do, and hate himself for love."

"You," Suzette said, chucking Fatima under the chin, "are a remarkably perceptive young lady."

"I learn from you, Lady Whitehall. Gerrin talk to me a lot too, and I learn," she replied. Her head tilted to one side. "Why is it, lady, that man who want bed woman all the time, very much, what's the word?"

"*Muymach.*"

"Ah. Muymach man, often not want to *talk* to woman? Like, oh, Kaltin?"

"Kaltin Gruder's a loyal Companion," Suzette said. *Who hates my guts, but that's neither here nor there.* Kaltin Gruder had lost a brother and acquired scars external and mental in Raj's service, but he remained very . . . straightforward. Intelligent, but not subtle.

"Yes, a man-of-men. I friend with his concubine; they say he like bull in bed, but they lonely — he never *talk* to them. Back home," she went on, "man never talk to woman, not even father to daughter."

"And I have the best of both worlds," Suzette said with a fond smile for an absent man. "Do keep talking to Cabot," she went on. "You've been very helpful."

She touched a handbell. The door opened and a man looked through; for effect with the locals, he was dressed in his native costume of jellabah and ha'aik, with a long curved dagger and sheath of chased silver thrust through his belt. The Star amulet around his neck was protective camouflage; Abdullah al'Azziz had been born a Druze, and was authorized by the tenants of his own faith to feign the religion of any region in which he lived. Suzette had seen him imitate an Arab shaik of Al Kebir, a Sufi dervish, a fiercely orthodox Star Spirit-worshipping Borderer from the southeastern marchlands of the Civil

Government, an East Residence shopkeeper, and a wandering scholar from Lion City in the Western Territories. No, not imitate, *be* those things. Though she had saved him and his family from slavery, she suspected that the man served her as much for the opportunity to use his talents as much from gratitude.

"Who's next, Abdullah?" She switched to Arabic; hers was far better than Fatima's Sponglish, and the tongue was little known this far west outside enclaves of Colonial merchants.

"A lord of the Brigade, *saaidya*," he said. "And the merchant Reggiri of Wager Bay."

"Ah," Suzette said, frowning. "The *Brigadero*, my Abdullah; does he give his name?"

"No, lady. He is of middle years, with more grey than black in his beard, and wears a bandana, thus." The Druze covered his lower face. "He seeks to show humility but walks like a man of power; also a man who rides much. The guards hold him in an outer room."

"I'll bet they do," Suzette murmured.

Reggiri has the information we need, she thought. He'd been most generous with information before the invasion of the Southern Territories, information he'd gotten through his trading contacts. Crucial information about Squadron movements. *Of course,* she thought coldly, *he was paid in full, one way or another, after that little supper-party of his I attended. Doubtless he'd like another installment.*

Decision crystallized. "Bring the Brigadero. Send refreshment and entertainment to Messer Reggiri and tell him . . . ah, tell him my chaplain and I are Entering my sins at the Terminal." *He would laugh at that. Let him.* He would be far from the first man she'd had the final and most satisfying laugh on.

The Brigadero entered between three of the 5th Descott troopers assigned as her personal bodyguards. He was a stocky man, not tall for one of the barbarians, and wrapped in a long cloak. Together with the bandana and broad-brimmed leather hat, it was almost comically sinister. Conspicuous, but effective concealment for all that.

"Thank you, Corporal Saynchez," she said. "You searched him for weapons, of course."

"Yis, m'lady," the noncom said in thick County brogue. "Says ye'll know him an' wouldna thank ussn fer barin' his face."

"You can leave, now. Wait outside."

"No, m'lady," the man said. He stood three paces to the rear of the stranger, with drawn pistol trained. The other two rested their bayonetted rifles about a handspan from his kidneys.

A dozen generations of East Residence patricians freighted her words with ice:

"Did you hear me, corporal?"

"Yis, m'lady."

"Then *wait out in the hall.*"

"No, m'lady. Might be 'n daggerman, er sommat loik that. Messer Raj, he said t' see ye safe."

The stolid yeoman face under the round helmet didn't alter an iota in the searchlight of her glare. Suzette sighed inwardly; she was part of the 5th's mythology now, the Messer's beautiful lady who went everywhere with him, bound up troopers' wounds . . . *flattering as hell and extremely confining.* This bunch would obey any order except one that put her in danger.

"Very well, corporal . . . Billi Saynchez, isn't it? Of Moggersford, transfered from the 7th Descott Rangers last year?" She smiled, and the young trooper swallowed as if his collar was too tight as he nodded. "Now, if you would stand off to one side, in the corner there? And you, messer, whoever you are, pull up that stool."

She rang the handbell again; her servants came and placed kave, biscuits and brandy. Fatima looked up at her for a moment with shining eyes; she'd told her patroness once that the cruelest thing about harem life was that nothing ever happened.

Softly, she began to sing to the sitar, a murmur of noise that would drown out the conversation to anyone more than a few paces away. It was a reiver's ballad from the debatable lands below the Oxhead mountains, the long border between the sea and the Drangosh where Borderer and Bedouin fought a duel of raid and counter-raid nearly as old as man on Bellevue. Suzette had heard a version sung in south-country Sponglish with the names and identities reversed. The Colonial's started:

> *O woe is me for the merry life*
> > *I led beyond the Bar*
> *And trebble woe for my winsome wife*
> > *That weeps at Shalimar.*

"The girl speaks no Namerique," she said in that language. "And I don't speak to men with masked faces."

"Lady Whitehall," the man said. He lowered the bandana; the hat would hide him from view from the rear. "A pleasure to see you once again."

"And the same for me, Colonel Boyce," she said softly. The square-cut beard was greyer than she remembered, but the little blue eyes were still cool and shrewd.

"No names . . . and the circumstances are less fortunate than our last meeting." Boyce had been rather more than a friendly neutral as commander of the Brigade forces on Stern Isle when Raj passed through to the Southern Territories.

"I've been relieved of command, as of last week. Colonel Courtet is now in charge of Stern Isle, or at least of Wager Bay, since that's all the idiot has been able to keep."

"Would you have been able to hold more, against my husband?"

"No, I would have surrendered on demand," Boyce

said. "Which is why the local command council deposed me, the fools. The Stern Isle garrison was here to keep the natives down and guard against Squadron pirates. With the Southern Territories in Civil Government hands, we're indefensible against a determined attack. Outer Dark, we're an island with no naval protection!"

They have taken away my long jezail,
My shield and saber fine,
I am sold for a slave to the Central Rail
For lifting of the kine.

"Do have some kave," Suzette said, pouring for them both. "That's very intelligent of you, I'm sure," she went on. "I expect you'll be taking the amnesty, then?"

"Only if nothing better offers," he said. "Two sugar, thank you. The terms of the amnesty specify that those who surrender don't have to take active part in operations against the Brigade."

"I take it you also object to the provision for the surrender of two-thirds of landed property?" she murmured, taking a brandy snifter in her other hand.

"By the Spirit of Man of . . . the Spirit, I do, Messa! So will my sons, some day; they'll find that real estate wears better than patriotism."

"Let me see if I understand you, Messer Boyce," Suzette said. "Your main properties lie on the mainland, don't they?" He nodded. "If the Brigade wins this war, you stand to recover the mainland properties at least — even if you take the amnesty, and even if we retain this island. On the other hand, if you aid us openly, those lands will be forfeit to the General. Unless we win. You're telling me you expect us to win? And want to be on the winning side, of course."

"Of course." Boyce sat silent for a moment, and the throaty Arabic music rang louder:

The steer may low within the byre
The serf may tend his grain,

For there'll be neither loot nor fire
    Till I escape again.

"Messa," he went on slowly, "I know you call my
people barbarians. The Squadron are — were, rather.
The Guards are, since they haven't had our contact
with the Midworld Sea; the Stalwarts most *assuredly*
are. We of the Brigade have ruled the Western
Territories for a long, long time, though. Give us credit
for learning something. Give me credit, at least.

"Yes," he continued, "I think your Messer Raj —" he
used the troops' nickname "— may win this war. *May*.
It seems unlikely from the numbers, but I've visited
the Civil Government. I know its potential strength
when there's a strong Governor with an able commander. That's happened now, and we, well. I wouldn't
trust General Forker to lead a sailor into a whore-
house, to be blunt. Most of the possible replacements
are worse, we've managed to turn Carson Barracks into
a stew of intrigue as bad as East Residence, only with
less sense of long-term interests. Most of all, I've seen
Raj Whitehall. I've studied his campaigns in the east,
and I had a ringside seat for the destruction of the
Squadron.

"You *may* win. Even if you don't, the war will be
long and bloody. If we kick you out, we'll still be so
weakened the Stalwarts will roll over us like a rug.
We're having more and more trouble holding the
border against them anyway."

He leaned forward, the blunt swordsman's fingers
incongruous on the delicate china.

"And win or lose, the worst thing that could happen to
us is a long war. If we win, the Stalwarts will pick our
bones. If we lose, the Western Territories may be so
weakened that you can't hold them against the northern
savages either. And in any case, if we lose after a long
struggle we may just . . . vanish as a people, the way it's
happening to the Squadron. Ordinary nations can lose
their nobles and soldiers and priests —" he snapped his

fingers "— and they'll produce a new set of 'em in a few generations, even if they have to throw off a foreign yoke first. We of the Brigade, we haven't had a peasant class of our own since we left the Base Area. If we lose our lands and positions, we lose *everything*."

And God have mercy on the serf
  When once my fetters fall
And Heaven defend the noble's garth
  When I am loosed from thrall.

Suzette looked at him with new respect. "So since you *know* that General Whitehall can't be beaten easily, you think a swift Civil Government victory is the best thing for your people?"

"Exactly, my lady. You'll *need* us. Need our fighting men, not least. In a generation or two, who knows?" He hesitated. "I wouldn't describe myself as an idealist, Lady Whitehall. Let's say I value civilization, if nothing else because it's so much more comfortable than sitting in a drafty log hall eating bad food and listening to worse poetry. The more thoughtful members of the Brigade have always considered themselves guardians of the culture we took over. General Whitehall claims to be defending civilization by uniting it. The Stalwarts have taken a third of our mainland possessions since my grandfather's time — they're like ants. As I said, I'm interested in preserving my sons' heritage."

"And your lands," Suzette said.

It's woe to bend the stubborn back
  In a coal-mine's inky bourne
It's woe to hear the leg-bar clack
  And jingle when I turn!

"And my lands. All of them, not one-third. The information I have is worth it."

"Why come to me?"

"Too many eyes on your husband, my lady. Too many patriotic fools ready to kill a middle-aged traitor; my excessively honorable sons, for starters. I don't want to see them buried in a ditch and my grandchildren sold as slaves; on the other hand, I don't want them to kill *me*, either. They'll quiet down when it's over."

Suzette sat in silence, setting down the empty kave cup and sipping at her brandy. Beads of sweat ran down from the Brigade noble's hairline, but his features were very steady.

But for the sorrow and the shame,
  The brand on me and mine,
I'll pay you back in the leaping flame
  And loss of the butchered kine.

"Corporal!" she called. The Descotter gunmen came over at the trot, weapons poised.

"M'lady," Saynchez said, bracing to attention.

"This man is to be put under arrest . . . there's a vacant room with an iron door in the cellars here, isn't there?"

"Yis, m'lady."

For every sheep I spared before —
  In charity set free —
If I may reach my hold once more
  I'll reive an honest three.

"Take him there. Let nobody see his face. He's to have food, water and bedding, but nobody, and I mean *nobody*, is to enter his cell or have conversation with him until I or General Whitehall authorize it. You will see that he's guarded by men who know how to keep their mouths shut. Do you understand?"

"Yis, m'lady." Corporal Saynchez quivered with eagerness, like a war-dog just before the charge is sounded. "T'barb 'ull vanish offn t'earth."

For every time I rasied the lowe
  That scarred the dusty plain,
By sword and cord, by torch and tow
  I'll light the land with twain!

"Abdullah," she called, when the soldiers had gone. Not quite at a run, and their hobnails grinding on the pavement.

"Saaidya."

"Messer Whitehall should be back in —" she looked out the window; Miniluna was three-quarters, and a hand's breadth above the horizon "— five hours. Please set a table for three in the lower alcove in time for him. Serve us yourself, please." That room had a stair to the cellars. "And take this to Messer Reggiri."

She pulled a ring from her finger; it was in the shape of a serpent biting its own tail, ruby-studded. "Tell him," she went on, after a pause for thought, "that I will give him a better gift than this, and a sweeter. But not here, in Wager Bay; and that I trust his discretion absolutely."

The dog runs better if you dangle the bone, she thought cooly. Her mind felt sharp as crystal, completely alive. The puzzle in her brain was not solved, but the pieces were there, and she could feel her consciousness turning and considering them. She had no genius for war; that was Raj's domain, and no human living could match him. At plot and counterplot and the ways of devious treachery, she was his third arm. She would give him what he needed to know, and he would wring victory out of it.

Spur hard your dog to Abazai,
Young lord of face so fair —
Lie close, lie close as Borderers lie,
Fat herds below Bonair!

"And Cabot?" she said, in answer to an unasked question. "I don't know. There's a great many things I don't know."

The one I'll shoot at the twilight-tide,
At dawn I'll drive the other;
The serf shall mourn for hoof and hide
The March-lord for his brother.

"But I do know what my Raj can do, if he has the tools he needs to work with. What he needs. And I'll bring him what he needs, whether he knows it or not."

'Tis war, red war, I'll give you then,
    War till my sinews fail;
For the wrong you have done to a chief of men,
    And a thief of the Bani Kahil.
And if I fall to your hand afresh
    I give you leave for the sin,
That you cram my throat with the foul pig's flesh
    And hang me in the skin!

CHAPTER SEVEN

"Not as enthusiastic as they were in Port Murchison," Raj said.

The capital of the Southern Territories had greeted his army with flowers and free wine; the men still talked about it with wistful exaggeration. Here the streets were mostly empty, save for a few knots of men standing on streetcorners watching the Civil Government's army roll by. The ironshod wheels of guns on the cobbles and the thunder-belling of nervous dogs rattled oddly through the unpeopled streets, a nighttime sound on a bright summer's morning. Hobnailed boots slammed in earthquake unison as the infantry marched; he was keeping most of his cavalry bivouacked outside, in villages and manors in the rich coastal countryside. Less chance of disease breaking out, and better for the dogs.

"They're not as sure we're going to win as they were in Port Murchison," Kaltin Gruder pointed out.

They all snapped off a salute as the banner of the 24th Valencia Foot went by, and the standard dipped in response. The Companion considered them with a professional eye.

"Their marching's certainly sharp," he said dryly; cavalry in general and Descotters in particular didn't spend much time on it.

Raj shrugged. "It helps convince them they're soldiers," he said.

The foot-soldiers were mostly conscripted peons from the central provinces, several cuts below the average cavalry recruit socially. *You just have to know how to treat them*, he thought. Tell a man he's worthless often enough, and he'd act like it. For initiative and quick response, the infantry were never going to match a mounted unit like the 5th or Kaltin's 7th Descott Rangers. But they could be solid enough, if you handled them properly.

His eyes went back to the fort. "Well, the good citizens certainly got some evidence for doubting our chances," he pointed out.

The main north gate of Wager Bay gave them a good view downslope and to the east, where Fort Wager sat atop its headland. Every ten minutes or so a cannon would boom out, and a few seconds later a heavy roundshot would crash through a roof in the town below. Mostly they were falling in the tenement-and-workshop district of the town, narrow streets flanked by four-storey limestone apartment blocks, soap works, olive-oil plants and sulfur-refineries. Columns of black smoke marked where fires had started.

"Kaltin, see to getting those out, would you? There's a working aqueduct here, so it shouldn't be so difficult. Coordinate with the infantry commanders if you need more manpower."

The Companion nodded. "At least we know that they're not short of powder," he went on.

"That and a good deal else," Raj said absently.

He trained his binoculars on the harbor, studying the narrow shelf below the bluff and the fort. There were piers at the cliff-face nearest the harbor, but the ground rose steeply, no access except by covered staircases in the rock. Impossible to force; the defenses were built with that in mind. The main guns of the fort couldn't bear on the beach, but anyone trying to climb the cliff would face streams of burning olive oil out of force-pumps, at the very least. Further on, the cliffs bent sharply to the east; even steeper there, and waves frothed in complicated patterns on rock and reef further out.

following changes since last data update, Center said.

I hate it when you suddenly drop into Church jargon, Raj grumbled. He counted himself a pious man, but he'd never understood why the priests had to call commonplace facts "data." It wasn't as if they were speaking of something from the Canonical Handbooks, for the Spirit's sake. Center had the same unfortunate habit at times. One had to make allowances for an angel, of course. . . .

thank you. The water vanished from his sight, leaving the pattern of underlying rocks clear; then schematics showed the flow of currents.

"Hand me that map, would you?" he asked. A clipboard braced against his saddlebow, and he sketched without looking down. "There."

"Also the Brigade's not as unpopular with its subjects as the Squadron was," Muzzaf Kerpatik said as he reclaimed the papers.

"Details?" Raj said.

"I have used my contacts," the little man said; he seemed to have an infinity of them, from Al-Kebir and the Upper Drangosh to all the major ports of the Midworld Sea. As usual, he was dressed in dazzling white linen, a long-skirted coat after the fashion of Komar and the southern border Counties; he was one of the new class of monetary risk-takers growing up there in recent years. The white cloth and snow-white fur of the borzoi he rode contrasted with the carefully curled blue-black hair and goatee and the teak-brown skin.

The pepperpot revolver tucked into his sash had seen use, however.

"The Brigade commanders here have followed general policy; no persecution of Spirit of Man of the Stars clergy unless they meddle in politics."

Raj nodded; the Brigade depended on the old civilian power structure to maintain administration, and the civilian magnates stubbornly refused to abandon the orthodox faith for the heretical This Earth cult. Down in the Southern Territories the Squadron had run a purely feudal state; they had dispossessed the native aristocracy completely, and didn't much care if urban services went to wrack and ruin. They'd had a nasty habit of burning Star Spirit churches with their clergy in them, too. The piratical heritage of old Admiral Geyser Ricks, and one which had simplified Raj's task.

"In fact, there are large colonies of Colonial Muslim merchants, and even Christos and Jews, here and in most Brigade-held port cities. Merchant guilds are in charge of collecting the customs dues and urban land-tax, since the Brigade commanders care little as long as the money comes in. This arrangement is less, ah, *rigorous* than that common in the Civil Government."

Raj nodded again. The Civil Government's bureaucracy was corrupt, but that was like caterpillars in a fruit tree, tolerable if kept under reasonable control. What was important was that it *worked*, which gave the State a potentially unbeatable advantage. The laxness of the Military Governments was a compound of sloth and incompetence, not policy — they couldn't tighten up much no matter what the emergency.

"Speaking of religion, Messer . . . a delegation of priests in East Residence has presented a petition to the Chair and the Reverend Hierarch Arch-Sysup Metropolitan of East Residence, protesting your policy of toleration towards This Earth cultists in the Southern Territories."

"Damn!" Raj bit out. Barholm took his ecclesiastical duties as head of Holy Federation Church quite seriously. Theology was a perennial hobby of Governors, Church and State being as closely linked as they were. He didn't need Center to tell him what the consequences would be if the Chair tried to reunite the faiths by force and overnight —

revolt in former military government territory, probability 72% +/-5, Center said. **mutiny among ex-squadron personnel with expeditionary force, probability 38% +/-4. mutiny among ex-squadron troops elsewhere in civil government area, probability 81% +/-2.**

And there were six battalions of former *Squadrones* on the eastern frontier, keeping watch on the Colonists. Wouldn't *that* be a lovely gift to Ali, hungry for vengeance for his dead father! The Fall seemed to continue by mere inertia. There were times when he felt like a man condemned to spend eternity trying to push an anvil up a slope of smooth greased brass.

indeed. i have done so for a thousand years.

"Tzetzas," he said aloud.

"The Chancellor may have been involved in gathering the petition," Muzzaf said, and grinned whitely.

Back when he'd been the Chancellor's flunky and accomplice he had lived in terror, and in the certain knowledge that Tzetzas would throw him aside like a used bathhouse sponge whenever he ceased to be useful. Now he was one of the Companions of Raj Whitehall, and he knew with equal certainty that Tzetzas would have to come through Raj and every one of the Companions to get him — and had better make sure that none of them survived to avenge him, either. That didn't make him feel immortal; the casualty rate among the Companions was far too obvious. It did make him feel just as dangerous as Chancellor Tzetzas, which was *better* than feeling safe. If he'd wanted to be safe, he would have stuck to running a date-processing business like his father.

"However," he went on, "Governor Barholm has stated that any reversal of policy is premature." Raj relaxed.

"Not until we've got the Brigaderos safely under his thumb," Kaltin said with cold cynicism. "Then he'll send in the Viral Cleansers."

probability 96% +/-2 within five years of suc-cessful pacification, Center said. **consequences —**

I can imagine. "We'll take the problems one at a time," Raj said.

Muzzaf turned pages. "The soldier's market will be held in the main square," he went on. Troopers were generally expected to buy their own rations out of their pay when the army wasn't on the march, and an efficient market was important to morale and health. More armies had died from bad food and runny guts than all the bullets and sabers ever made. The markets Muzzaf supervised were generally very efficient. "Bulk supplies are coming in with acceptable speed, since we pointed out that the Government receipts used to pay for them are exchangeable against taxes. In fact, a secondary market in receipts has arisen."

Raj blinked in bewilderment, then waved aside the explanation. He'd abandoned attempts to understand that sort of thing when Kerpatik tried to tell him how you could make money by buying tobacco that hadn't been planted yet on land you didn't own and then selling it before it was harvested. Every word he'd said had been in Sponglish, but it might as well have been an Azanian witchdoctor explaining the esoterica of his craft. *The cobbler should stick to his last, and I to the sword,* he thought.

"And I have coordinated the six-month receipts for your personal accounts with Lady Whitehall and your clerks."

Raj accepted the paper, raised his brows at the total, and handed it back. For himself he'd as soon have just bought land with his share of the plunder; it was the traditional safe investment, even successful merchants always tried to buy an estate. Kerpatik had convinced him — convinced Suzette, actually — that it would be better to spread it out in part-shares of the new combined capital ventures all over the Civil Govern-ment. It certainly seemed to work, and was less trouble even than collecting rents. For that matter, he'd be content to live from his pay and the income from Hillchapel, the Whitehall estate in Descott. Wealth was a tool, occasionally useful but not central to his work.

"And the special equipment will arrive from Hayapalco within the month."

"Good work, Muzzaf. My thanks."

"Oh, and Kaltin," Raj said.

They heeled their dogs out to follow the last infantry unit; the 7th Descott Rangers were bringing up the rear, and the troopers raised a baying cheer to see their Major and Raj fall in below their banner, a running war-hound over the numeral seven and the unit motto: *Fwego Erst* — Shoot First. The dogs joined in, a discordant but somehow musical belling.

"Suzette and I are having a small get-together tonight," Raj went on. "Provided we can get those imbeciles —" he nodded toward the fortress "— to stop showing how brave they are by shelling the slums. The usual thing, reassure the local grandees; we need them cooperative. I know you're busy, but why don't you drop by?"

Gruder looked over at him; the left side of the Companion's face was lined with parallel white scars, legacy of the Colonial pompom shell that had also scattered his younger brother's brains across his torso.

"I, ah, have —"

"A billet that just happens to contain a pretty young widow?" Kaltin Gruder was not nicknamed "The Rooster" by his men for nothing.

Kaltin coughed into one hand. "Grass widow, actually."

"Leave her or bring her," Raj said offhand. The Companion eyed him narrowly. "Everyone will be there. Old friends, like Messer Reggiri."

They were passing a lone Star Spirit priest, come out to bless the representatives of Holy Federation

Church. Kaltin's sudden clamp of legs around the barrel of his dog made the animal skitter sideways in an arc that nearly smashed the unfortunate cleric against the wrought-iron grillwork of a courtyard door.

"Sorry, Reverend Father," the Descotter cast over his shoulder, as his usual skills reasserted themselves and the mount went dancing back in a sidling arc to Raj's side.

"I don't need a new dog, or a slavegirl," Gruder said. Kaltin had led the escort party that took Suzette to Reggiri's manor for a dinner-party Raj was *too busy* to attend. The officers in that escort had all been sent off with lavish gifts; it was notable that Kaltin Gruder had sold the dog immediately. Although he'd kept the girl, a redhead of Stalwart background named Mitchi.

"Oh, I somehow suspect Messer Reggiri will be giving us *all* gifts," Raj said quietly.

The two Descotters met each other's eyes. After a moment, they began to smile.

"Why thank you, Cabot," Suzette said, fanning herself and taking the glass of punch.

The ballroom was bright with oil lanterns and hot, despite the tall glass doors that stood open to the early summer night. Couples swirled across the marble, bright gowns and jewels and uniforms glittering under the chandeliers. A band of steel drums, sitars and flutes filled the room with soft music; few of the revellers bothered to look up at the fortress on the bluffs, silhouetted against the great arc of Maxiluna. Suzette sang softly to the slow sweep of the music:

"If every man does all he can —
   If every man be true
Then we shall paint the sky above
   In Federation blue . . ."

"Are those the words to that tune?" Cabot asked.

They were leaning on the railing just outside the windows, looking down over the city. There were fewer lights than usual, except the reddish glow of the fires that persisted long after the shelling had ceased in accordance with the twenty-four hour truce. The flames gave a brimstone tinge to the air, under the breeze coming in from the sea and the gardens of the Commander's palace.

"Very old words, but old songs are a hobby of mine," Suzette said, leaning a little closer.

"Very true, too," Cabot replied. He looked up at the fortress, and his strong young swordsman's hands closed on the fretted bronze and iron of the rail. "If we'd all just work at it, that barb wouldn't be up there laughing at us."

Suzette put a hand on his forearm. "I rather think Colonel Courtet is feeling more inclined to gnash his teeth, at the moment, Cabot. Since this *is* his residence we're dancing in."

The young man shook off his mood. "Another dance?" he said.

She shook her head, laughing and tapping him on the shoulder with her fan. "Do you want the other ladies to scratch my eyes out? Four quadrilles in a row with the Governor's nephew! Poor things, it's not often they get the chance to whirl in the arms of a handsome gallant from the capital, and here I'm monopolizing you."

"Provincial frumps," Cabot said, bowing over her hand. "Let them suffer — and make me happy."

"Later, you scamp. Let an old woman have a chance to catch her breath."

"Old!" he said breathlessly, tightening his grip on her hand. "You — you're as ageless and as beautiful as the Stars themselves."

"Now you'll get me in trouble with the Church."

Not to mention that at several years short of thirty it was early days to be calling her *ageless*.

"Nonsense; I'll proclaim a new dispensation from the Chair."

Don't let your uncle hear you talking like that, she thought. *He doesn't have much of a sense of humor.*

"Later, Cabot. I really do need some rest, and it's a sin for a dancer like you to be wasted even for an hour. I'll meet you later by the fountain."

She watched him go, tapping her chin thoughtfully with the fan. "Hello, Hadolfo," she said, as Reggiri leaned against the railing in turn.

The black and silver of his jacket and breeches made a contrast with her white-on-white torofib silk and the platinum-and-diamond hairnet that drifted in veils of mesh around her bare shoulders. He had a weathered seaman's tan, and there were calluses on the hand that held hers as he made his bow.

"You seem to be seeing a lot of that young spark," he said.

"Well, he *is* the Governor's nephew, Hadolfo. I can scarcely throw a drink in his face."

"My dear, you not only could, you could make him — or any man — thank you for it."

She laughed, a low musical chuckle, and tucked her arm through his. "Maybe I should work my witchery on Colonel Courtet," she said, nodding toward the fort.

"You might," he said. "I've had considerable dealings with the good Colonel, and in my experience he's extremely susceptible to feminine charm; unfortunately, also to Sala brandy and to whoever talked to him last."

"You know a great deal about affairs here," she said.

"I try to keep informed . . . as you may remember, dear Suzette."

"Then why don't we go somewhere a little more private for conversation, Hadolfo?"

He looked at her sharply, flushing. "*Here?*" he said.

"Well, not *exactly* here," Suzette replied, steering him around the couples sitting out the dance and crowding to the punchbowls and buffets. "But it is a fairly large mansion, and one learns the way of things at Court; there's far less privacy in the Governor's Palace, believe me."

She snapped open her fan, and flicked a breeze across his neck. "You're glowing, Hadolfo. Now stroll along with me, and tell me *all* the gossip, and we'll find a sofa somewhere for a cosy chat."

Hadolfo Reggiri felt himself flushing and fought not to stammer as they pushed open the doors to the lower room; it was a storey down from the ballroom and across a courtyard, close enough to hear the music, but shadowed with the black velvet curtains. His tongue felt thick, far more so than a few glasses of wine would account for, caught between memory and desire.

Get a grip on yourself, man! he thought. *You're not Spirit-damned sixteen any more!*

He could see how the witch kept the great General Whitehall dangling at her skirts. He could almost feel sorry for the man.

The glow of two cigarettes in the far corner of the darkened room was like running into a wall of cold salt water. He stopped dead, his hand tightening unconsciously on Suzette's where her fingers rested on his right arm. She rapped him sharply across the knuckles with her fan, and walked to the waiting men with the same slender swaying grace, her gown luminescent against the dark woodwork and furniture. Reggiri kept walking numbly forward, because there simply didn't seem to be much else to do. His mind was like a ship he had once seen, whose cargo shifted during a storm. Staggering, everything out of alignment suddenly.

He recognized the men as he approached; Raj Whitehall, and one of his officers, Kaltin Gruder. The scar-faced one he'd been convinced for a moment was going to shoot him last year, until Suzette's voice whipped him into obedience like a lash of ice. The self-appointed guardian of his master's honor.

Both the officers were wearing long dark military-issue greatcloaks, probably to disguise the fact that they were also wearing saber and pistol — real weapons, not the fancy dress cutlery appropriate at a ball. Behind them were four cavalry troopers; they'd been washed up and their uniforms were new, but they carried rifles in their crossed arms. Bull-necked, bow-legged Descotters, as out of place at a party in the mansion as a pack of trolls at an elf convention. Their eyes stayed fixed on the merchant, more feral than any barbarian of the Brigade he'd ever seen.

Hadolfo Reggiri was a good man of his hands; nobody could trade so long in the wilder parts of the Midworld Sea and survive unless he was. He also had no illusions about his own chances with Raj Whitehall or one of his picked fighting comrades; the troopers were a message, not a precaution. They paced out behind him now, hobnails grating on the parquet, looming presences at his back.

"*Bwenyatar, heneralissimo,*" he said, sweeping a bow. "Good evening, Most Valiant General. I've been hoping you'd have the time to speak to me for several days; as a loyal man, I've information on the enemy —"

"I don't doubt you do," Raj said. He flicked at his cigarette and considered the ember. "Eighteen hundred men in the fort, half regular gunners, about four thousand refugees . . ."

It was considerably more complete than the file Reggiri had been compiling.

"Then, if I can't be of assistance, and since you're undoubtedly very busy," he began.

Raj drew another puff. "Actually, messer, there is something you could help the war effort with. My aide Muzzaf Kerpatik tells me you have four ships currently at Sala."

"Preparing to load sulphur, ornamental stone and fortified wine for East Residence," he confirmed.

"They're needed for the war effort. I'd appreciate it if you'd send orders to their captains. They're to report to my base on the north coast and place themselves under the orders of Colonel Dinnalsyn of the Artillery Corps."

"Artillery," Reggiri whispered. "You're going to waste my ships against that bloody fort!"

"That's *Messer General*, t'yer," one of the troopers growled. Raj waved him to silence.

"What," Kaltin said, "would be the penalty, sir, for denying aid to officers of the Civil Government in time of war?"

"Oh, crucifixion," Raj said pleasantly, "for treason. But that doesn't arise, I'm sure. Not waste, Messer Reggiri. *Use*. But I do think they'll be used up. War does that; ships, ammunition, men."

"My ships," Reggiri said. They didn't carry insurance against war losses or acts of government; losing them would wreck him. "You can't steal my ships! Messer General," he added hastily as the soldiers stirred behind him. "I have friends at court."

"I wouldn't dream of stealing them," Raj said. Beside him Suzette pulled a document from her recticule and handed it to her husband. He extended it to the merchant.

Reggiri strained to read it; one of the troopers helpfully lit a match against his thumbnail and held it over his shoulder. The hand stank of dog and gun-oil.

Three thousand gold FedCreds, he read. Not quite robbery, but not replacement value for the ships either. And —

"This is drawn on Chancellor Tzetzas!" he blurted. "I've a better chance of getting the money out of Ali of Al-Kebir!"

"Not satisfactory?" Raj said.

He plucked it back out of the other man's fingers and tore it in half. Suzette produced another sheet of parchment, and handed it to Raj. Reggiri took it with trembling fingers. It was identical to the first, except that the amount had been reduced to twenty-five hundred.

Reggiri looked up at Suzette; she stood beside her husband, one delicate hand touching fingertips to his massive wrist. Her eyes had seemed like green flame earlier; now they reminded him of a glacier he had seen once, in the mountains of the Base Area in the far north.

"Bitch," he said, very softly. Then: "*Unnhh!*" as a rifle-butt thudded over his kidneys. White fire turned his knees liquid for a moment, and ungentle hands beneath his arms steadied him.

"Watch yer arsemouth!" the trooper barked. "Beggin' yer pardon, messer, messa."

"Kaltin," Raj went on, his expression flat. "Messer Reggiri seems to have had a bit too much to drink, since he's forgotten how one addresses a messa. I think he needs an escort home."

Gruder nodded: "Well, he is a slave-trader," he said in a pleasant tone. "Probably learned his manners pimping his sisters as a boy."

Reggiri's hand came up of its own volition. Gruder's face thrust forward for the slap that never came, the scars that disfigured half of it flushing red.

"Please," he said, his voice husky and earnest. His lips came back from his teeth. "Oh, *please*. One of my men will lend you a sword."

Raj touched his elbow. "Major," he said, and Gruder's hand dropped from the hilt of his saber. "I really do think Messer Reggiri needs that escort. And a guard for the next week or so, because he seems to be remarkably reckless in his cups."

"I gave you Connor Auburn on a platter!" Reggiri burst out. The troopers fell in around him, as irresistible as four walking boulders.

"And you're not dying on a cross right now," Raj said in the same expressionless tone. Only his eyes moved, and the hand bringing the cigarette to his lips. "Now leave."

❖   ❖   ❖

Suzette's fingers unfastened the buckle of Raj's military cloak and tossed it on the chaise-lounge behind them. She backed a step and curtsied deeply; Raj replied with an equally deep bow, making a courtier's leg. Music drifted through the open windows behind the black-velvet curtains, and the fading tramp of boots through the door.

"Messa Whitehall, might I have the honor of this dance?" he said.

"Enchanted, Messer Whitehall."

Their right hands clasped, and she guided his left to her waist before they swirled away, alone on the dim-lit floor.

CHAPTER EIGHT

"I told you these'd come in useful," Grammek Dinnalsyn said.

The weapon in the revetment of sandbags, timber and sheet-iron on the forecastle of the *Chakra* was a stubby cast-steel tube nearly as tall as a man, joined to a massive circular disk-plate of welded wrought iron and steel by a ball-and-socket joint. It was supported and aimed by a metal tripod, long threaded bars and handwheels to turn for elevation and traverse. The bore was twenty centimeters, more than twice that of a normal field-gun, and rifled. Beside the weapon was a stack of shells, cylinders with stubby conical caps and a driving band of soft gunmetal around their middle; at the rear of each was a perforated tube. The crews would wrap silk bags of gunpowder around the tubes before they dropped them down the barrel, a precise number for a given range at a given elevation. The base charge was a shotgun shell; when it hit the fixed firing pin at the bottom of the barrel, it would flash off the ring charges around the tube.

One thing Boyce had told them was that the casements of Fort Wager had no overhead protection. None was needed with normal artillery, given the placement of the fort.

"I know they're useful, Grammeck," Raj said. "Their little brothers were extremely handy in the Port Murchison fighting." It had been more like a massacre, but never mind. "They're also extremely *heavy*. Get me one that can move like a field gun, and I'll take dozens of them with me wherever I go."

He walked down the deck of the *Chakra*, striding easily; it had been two days from the north coast to Port Wager, more than time enough to get his sealegs back. Many of the platoon of 5th Descott troopers aboard were still looking greenly miserable, landsmen to the core. They'd do their jobs, though, puking or not, and he intended to give them a stable firing platform. The huge sails of the three-master tilted above him; she was barque-rigged, fore-and-aft sails on the rear mast and square on the other two. Water, wind and cordage creaked and spoke; he squinted against the dazzle and made out the tall headland of Fort Wager to the north. There was a brisk onshore breeze, common in the early afternoon. Center had predicted it would hold long enough today —

probability 78% +/-3, Center corrected him. **i am not a prophet. i merely estimate.**

— and at worst, they could kedge in the last little way, hauling on anchors dropped out in front by men in longboats.

He leaned on the emplacement. The crew looked up from giving their weapon a final check and braced; most of them were stripped to boots and the blue pants with red-laced seams of their service.

"Rest easy, boys," he said, returning their salute.

Artillerymen were mostly from the towns, and their officers from the urban middle classes; both unlike any other Army units in the Civil Government's forces. Many cavalry commanders barely acknowledged their existence. *Pure snobbery*, he thought. *They're invaluable if you use them right*. Their engineering skills, for example, and general technical knowledge. Far too many rural nobles weren't interested in anything moving that they couldn't ride, hunt or fuck, like so many Brigaderos except for basic literacy.

"This one's all up to you," he went on to the gunners. "Infantry can't do it, cavalry can't do it. You're the only ones with a chance."

"We'll whup 'em for you, Messer Raj!" the sergeant growled.

"So you will, by the Spirit," he replied. "See you in the fort."

Inwardly, he was a little uneasy at the way that verbal habit had caught on; *Master Raj* was the way a personal retainer back on the estate would have addressed him. His old nurse, for example, or the armsmaster who'd taught him marksmanship and how to handle a sword. *Curse it, these men are soldiers of the Civil Government, not some barb chief's warband!* he thought.

you are right to be concerned, Center said. **however, the phenomenon is useful at present.**

He took a slightly different tack with the cavalry troopers waiting belowdecks. The ship's gunwales had been built up and pierced with loopholes, but there was no sense in exposing the men or hindering the sailors before there was need.

"Day to you, dog-brothers," he said with a grin, slapping fists with the lieutenant in command. "Done with your puking yet?"

"Puked out ever-fukkin'-thin' but me guts, ser," one man said.

"It'll be tax-day in Descott when you lose your guts, Robbi M'Teglez," Raj said. He'd always had a knack for remembering names and faces; Center amplified it to perfection. The trooper flushed and grinned. "You're the one brought me that wog banner at Sandoral, aren't you?"

"Yisser, Messer Raj," the man said. "Me Da got it, an' the carbine 'n dog ye sent. 'N the priest back home read t' letter from the Colonel on Starday 'n all."

The trooper's comrades were looking at him with raw envy. Raj went on: "We'll be sailing in through the barb cannonade; oughtn't to be more than twenty minutes or so. Not much for those of you who saw off the wogboys at Sandoral. For those who weren't there — well, you get to learn a new prayer."

"Prayer, ser?" one asked.

He had the raw look of a youth not long off the farm, barely shaving, but the big hands that gripped his rifle were competent enough. Most yeomen-tenants in Descott sent one male per generation to the Army in lieu of land-taxes. There were no peons in Descott, and relatively few slaves. Widows, however, were plentiful enough.

A squadmate answered him. *"Fer whut weuns about t'receive, may t'Spirit make us truly thankful,"* he said. "Don't git yer balls drawed up, Tinneran. Ain't no barbs got guns loik t'ragheads."

That brought a round of smiles, half tension and half anticipation. Those who'd waited all day in the bunkers while the Colonist guns pounded them, waiting for the waves of troops in red jellabas to charge through rifle-fire with their repeating carbines . . . they'd know. Those who hadn't been there couldn't be told. They could only be shown.

"Once we're through, the gunners have their jobs to do. It's our job to make sure the barbs don't come down the rocks, wade out and take 'em the way the wild dog took the miller's wife, from behind. You boys ready to do a man's work today?"

Their mounts were back at the base-camp, but the noise the men made would have done credit to the half-ton carnivores they usually rode.

"So commend your souls to the Spirit, wait for the orders, and pick your targets, lads," he finished. "To Hell or plunder, dog-brothers."

"I thought they were about to mutiny, from the sound," Dinnalsyn said as Raj came blinking back into the sunlight on the quarterdeck.

"Not likely," Raj said.

The headland was coming up with shocking speed, and the four ships were angling in on the course he'd set, the one that would expose them to the least possible number of guns as they cut in toward the cliffs. *Spirit of* Man, *but I feel good*, he thought. Frightened, yes. Harbors attracted downdraggers, and he still had bad dreams about the tentacles and gnashing beaks and intelligent, waiting eyes crowding around the wharfs when they tipped the Squadron dead into the water after Port Murchison. Eight thousand men dead in an afternoon; the sea-beasts had been glutted, dragging corpses away to their underwater nests when their stomachs wouldn't take any more flesh.

So he wasn't easy about the chance of going into the water here, no. But after the grinding anxiety of high command, the prospect of action on this scale made him feel . . . young.

Starless Dark, he told himself. *I'm not thirty yet!*

"You shouldn't be here, sir," Dinnalsyn said, lowering his voice.

"You aren't exactly the first one to tell me that, Colonel," Raj said. His exuberance showed in the light punch he landed on the East Residencer officer's shoulder. "But I *have* to take it when my wife says it. Let's get on with the job, shall we?"

The *Chakra* was commanded from the stern, where the quarterdeck held the tall two-man wheel that controlled the rudder and the captain could direct the first mate. Nothing could be done about the vulnerability of the deck crew, who trimmed the lines and climbed into the rigging to wrestle with canvas in response to orders bellowed through a megaphone. Dinnalsyn had seen to putting a C-shaped iron stand around the helm itself, though, with overhead protection and vision-slits, boiler-plate mounted on heavy timbers.

The captain turned to Raj. "Rocks 're bad here," he said. In Spanjol, with a nasal accent; he was a tall ropey-muscled man with flax-pale hair shaven from the back of his head and long mustaches. The tunic he wore was striped horizontally with black and white, heavy canvas with iron rings the size of bracelets sewn to it. With fighting possible, he had shoved the handles of short curve-bladed throwing axes through the rings, and had two long knives in his belt.

A Stalwart wandered down from the north, one of the latest tribe of barbarians to move south out of the Base Area. Possibly the fiercest of all; they would have been much more dangerous if fratricide and patricide hadn't been the national sport of their kings. The day one of them managed to kill off all his rivals and unite the tribe would be a dangerous one for the world.

Raj was not particularly worried about treachery from Captain Lodoviko; offshore, the black plumes showed where the Civil Government's steam rams waited. They were too deep-draught to do this job themselves, but he'd given instructions that any ship which turned back without orders was to be sunk and everyone knew it. He'd also promised every man on board a bonus equivalent to a year's pay, with new berths and commands for the mates and captains and enough to buy a share in their ship. Plus, of course, he had forty of his own troops on each ship, ready to shoot down any man who abandoned his station. Everyone knew that, too.

"Steer this course," Raj said. A colored grid dropped down before his eyes, and he swung his arm to align with the pointer Center provided. "*Precisely* that course, Captain Lodoviko, and change *precisely* when I tell you. Understood?"

Lodoviko squinted at him, and murmured something in his dialect of Namerique; probably an invocation to one of the dozens of heathen gods the Stalwarts followed. Glim of the Waves, perhaps, or Baffire of the Thunder. Then he grunted orders to the helm and his first mate. The wheel swung, and feet rushed across the deck. Men swarmed into the ratlines, agile as cliff-climbing rogosauroids.

The ship's bow swung and its motion altered as it

took the waves at a different angle. The three ships behind swung into line, following as nearly as they could in line astern.

"We're going too fast," Raj said again, his tone remote. "Reduce by . . . two knots, please. Make ready to turn the boat to the left."

"Ship to port. This ain't steered from the same end as a dog, General." Another set of orders from the megaphone, and canvas was snatched up and lashed to spars.

"Whatever. That's right. Now turn to this angle." His arm swung.

Ahead, they were close enough to see the tall cream-colored limestone cliffs, scarred and irregular but nearly vertical; the stone of the fort was the same color, only the smoothness and block-lines marking where it began and the native rock left off. Surf beat on the shingle beach below, and more white water thrashed over rocks and reefs further out. Any one of them could rip the timber bottom of the *Chakra* open the way a bayonet did a man's belly.

I don't envy Gerrin trying to make them think he's going to do a mass attack in broad daylight, Raj thought, at some level not occupied with his passionless translation of Center's instructions.

Dinnalsyn and his aide had quietly drawn their revolvers, standing behind the binnacle that held the wheel. "Spirit, it's really working," the gunner whispered, in the abstracted tones of a man speaking to himself. "Spirit, maybe he *is* a bleeding Avatar."

"This heading. Keep this heading."

They were slanting in towards the cliffs at a sixty-degree angle, still more than a kilometer out. The breeze freshened. A cannon boomed, and everyone except Raj jumped. He was too fixed in the strait world of lines and markers Center had clamped over his vision.

"Colonel Staenbridge is demonstrating against the

fort, and they're warning him off," he said calmly.
"They don't have enough men to crew all their guns.
They'll see we're coming in soon enough."

The path to the little pier around the harbor-side
angle of the cliffs was much easier sailing, but the last
thing he wanted was to be right at the foot of the
covered staircase up to the fort. For one thing,
small-arms fire from the ramparts could reach a ship
there; for another, he was fairly sure the garrison wasn't
going to let him sit and shell them without trying to pay
a visit.

His back was to the stern rail; he drew his own pistol
and thumbed back the hammer. Lodoviko scratched
his ribs; he *might* not have been toying with the haft of
one of his axes.

BOOM. Smoke vomited from an embrasure on the
seaward side of the fort.

"Think they've seen us," Dinnalsyn said. The air
ripped, and water fountained white two hundred
meters off the *Chakra's* bow.

BOOM. It went overhead this time, and the ball
struck rock barely submerged a few hundred meters to
their left, with a sound like an enormous ball-peen
hammer on granite. It bounced back into the air and
wobbled another hundred meters to splash in deeper
waves.

"Yep, they've seen us all right," the gunner went on
dispassionately. "Undershot and overshot. Tricky, with
a moving target like this."

"Turn right. This far."

"Y'heard the lubber, port ten!" Lodoviko snapped.
Sweat was running down his boiled-lobster face and
soaking his tunic, but his directions were precise.

BOOM. BOOM. BOOM. BOOM. BOOM. BOOM.

A wall of smoke along the gunports of the fort where
the wall faced them.

Inside, the gunners would be leaping through their
intricately choreographed dance. Swabbers to push

sponge-tipped poles down the barrels to quench the
sparks. Gunner standing by with his leather-sheathed
thumb over the touch-hole to keep air out. Linen bags
of gunpowder rammed down the muzzle next. The
gunner lifting his thumb and jabbing the wire pricker
down the hole to split the fabric. A wad going in, a
heavy circle of woven hemp rope. Then the ball —
four men with a scissor-grip clamp, on guns this heavy.
Ram another wad on the ball, as the gunner pushed
home the friction fuse and clipped his lanyard to it.
Men heaving at ropes and the block-and-tackle squeal-
ing as the long black pebbled surface of the cast-iron
barrel came back to bear, and the gunner standing on
the platform at the rear to aim as the officer called the
bearing and men spun the screws.

Fire, as the crew sprang back from the path of
recoil, mouths open and hands over their ears. Noise
and choking smoke, and the whole thing to do again
and again. . . .

BOOM. BOOM. BOOM. BOOM. BOOM. BOOM.
BOOM. BOOM.

"Turn right. Hard right, for the beach," Raj said.

He shook his head as the visions faded, and had to
grab the captain and scream the directions into his ear;
the man turned eyes gone almost black as the pupil
swallowed the iris, but he shouted in his turn — then
cuffed the helmsman aside and spun the wheel
himself, ropy muscle bulging on his bare arms. This
time the ripping-cloth noise was much louder, almost
shrill, and water splashed across the deck as spouts half
as high as the masts collapsed onto them. Instinct
made him cover his revolver with his hand as the salt
water drenched him.

Dinnalsyn was looking aft. "Damnation to the
Starless Dark," he said. "They got the *Ispirto dil Hom.*"

The next ship in line was turning around the pivot of
the toppled mainmast, a tangled mass of wood and
canvas leaning over the side into the waves. As he

watched two more balls struck. One into the deck, but the next was a very lucky accident. It hit the mortar tube square-on, and the piled ammunition went up in a ball of orange fire. When it cleared the whole front of the ship was missing; the stern slid forward on the same course. Men climbed frantically as the rudder flapped into view; then the merchantman slid out of sight. The water was scattered with floatsam, some of which screamed for help to the next vessel through.

Smooth flukes tossed water upward as the down-draggers came, the only help those men would receive today. Tentacles lashed around a floating spar and the men clinging to it. Their shrieks carried a long way over the water.

Raj turned, stomach knotting. Lodoviko was scream-ing to the sailors in the rigging to drop sail; the bow rose and fell in a choppy motion as the spars came down in a controlled disaster of crashing weight.

"We have to get in," Raj said, grabbing the man by the shoulder.

"We *will*, you lubber of a soldier! Double-moon tide and an onshore breeze: if we come in too fast, the masts'll come down on your precious popgun when she grounds her belly."

Lodoviko seemed to be an intelligent savage. If that mortar didn't work, they would all be joining the crew of the *Spirit of Man* very soon.

BOOM. BOOM. BOOM. BOOM. BOOM. BOOM. BOOM. BOOM.

"Over," Dinnalsyn said, tracing the trajectories. "Over, over, over . . . over . . . over, *over*! Overshot, by the Spirit! Their guns can't depress this far."

Raj cast a look back. The next ship, the *Rover's Bane*, was coming through the gauntlet of waterspouts. *Crack*. Not undamaged; the top of the middle mast — mainmast, he reminded himself — went over the side, and broken staylines snapped across the deck like the whips of a malignant god. They were turning, now, turning straight in for the beach. *City of Wager* right behind.

BOOM. BOOM. BOOM. BOOM. BOOM. BOOM. BOOM. BOOM.

"Hit, she's hit," Raj said, peering through distance and spray.

"Took out her wheel and the second one smashed her rudder," Dinnalsyn said grimly. Then: "She's still steering, Spirit bugger me blind!"

Lodoviko showed teeth like an ox's, yellow and strong. "Florez. That he-whore is a seaman, by Glim. He takes her in with the sails alone — onshore wind, it can be done. He has balls, that one."

The Stalwart drew two of his axes and turned, clashing them together over his head at the fortress. He brayed out a long war-cry, the overhanging yellow fuzz of his mustache standing out from his lip in food-stained glory with the volume.

"Come out and fight, you Brigade heroes! You pussy-whipped suckers of priest's cocks! Come out of that stone barn and fight — *everyone grab a line.*"

The final rush to the cliff was shocking; a pitching glide, and the rough stone rising to blot out the sky above. The keel caught and grated, then caught again in a chorus of groans and snaps and rending noises. Rigging gave way with sounds like gigantic lute-strings, but none of the masts went over. The impact seemed slow and gentle, but Raj felt his feet jerked out from under him by inertia, and only the iron grip of his sword-hand on the tarred cordage by his side kept him from falling forward. One seaman still in the rigging screamed as he described a long arc shorewards, ending in abrupt silence as he impacted on the cliff and fell limply to the narrow strip of stony beach.

Silence fell for an instant, and then the ship quivered as it settled. The hulls of all four — all three — were U-shaped in section with edge-keels rather than a single deep keelson-mounted fin. The *Chakra* ground her way down into the loose rocks of the shore and settled almost level. The comparative absence of noise seemed unnatural, like a ringing in the ears. Off to the left the other two ships were grounded rather further out; there was twenty meters of water between the *Chakra* and dry land, twice that for each of the others.

Dinnalysn picked himself up. "We made it," he said. "They can't touch us now."

"Professional tunnel-vision, Grammeck," Raj said with a grim smile. He checked the loads in his pistol and wiped the surfaces dry with the tail of his uniform jacket. "You mean their *artillery* can't touch us," he went on, and pointed to their left. The rock bulged out and then curved away; most of Port Wager was hidden by it.

"Nothing to prevent them coming down the stairways around that corner of the cliff and trying their best to beat us to death. Nothing at all."

"No, up two more turns with the same charge," Raj said.

The mortarman looked at him with awe and spun the elevating screw. The four loaders lifted the heavy shell with its sausage-rings of gunpowder at the base and eased it into the muzzle. Everyone else in the sandbagged emplacement on the forecastle bent away, closing their eyes and opening their mouths, jamming thumbs against their ears.

"Fire in the hole!"

Fffumph. The 20-cm tube belched a blade of fire taller than a man; everyone was coughing and waving to clear the dense cloud of smoke. The projectile was visible as a dark blur through the air, then a dot that hesitated high above, and then a blur again.

crump. Muted, because it was exploding within the walls of Fort Wager, but still loud. The shells had a ten-kilogram bursting charge, and their target — the land-facing guns of the fort — had no overhead protection. Only thin partitions between each of the guns on the firing deck, as well. The seaward-facing guns might as well be in Carson Barracks for all the good they were doing the Brigade now.

The problem was that there was no way to observe the fall of shot from the ships; the target was not only half a kilometer north, it was three hundred meters higher up and behind a thick stone wall. The main Civil Government force, massed just out of cannon-shot of the fort walls on the other side, *could* observe roughly where the shells landed. The signals were rough as well, color-coded rockets; green for "too far," red for "short," white and black for "left" and "right." Even with Center to help with the calculations it was taking time to walk the shells of each gun onto the target. Time they might not have.

"Ser! Here t'barbs come agin!"

Raj vaulted over the sandbags, pivoting on his left hand, and landed in a crouch on the deck. That put him below the level of the built-up railings, which were turning out to be a very good idea. The cluster of boulders at the bulge of the cliff was four hundred meters away. The Brigaderos had gotten set up in there, and proved to be deadly accurate. Not very fast, but there were a lot of them, and they tended to hit what they aimed at. Tinneran, the recruit with the big hands, had found out the hard way when he stood up to get a better shot; he was lying wrapped in canvas and out of the way, with a round blue hole in his forehead and the back blown out of his head. The lieutenant was dead, too. Exactly according to the odds. The two most dangerous positions in a cavalry platoon were junior officer and raw recruit.

Two other fatals, and two too badly hurt to shoot even kneeling and through a loophole. That left him thirty rifles. The loopholes had saved their *butts*. It was a good thing there was no way to hide coming down the cliff directly overhead, and a man rapelling down on a rope had proved to be a very good target.

He duckwalked to the side of the ship and squinted through a narrow slit in the wooden barricade. Bullets made their flat *crack* overhead, or thocked into the ship's timbers, or peened as they struck metal. Puffs of smoke rose from the rocks as the marksmen increased their covering fire; at a guess, each was a picked man with two or three others passing him loaded rifle-muskets. The 5th troopers kept hunched down behind the bulletproof sheath of planking that Center had added to Raj's plan. It wasn't worth the risk to stick their rifles out the firing slits until they had better targets.

Which would be shortly. None of the bodies from the last attack was floating; the downdraggers had gotten them all. They'd even gone for the ones on the narrow strip of beach, until both sides shot half a dozen of the repulsive beasts while they dragged themselves half-out of the water to seize their prey.

"Here t' bastids come," called the NCO.

"Pick your targets," Raj said, loud but calm. "Fire low."

A first wave came pelting up the beach beneath the cliffs. They wore green-gray jackets and black pants, lobster-tail steel helmets with nasals and cheek-flaps. General's Dragoons, part of the Brigade's regular army. Their rifles were slung, and they carried short ladders.

"Now!"

The Armory rifles began to speak, a steady beat. Men fell, others picked up their ladders and came forward again. Another hundred and another, and the third had no ladders but waded out into the water directly towards the *Chakra*. The bow was thigh-deep, but there was another four meters or so of sheer hull to climb if they made it that far. The midships railing was half a deck lower than the forecastle, but the water there was waist-to chest deep.

Damn, but those are brave men, he thought.

The downdraggers were out there; the men had to come in a dense phalanx and prod with their bayonets. Even so some went down in the tentacles at the edge or rear of the formation, and more stayed to stab and hack at the smooth grey flesh of the predators. For a moment, because the water was being whipped to froth by fire from the *Chakra* and the other two ships. They were too far out to be attacked, but they could support their sister.

A slapping sound and a grunt. Just down from him a trooper slumped backwards twitching and coughing out sheets of blood from a soft-lead slug through the upper chest. Bullets were cracking into the planking like hail, and if enough came your way one was going to get through the loophole. He switched positions. The hundred men in the first wave were more like thirty now; one turned and tried to run back the way he'd come, and an officer shot him at point-blank range with his pistol. Now they were level with the *Chakra*'s bow and curving out into the water with their ladders, knees coming up high as if in unconscious reluctance to let their feet touch the surface.

"First squad, *follow me!*" he called, and led them to the bows.

Past the mortar, where another shot came, and another — they were firing for effect, how had he missed the signal they were on target? Up to the bows, and the rough pole ends of an improvised ladder slapping against the boards. He stuck his revolver over the edge and squeezed off three shots; somebody screamed, and a dozen bullets hammered the edge of the planking as he snatched the hand back. *Good. Decoyed, by the Spirit.* There might be something in the world more futile than trying to reload a musket while standing in a meter of monster-haunted water, but he couldn't think of it offhand.

A Brigadero head came over the rail. He shot, and the bullet keened off the lobster-tail helmet; the man's head jerked around as if he'd been kicked by a riding dog, and he vanished to splash below. One more shot; it missed, but the trooper beside him didn't. The

Brigade warrior folded around his belly and jackknifed, flopping across the rail. Raj holstered his revolver and swept out his saber.

"Come on!" he said, and set the point against the ladder.

The trooper did likewise, putting the tip of his long bayonet against the other upright. They pushed — sideways, not straight back. The ladder slid out of sight, and the timbre of the screams below changed from fury to terror. Raj risked a look; something like a mass of animated worms around a serrated beak the length of an arm had the man who'd held the ladder at the base. It was pulling him seaward and biting chunks out of him at the same time; three of his comrades were hacking at it with their swords although the victim was obviously dead; even *following* it. Which he wouldn't have believed, if he hadn't seen some of the things men would do in combat. . . . The squad with him fired point-blank at the next set of men with a ladder.

"*Ser.*"

He whipped around. A Brigadero had gotten to the deck, twenty feet away where the sailors were holding a section with cutlass and boarding axe. Down in the waist of the ship, the ones who'd come without ladders must be climbing over each other's shoulders to get on board. The first man on jerked two revolvers from crossdraw holsters. Raj and the trooper beside him ran back toward him. The Brigade warrior took a careful stance and shot the trooper. The man went over with a yell, clutching his thigh as if to squeeze out the pain and rolling into a tangle of sailcloth and rope hanging to the deck. Raj dove forward over the edge of the forecastle half-deck, kept hold of his saber but landed with his ribs on something *hard*, and came up wheezing.

Not ten feet from the Brigadero. The man was grinning, or snarling, impossible to say. He aimed with care, as much outside the range of Raj's saber as if he'd been on Maxiluna or lost Earth itself —

Something bright flashed by, rotating into a blur. It stopped at the pistoleer, turning into one of Lodoviko's axes. The bit took the Brigadero at a flat angle between neck and shoulder. Blood jutted through the cut cloth and flesh, spurting; shock convulsed both the man's hands, and the pistols fired. By luck, good or bad, one barked into the deck-planking by Raj's foot, turning a thumb-sized patch into a miniature crater.

He hurdled the dying man's body and turned the next stride into a full-sweep kick at the next man coming over the low rail. The steel-reinforced toe of Raj's riding boot thudded into his chest with an impact that brought a twinge of pain to Raj's lower back. The Brigadero toppled backward and splashed into the water. He came up bent over and gasping with his mouth barely above the surface, wading back towards shore with empty hands. Raj leaned over the rail.

He met the eyes of the man there, the one who had been standing chest deep so his comrades could climb up him and onto the ship. The bearded snarling face showed only an intense concentration; his right hand went back for the sword slung over his shoulder. Raj could see something else; a smooth upwelling in the water, a track heading straight for the enemy soldier's back. He leaned and thrust; the point punched into the standing man's neck. His eyes were turning up as he slid off the point.

A mercy, Raj thought

Fdump. Much louder than the previous mortar-shells. A column of black smoke atop a dome of fire rose over the edge of the cliff, over the barely-visible wall of the fort beyond. Red dots trailing smoke and sparks shot skyward, and heavier debris tumbled briefly into sight.

secondary explosion, Center said. **gun bay three, frontal sector to the right of the main gates.**

Then something much heavier went off. Shards of rock as big as dogs quivered loose from the cliff, and the noise thumped at his face.

Raj nodded, wheezing back his breath. A fragment of red-hot iron slicing into a bagged charge . . . ripple effect. Massive guns flipping out into the air, and pieces of the crews with them. Chunks of rock and concrete blasting in all directions.

A yell went up from the sandbagged mortar enclosure. Nobody noticed along the sides of the ship for an instant. There was a final snarling fury of shots fired with the muzzles touching flesh and bayonet clashing on swords. The enemy fell back, realizing by instinct that there were too few of them to push home their attack. They saw the pillar of fire as they retreated, and ran.

Then the crew and soldiers were cheering too; another trio of mortar shells puffed upwards, and the sound of their firing slapped back from the cliffs like the applause of giants.

"Cease fire, riflemen," Raj croaked, keeping well down — the marksmen among the tumbled boulders could shoot again now, with their own men dead or out of the way. Lodoviko looked up from bandaging a gash in his hairy thigh and hooted laughter; Raj nodded.

"Ser?" the platoon sergeant said. "We could git sommat more of 'em —"

"No," Raj said. He remembered the man standing in the water, waiting while others climbed to safety over him. Or at least out of reach of the tentacles. "I need men like that. All I can get."

as do i, raj whitehall, Center said. **as do i.**

Colonel Courtet had probably been a fine figure of a man, back before twenty years of inactivity and Sala brandy took their toll; the vast bush of beard that hid his face was probably a mercy. He hadn't been drinking recently, but that probably only worsened the trembling of his liver-spotted hands. His body was large and soft, straining against the silvered armor he wore, and his dog shifted as if sensing its rider's unease.

"Colonel Gerrin Staenbridge," the Civil Government officer said, saluting crisply.

The other man's reply was a vague wave followed by silence. Gerrin was in no particular hurry, within reason. The two parties were meeting under a white flag in the cleared no-man's-land in front of the fort, which gave a wonderful view of the tumbled ruin of the main defensive bastion beside the gate. Eroded-looking stumps stood up above rubble that had filled in the moat and made a perfect ramp up into Fort Wager. In fact, it even looked accessible on dogback. Every minute that Courtet had to watch it from this angle was a blow struck at his morale, which looked none too steady to begin with. According to the intelligence, he'd been pushed forward by the local military council because he was the only officer of sufficient birth and rank who wasn't as defeatist as Colonel Boyce.

As completely defeatist as Boyce. Senior officers with military ability or ambition didn't come to Stern Isle.

Besides, Courtet's aide was worth a little attention: he looked the way a noble Military Government warrior was supposed to in the legends and so rarely did in practice. Twenty, broad in the shoulders and narrow in the hips, regular bronzed features and tourmaline eyes, long blond hair flowing to his shoulders and close-trimmed barley-colored beard. Uniform of beautiful materials, elegantly understated, but the breastplate commendably hacked, battered and lead-splashed.

Gerrin fought down a friendly smile; besides, Bartin was acting as *his* aide. The senior officer, a junior, and a bannerman, as was traditional.

"There's no point in wasting time," Staenbridge went on, when it was plain Courtet would not speak. Possibly could not. "You're getting the third and last chance to surrender."

"Ah . . ." Courtet coughed rackingly. "Same terms?" He wet his lips, visibly thirsty. Out of the corner of his eye, Gerrin could see the fine-drawn lip of the Brigadero aide curl.

"Of course not," Staenbridge snapped. "You know the laws of war concerning fortified places, colonel. We summoned you first when we invested the fort, and again before we commenced firing. Terms become more strict with each refusal."

He pointed with a gauntleted hand. "Now we've put a workable breach in your defenses. If you refuse and we storm the position, your lives are forfeit. And believe me, if you force us to take unnecessary casualties, we'll throw any survivors over the cliffs and their families will be turned over to the men. Who will *not* be in a gentle mood."

Courtet looked from one Civil Government officer to the other, from the dark suave face of a killer to the cheerful, handsome young man with the razor-edged steel hook for a left hand. The flower tucked behind his ear made the sight worse, not better.

"What terms, gentlemen?" he said hoarsely.

"Personal liberty for your families. All able-bodied males and their households to be sent to East Residence, men to be enrolled in our forces under the usual provisions — no service against the Brigade. The remainder to be released after giving their parole never to bear arms against the Civil Government. Personal property except arms to be retained by the owners, and officers' sidearms and dogs for those discharged. Forfeiture of real property beyond one house and forty hectares. And if that seems harsh, messers, consider the alternatives."

"Can I, ah, consult with my officers?"

"With this gentleman and no others." *Although I wouldn't mind consulting with him myself, under other circumstances.* "Are you in command, Colonel Courtet, or not?"

Probably not, but he could lead his men in the obvious direction. There was nothing more demoralizing than being shelled without a chance to reply, except possibly knowing your family was there with you. The blond aide drew Courtet aside and whispered urgently in his ear.

When he turned back, the Brigade commander's face was like gellid fat. His aide dismounted and helped him to the ground; they both drew their swords and offered them hilt-first across their forearms.

A huge roaring cheer rose from the Civil Government troops downslope, in their hasty fieldworks. Even with the mortars in support, taking the fortress would enact a big enough butcher's bill to daunt anyone. The fort's ramparts were black with watchers as well, and the sound that came up from them was a long hollow groan, the sort of noise you hear on a battlefield after dark when the wounded lie out. Calling for water, or their mothers, or in wordless pain.

The Civil Government officers each took his counterpart's blade, flourished it overhead, and returned it. Then Staenbridge pulled out his watch.

"My felicitations on an honorable but difficult decision," *which you should have made yesterday, you butchering moron,* "Colonel Courtet. Your men will march out within twenty minutes and stack arms," he said, "or you'll be in violation of the truce. Colonel, you'll remain with me until that's done. Sooner begun, the sooner we can get the wounded attended to and your women and children settled."

Courtet nodded heavily, resting one hand on the saddle of the dog beside him.

"Where's Whitehall?" he burst out.

The two Descotters looked at him expressionlessly. He blinked, and amended: "Where's Messer General Whitehall? They say," the Brigadero went on, "the demons fight for him. I could believe that."

"General Whitehall is where he thinks best," Staenbridge said. *And I violently disagree; he should be here, and I on that boat.* "And the holy Avatars fight for him,

Colonel. He is the Sword of the Spirit of Man —
hadn't you heard?"

Courtet was silent but his aide bowed courteously. "I
had heard that, sir," he said, in fair if slow Sponglish.
"We yield our swords to the might of the Spirit, then,
to take them up again against Its enemies, heathen and
Muslim." He turned and spurred for the gates.

They opened, and remained that way. A squad came
forward to put Courtet under guard; Bartin Foley
murmured to the lieutenant in charge, and a table,
chair and tumbler of brandy appeared. The fat old man
in too-tight armor looked at them and then put his face
in his hands, his shoulders heaving.

Staenbridge heeled his dog off to one side. Bartin
leaned toward him.

"You said that as if you meant it," the younger man
said. "About Messer Raj being the Sword of the Spirit;
and here I thought you were a sceptic."

"I find myself growing less sceptical, comrade of my
heart. Less sceptical than I would wish."

"Envious?" Bartin grinned.

Gerrin Staenbridge shuddered elaborately and
began stripping off his gloves. "Merciful Avatars — if
there are any — no! Plenty of fame in being one of the
selfless, faithful Companions, as I don't doubt the lying
histories will call us all, forgetting we're each the
central characters of our own stories." He thought for a
moment, watching the screeching gulls and scawing
dactosauroids over the harbor.

"Bad enough to be a hero, and carry the burdens of
human expectations. To shoulder those of Something
Else . . . even a soul like Raj's will crack under the
burden in the end. No matter that all of us do what we
can to help."

He looked at the younger officer and smiled. "The
flower's charming, by the way. And since it's on the left
today . . . ?"

CHAPTER NINE

Raj Whitehall looked past his booted feet where they rested on the table, down the long conference chamber and out the french doors and balcony at the other end. From here you could just see the blue-and-silver Starburst banner of the Civil Government floating over Fort Wager against the violet morning sky and the pale translucent globe of Maxiluna. Soon to be renamed Fort Tinneran, for all the good it would do. There *was* something satisfying in the sight. Also in getting some honest work done. This meeting was informal, the Companions and one or two others, but there were things that needed doing.

Grammeck Dinnalsyn ruffled a stack of papers. "Just mason's work for now, general," he said. "The fort's sound."

"Not until it gets overhead protection for the guns, and something that can drop plunging fire on the beach," Raj said crisply. "Cursed if I'll see it taken back by the same tricks *I* used, Grammeck."

Although that would be a lot more difficult without Center. It had been close enough even with the Spirit lending a direct hand.

i am not god.

No, but you're the closest approximation available within current parameters, Raj thought.

"I do have an idea about that," the gunner said. "It'll be a while before we can get real howitzers or mortars there; they'll have to be ordered from East Residence Armory or the Kolobassian forges. Which requires formal funding from the Master of Ordnance . . ."

Half a dozen people groaned. "Exactly. You can steal money for yourself, but Star Spirit help you if you spend money irregularly for the State. What we *can* do, is take some of the surplus smoothbores, cut them down, and mount them in pits. Some sort of turntable, but that's blacksmith level work. Then timber-and-earth covers, with removable sections. Solid shot, and time-fused shell, of sorts. I wouldn't care to have forty kilograms of either dropped on my head."

Raj nodded. *Spirit, but I like a man who can think for himself.* With Center's matchless ability to store and sort information, he really didn't need all that much of a staff. He had set himself to train one anyway; the Civil Government *needed* something better than ad-hoc organizations whenever a field army was set up. There was a big gap in the table between the administrators who saw to pay and garrison work, and the battalion-level unit organizations.

a deliberate one, Center observed. Field armies made coups easier.

We get the coups anyway, Raj replied.

"Draw up the plans," he said. "We may not have time for it, but at least our successors will get some help. How are the public works, town water supplies, that sort of thing?"

"In fair-to-good shape, no new work but maintenance is sound. Nothing like the pigsty we found down in Port Murchison; but the roads are pretty bad."

"See if you can get the same organization working on transport, then," Raj said.

"Sir," Ludwig Bellamy cut in, "speaking of Port Murchison —"

Raj nodded, and the ex-*Squadrone* went on, "I've had a letter in from my father."

He smoothed the sheaf of crinkled pages out; they were covered with a thick quasi-literate scrawl. Karl Bellamy had had expensive tutors shipped in from East Residence for his son, as he might have had a concubine or swordsmith. In fact, most *Squadrone* fathers would much rather have spent the money on girls or guns than possibly sissifying *grisuh* learning. The elder Bellamy had seen no need for such polish for himself, and the letter was too confidential for secretaries.

"Colonel Osterville has been removed as Vice-Governor of the Territories," he said.

There was a general murmur of satisfaction around the table. Osterville was one of Barholm's Guards — a semi-official group of troubleshooters-cum-enforcers of good birth, usually men with few prospects save the Governor's favor. Raj had been a Guard, to begin with. Osterville still was, and he'd been sent to relieve Raj at the end of the reconquest under what looked suspiciously like official disfavor.

"The man's got the soul of a pimp," Kaltin Gruder said flatly. "I had to spend six months under his command, and the Spirit spare me any such service again. Who got him, Ludwig?"

"Administrator Berg," Ludwig said, raising his brows. "Malfeasance in office, peculation, suspicion of usurpation of Gubernatorial honors." The last would be the decisive one. Far more dangerous to wear the wrong color shoes than to strip a province bare. "He's being posted as garrison commander to . . . ah, Sandoral."

More satisfied smiles. A hot, dusty town uncomfortably close to the Colony. None of them expected Osterville to shine if it came to serious skirmishing.

observe, Center said. A brief flash; Osterville's face streaked with sweat and dust, bracing himself against the rocking of a railway car. The view out the window was not unlike central Stern Isle, but Raj recognized it as the plateau north of the Oxheads, east of salt-thick Lake Canpech. On Governor Barholm's new Central Railway, heading east away from East Residence and the rich lands of the Hemmar River country.

"*Hingada* Osterville," Hadolfo Zahpata said, in his sing-song southern accent; he was from northwest of Sandoral, and so were most of his 18th Komar Borderers. "I would wish a more able man in the post, though. Ali will be moving sometime. Malash; the Spirit appoints our coming up and our going down."

"Endfile," Raj said, and rapped his knuckles on the table. That was pleasant news, but not strictly germane. "Now, Muzzaf?"

The Komarite cleared his throat. "There is a machine shop which can do the work you requested," he said, setting a Brigade cap-and-ball revolver down on the table. It was a five-shot weapon, loaded with paper cartridges from the front and with nipples for the percussion caps on the back of the cylinder.

"The original design was copied from the Civil Government model," he went on, "so the calibre and pitch of the rifling are the same. Once the cylinder is bored through and tapped, and the hammer modifed, it will accept the standard brass cartridge case — and ammunition is available in sufficient quantity if we indent for it now. I, ah," he coughed, "know of certain channels to expedite matters."

"Go for it," Raj said. "Initial order of six thousand, we certainly captured enough. I want every cavalryman to have one by the time we ship out of here; we don't want melee actions, but I'm damned if I'm going to have my lads facing a man with four revolvers and them with nothing but a sword. Messer Historiomo?"

"I see no reason not to authorize the expenditure," the Administrative Service representative said cautiously; but then, he did *everything* cautiously.

"Which brings us," Raj went on, "to the fund. My lady?"

"Every battalion has agreed to contribute in proportion to their losses," she said. "I talked to the officers' wives . . ."

"Good, very good." The Civil Government made

little provision for the families of casualties, or for men rendered unfit-for-service. He'd established a tradition of using plunder to set up a pension fund; the men trusted him not to steal it. "Muzzaf, put it in something suitable. Land, I suppose, or town properties. Arrange for trustees, trustworthy ones."

"My love?" Suzette went on.

He nodded. Some people found his conferences a trifle eccentric — Fatima, for example, was acting as secretary to Suzette and had her nine-month-old daughter, named Suzette for her patroness, in a cradle beneath the side table they were using — but they got the work done.

Raj's wife produced a list of her own. "We have about fifty troopers who've got injuries that make them unfit-for-service but not really incapacitated — ones without somewhere to retire to back home, that is. I've looked up about the same number of young Brigaderos widows or orphaned maidens of good reputation and appropriate rank who were covered by the amnesty; there were a fair number of men with medium-sized farms held in fee simple, here. Widows and daughters wouldn't inherit in the absence of male offspring under Brigade law but would under ours; the ones I've talked to are willing and ready to convert to orthodoxy to avoid ending up as spinsters living on their relatives. For that matter, there are a couple of hundred who'll settle for a man on active service; that's a Brigade tradition too. If you know some unmarried troopers you'd like to see get a farm to come back to eventually . . ."

Raj nodded. The same thing had happened spontaneously in the Southern Territories after the conquest, and worked out surprisingly well. Soldiers and their relatives had solid legal status under the Civil Government, and could hold land under low-tax military tenure; desirable qualities in a husband, in uncertain times. Having a farm to retire to after mustering-out was the dream of most troopers who didn't stand to inherit one or a good tenancy. It was a good way to start integrating new territory into the Civil Government as well.

"See to it, then, my sweet. Ah — we could hold a mass ceremony here. The men would like that, and it'll make them remember they're soldiers first and foremost, active or on the invalid list."

Kaltin laughed. "Advise the active-service men to get the brides pregnant before they leave," he said.

"I don't doubt they'll try, Kaltin," Gerrin said. "The dispositions, Raj? We're still scattered to hell-and-gone."

He swung his feet down as servants brought in the breakfast trays. "That is next," he said, accepting a plate and shoveling it in without looking. After a moment he tasted what he was eating and looked over at his wife. "How *do* you manage to dig up a good cook wherever we go?" he asked. Their regular was an East Residence native who refused to leave the walls for whatever reason.

"Hereditary talent, my sweet."

"Well. Now, I'm sure all you gentlemen are having a wonderful time relaxing, but we've got to get Kaltin back into the field before he fades to a sylph and gets worn down to a nub."

"You underestimate me, sir. It's only been a week."

"Nevertheless. Gerrin, you are hereby appointed Purple Commander." He slid a clip of papers down to the other Descotter, who looked through them and began to hand them out to the men who would be his subordinates for the field maneuvers.

"I will be Orange Commander," Raj said, and did likewise.

"Jorg, you'll be in charge of the referees, and I want it as realistic as we can get without massive casualties. We'll do a thorough briefing this afternoon, but in essence I want to get us better at marching divided —" he held out a hand, fingers splayed "— and fighting united." The hand closed into a fist.

"Oh, and we'd better arrange some sort of substantial prize for the best units; the men are starting to think this is going to be a military picnic like the Southern Territories."

"I doubt many who were in those boats with you think that, Raj," Gerrin said soberly.

"Learning by experience can be prohibitively expensive," Raj said. "Next, the *Brigaderos* we sent back to East Residence. They'll need to be retrained, and then they'll need officers. We won't be in charge of that, but between us I think we can have some influence, and it'd be a shame to waste material that good under incompetents. Messers, I'd appreciate it if you'd each prepare me a list of men you think suitable, and we'll see what we can do. Next, promotions, demotions, and gold-of-valor awards."

They worked their way through the *huwacheros*, toast and kave, then through a round of kave and cigarettes. He saved the disagreeable signing of death-warrants for last. There was always someone who didn't believe the stories about how hard-ass Messer Raj was about mistreating locals. None from the 5th Descott this time, thank the Spirit . . .

"Does that wrap up the military end of it?" Raj said. He looked out the window; with a little luck, he could get his butt into the saddle this afternoon and do some hands-on work. A chance to avoid Bureaucrat's Bottom a little while longer.

"All but the Star question, oh Savior of the State," Gerrin said. "When do we get on with the rest of the bloody campaign?"

"According to the latest dispatches from East Residence," Raj said judiciously, "negotiations between the Ministry of Barbarians and General Forker are proceeding, mmmm, *in an orderly but discrete fashion* due to *turbulent elements* in Carson Barracks. Interpret that as you will."

"Meaning, Messer," Dinnalsyn said sourly, with the

experience of a man brought up in East Residence, "that Forker can't decide whether to crap or get off the pot, because the barb commanders are running around rubbing their heads and wondering what hit them. And the Ministry bureaucrats are sending each other memos consisting of competitively obscure literary allusions and strings of references to precedents back six hundred years. Which is probably what their predecessors were doing six hundred years ago when we lost the Old Residence to the Brigade in the *first* place."

"Pen-pushers," Zahpata said, striking his forehead with his palm.

"I'm assured that the *relevant experts are working earnestly for a peaceful solution to the issues in dispute*," Raj went on dryly.

"That bad?" Kaltin said. He tore open a roll. "With the relevant experts working for peace, you *know* we're going to have war, Messer — but not until the worst possible time."

"Bite your tongue, major," Raj said. "My estimation is that between them Forker and the Ministry will do exactly that, string things out until the onset of the winter rains and then decide to fight after all. Decide that *we* should fight."

This time the curses were genuine and heartfelt. With local variations the whole Midworld basin had a climate of warm dry summers and cool-to-cold wet winters. The northerly sectors of the Western Territories got snow, and the whole area had abundant mud. On the unmaintained roads of country under barbarian rule that meant morasses that clogged dogs' feet, sucked the boots off men and mired guns and wagons. Plus foraging would be more difficult, that long after harvest, and even hardy men were more likely to sicken with chest fevers if they had to sleep out in the rains. Disease had destroyed more armies than battle, and they all knew it.

Spring and fall were the best seasons for campaigning;

early summer after the wheat harvest was tolerable, although bad water meant cholera unless you were very careful about the Church's sanitation edicts. High summer was bad. Winter was a desperation-only nightmare.

"Nevertheless, if it has to be done, we'll do it," Raj said. He quoted from an ancient Civil Government military handbook: *"Remember that the enemy's bodies too are subject to mortality and fatigue; they are initiated also into the mysteries of death, as are all men.* And even their rank-and-file include a good many landed men, their reservists particularly, who won't be used to living hard. I want us *ready*.

"Ehwardo," he went on. The last living Poplanich looked up. Raj tapped several red-covered ledgers beside him. They had the Ministry of Barbarians seal on their covers, with the odd grain-sheaf subseal of the Foreign Intelligence division.

"Coordinate with Muzzaf and see what you can do about these intelligence reports. I want digests, including what new information you can get from local sources. Chop out the political bumpf and verbiage and the unfounded speculation; give me hard information. Manpower, weapons, road conditions, weather patterns, regional crops and yields and foraging prospects, what railroads the barbs have running, local landowners and Sysups and how they lean."

"General," Ehwardo said, already looking still more abstracted. Raj nodded; Thom's cousin was one of the few noblemen he knew who really appreciated numbers and their uses.

"Messers . . . to work."

The room felt larger after the officers had left, with a clack of the heel-plates of their boots and a jingle as they hitched at their sword-belts. Historiomo cleared his throat and glanced at Suzette and her protege.

"Messa Whitehall has my complete confidence," Raj said.

"Ah. So I was given to understand." A long pause. "I am to understand, then, that the Most Valiant General is pleased with mine and my colleagues' work?"

"Pleasantly surprised," Raj said. "It's important to this war that we have a secure and productive forward base; Stern Isle is the obvious candidate."

He ran his hand over a preliminary report on land tenure on Stern Isle as it had been under the Brigade and would be with the massive transfers of ownership following the conquest. Dry stuff, but crucially important. Cities and trade were the way a few people made their living and the odd merchant grew rich, but land was absolutely crucial to everything. Not just that the overwhelming majority everywhere were peasants, land tenure was the foundation of revenue and political and military power. His own studies, his instincts, and everything Center had taught him agreed that there was nothing more useless than an unconsolidated victory. Conquest without follow-up would crumble away behind him.

The problem was that he was to expert administration what say, Colonel Boyce was to combat command — he could recognize it when he saw it, but lacked inclination and talent himself for anything but the rough-and-ready military equivalent. Which was to the real thing as military music was to music.

"Yes." Historiomo pushed his silver-rimmed glasses up his nose. He was the sort of soft little man you saw by the scores of thousands on the streets of East Residence, with carefully folded cravats and polished pewter buckles on their shoes and drab brown coats. So nondescript it was always a bit of a surprise to see him, as if you'd never met him before.

"Yes, Chief Administrator Berg did tell us that you and your household were not the general run of military nobility, Most Valiant —"

"Messer will do."

"Messer General, then."

"Berg," Raj said with a cold smile, "struck me as being not in the ordinary run of bureaucrat. Once he'd been convinced that I wanted him to cooperate, but intended to get the job done whether he did or not."

"Indeed." Historiomo took the glasses off again and polished them. His voice grew a touch sharper, as if the blurring of vision removed some constraint. "You find us of the Administrative Service, ah, excessively cautious, do you not, Messer Whitehall?"

Raj shrugged. "I have a job of work to do in this world," he said. "To do it, I have to take men as I find them."

"We're used to being despised," Historiomo said with polite bitterness. "The military nobility always have; it's *find us supplies for twenty thousand men*, or *why aren't the roads ready*? But do they listen when we explain? Never. They worship action at the expense of thought, and think that you can overcome any problem with a sword and willpower. They impose solutions that make problems *worse* and we have to work around the wreckage. Or a Governor shoots his way to the Chair and then thinks he can order us to do the impossible. We're the ones who have to tell them no.

"The patricians —" he cast a cautious look at Suzette; the urban nobility was her class, and that of Chancellor Tzetzas "— make an art of intrigue and a god of form at the expense of content. They monopolize the great offices of State and plunder them without shame or thought for long-term consequences, and *we* take the blame. And everybody mocks us, our forms and paperwork, our fussy little precedents. Yet who is it that preserves the institutional memory of the State, who keeps the Civil Government from turning into another feudal hodgepodge of squabbling barons? Who keeps things together and the public services functioning through defeats and civil wars and bad Governors? We do."

"Agreed," Raj said.

Historiomo started, cleared his throat and fiddled

with his pen-case.

"Messer, I'm called the Sword of the Spirit of Man. That means I know what you *can't* do with a sword. I'm *not* the pen, the voice, or the conscience of the Spirit. I'm the Sword; I chop obstacles out of the way; I keep the barbarians from burning the cities around the ears of people like you. I do my job; and when I find someone else who can do *his*, then I don't care if they're nobleman, patrician, clerk, merchant, Starless Dark, I don't give a damn if they're Colonists or barbs."

"Most Valiant General," Historiomo said, rising and neatly stacking his document boxes before fastening them together with a leather strap, "I won't say it's a pleasure to work with you. Alarming, in fact. But it is a *relief*, I assure you. Messa Whitehall."

He bowed deeply and walked out with the strap over his shoulder.

"Well, that'll teach us not to judge a scroll by the winding-stick," Suzette said. She bent over the crib beneath her table. "I think this young lady needs to be changed, Fatima."

When they were alone, she smiled at Raj. "And what, my darling, is *my* function with the Sword of the Spirit?"

"You keep him from going completely fucking insane," Raj said, smiling back.

"So far."

"So far."

CHAPTER TEN

"You are all conspiring to drive me *mad*," Filip Forker said, pulling off the light ceremonial helmet and throwing it to the floor with a clang. "Mad, mad!" Shocked murmurs rolled for a moment down the long chamber, until the armored guards along the walls thumped their musket-butts on the floor. Once, twice, three times; when they returned to immobility, the silence was complete.

Attendants closed in around the Brigade monarch; one passed a damp cloth over his face, and another got in a lick with a polishing cloth at the thin silver breastplate the slight little man wore. A minister murmured in his ear; after a while Forker's face set in an expression of petulant resignation, and he sat again.

"Go on, go on."

Even the high arched ceiling and meter-thick walls of the Primary Audience Hall couldn't take any of the muggy heat out of a Carson Barracks summer. The temperature outside was thirty Celsius, and the city was built out of dark basalt blocks and set in the middle of a swamp; in winter the building would be chilly and dank instead, for all the great arched fireplaces at either end of the Hall. The skylights sent shafts of light ten meters down into hot gloom, with the wings of insects glittering as they crossed from shadow into sun. Very little light or air came in through the narrow slit windows.

The men who had built — ordered the building — of the Hall hadn't exactly intended it as a fortress. If anything, it had originally been designed to hold large assemblies for public address, and incidentally to intimidate petitioners. Standing off attackers had not been far from the builders' minds, though, and ordinary comfort just wasn't something to which they had attached much importance.

The Civil Government embassy rose from their stools below the Seat and bowed, hands on chests.

"If Your Mightiness will deign to examine these documents once again," their leader began again, with infinite patience. "Much will be made clear, as clear as the Operating Code of the Spirit."

His Namerique so perfectly adjusted to upper-class Brigade ears that it was more conspicuous than an accent, coming from a dark clean-shaven man in a long embroidered robe. A gesture suggested the age-yellowed papers on a side table below the Seat without the vulgarity of actually pointing.

"You will see that by agreement between your . . . predecessor His Mightiness General Oskar Grakker and the then Admiral of the Squadron Shelvil Ricks, in the time of our Sovereign Lord and Sole Autocrat Laron Poplanich, Governor of the Civil Government of Holy Federation, may the Spirit upload the souls of the worthy dead into Its Nets, the bulk of Stern Isle was granted as dower property to Mindy-Sue Grakker and the heirs of her body and Shelvil Ricks. Which is to say, the Admirals of the Squadron, which is to say — since ex-Admiral Connor Auburn has been persuaded by grace of the Spirit to lay down the unseemly usurped sovereignty which Geyser Ricks unrighteously seized — which is to say, the heir is our Most Sovereign Mighty Lord Barholm Clerett, Viceregent of the Spirit of Man upon Earth. In no way, most Mighty General, could the repossession of Stern Isle therefore be held a usurpation or aggression; for on the contrary righteousness consists of acting rightly —"

The voice droned on for another twenty minutes of rhetorical strophe and antistrophe, spiced out with appeals to truth, justice, reason and comparisons to events that no Brigade member in the Hall besides Forker himself had ever heard of. Unlike most of his nation, General Forker had had a comprehensive classical education; it was one major source of his unpopularity.

At last he broke in peevishly: "Yes, yes, We will read your position paper, Ambassador Minh. At our leisure. These matters cannot be settled in a day, you know."

"Your Mightiness," Minh said, bowing again in profound agreement.

"Who's next?" Forker asked, as the Civil Government ambassadors bowed themselves backward, as neatly choreographed as dancers. Despite the heat and the prickly rash under his ceremonial uniform, the sight mollified him a little.

They know how to serve, he thought.

"Your Mightiness, the inventor and newsletter producer Martini of Pedden, currently dwelling in Old Residence, desires —"

"No!" This time Forker brushed aside the helping hands as he rose. "When will you learn not to waste my time with trivialities?" The minister leaned close again, but the Brigade ruler interrupted him: "I don't care *how* much he paid you. This audience is at an end. We will withdraw. Send the Chief Librarian Kassador to my quarters, *after* I've had a bath."

Stentor-voiced, a Captain of the Life Guards called: "Hear the word; this audience is at an end. So orders our General, His Mightiness Filip Forker, Lord of Men."

The great hall echoed, cracking as the guards stamped their musket butts again on the floor and then brought the long weapons to port arms. Two platoons along either wall marched up to the Seat and out across the vacant space between the petitioners and the commander's dais, then did a left-wheel to face the crowd. The captain snapped another order, and they

began to march forward in slow-pace: step-*pause*-step,
with the foot remaining poised for an instant before it
came down in a unified hundredfold crash. It was a
showy maneuver and perfectly timed. It also let
everyone get to the big doors at the rear in an orderly
fashion, without allowing any loitering. Nobody who
saw the Life Guards' faces doubted that getting in their
way would be a bad idea.

Forker and his entourage left by exits in the high
arch behind the Seat. The remaining men were
officers and nobles too important to be hustled out
with the bulk of the petitioners and not close enough
to Forker to leave by the VIP entrance within the royal
enclosure. They made their own way out the main
doors, as the Guards countermarched back to the walls
and settled into position again. Footsteps echoed, with
most of the sound-muffling human bodies out of the
barn-like structure. Banners hung limp above their
heads in the still, musky air. The bronze clamps that
held ancient energy-weapons to the walls were green
with verdigris; the lasers themselves were as bright as
the day reverent hands had set them there, down to
the stamped *591st Provisional Brigade* on the stocks.

"What do you know, Howyrd," Ingreid Manfrond
said, lowering his voice slightly as they walked out past
another line of guards onto the portico. "His Maybe-
ness actually made a decision without countermanding
it."

"Wrong, Ingreid," Howyrd Carstens replied.

His friend wore the fringed jacket and tweed
trousers of an off-duty noble, the leather strips ending
in gold beads; there were gold plaques on his swordbelt, rubies on the elaborate basket guard around the
hilt, and his spurs were platinum. The sword-hilt and
the hand that rested on it had both seen real use.
Carstens was in the green-grey-black uniform of the
General's Dragoons, with Colonel's insignia.

"He must've settled something with the *grisuh* last

night," the officer said. "This was to confirm it publicly. And he chickened out; probably afraid we'd hack him to pieces on the Seat." A rare occurrence but not entirely unknown in Brigade history.

They paused and lit their pipes, two gentlemen with gray in their beards and long clubbed hair talking idly in the shade of the portico on a hot summer's day, beneath one of the three-story columns hewn in the shape of a Federation assault landing boat. Ushers came and returned their revolvers: nobody but the Life Guards carried firearms inside the Hall.

The parade square ahead of them was five hundred meters on a side; the black bulk of the Palace behind them, the four-square Cathedron of the Spirit of Man of This Earth to their left, with its facade of glass mosaic, and the Iron House of War to the right. Dead ahead to the north was a gap, where the road ran down off the artificial mound into the main part of the city. Canals were as numerous as roads, and the houses were squat two-story structures with few exterior windows but a good deal of carving and terracotta-work painted in bright colors. Carson Barracks was the only major town in the Western Territories built wholly since the Brigade arrived down from the Base Area two centuries after the Fall.

The low-sunk defenses were a lip in the earth from here; they'd been modernized a century or so ago. Carson Barracks didn't really need walls. It stood at the center of several thousand square kilometers of marsh and bog, hardly a hectare of it capable of bearing a man's weight and much of it quicksand. Melancholy wastes of swamp were visible from where they stood, with only the arrow-straight causeway and canal that led north to the railhead on solid ground near the Padan river to vary the landscape. Waving reddish-green native reeds, the green-green Terran variety, an occasional glint of water through the thick ground-haze. The air stank of vegetable decay and the sewage that drained into the swamp and moved, very slowly, downslope toward the river.

Not many Brigade members lived in Carson Barracks by choice, although duty brought many there for a time. Most of the permanent population were slaves, or administrators drawn from the old native upper classes.

"It's probably a good thing fuckin' Forker waffled again," Ingreid went on. "The only thing he could make up his mind on would be to sell us out to the civvies."

"Yeah. What we *ought* to be doing is mobilizing. You remember my cousin Henrik?"

Ingreid rubbed his bearded chin. Hairs caught in the thick layer of horny callus that ringed the thumb and forefinger of his right hand where it controlled his sword.

"Bit younger than you? Had a captaincy in the regulars, then killed . . . shit, what's-his-name —"

"Danni Wimbler's son Erik."

"— over a woman, had to make tracks. Good man, as I remember." Ingreid snapped his fingers. "I do remember. He's the one cut the head off that Stalwart chief at, oh, up near Monnerei."

"Yeah; good man, but no luck. The *grisuh* killed him on Stern Isle."

"Spirit of Man of This Earth download his core," the other man said.

Howyrd touched a lump of blessed agate he wore around his neck. "Yeah. Thing is, one of his men lived, knocked out by a shell. Got shipped out on a slaver after the *grisuh* caught him, then pirates jumped the ship and sold crew and cargo in Tortug. This guy, Eddi, he killed a guard and stole a sailboat, turned up half-dead . . . anyway, he told me about the fighting. More like what a sicklefoot pack does to a herd of sheep. The Squadron wasn't any accident. Ingreid, we ought to be mobilizing. Right now."

The other noble shook his head. "Damned if I thought we'd ever be running scared of the civvies," he mused.

"More like running scared of this Whitehall."

"Think he's really got the Outer Dark workin' for him?"

They spat and made a gesture with their left hands. "*Ni*, he's just one grenade-on-toast of a fighting man," Howyrd said. "They say when he had some Skinners fighting with him, he hung one for killing a civvie trooper, then rode into their camp alone — and they made him a blood-brother or something."

Ingreid winced. "I fought the Skinners once. In maybe a hundred years, I'll want to do *that* again." He shook his head. "Tell you what I'm going to do, I'm going to hire and outfit another regiment of guards, and start buying powder and lead, and check that all my tenants-in-chief and freeholder-vassals have their rifles ready and their swords sharp. *And* I'll tell everyone I know to do the same, down to the petty-squires and fifty-hectare men. And if Forker doesn't like it, Forker can go suck a dead dog's farts. He's not going to have *me* drowned in my bath like he did Charlotte Welf."

Carstens sighed and knocked the dottle out of his pipe against his heel; the spur jingled sweetly as he did. "Watch out you don't get a native uprising," he cautioned. His friend was wealthy even by the upper nobility's standard, but he would have to squeeze his serfs fairly hard to support an extra twelve hundred men and their dogs and gear.

"Then we get practice whipping peon butt," Ingreid snorted. "Heretic bastards deserve it, anyway. They're all civvie-lovers, from the ploughboys to the so-called gentry — whatever they say to your face. *He's* no better," he went on, jerking a thumb over his shoulder at the Palace. "Books, librarians, it's enough to make a real man puke. Outer Dark, he's got to look at some book before he knows what hole to put it in. If he's got anything to put."

"Yeah, and I've got to waste my time and my regiment's back on the border," Howyrd said.

"They're not coming by land?"

"*Ni*. Nothing but rocks up there, or swamps worsn' this."

As if to counterpoint his words, a distant honking roar came out of the reedbeds. A hadrosauroid herd by the sound; the big grazers had been preserved around Carson Barracks for hunting and as emergency food supplies. Hadrosauroids ranged up to four or five tons each, and they flourished on the reeds. Howyrd flipped a finger at an entirely different sort of sauroid tooth hanging on his amulet chain, a curved cutting dagger serrated on both sides and long as a woman's hand.

"Only there's still a lot of big meat-eaters around there, so you have to build palisaded camps. Not enough cleared land or farmers for major campaigning; most of what the civvies've got there is tribal stuff, mercs. Naw, when they come, they'll come by sea."

Grooms brought up their dogs, big glossy mastiffs standing chest-high to a tall man at the shoulder. A squad of Carsten's dragoon Regulars rode up as escorts for their colonel, armed with rifle, broadsword and revolver; they had the worn look of a weapon that fits a man's hand easily when he reaches. Ingreid's guards were in the buff and gray of his household regiment; half the hundred-man detachment were dragoons, half heavy cavalry on Newfoundlands, with steel back-and-breasts, helmets, arm-guards and thigh-tassets. They carried twelve-foot lances as well as the usual swords and firearms, and the long slender ashwood poles stood like a steel-tipped thicket above the square.

"Off to see Marie?" Howyrd said.

Ingreid gathered his reins. "No such luck. Marie Welf tells me that I'm old enough to be her father — my sons *are* older than her — and I should go looking for a nice widow of forty with tits like pillows if I want to marry again."

They exchanged a look. Whoever married Marie Welf would be technically an Amalson, and eligible for the Brigade's elective monarchy. Those elections were settled by weight of shot as often as numbers of votes, but that was one rule always observed. Forker was childless and getting old. Any sons Marie bore . . .

Ingried shook his head. "She's got guts, have to say that for the bitch."

"Not the only thing she's got, by the Spirit," Carstens said with a man-to-man grin. More harshly: "And she'd better get a protector soon. Does she think she can breathe bathwater, just because her momma got the chance to try?"

"*Women*," Ingreid said. "Hail and farewell, friend. See you on the battlefield."

"And some people think he's a simple soldier," Cabot Clerett said bitterly, beside her on the church steps.

Fatima wiped at her eye with a lace handkerchief, managing a final sniffle. Civil Government convention was for ladies to weep when a guest at other people's weddings; it seemed bizzare to her, but custom was custom. The ceremony had been beautiful, she had a lovely new dress of light-blue silk, torofib woven in Azania, and Gerrin and Bartin — she smiled to herself — had promised her another present as well, fitting to the occasion. It was *hard* to cry under those circumstances.

The newly married couples were parading two by two out of the high brass-and-steel doors of the Wager Bay Cathedron, newly converted back to the Spirit of Man of the Stars; only fair, since there had been barely enough Earth Spirit cultists in town for a congregation. The newlyweds passed beneath an arch of sabers held by their comrades, on to awnings and trestle tables.

Whole oxen and pigs were roasting over portable grills; there was to be a feast for the battalions of the men concerned, courtesy of the commanding officers of the units and Messer Raj.

"They *are* simple soldiers, Messer Cabot," Fatima pointed out ingenuously.

It was just going on for sundown, but the post-siesta crowds of townsfolk were kept out of the square by pickets tonight. Both moons were up, and paper lanterns had been strung from the official buildings which ringed the plaza. A breeze from the sea tempered the day's late-summer heat to a langorous softness.

The troops were on their best behavior, with detachments in *guardia* armbands to see that they stayed that way later after the wine had flowed. The wedding songs they were bawling out ranged from the bawdy to the obscene, but that was customary in most places. That the couples had barely met before the ceremony was also common enough; and if the grooms had been among those who slaughtered the brides' fathers or former husbands in the fighting around Fort Wager, that too was not unknown among a warrior people like the Brigade. Nobody knew for sure who had killed who . . . and life would not be easy for Brigade women without protectors among a hostile native populace, in a province newly conquered by aliens of a different faith.

"No, not them," Cabot said. "The men are all right; good soldiers, they deserve a holiday, they've been working hard."

"Too hard, some," Fatima said.

She generally helped out in the 5th's field hospitals, and there had been a full complement of broken bones and heatstroke during the field exercises. Moving thousands of men at speed through rough country was dangerous even without live ammunition. Plus cracked heads and ribs from over-enthusiastic encounters with practice sabers, sheathed bayonets and rifle butts during the melees. Especially between units with a history of bad blood like the 5th Descott and the Rogor Slashers.

"Well, if they didn't like to fight they wouldn't be much use, would they?" Cabot said.

His voice was friendly in a patronizing way. Fatima suspected he talked to her only because he was fairly sure she didn't understand him most of the time; doubly sure, since she was both a woman and a Colonist. Also he was lonely in the Expeditionary Force, close only to Ludwig Bellamy and constrained with him. Most of the men of comparable rank were either Companions or professionals deeply respectful of the General's abilities; they were older, too. For all that, he was a nice enough young man, she thought. No problems after her firmly polite refusal of a *pro forma* attempt at seduction, the sort most men felt obliged to make toward another's mistress. Of course, Fatima was often near Lady Whitehall. . . .

"No, it's the *land*," Cabot Clerett said. "I can't think what Historiomo is thinking of, to let him distribute *land* to men under his command! Cash donatives are bad enough, but if you give a man a farm you've got him for life. *And* it makes all the others hope for the same thing." The faint hope of saving enough for a homestead out of plunder was one major reason so many younger sons of yeoman-tenants and freeholders joined the cavalry.

"Government would give them farms?" Fatima asked, making her eyes go wide. Suzette had shown her how to do that.

"Ah, no." His face lit. "There's Lady Suzette —"

His eyes sought her out. Raj and his wife were strolling between the tables, exchanging a word here and there and toasting the couples. It wouldn't be appropriate or dignified for a man of his rank and birth to actually sit at table with enlisted men in a social gathering, unlike a campfire on a battlefield. The first table started to raise a cheer, then quieted at a single motion of Raj's hand. The singing immediately grew less raucous when Suzette came by; two of her maidservants followed her with sacks, and she was handing gifts to the brides, small things like shawls or brooches. Words of reassurance probably meant more, to young women now alone with men with whom they might not even share a common language beyond a few words of the Spanjol foreign to both.

"I don't understand it," Cabot muttered, half to himself. "One minute he's trying to buy their favor, and then . . . He works them like peons right after they've won a battle; he keeps the strictist discipline I've ever seen, flogs and hangs for minor offenses against peasants —"

"He make them win," Fatima said.

"Yes," Cabot said; again to himself. "He's got guts and he knows his trade, I'll grant him that. And he wins. That's what makes him dangerous."

"General who lose is not dangerous to his *Sultan*?" Fatima asked. Cabot shot her a sharp glance, then relaxed at her palpable innocence.

"Yes, Fatima," he said. "That's the problem, you see. Bad generals may ruin you; good ones may overthrow you. Now, a *Governor* who was a successful general . . ."

"Besides," Fatima went on, frowning, "I think — thought — Lady Whitehall have the idea for the weddings."

"Oh, Lady Suzette," Cabot said, the throttled anger in his voice vanishing. "Suzette. She's an angel. I'm sure she didn't have anything in mind but helping —"

"Excuse me, Messer Clerett," Gerrin Staenbridge said. "I've come to collect my mistress."

"Of course," Cabot said, bowing. "And I complement you on your taste, Messer Staenbridge . . . in this at least."

Gerrin's grin was toothily insincere as he bowed the

other man on his way. "No style at all," he murmured to himself after the Governor's nephew had moved out of earshot. "Bottom like a peasant, to boot. Very boot-able, in fact."

Fatima was thinking over Cabot's last remark to her. "Gerrin," she said, "tell me: why smart young man stupid about a woman?" *My lady Suzette is a djinni, not a houri*, she thought in her mother tongue.

"What was that?" Bartin Foley said, coming up on her other side.

"I ask why all young men so stupid," Fatima said, taking his arm as well.

"Imp," he said. She stuck out her tongue at him.

"Are you sure you will not need me more here, saaidya?" Abdullah said.

Suzette looked around her sitting room; while she did, her hands straightened the pile of papers before her. The punkah overhead made a languid attempt to stir the air, and hot white light speared in through the slats of the shutters. A cat on a pile of silk cushions beneath writhed in its slumber, spreading a paw. From the courtyard garden came the sound of splashing water and a rake slowly, very slowly, gathering leaves.

"We won't *be* here much longer, my faithful one," she said.

"Now: here is the report from Ndella. Read and destroy it."

"Ah, that one," Abdullah said with professional appreciation.

Ndella cor Whitehall had been born in the Zanj city of Liswali and trained as a physician, before being captured by Tewfik's men and sold north to Al Kebir. As a freedwoman of Suzette Whitehall she plied her old trade and a more discrete one among the servants of the Gubernatorial Palace.

"Men tend to ignore women and servants," Suzette said judiciously.

"Fools do," Abdullah conceded. "But then, most men are fools. Even the wise among us can be led into folly by the organ of generation. Or so my wife claims."

"So I've found," Suzette agreed. "Now, there are some juicy details in there on just how far along Forker went toward surrender at one point. Use them with extreme discretion, but anyone who knows him will probably believe it.

"Here," she went on, "are *ayzed* and *beyam*." Zanj, an abortificant and poison respectively; brewed from native Bellevue herbs known only in the far south and utterly untraceable in the western Midworld. Suzette sighed: "I only wish there were two of you, Abdullah."

The Druze smiled. "Am I not multitudes, saaidya?"

Right now he was a Spanjol-speaking merchant of Port Murchison; down to the four-cornered hat with modest plume, green linen swallowtail jacket with brass buttons, striped cravat and natty chiseled-steel buckles on the shoes below his knee-breeches. He made a flourish with the hat, bowing and letting his hand rest on the hilt of a plain sword.

"I shall be welcome in Lion City." Particularly bringing a sloop with a cargo of Stern Isle sulfur and Southern Territories saltpeter. Both restricted cargoes in time of war, of course, but a few hundred pounds would make no real difference.

"Less so in Carson Barracks," she said. More briskly:

"Now: unless I miss my woman and your reports are false, Marie Welf is well aware that she's the sheep at the carnosauroid's congress. Forker and half the nobles in the Brigade want to murder her, the other half to marry her and father an heir to the Seat — and once she's had a male child, she's an inconvenience and danger. None of the prospects pleases, and most of the men are vile.

"You will approach her *only* when she's desperate. This isn't a girl who waits for a rescuer, but she's inexperienced. She'll jump at a way out. Forker keeps

her isolated, but she has friends, and the Welfs have
partisans. Investigate them also."

"Ah, saaidya," Abdullah said, tucking the small case
of vials into an inside pocket of his tailcoat. "Were you
a man, what a ruler you would be!"

"Were I a man," Suzette said tartly, "I'd have better
sense than to want to be a ruler."

"As I said, my lady."

She extended a hand, and Abdullah bent over it in
the style of the Civil Government. Suzette dropped
back into Arabic:

"Go, thou Slave of God," she said, which was what his
name meant. "May my God and thine go with thee."

"May the Benificent, the Lovingkind, be with thee
and thy lord."

Alone, Suzette picked up a packet of letters — they
were copies of Cabot's reports to his uncle — and put
them down again. Raj was out with most of the
Expeditionary Force, on maneuvers again. Cabot and
she were to meet at a little cove, where the swimming
was safe. Quite respectible, since several of her women
would be along; the Civil Government had a nudity
taboo but not during bathing.

"Some men," she murmured, stroking the cat, "are
governable by the fulfillment of their desires, and
some by their frustration." For the present, Cabot
Clerett *wanted* to worship from afar; his concubine
was probably sitting down rather carefully these days.

How long he could be controlled that way was
another matter, of course. A man who knew himself
able, but also knew he owed everything to his uncle's
preferment. Wild to accomplish something of his own
. . . and dangerously reckless in his hate, from the
evidence in the letters. Far too dangerous to Raj to be
tolerated.

"That Bureaucrat's Bottom is slowing you down,
Whitehall," Gerrin Staenbridge taunted, and lunged.

Clack. The double-weight wooden practice sabers met, touched. Lunge, parry from the wrist, feint, cut-stamp-cut. They advanced and retreated across the carefully uneven gravel-rock-earth floor of the salle d'armes. The scuff of feet and slamming clatter of oak on oak echoed from the high whitewashed walls. For a moment they went corps-a-corps.

"Save your breath . . . old man," Raj grunted. A convulsive heave sent them to blade's length again.

In fact, neither man was carrying an ounce of spare flesh, something fully apparent since they were stripped to the waist for the exercise, with only face-masks as protection. Staenbridge was a little thicker through the shoulders, Raj slightly longer in the arm; both big men and hugely strong for their size, moving with the carnivore grace of those who had killed often with cold steel and trained since birth. Raj was drilling hard because it was a way to burn out the poisons of frustration that were worse with every passing week. Staenbridge met the fury of his attack with six extra years of experience. Sweat hung heavy on the dry hot air, slicking down torsos marked with the scars of every weapon known on Bellevue.

"Ahem." Then louder: "Ahem!"

They disengaged, leaped back and lowered their blades. Raj ripped the face-mask off and turned, chest pumping like a deep slow bellows. The salle d'armes of the Wager Bay commandants seemed frozen for a moment in time; Ludwig Bellamy practicing forms before a mirror, Kaltin Gruder on a masseur's table; Fatima on a bench keeping a careful grip on young Bartin Staenbridge, the three-year-old was supposed to be getting his first taste of training but showed a disconcerting tendency to run in wherever there was action. Outside in the courtyard Suzette wrote a letter at a table beneath a trellis of bougainvillea. Her pen poised over the paper. The slapping of the masseurs' hands ran down into silence.

Bartin Foley was sweating too, as if he had run some way in the heat.

"Far be it from me, Messers, to disturb this tranquil scene —"

Raj made a warning sound and snatched at the paper that the younger man pulled out of his helmet-lining. Everyone recognized the purple seal. Raj's hands shook very slightly as he broke it.

He looked up and nodded, then tossed the Gubernatorial Rescript back to Foley and accepted the towel from the servant.

"The Brigaderos won some skirmish on the frontier," he said. "A regiment of their dragoons whipped on some tribal auxiliaries of ours. Forker is claiming that indicates who the Spirit of Man favors. The Governor has ordered me to reduce the Western Territories to obedience, commencing immediately. With full proconsular authority for one year, or the duration of the war."

A sigh ran through the room. "Everything but the men, the dogs and a change of underdrawers is on the ships," Staenbridge said.

Raj nodded again. "Tomorrow with the evening tide," he said softly.

The main municipal stadium of Port Wager had superb acoustics; it was used for public speaking and theatre, as well as bullfights and baseball games. It was well into the morning when the last unit filed in; since there were so many This Earth cultists in the ranks now, Raj had held religious services by groups of units rather than for the whole force. And dropped in on every one of them personally, and be damned what the priests would say back in East Residence.

He knew what the Spirit of Man, of This Earth *and* the Stars, needed. What his men needed.

Silence fell like a blade as he walked out. The tiers of seats that rose in a semicircle up the hillside were blue with the uniform coats of the troops; the paler faces turned toward him like flowers towards the sun as he walked up the steps of the timber podium. The blue and silver Starburst backed it; beyond that was the harbor and the masts of the waiting ships. In front the unit banners of thirty battalions were planted in the sand.

Raj faced his men, hands clenched behind his back.

"Fellow soldiers," he began. A long surf-wave of noise rose from the packed ranks, like a wave over deep ocean. The impact was stunning in the confined space. So was the response when he raised a hand; suddenly he could hear the blood beating in his own ears.

"Fellow soldiers, those of you who've campaigned with me before, in the desert, at Sandoral where we crushed Jamal's armies, in the Southern Territories where we broke a kingdom in one campaign — you and I, we know each other."

This time the sound was white noise, physically painful. He raised his hand again and felt it cease, like Horace answering to the rein. The raw intoxication of it struck him for a moment; this was true power. Not the ability to compel, but thousands of armed men willing to follow where he led — because he could *lead*.

remember, you are human, Center's voice whispered. They would follow; and many would die. Duty was heavier than mountains.

"You know what's demanded of you now," he went on. "For those of you who haven't been in the field with me before, only this: obey your orders, stand by your comrades and your salt. Treat the peasants kindly; we're fighting to give them right governance, not to oppress them. Treat captive foes according to the terms of their surrender, for my honor and yours and the sake of good faith between fighting men.

"And never, never be afraid to engage anyone who stands before you. Because nowhere in this world will you meet troops who are your equal. The Spirit of Man marches with us!"

The shouting started with the former *Squadrones*, the 1st and 2nd Cruisers.

"Hail! Hail! Hail!"

Their deep-chested bellows crashed into the moment of silence after Raj finished speaking. The 5th Descott and the 7th, the Slashers — one by one they rose to their feet, helmets on the muzzles of their rifles.

"RAJ! RAJ! RAJ!"

"By the Spirit, these are good troops," Gerrin Staenbridge said, watching the troopers lead their mounts onto a transport. The big animals walked cautiously onto the gangplanks, testing the footing with each step.

"About the best fighting army the Civil Government's ever fielded," Raj said.

using reasonable equalizing assumptions, that statement is accurate to within 7%, Center observed.

Staenbridge rapped his knuckles on the helmet he carried in the crook of his arm. "My oath, with sixty thousand like them we could sweep the earth."

bellevue, Center corrected in Raj's mind. **so restated, and speaking of the main continental mass, probability of victory for such a force over all civilized opponents would be 76% +/-3, under your leadership**, Center said.

"Unfortunately, Gerrin," Raj said, settling his own helmet and buckling the chinstrap.

A groom brought up Horace; was towed up by Horace, rather, when the hound scented its master. He put a hand on the smooth warm curve of the black dog's neck.

"Unfortunately, the question isn't whether we can conquer the world with sixty thousand — it's whether we can conquer two hundred thousand Brigaderos warriors with less than twenty thousand."

probability of successful outcome 50% +/-10, with an exceptionally large number of overdetermined individually contingent factors, Center admitted. **in colloquial terms, too close to call.**

Raj took Horace's reins in his hand below the angle of his jaw. Suzette was coaxing her palfrey Harbie towards the gangplank as well; the mounts knew they would be separated from their riders for the voyage, and were whimpering their displeasure. That was why it was best for the owner to settle the dog, if their primary bond was to the rider and not the grooms.

He took a deep breath. "Let's go find out."

CHAPTER ELEVEN

Sixty or so dogs waded out on the beach in a group; they shook themselves in a salt-water thunderstorm and fell to greeting each other after the voyage in an orgy of tail-wagging, behind-sniffing, muzzle-licking, growling and stiff-legged hackle-showing.

"Just like a bunch of East Residence society matrons at a ball," Suzette observed in passing, shouldering her Colonial-made carbine.

The command group gave a harsh collective chuckle and turned back to the map pinned to the stunted pricklebark tree.

"Landing's going well," Jorg Menyez observed.

"Ought to, the practice we've had," Raj said.

The Civil Government fleet lay off a low coastline of sand, scree, heather and reddish native groundrunner; inland it rose to clumps of dark oakwood separated by meadows where the grass was thigh-high and straw yellow. Sandspits a kilometer offshore broke the force of the surf, and a gently shelving sandy bottom made it easier to beach the smaller vessels. Those had been run in at high tide a few hours ago, and a steam ram was already towing an empty one off stern-first to make room for the others. Piles of bales and crates and square-sided, rope-handled ammunition boxes were going up above the high-water mark; there were even a few determined camp-followers, soldiers' women and servants — cavalry troopers were allowed one per eight-man squad — wading ashore already as well.

A 5th master-sergeant and two other troopers came up to the dogs; they each bridled the dominant animal in a platoon-pack and led it off after a few warning nose-thumps with the handles of their dogwhips convinced the beasts that it was time to go back to work.

"Follow t'heel, ye bitches' brood!" the noncom shouted, and set off at a trot upslope to the perimeter the first-in units had established. Cavalry might fight mostly on foot, but they felt extremely uncomfortable without their mounts to hand. The rest of the giant carnivores followed along after, heads up and sniffing the wind blowing from inland. More dogs were swimming for the shore; from the way a few pursuing longboats darted about out by the skerries, the usual scattering of animals determined to try swimming back to their last port of call were being rounded up.

The larger ships, four hundred to eight hundred tons, were anchored offshore. Cargo nets swung stores and equipment down to boats; or a field-gun down to a stout raft of barrels and timbers Dinnalsyn's men had knocked together. Rowboats towed it toward the shore, the brass fittings of its breech glittering in the morning sun, as bright as the droplets of spray cast up by the oars. Company after company of infantry scrambled down nets from the grounded ships, fell in to the shouts and whistles of their officers, and marched upslope. The metal-leather-sweat-dogshit smell of an Army encampment was already overlaying the clean odors of sea and heath.

Twenty thousand humans and ten thousand dogs were coming ashore, and Raj intended to have the whole process completed by nightfall.

"Jorg," he went on. The infantry colonel sneezed and nodded. "I want your infantry to —"

"Make the standard fortified camp, I know," he said. "We also serve who only dig ditches." The ground was fairly flat, so the men would scarcely need the artillery to drive stakes for layout; they could make a standard camp in their sleep, and sometimes did after a forced march. He looked around; there were no large Brigade settlements within a day's march, by the map.

"Since we're only staying a few nights, is that entirely necessary? There's a great deal else for the men to do."

Raj grinned like a carnosauroid. "That's what I thought at Ksar Bourgie," he said. "And nearly got converted to a hareem attendant by Tewfik. Dig in, if you please. The men can set up their tents or not, the weather looks to stay fine, but I want the firing parapet, the pit-latrines and the water supply laid on as if we were going to be here a month."

"*Ci, mi heneral.*"

"The armored cars are coming ashore," Dinnalsyn noted. "Do you want them assembled?"

The artilleryman sounded slightly ambivalent. Raj knew how he felt. The vehicles were boiler-plate boxes on wheels, propelled by the only gas engines in the Civil Government, expensively hand-made. They were temperamental and delicate, required constant maintenance, and had to be hauled by oxen if they moved any distance overland. They were a hell of noise and fumes and heat for the crews in operation. Still, with riflemen or light cannon firing from behind bulletproof cover, they could be decisive at a critical point — and that made up for the endless bother of hauling them around.

Raj nodded. "Just the frames and shells," he said. The engines and armament could be fitted in a day or two and the empty shells were much easier to transport.

"Right," Raj went on, "this is the Crown Peninsula." He tapped the thumb-shaped outline on the map; it stuck out from the main coast of the Western Territories on the eastern fringe. "We're here." On the west coast, a hundred kilometers up from Lion City, the provincial capital, and across five hundred klicks of open water from the coast nearest the Old Residence.

"We'll secure the Crown and Lion City, then advance north" — he traced a line northwestward — "cross the Waladavir River at the bridge here or here where it's fordable, then move southeast toward Old Residence. What exactly we do then depends on opportunity and the enemy, but I intend to have the city before the winter sets hard.

"Our immediate objective is to pacify the Crown outside Lion City. The city has the only real garrison, about four thousand of the General's regulars; for the rest, it's the landowners' household troops we'll be facing. I expect most of them to give up, but don't count on it in any particular case.

"Gerrin, you take two-thirds of the 5th, the 2nd Residence Battalion and two guns, and head northwest up the coast road." His other hand pointed inland. "Hadolfo, your Borderers and the 1st Cruisers, two guns, northeast. Kaltin, you take the 7th Descott and three guns — you've got a couple of crossroads towns and may need them — and head directly east. Ehwardo, you've got Poplanich's Own and the Maximilliano Dragoons and a battery. Go southeast, to the other side of the Crown, down the main spinal road. Ludwig, you take the 2nd Cruisers and the Rogor Slashers and two batteries. Head straight south down to the gates of Lion City, and make sure nobody gets in or out. The city's going to be enough of a problem without too many household units stiffening their defense."

Suzette returned, with a string of HQ servants bearing trays of grilled sausages in split rolls. Everyone grabbed one; Raj used his to gesture between bites.

"You've all seen the sicklefoot and trihorn matches?"

A chorus of nods. Trihorns were browsing sauroids with bone armor on their head and shoulders, up to six tons of vile temper, common in thinly-peopled wilderness. Sicklefeet were smallish carnosauroids, a little more than man-size with a huge curved dewclaw on

their hind feet, usually held up against the leg; they
hunted in packs, vicious and incredibly agile, leaping in
the air to extend their claws and kick-slash their prey to
death. The two species rarely interacted in their
natural habitats, but they were often matched in large
city stadiums in the Civil Government.

"We're the sicklefeet, the Brigaderos are the trihorns. If we let them use their strength, they'll crush
us. We slash and move and let them bleed to death."

Raj put his hand on the map, palm on the landing
ground and fingers splayed out across the map. Then
he rotated the hand, pulling the fingers together as
they approached Lion City.

"You'll move south clockwise, sweeping the countryside repeatedly; Ludwig, you're the anvil for any who
filter past. Speed and impact, everyone — don't pee on
them, boot their heads. If we give them time to catch
their breath, we'll have bands of them hiding in the
woods for years, and we do *not* have enough troops to
garrison. Stamp on anyone who actively resists; stamp
hard, strike terror. Strip those who surrender of every
weapon down to their belt-knives and every man who
even looks like a soldier and send them back to base;
we'll run them to East Residence in the returning
transports and comandeered shipping. I don't want an
ounce of powder or lead left available, either. Destroy
whatever weapons you can't easily cart away; once
we've got the area pacified, Administrator Historiomo
will be raising a police and militia from the native
population, and we can use the captured weapons to
arm them.

"Again, messers, the *only* way we can dominate so
large an area with so few troops is to roll them up
before they realize what's hit them. If we look like
winners, the native population will also rally to us, and
we *need* their active support against the Brigaderos.
What happens in the Crown will be crucial to the
whole campaign.

"Jorg, there's going to be plenty for you to do as well. All the flying columns will be sending back prisoners by the hundreds; they'll also be calling on you for temporary infantry garrisons to hold confiscated supplies, weapons, and strategic spots.

"You've all got the intelligence reports," he went on. "I've noted the magnate families I want hostages from. We'll move them back here on a temporary basis until we have something better available, along with the soldiers, but they can't be mixed in. Suzette —"

"I'll see to it," she said.

Keeping the hostages — not happy — but not impossibly demoralized would be difficult, with the stringent limits on resources available. A dead hostage was worse than a dead loss, and a mistreated one could provoke suicidal resistance among the Brigade nobility. Most of them would be women and children, and of noble birth; Lady Whitehall would sooth some of the fears and prickly status-conciousness. Thus keeping them out of his hair, and the families they stood surety for quiet as well. That could be worth more than battalions of troops in garrisons in pacifying the area.

"Muzzaf?" Raj went on. The Komarite had been ashore for a day, operating under cover.

"*Seyor*, I've already contacted some of the local merchants in the farm-towns. We can expect them, and local peasants and native landowners, to be bringing in supplies within a day at any point we designate. I didn't tell them where, of course."

Raj nodded approval. "Do so now. What with prisoners, camp followers and troops we'll have to feed forty thousand or better soon. Now, you may all have noticed that it's cooler here." They all nodded; the temperature was warm-comfortable, rather than the blazing heat of Stern Isle in late summer. "The rains start earlier here — and it rains more than back home. We're racing against time. Questions?"

"Sir," Cabot Clerett said. "My mission?"

Raj looked at him for a moment, then slid his finger up the map. "Major Clerett, I'm giving you a rather different role. You'll take your 1st Residence Life Guards, and the 21st Novy Haifa, and move right up here to the Waladavir River."

Clerett looked crisp and warlike in the bright sun, helmet tucked under one arm and black curls tossing. "I'm to perform a screening function, sir?"

"Rather more than that," Raj said. "I want you to secure the bridge over the Waladavir at Sna Chumbiha and the fords — put in earthworks and your guns — then send appropriately-sized raiding parties from the two cavalry battalions over the river westward to attack the magnates' estates and small garrisons. Colonel Menyez will be moving four battalions of infantry up to occupy the bridge and the fords and relieve your men; they and the 21st Novy Haifa will anchor our line of advance.

"We want to conceal our intentions, and hopefully to panic every Brigadero between the Waladavir and the Padan River into thinking we're on their doorstep. I want them running for Carson Barracks, carrying the family silver and howling about the boogeyman. Don't try to hold territory west of your bridgeheads; kill and burn, but selectively, just the Brigaderos and men only as much as you can. I don't want to have to march across a desert in a couple of weeks. Make the refugees overestimate your numbers by moving quickly so they think you're everywhere at once. With luck the natives will rise on their own."

"Sir!" Cabot was quivering with surprise and suspicious delight. It was an assignment with plenty of opportunities for dash and daring; he'd expected to be kept to something dull and safe.

"Major Clerett," Raj went on. "Pay careful attention." He waited an instant. "I'm confident of your courage and your will to combat; a cavalry officer without aggression is a sorry thing. This mission will also test your skills; I'm familiar with the weaknesses of aggressive young commanders, having been one myself back in the dawn of time."

There were grins at that; Raj Whitehall was the youngest general in five hundred years, and his battalion commanders were nearly a decade below the average age. Only two of the Companions were over forty.

"Remember that the Brigaderos are thicker on the ground the further west you go; some of the great nobles have private armies of battalion size or better. Do *not* get out of touch, do *not* go too far in, and do *not* let your men get out of hand — a raid makes discipline difficult but more essential than ever. Colonel Staenbridge will be in constant communication, and he's your reserve if you run into something bigger than the intelligence reports indicate; do *not* hesitate to call for help if you need it. You're being sent to give an appearance of strength, so if any of your units is mousetrapped we'll have a *real* problem up there. Give them the taste of victory, however small, and they'll be attacking us instead of running away. We can beat any nobleman's following, but that would take *time*. Keep your men moving, and don't let yourself get bogged down."

Which meant, among other things, keeping them from burdening themselves with too much loot; a real test of command skills, when they'd be fanning out on *razziah* across rich countryside.

Suzette spoke softly. "I'm sure Major Clerett won't disappoint us, Raj."

probability clerett will act according to instructions within acceptable parameters 82% +/-4 based on voice-stress and other analysis, Center said.

And Barholm can't complain I'm not giving his nephew an opportunity to shine.

Cabot clicked heels. "Rest assured, Messa."

Raj nodded. "I'm giving you no more than one week of raiding," he went on. "Then I'll need you back at Lion City. Throw out a wide net of scouts west of the river — the native locals will probably give you information enough, especially with some —" he rubbed finger and thumb together "— but you'll have to check. Then turn over command to Major Istban and make tracks for the city, which will be invested.

"This is a complex set of movements, gentlemen, to be carried out at speed, but you're all big boys now. Exercise your initiative."

Gerrin cleared his throat. "What'll you be doing, Raj?"

"Ah, well, our tribal auxiliaries have arrived. Including eight hundred Skinners."

"The gentle, abstentious people," someone muttered.

"A two-edged sword, but a sharp one," Raj admitted. "They, and the two companies of the 5th, will form a central reserve under my direct command. When you run into anything unusual, gentlemen, tell me and I'll bring them up. After that happens once or twice, even the most onerous surrender terms will start looking very good indeed.

"No more questions? Then let's get our men together and be about our business." The Companions and a few of the other battalion commanders stepped closer, and they slapped their raised fists together in a pyramid. The leather of their gauntlets made a hard cracking sound.

"Hell or plunder, dog-brothers."

"Anither seven in t' trees, ser," M'lewis said, without turning his head. "Half a klick, loik."

"Good eyes, Lieutenant," Raj nodded.

Skinners didn't set lookouts, really. It was just that there were always groups of men lying-up around one of their camps, and they saw and heard and probably scented everything. At home on the plains of the far northeast they lived by hunting sauroids. All shapes and sizes, from sicklefoot packs to the big grazers to carnivores ten meters tall. Bellevue's sauroids hadn't had a million years of exposure to hominids to give them an instinct to avoid men. Most inhabited areas had to be kept shot out of all the larger types; the Skinners lived *among* the native life, and throve.

"Trumpeter, sound the canter. Remember the instructions."

The cool brassy notes sounded, and the two hundred men broke into a swift lope, the butts of their rifles resting on their thighs. As they broke through the screen of brush around the big meadow, they raised them and fired them into the sky, then flipped the long weapons down and sheathed them in the scabbards before their knees. A gesture of contempt, not reassurance . . . a statement: *you're not worth carrying a loaded gun to meet.*

There was an etiquette to dealing with Skinners.

Nobody got up as the soldiers approached, unless they happened to be standing at the moment. Those who wanted to stare did; those who were sleeping or drinking kept on doing so. One man did amble out, peering as if in surprise.

"Eh, *mun ami!*" Chief Juluk Paypan said. He turned and shouted in Paytoiz, the Skinner tongue:

"*Iles de Gran' wheetigo! E' sun bruha. L'hum qes' mal com nus!*"

Many of the Skinners looked up at that; a few gave quick yelping barks of greeting, and started drifting toward their chief and the general who was — theoretically — their commander.

"Which means?" Suzette asked. She had ridden into a near-riot in the Skinner camp with him on the last campaign, to face down their chiefs after Raj hung two Skinners for murder. This was her first glimpse of them in a peaceful mood.

Of course, on that occasion they'd had four battalions with leveled rifles and a battery of artillery behind them.

Raj translated: "It's The Big Devil and his witch. The man who's *bad like us*."

"Is that a compliment?"

Raj grimaced. "To a Skinner."

He had never learned the Skinner tongue, not himself — the knowledge had the ice-edged hardness of something Center had implanted. Thinking about that always gave him a queasy feeling, like a mental image of bad pork.

It was not a good idea to think of smells when you were around Skinners. The bandy-legged little nomads had only been ashore a day, but the stink of their camp was already stunning. One man was standing in his sketchy saddle to urinate as they entered; he waved cheerfully and readjusted his breechclout without embarrassment, then rode off with a whoop. A few of them had put up leather shelters on poles, but most of the nomad mercenaries slept as they ate, defecated and fornicated — as and where the impulse took them. Dung, human and canine, and bits and scraps of things unidentifiable dotted the encampment. A monohorn carcass lay in the center of a ring of fires; those were medium-sized browsers, about twice the weight of a large bull, with columnar legs and a bone shield that extended from the long horn on their nose to the top of their humped shoulders. A single round hole above one eye showed what had killed it; the Skinners had probably camped where it died. The body and the ground for meters around was black with a carpet of flies.

As Raj watched, a Skinner backed out of its stomach cavity with a length of huge glistening purple-grey intestine in his teeth. He sawed it free a foot or so from his mouth, then threw back his head to swallow it without chewing. A visible bulge went down his throat to the already rounded stomach as they watched.

Juluk was grinning from ear to ear. He was fairly typical of his race, shorter than Suzette but twice as broad, a normal man compressed halfway down to dwarf size. Face and body were the color of old oiled leather; it was difficult to tell what his shaven scalplocked head and round button-nosed face would have looked like naturally, because of the mass of scar tissue. About half of it was tribal markings. He wore fringed leggings and breechclout of soft-tanned sauroid leather, with long knives on his thighs; crossed belts on his chest held shells for the two-meter tall rifle he leaned on, and each brass cartridge was longer than a man's hand, each bullet bigger than Raj's thumb. His hound lay at his feet; it cocked an eye up at Horace and went back to sleep.

Only Skinners habitually rode hounds, and entire males at that. Horace was one reason they regarded Raj as a human being. Most of it was the number of bodies his battles had piled up, impressive even to the tribes the Church called the Scourge of the Spirit's Wrath.

Juluk drank and passed him up the leather flask. "Hey, mebbe we kill you now, sojer-man, wait too long anyway. You come to hang more of *mes gars* for killing farmers? That why you bring half-men?"

He jerked his head at the two companies of the 5th sitting their dogs behind Raj and Suzette. Half-men was a complement; the Skinners had a quasi-respect for Descotters. Their name for themselves translated into Sponglish as Real Men. Or The Only Real Men.

Raj took a long swig of the *arrak*, date gin yellow with distilling byproducts and spiked with cayenne peppers, chile and gunpowder. Then he leaned over and spat half of it on the nose of the Skinner's dog. The big animal leapt to its feet, growling: Raj's boot and stirrup-iron met its nose with a nicely-timed swing, and Horace showed teeth as long as a man's fingers centimeters from the other animal's throat. It reconsidered, turned its back and ambled off, dishcloth-sized ears flapping.

"I only keep you alive to make me laugh, Juluk," Raj said, drinking again. He'd eaten half a loaf of bread soaked in olive oil just before coming to the Skinner camp. "I brought real men here to show your little boys how to fight. Where'd you get this sauroid-vomit? I piss it out on your bitch-mother's grave."

This time he swallowed most of it, forcing himself not to gag. To his surprise, Suzette took the skin next and managed a healthy swallow. Some of the Skinners frowned at her presumption, and one or two shook medicine bags at her, but most of them laughed uproariously, Juluk included. A woman with *baraka*, spirit-power, was an even bigger joke than a non-Skinner with real balls. His necklace of finger-long sauroid fangs clattered against his bandoliers.

"Eh, even your woman got balls, sojer-man! Big stone-house chief, he tell me you make war on the long-hairs of the west. Good fighting where you make war."

"Where's your friend Pha-air?" There had been two chiefs with this band on the last campaign.

"Oh, I kill him a season ago," the Skinner chief said with a shrug. "He give me this — good man with knife." A grimy thumb traced a new scar, still shiny, across the chief's belly.

Raj raised his voice: "Are you women ready to go fight, or are you only good for drinking and eating sauroids that die of disease?"

More hoots and trills of laughter; the Skinners looked and smelled like trolls but their voices had the high pitch of excited schoolgirls.

Juluk fired the huge rifle over his shoulder without bothering to move it. The brass-cored 15mm slug cracked by within a meter of Raj's head, but he was as safe as if the weapon had been in East Residence. The Skinner chief would slit his own throat in shame if he ever shot a man without intending to.

Men and dogs boiled out of the camp, and out of thickets roundabout. It was chaos, an instant change from sleepy lethargy to whooping, screeching tumult — but in less than five minutes the liquor and ammunition had been thrown on spare dogs, and the warriors were mounted and ready to move.

Center had taught him Paytoiz, but Raj had always been able to get on with the Skinner mercenaries.

"Are they really worth the trouble?" Suzette asked, as her escort fell in around her for the short journey back to the base camp.

"My sweet, you've only seen them twice, and in camp," Raj said. "As soldiers, they're a disaster — they devastate any place you station them, and you might as well try to discipline sauroids, and when they're drunk, which is usually . . . But if you could see them *fight* —" He shook his head. "Yes, they're worth the trouble."

"Why's the road so far inland?" Bartin Foley asked.

"Pirates," Gerrin Staenbridge replied. "More profit in longshore raiding than attacking ships, if you've got a target that doesn't have signal heliographs, a fleet of steam rams and quick-reaction forces the way the Civil Government does."

Company A of the 5th was lead unit on the ride north, next to the battalion banner and the HQ squad. They were staying in column, for speed's sake, with outriders flung out ahead and to either side; they could see them dodging into small woods and jumping fences occasionally, off at the edge of sight.

"*Squadrone* pirates?" Bartin went on.

"Probably not the last generation, but there are plenty of freelancers operating out of islands like Blanchfer and Sabatin, just south of here . . . Ah, that should be our Hereditary Colonel Makman's place, coming up."

The maps said this was a main military highway; in the Civil Government, even in Descott, they'd have called it a track and left it at that. Mostly it was beaten earth, possibly it had been graded with an ox-drawn scraper within the last couple of years, and somebody had scattered gravel on the low points at some time in the past. Snake-rail fences edged it on either side; inland of the belt of forest along the coast the country opened up into rolling fields. Small shaws of oak, hazelnut and some native tree with hexagonal-scaled bark and scarlet leaves topped an occasional hill. The wheatfields were long since reaped, but there were many fields of *mais* — *kawn* in Namerique and *gruno* in Spanjol — full of dry, rustling stocks chest-high to a rider.

A hogback ridge rose ahead and to the right, eastward of the road. The two officers raised their binoculars; the manor was a big foursquare building, whitewashed stone, with a squat tower rising from one corner flying the double lightning flash banner of the Brigade and a personal blazon of complicated inter-woven loops, white on dark gray. The lower story was pierced only by narrow windows, but the upper had balconies and broad stretches of glazing. A number of long low structures stood nearby; stables undoubtedly, and the barracks.

"Almost homelike," Gerrin said dryly.

Descott architecture had some of the same features and for the same reason, except that things had never been either peaceful or prosperous enough for long enough to widen the second-story windows.

Staenbridge threw up a hand, and the trumpet sounded. "Battalion —"

"Company —"

"Walk-march . . . *halt*."

"Let's hope Makman sees sense," the commander of the 5th said.

"I hope so too," Foley replied. He turned in the saddle: "Flag of truce, Lieutenant, and follow me if you please." He turned back to Staenbridge. "Probably won't, though. Not the first one we call on."

❖   ❖   ❖

"You *what*?" the old man roared.

"Summon you to surrender in the name of the Civil Government of Holy Federation," Foley said tightly.

His hand was on his pistol, but he was fully conscious of what a sniper could do. The white pennant snapped from his bannerman's pole. That been cold comfort to poor Mekkle Thiddo last year, after he'd delivered Connor Auburn's head to his brother the Admiral. His mind tried to replay scenes of the Squadron blunderblusses belching smoke, the white flag falling . . . and instead it insisted on showing him Raj Whitehall's face, as he rode down the row of thirty-one crosses, each bearing the twisting body of one of the men responsible for that violation of the laws of war.

That had probably been cold comfort to Thiddo too.

A bell was tolling in the tower of the estate; frightened faces peered out at him from the second-story window, and dogs were *yowrp*ing in the stables as men rushed to saddle them. Behind him the platoon's mounts shifted and growled softly, conscious of the aggression of intruding on another pack's territory but trained out of instinctive reluctance. The gravel of the driveway crunched under their paws; the smell of their massed breath was rank, overpowering the scents of woodsmoke and garden.

Hereditary Colonel Makman was tall, about a hundred and ninety centimeters, with little spare flesh on his heavy bones, and his red face contrasted violently with the white muttonchop whiskers that framed it. The unexpected visitors had evidently surprised him at lunch, and a napkin was tucked into the collar of his shirt.

He glared at Foley. "*Grisuh*, you've got your nerve, coming on to *my* land with a story like this," he snapped, in the tones of a man who hasn't been contradicted in a very long time.

Foley smiled and raised his hook. "Messer, that term

grisuh is impolite, not to mention inappropriate. The last man to use it to me was one of Curtis Auburn's house-troops, and he came to a bad end." Sudden doubt washed over Makman's face.

"*Seyor*," the platoon commander said. *Sir.*

Foley turned his head; a group of men was double-timing up the grassy slope to the right. In bits and pieces of hastily-donned uniform, but all carrying rifles and wearing their swords. They checked at the sight of the mounted men, then came on again at a more measured pace.

The young captain nodded. The lieutenant barked an order, and half the platoon turned their dogs with a touch of the foot. Another, and the animals crouched; the men stepped forward with their rifles at port.

"Slope arms! Fix bayonets!" Smooth precision as butts thumped and hands slapped the hilts, not parade-ground stiffness but the natural flow of actions performed as part of a way of living, a trade practiced daily. The bayonets came out, bright and long as a man's forearm, and rattled as they clipped to the ring-and-bar fasteners. "Shoulder arms — front rank, kneel — ready — present — pick your targets — prepare for volley fire. On the word of command!"

Hands slapped iron and the long Armory rifles jerked up to shoulders. Behind the kneeling riflemen the second file drew their sabers and sloped them back, resting on their shoulders. The dogs barred their teeth and growled like boulders churning in a flooded river, long strings of slaver running from their opened half-meter mouths.

Makman surprised Foley; he spoke quietly. "You came under a flag of truce."

Bartin Foley's face had been delicately pretty once; it was still slim-lined and handsome in an ascetic fashion. Black eyes met blue, and the Brigade nobleman's narrowed in memory. From the battered look of his thick-fingered hands he had seen action enough once; enough to recognize the look of a man poised on the edge of killing violence.

"Messer, I also once saw an officer murdered under flag of truce by the barbarians of the Squadron," the young man said.

Makman snatched the handkerchief from his shirt and half-turned. "Siegfrond!" he snapped. "Ground arms, you fool."

The Brigadero troopers had formed a ragged firing line. Now their muzzles came down; there were about thirty of them, with more straggling up from the barracks by ones and twos, like crystals accreting in a solution.

"And somebody stop that damned bell."

A servant from the crowd around the Brigade nobleman scampered away, and the bronze clanging faded away to silence.

A woman came out onto the broad verandah of the fortified manor; she was in her twenties, in along white dress with a yoke of pearls, and a child of four or five was by her side.

"Grandfather," she began, "what's — oh!" She swept the child behind her and put one hand to her throat.

Makman was studying the soldiers before his house, *seeing* them for the first time, Foley suspected. "*Gubernio Civil*, right enough," he said, and looked up at their officer. "Is this some sort of raid? You've a good deal of brass, young man, coming this far inland with less than forty men."

"This is the vanguard of General Raj Whitehall's army," Foley said, with a coldly beautiful smile. The woman gasped, and Makman's ruddy face paled.

"He's on Stern Isle," he whispered.

"*Was*," Foley corrected. "The Sword of the Spirit of Man is swift. And in case you doubt that there are more of us here —"

He drew his saber and turned in the saddle, waving the blade slowly overhead. Downslope of the house gardens was an open field, full of black-coated cattle grazing. Beyond that was cultivated land, with a scattering of small half-timbered thatched cottages, and a line of trees. Red light winked from the edge of the forest. Half a second later the flat *poumpf* of a 75mm field gun came, and the ripping wail. A tall bottle-shape of dirt fountained out of the pasture; cattle were running and bawling, except for three that lay mangled, blood red and intestines pink against their black hides. Steel twinkled all along the distant field edge as five hundred men stepped into the open and the sun caught their bayonets. A frantic voice called from the tower that more were in sight behind the manor, among the peon village.

2nd Residence, right on time, Foley thought.

"What . . ." Makman rasped. "What are your terms?"

"General Whitehall's terms are these; you are to take oath of obedience to the Civil Government and cooperate fully with all its officers and administrators in furnishing supplies and war levies. All arms and armed men to be surrendered; soldiers to be sent to East Residence for induction into our army. You personally will accompany our troops to encourage surrender among your military vassals and neighbors. In return your life and liberty, and one-third of your real property, are spared."

"One-third!"

"It's a great deal more than you'd enjoy in the grave, Messer. Because my orders are that if you refuse this place will be sacked and any survivors sold as slaves." He looked up at the young woman. "I doubt your granddaughter would find life as a whore in a dockside crib in East Residence very pleasant." He cut off the beginnings of a roar. "I've seen it, Messer. I've *done* it. Believe me."

The old man slumped. Foley's voice went on inexorably; "You will also deliver a hostage of your immediate family as surety for your good behavior."

"Who?" Makman said, scrubbing a hand over his face. "My son is ten years dead, my daughters with their own husbands, and my grandson holds a commission with the Makman Mounted in Carson Barracks —" He halted, frowning.

The young woman turned white and glared at Foley, and Makman's great age-spotted hands clenched. The young man almost laughed, but managed to keep his face grave. Things were not *quite* out of the woods yet; these were barbarians, after all.

"Your granddaughter-in-law and great-grandson will be under the protection of Lady Suzette Whitehall," he soothed. "She may take one maidservant and a suitable chaperone, and since you'll have to come in to swear allegiance with General Whitehall, you may deliver her to Lady Whitehall yourself. And rest assured, on my word as a gentleman and officer, that her honor is safe with me."

If you only knew how very *safe*, he thought.

"*Upyarz! Upyarz!*"

The Brigaderos roared as they fought. Clerett's Life Guards used their sabers with bleak skill; the Governor had carefully picked the men to send to war with his heir. Steel crashed on steel across the fields, pistols banged, dogs howled and men shrieked in sudden agony too great for flesh to bear. The failing light of sundown was blood-red, but the true red of blood was turning to black despite the flames from the burning farmhouse on the north side of it. The wagons the refugees had tried to draw into a circle for defense burned too. Powder-smoke drifted pink-tinged over the heads and thrashing blades of four hundred men. The air smelled of sulphur and feces, the wet-iron stink of blood, and burning thatch.

Cabot Clerett watched narrowly. His hand chopped down, and his heels clapped to his dog's ribs; with a hundred men behind him he swept out of the timber and put his mount at the rail fence. The big mastiff gathered itself and soared as its rider leaned forward in the saddle. The banner of the 1st Residence Life Guards streamed at his side, and all around him the blades of the sabers snapped down in unison to lie along the necks of the dogs, point toward the enemy. They were turning to meet him, a lancepoint flashed by, *trannggg* and a breastplate shed the point of his Kolobassian blade and nearly dragged him out of the saddle. The Civil Government line smashed into the melee.

A dismounted trooper was before him, backing with sword working while a Brigadero lancer probed for his life and another kept the soldier's dog at bay.

Cabot spurred forward again. This time the enemy warrior could not turn in time, the inertia of his lance too much for his arm. The young officer poised his hilt over his head and stabbed, down into the neck past the collarbone to avoid the armor. The resistance was crisp and then heavy-soft; he wrenched the blade free and the barbarian reeled away on a bolting dog, coughing blood in sheets down his breastplate. The loose Life Guards dog snapped, its neck extending like a snake and closing on the lance-shaft below the steel lappets. Ashwood crunched and the Brigadero was backing and cursing as he drew his sword. Cabot let him escape, dropped his reins, and clamped the bloody saber to his side while he drew his pistol and tossed it to his left hand.

"Thankee, ser!" the trooper yelled, straddling his dog as the animal crouched for him to mount.

Cabot flourished the saber with a grin. *I'm not afraid, I'm not afraid!* he realized exultantly. A sword flickered in the corner of his eye; he blocked the blow with his own near the hilt. The force of it slugged him to one side, leaning far over; he pointed the revolver under his own armpit and fired into the Brigadero's torso. The enemy dog locked jaws with his dog's, both

animals slamming at each other's legs with clawed paws
the size of plates. Cabot heaved himself back erect and
leaned forward to fire again with the muzzle half an
inch from the other dog's eye. It collapsed in mid-
growl, falling with a thump that made his own mount
jump backwards.

The HQ group had caught up with him, stabbing
and shooting; the enemy were recoiling under the
weight of the flank charge, but they still had numbers
and weight of metal on their side. He signaled the
trumpeter and the brassy notes rang out over the
lessening clamor. Almost as one man the Civil Government troops turned and fled in a rout, pouring across
the meadow and into the narrow road that spiked into
the forest on the south.

The Brigaderos, household guards and part of a
dragoon garrison regiment, scrambled after them four
hundred strong. Here the lighter gear of the easterners
was their advantage; the big Airedales and Newfoundlands were fast enough, but slower off the mark than
the rangy Descotter farmbreds and Colonial-style
Banzenjis the invaders rode. Slather flew from the
mouths of the dogs as they lunged for the shadowing
trees. The narrow wedge of open land at the road's
mouth squeezed the larger Brigade force harder than
their quarry, and for a moment the whole mass of men
and dogs slowed as the warriors on the outside pressed
inward.

Four hundred riflemen volley-fired from the edge of
the woods into the clumped Brigade troops. In the
dusk the muzzle-flashes were long and regular, like
spearheads of fire along an endless phalanx. Crisp
orders sounded, pitched high to carry. Platoon volleys
slammed out like a crackle of very loud single shots,
each one a comb of flame licking toward the enemy.
Bullets hammered into dogs and men; a few spanged
off armor, red sparks flicking up into the gathering
night, but the range was close — and for this

campaign, half of the standard-issue hollowpoints had been replaced with rounds carrying a pointed brass cap. Four companies of trained men with Armory rifles could put over three thousand rounds in a single minute. None of the Brigaderos was more than a hundred meters from the forest edge when the firing started, and the barricade of burning buildings and wagons was less than six hundred meters away. At that distance a bullet aimed level would strike a mounted man anywhere along its flight path.

The trumpet rang again in darkness, behind the firefly glimmer of the crossfire raking the Brigade men from two sides of a triangle. Panting dogs and cursing men sorted themselves into ranks. Snarls and snaps like wet coffin-lids falling punctuated the jostling, until men soothed their mounts to obedience.

"Damned if it didn't work, sir," the Senior Captain of the 2nd said in Cabot's ear.

He jumped slightly, glad of the darkness; he could feel the glassy stare of his eyes. His hands were steady as he reloaded.

"I rather thought it would, Captain Fikaros," the Governor's nephew said hoarsely. "I rather thought it would."

Both moons were up, enough to see a few survivors scattering across the meadow. Few made it past the burning buildings on the other side, although a number of riderless dogs with jouncing stirrups did.

"Let's collect our wounded and head for the river," Cabot said. "This bunch were a little too numerous for my taste."

"Sir!"

The men cheered as he rode past with the unit banner and the trumpeter.

Wait until Uncle hears about this, he thought. *Wait until Suzette hears.*

Glory!

CHAPTER THIRTEEN

Major Ehwardo Poplanich looked up at the row of shackles that rattled along the stone wall of the courthouse, below a bricked-in sign reading *runaway* in Spanjol and Namerique. The cuffs hung at about two meters off the ground. A meter and a half below each set the stucco was scored with a half-moon of smooth wear from flailing feet. A man hung by his hands with no support beneath cannot draw air into his lungs if he lets his full weight fall on his wrists; his chest crushes the diaphragm with the weight of his lower body. He must haul himself up at least a little with every breath. Once fatigue sets in, suffocation follows — a slow, gradual suffocation, as each despairing effort brings less oxygen and burns more.

"Well, that's one way to make sure a serf regrets it if he leaves the estate," he said mildly.

The set smile of the Brigadero magistrate did not alter; he bobbed his head in agreement, as he would have to anything Poplanich said at that moment. A big burly man, he was a noble by courtesy under Brigade law because he was on the muster rolls, but most of the native members of the town council had owned more land than he. Town marshall was not a rank true nobles, the *brazaz* officer class of the Brigade, aspired to. Now the councilors owned *much* more, and what had been a substantial farm if not an estate for the magistrate would shrink to a smallholding as soon as the new administration produced a cadastral survey.

With a battalion of Poplanich's Own in town, he wasn't going to object very forcefully. A few had tried, and their bodies hung from the portico of the This Earth church as a warning.

Ehwardo looked at the fetters again. A strong man, or a light wirey one, could probably live quite a few hours hanging there. *I shouldn't be upset*, he told himself. Serfdom — debt-peonage — was close to a universal institution around the Midworld Basin; back home a runaway who couldn't pay his impossible, hereditary debts would be flogged and turned back to his master. That had started long ago to prevent peasants from absconding from their tax obligations; and Spirit knew there didn't seem to be any other way to keep civilization going in the Fallen world. Not that anyone had told him, at least . . . but there was nothing like this on the Poplanich estates. A landlord who was willing to stand between his people and the tax farmers didn't have to flog much to keep order.

And where *was* that damned infantryman? He had better things to do than stand here talking to a gang of provincial boobies. He was supposed to be turning everything over to an infantry battalion so he could move on south, and it was taking a *cursed* long time.

In normal times he supposed Maoachin was a pleasant enough little place, a market town for the farms and estates roundabout. There was a large, gaudily decorated church for the This Earth cultists, and a more modest one for the Star Spirit worshippers; a few fine houses behind walls, a few streets of modest ones mixed with shops and artisan crafts, cottages on the outskirts. No fountain in the plaza, but the streets were cobbled and lined with trees.

Now the streets were jammed solid. With oxcarts full of grain in sacks and flour and cornmeal in barrels, and sides of bacon and dried beef and turnips and beans. Furniture and silverware too, and tools; many, many wagons of swords and rifle-muskets and shotguns and revolvers, ammunition, kegs of powder and ingots of lead. Riding dogs on leading chains, muzzled with steel-wire cages over their jaws and driven frantic by stress, and palfreys for the hostages. Hundreds of prisoners, Brigaderos fighting men going back to be packed into transports and shipped across the Midworld and inducted into the Civil Government's army. They walked with their eyes down, avoiding looking at the smaller groups, battered and bloody and in chains, who'd tried to fight. *They* and their families were headed for slave markets.

The noise and dust, the howls of dogs and sobbing of children, were beyond belief; the harsh noon sun beat down without mercy.

He looked back down at the magistrate standing at his stirrup, and the town councilors. Most of them were natives, Spanjol-speaking followers of the orthodox faith they shared with the Civil Government. More than a few of them were smiling at the magistrate's discomfort. They had kept two-thirds of their land, and had pleasure of seeing the bottom rail put on top, as well. When the confiscated Brigade estates came on the market, they would be positioned to expand their holdings in a way that would more than make up for the initial loss.

"But, ah, with respect —" the bearded judge-gendarme said, his Sponglish clumsy and full of misplaced Spanjol endings "— you then leave me at all no armed men, how do I under put native risings?"

A councilor *did* laugh at that. The magistrate whirled on him, frustration breaking through in a scream as he dropped back into Spanjol. Ehwardo could follow that well enough. Out of sheer inertia the Civil Government had maintained it as a second official language all these centuries, and he had been trained to public service.

"*Iytiote!*" he screamed: *fool.* "Do your peons love you because you have the same priest and demand your rent in the same tongue? How many have I scourged back to their plows for you? If they taste a master's blood and he is a Brigade noble, won't they want yours?"

The councilors' smiles disappeared, to be replaced with thoughtful expressions.

"Don't worry, Messers," Ehwardo said. "The Civil Government will keep order."

It had to. Unless the peasants paid their landlords a share of their crop and forced labor, they would eat everything they produced. How could the armies and cities be supported then? Not to mention the fact that landlords were the ruling class at home, as they were everywhere. Still . . .

"Did you know," he went on in the local language, "that my great-uncle was Governor in East Residence?" They hadn't, and breath sucked in; he waved away their bows. "Listen carefully, then, to a story Governor Poplanich told my father, and my father to me.

"Once there was a mighty king, who ruled broad lands. His minister read the king's plans for the coming year, and went to his lord.

"'Lord,' the minister said, 'I see you spend millions on soldiers and forts and weapons, and not one *senthavo* to lighten the sufferings of the poor.'

"'Yes,' said the king. 'When the revolution comes, I will be ready.'"

A color-party of the 17th Kelden Foot was forcing its way through the press toward him; Ehwardo sighed with relief. He smiled down at the councilors, and tapped a finger alongside his nose.

"A wise man, my great-uncle," he said, grinning. *"Vayaadi a vo, Sehnors."*

The narrow forest lane was rutted even by Military Government standards, but the ground on either side was mostly open, beneath huge smooth-barked beech trees ten times taller than a man. Green gloom flickered with the breeze sighing through the canopy, but it was quiet and very still on the leaf-mould of the floor. The two companies of the 5th were spread out on either side of the road in platoon columns, moving at a brisk lope; the Skinners trickled along in clumps and clots around them, ambling or galloping. Three field-gun carriages followed the soldiers, with only half the usual six-dog teams; despite that they bounced along at a fair pace. The moving men started up a fair amount of game; sounders of half-wild pigs, mono-horns, a honking gabble of some sort of bipedal greenish things that stopped rooting for beech-nuts and fled with orange crests flaring from their long sheep-like heads and flat bills agape.

Luckily, there were no medium-to-large car-nosauroids around; those were mostly too stupid to be afraid, although there was nothing wrong with their reflexes, bloodlust or ferocious grip on life even when mangled. Killing one would be noisy.

Sentinels with the shoulder-flashes of the 7th Descott stepped out from behind trees.

"What've you got for me, Lieutenant?" Raj asked their officer, pulling up Horace in a rustle of leaves.

"Seyor," the man said, casting an eye at the Skinners who kept right on moving as if the sentry-line did not exist. "Major Gruder's got a pig-farmer for you."

"Took a while to get someone who could under-stand him, General," Kaltin Gruder said. "I *think* he's giving us pretty detailed directions to those holdouts."

The peasant — swineherd by profession — had an iron thrall-collar around his neck and a lump of scar tissue where his left ear should have been. His long knife and iron-shod crook were the tools of a trade that took him into the woods often, and his ragged smock and pants and bare callused feet wouldn't have been out of place in most villages in the Civil Government.

Raj listened closely to the gap-toothed gabble. The language problem was a little worse than he'd antici-pated. Spanjol and Sponglish were very different in their written forms and grammar, but the most basic terms, the eight hundred or so words that comprised everyday speech, were quite similar: *blood* in Spong-lish was *singre* and in Spanjol *sangre*, for instance, quite unlike the Namerique *blud* or Skinner *zank*.

The trouble was that neither the local peasants nor most of his soldiers spoke the standard versions of their respective national languages. When a Descotter trooper tried to talk to a Crown Peninsula sharecrop-per, misunderstanding was one of the better alternatives. Starless Dark, some of his Descotters had trouble in East Residence!

"Yes, that's what he's saying," Raj said after a moment. There was an icy feeling behind his eyes, more mental than physical, and the mouthings became coherent speech. "They're about . . . ten klicks that way. There's a valley . . . no, it sounds like a collapsed sinkhole. 'Many' of them — at least two thousand guns, I'd say. Possibly twice that; I doubt he can count past ten even barefoot."

Kaltin ran a hand through his dark bowl-cut hair. "Lucky thing I didn't go in with only the 7th," he said. "I *thought* I'd been running into an awful lot of empty manors." He looked up sharply. "If he's telling the truth, of course."

probability of 92% +/-3, Center said.

"He is," Raj replied flatly. "Let's see *exactly* where." That was an exercise in frustration, even when they brought in others from the circle of charcoal-burners and swineherds. They were eager to help, but none of them had even heard of maps; they could describe every creek and rock in their home territories — but only to a man who already knew the area that was their whole world.

"All right," he said at last. "It's about three hours on foot from here; call it ten kilometers. There's a low range of hills; in the middle of it's a big oval area, sounds like fifteen to thirty hectares, of lumpy ground with a rim all around it and a stream running through — it's limestone country, as I said. The axis is east-west. Natural fortress. Only one real way out, about two thousand meters across, on the eastern side of the oval. Evidently some native bandits — or rebels, depending on your point of view — used it until this man's father's time, then the Brigaderos finally hunted them down and hung them."

As he spoke, Raj sketched, tracing over the projection Center laid on the pad; training in perspective drawing was a part of the standard Civil Government military education, and he had set himself to it with unfashionable zeal as a young man.

Kaltin whistled through his teeth as he looked at the details. "Now that's going to be something like hard work, if we want to do it quick," he said. "Plenty of cover, lots of water, getting over the edge just won't do much good, not with all those hummocks. And if they're determined — well."

Which they would be, having refused the call to surrender. The problem with making examples was that it worked both ways; having looked at the alternatives, these Brigaderos had evidently decided that at seventh and last they'd rather die.

In which case they were going to get their wish.

"Then we'd better move quickly, before they have a chance to get set up," he said, with a slight cold smile. "We certainly can't afford to take a week winkling them out, or bringing up a larger force. The garrison in Lion City might sally if we did — four thousand trained men, and far too mobile for my taste if we let them loose."

Kaltin raised an eyebrow. "You think there's enough of us?" Slightly over six hundred in the 7th Descott, two companies of the 5th, and the Skinners. "For storming a strong defensive position, that is."

"Oh, I think so. Provided we're fast enough that they don't realize what's happening."

"Can we get the guns in there?"

"We can try; it's open beech forest for the most part, nearly to the sinkhole area. I'm certainly bringing those. Take a look; the ship missed us in Port Wager and pulled in here a few days ago."

Raj nodded toward three weapons on field-gun carriages, standing beside the rutted laneway. Kaltin looked them over, puzzled. At first glance they were much like the standard 75mm gun. At second, they were something very different.

"Rifle-barrels clamped together?" he said.

"Thirty-five of them, double-length," Raj said. "Demonstrate, Corporal."

The soldier threw a lever at the rear of the weapon, and a block swung back horizontally, like the platen of a letterpress. Another man lifted out a thin iron plate about the size of a book-cover with a loop on the top. The plate was drilled with thirty-five holes, and an equal number of standard 11mm Armory cartridges stood in them.

"Dry run, please," Raj said.

The crew inserted an empty plate; the gunner pushed the lever sharply forward and the mechanism locked with a *clunk* sound. He crouched to look through the rifle-type sights, spun the elevation and traverse screws, and turned a crank on the side of the breech through one complete revolution. A brisk *brttt* of clicks sounded. Then he threw the lever back again; the crew repeated the process another four times in less than thirty seconds.

"Three hundred and twenty-five rounds a minute, with practice," Raj said. "I know it works — that is, it'll shoot. Whether it's as useful as appearances suggest, the Spirit only knows and experience will show. I'm certainly not counting on it this time, not during the field-test, but it can't hurt."

Kaltin whistled again. "Turning engineer, Messer Raj?" he said. That would be beneath the dignity of a

landed Messer and cavalry officer, but Raj's eccentrici-
ties were legend anyway.

"No, a friend suggested it."

**provided schematic drawings suitable to current
technological levels,** Center corrected pedantically.
**after correcting certain design faults in the
original.**

Thank you, Raj thought.

you are welcome.

"It looks handy," the other officer said appraisingly.
"No recoil?" Cannon bounced backward with every
shot and had to be manhandled back into battery.

"None to speak of, and it's less than a quarter the
weight of a field gun. Muzzaf had some of his
innumerable relatives run it up — in Kolobassia
district, but out of the way. We're calling it the
splat-gun, from the sound."

The other man nodded; that southwestern peninsula
was one of the primary mining and metalworking areas
in the Civil Government.

"Don't tell me you got the Master of Ordnance to
spring for this," he said.

The last major innovation had been the Armory
rifle, nearly two hundred years before. The Civil
Government quite literally worshipped technology —
but technology was what the miraculous powers of the
UnFallen could accomplish, flying faster than sunlight
from world to world and inspired by the indwelling
Spirit of Man. Ironmongery did not qualify.

Raj's grin grew savage. "Tzetzas paid for it," he said.
"I used some of the surplus we got from his estates
when we sold him back his rotten hardtack and
waste-dump bunker coal."

He turned back to the map. "Let's get to work."

Hereditary Major Elfred Stubbins bent to look
through the telescope. One of his neighbors was an
amateur astronomer, and had imported the thing from

East Residence at enormous expense years ago; most
thought it mildly disgraceful, even religiously suspect
— wasn't the Spirit of Man of This Earth alone? Why
look at a heavens which held only the Outer Dark?
Stubbins considered himself an up-to-date and broad-
minded man, able to both read and write. He had
remembered the instrument when his neighbors met
in hasty conclave to plan their flight to the Crater, and
it was proving very useful. Clumsily, his sword-callused
hands turned the focusing screw.

A man leaped out at him, brought from two
thousand meters to arm's length. Round and brown
and button-nosed, with a tuft of scalplock on the crown
and bracelets of brass wire up the forearms. The rifle
he balanced across a bronze-shod shooting stick was a
joke, longer than the man aiming it. What in the Outer
Dark was —

CRACK.

The 15mm bullet drove the narrow final segment of
the telescope four inches into Stubbins' brain. He
pitched backward onto the gritty surface of the
limestone block, limbs thrashing like a pithed frog,
beating out a tattoo on the dusty stone. Men exploded
from all around him, to stand staring as the body
stilled, lying spread-eagled with a four-inch stub of
tattered brass protruding from one eye-socket.

CRACK. A man's head splashed away from the
monstrous sauroid-killing bullet.

The Brigade warriors didn't need a third prompt.
Every one of them was down behind cover within a
few seconds.

"What the fuck is happening here?" someone cried.
"Is it the civvies?" Kettledrums began beating the
alarm in the camps below them where the refugee
households had set up.

A few muskets crashed, firing blind towards the hills
to the north, then fell silent. The small figures moving
out of the low scrub there on the karstic hills were plainly

visible, but they were scattered, too far for any effective fire from the rifle-muskets that most of the men carried. More and more of the strangers were strolling forward; not looking in any particular hurry, calling to each other in high mild voices, yipping and hooting.

A Brigade officer came panting up the rocky way; there was a faint path worn just enough to be visible through the thirst-tolerant native vegetation that drove tendrils into the rock. Limestone drains freely; down lower where there was soil, trees grew. Many of them were fruit trees run wild, others spiky red-green Bellevue vegetation. Men had lived here before, the native forest-thieves of a generation ago, before that others from time to time, from century to century. The Brigade fugitives had found scraps of PreFall plastic and ancient charcoal beneath a deep overhang. Troops followed the officer, and further back women with their skirts kirted up and loads in their hands.

"Skinners," the officer said, as he stoop-crawled around the block Stubbins had used to set up his telescope. A ripple of curses ran along the waiting riflemen; most of them had heard of the tribe, at least. They were childhood boogies among the more northerly of the Brigade.

Another savage crack, and a man who had raised himself to fire slid backward with the top taken off his head the way a spoon does a hard-boiled egg. Freshly exposed brain oozed pink out of the shattered bone and white lining tissue; the limbs twiched for a second, the body hung in equipose, then began sliding further down the slope. Some of the women screamed as it bounced and rolled by, but they kept coming.

"Nomads from up northeast of the Stalwarts, east of the Base Area," the officer went on, for the benefit of those who *hadn't* heard of the Skinners. Few of their raids had penetrated to the edge of Brigade territory, although their pressure was one factor forcing the Stalwarts south.

"Spread out there, and keep your heads down. Adjust your sights for maximum and don't forget to shorten 'em again when they get closer."

The men obeyed, as they might not have the retainer of another landowner; the officer was a General's Dragoon. There was still a snarl in the voice of one who asked:

"What're they doing *here*? And what are those *gawdammit* women doing?"

"Coming up to load," the man called, raising his voice so everyone on the knoll could hear. "We're going to try and hold these high spots along the crater wall. Three women are going to load for each of you. Remember to check the sights. Shift rocks — they'll be looking for your powder-smoke."

"You can't bring women into a battle zone!" one man protested; a prosperous freeholder by his cowhide jacket.

"Fuckhead!" the officer screamed, frustration suddenly snapping his control. "Fuckhead! D'you think the Skinners will kiss their hands if they get through? They'll cut their throats and rape the dead bodies, you shit-eating civvie-breed, I've *fought* them before. The *grisuh*'ve brought them as mercs, Spirit eat their eyes for it.

"All of you!" he went on. "The only way we're gonna stop them is kill every one of them, because otherwise they'll keep coming till they blow away every swinging dick in this valley. Get ready!"

The Skinners ambled forward, climbing nimbly over the tumbled whitish-grey rock. Some of them were smoking pipes, and now and then one would stop to adjust his breechclout or take a swig of water from a skin bag. Big flop-eared brindled hounds walked behind them, some riding animals, some with wicker panniers of extra ammunition. Those came forward whenever a Skinner whistled, and the man would grab another handful of the carrot-sized shells. They were firing more often now; a nomad would stop, let the shooting stick swing down, aim, fire, reload, and start forward again in ten seconds or less. Most of them were catching their spent brass and tucking it into belt pouches. A Brigade warrior lurched back screaming with his hands to his face as rock-fragments clawed across his eyeballs from one near-miss.

The women had made it to the top of the trail, scurrying along well below the crestline to take positions below each rifleman before they set down their burden of hundred-round ammunition boxes. The men with them were carrying several muskets each; they used their swords to pry open the lids of the boxes and then handed out the weapons. Many of the women's palms were bleeding from the rough hemp of the rope handles, and some were crying silently, but they started loading immediately. More slowly than a trained fighter, but there were many of them. Two older women travelled from one clump of loaders to another, distributing small leather boxes of percussion caps they held in a fold of their skirts.

"Let 'em have it!" the officer shouted, as the Skinners came to about a thousand meters, maximum effective range.

Smoke jetted from hundreds of muzzles. Half a dozen of the Skinners were hit, of the hundreds swarming down the slope; some of those rose again. Some of those too badly wounded to rise — even a Skinner could not force a shattered thighbone to function no matter how indifferent to pain — tied rough bandages or tourniquets and started firing from a prone position. The rest of the Skinner force slowed their advance; not from fear, but because this was the optimum range. Their rifles were more accurate than their enemies', and nearly every Skinner could use his to the limit of the weapon's capacities.

The Brigade men reached behind for new weapons thrust into their hands, fired, fired again. Any man who

raised his upper body for a better shot died, and many
who showed only an eye and a rifle-barrel through a
crack in a boulder did too. The iron-and-shit stink of
death began to hang heavy; bodies bled out quickly
when fist-sized holes were blasted through their torsos.
Blood sank quickly into the porous rock, turning the
surface slick and greasy. Screams and moans from men
blinded or flayed by rock-fragments were continuous.
The women dragged wounded men backward, and
fresh riflemen — many of them boys and white-
bearded grandfathers, now — climbed the trail to take
their places. After a while, some of the women
themselves climbed up to take the spots of men who'd
been killed and not replaced. Few of them were as
accurate as the men, but the Skinners were much
closer now. Everyone could hear them hooting and
laughing as they walked forward, laughing and killing
with every shot.

The officer who had fought Skinners before lay
behind a rock; the tourniquet which had saved his life
let only a dribble of blood out of the shattered stump
of his left forearm. He kept his head well down the
rock; his face was mud-grey with shock and covered
with fat beads of sweat. His lip bled too, where he had
bitten it to make himself stay concious. Four revolvers
lay conveniently near his right hand, and his
unsheathed sword.

"Halt," Kaltin Gruder said, as the rise steepened to
twenty degrees, fissured water-rotted rock beneath
their feet.

No point in taking the dogs forward further. They
were sure-footed, much more so than a hoofed animal,
but size and the stiff backbone needed to bear the
weight of a man exacted its price in agility. A
saddle-dog had to watch its step on going like this, and
there was worse ahead. Mice can fall hundreds of feet
and walk away; a cat may or may not escape with

bruises or break a bone; a man dropped from the same height will almost surely die. A twelve-hundred-pound wardog would *splash*.

The officers and noncoms passed it down the line verbally; the Brigaderos would probably realize they were here soon, despite the continuous crackle of firing and thick pall of smoke from the far northern side of the crater, but there was no point in advertising with a trumpet-call designed to carry. The action was about three long rifle-shots from the southern rim, and as many more from his present position. The long slopes were thick with scrub oak, chinquapin, and witchhazel, too thin-soiled to support the big beeches that predominated further south. Ahead the scrub thinned to occasional patches dominated by reddish-green native climbers and many-stalked bushes. The slope was also littered with boulders from head-size to twice man-height, almost all the way up to the notched rim that stood like a line of decaying teeth a hundred meters high.

The dogs crouched, and men stepped out of the stirrups and loaded their rifles.

"Fix bayonets." Rattle and snap, and a subtle change in attitude. There was nothing like that order to drive home that it was about to hit the winnowing-fan. "Company A in reserve. B, C, and D will advance in extended skirmish order, by squads."

Eight-man squads moved forward cautiously, covered by the next; they took firing positions behind cover and waited alertly while their comrades leap-frogged forward. It was part of the drill, albeit not one used all that often. The dark blue of their jackets and the dull maroon of their pants blended well with the shade and varied colors of vegetation, soil and rock. In a minute or two nothing remained but an occasional glimpse, a stirring of leaves against the wind, or the clink of metal on stone. Back here the lines of dogs waited motionless, the riderless whining softly and staring with fixed attention at the direction their masters had taken.

Kaltin Gruder was nervous. Not about his men's performance. Even if this wasn't the most common form of combat, they'd trained for it . . . and they were all hunters at home, skirmishers when they or their squire had a quarrel with the neighbors. His own first smell of powder had come that way, stalking through a maze of gullys and canyons after a sheep-lifter, and you could die just as dead as in a major battle.

What worried him was the loss of control. He couldn't *see* more than a few of the men. In most situations a battalion commander expected to keep his whole force under observation, or at least ride around to his company-level officers checking on things. In this scrub even the *lieutenants* wouldn't have direct control over their units. Shouldn't be a problem keeping the advance going unless it got real sticky, no — although he pitied an infantry commander with a job like this. Men didn't join or stay in the 7th Descott Rangers unless they could be relied on to keep moving toward the sharp end without someone prodding them up the arse. The troops wouldn't stand for anyone like that, and they had emphatic and very practical ways of making it known.

The other thing that worried him was that his men knew the Skinner attack had got in before theirs. That was fine, keep the barbs' attention pinned one way, they'd still have men on the south fringe but not as many or as alert. But the Spirit of Man with a nuke in Its hand couldn't stop Skinners from lifting everything worth taking if they got into the refugees' stores first. His men wouldn't endanger the mission for loot . . . but since they were supposed to attack in that direction anyway, he knew they'd move faster than they should. Some of them, and the rest would keep up with their friends.

Everything's a tradeoff. Soldiers were useless

without the will to fight. But men trained to kill and too proud to show fear in the face of fire were never easy to control.

Starless Dark with this, he thought. He certainly wasn't going to maintain control if they couldn't see him.

"Captain." Company A was always overstrength and commanded by a captain rather than a senior lieutenant. "I'm taking the HQ squad forward. You'll act to prevent a breakthrough if the barbs counterattack, and advance on order or signal" — a red rocket — "or at your discretion after one hour."

"Yes, sir," Captain Falcones said with notable lack of enthusiasm.

"Your turn will come, Huan. You men, follow me!"

The signaler brought his trumpet, but he licked his thumb and wet the foresight of his rifle as they moved forward. A crackle of shots broke out, nearer than the slamming firefight along the north edge of the crater. Echoes slapped back and forth from the rocks.

"This way."

Braaaaaaaap.

The splat-gun to Raj's left fired. Thirty-five rounds slapped into the Brigaderos rush, and men went tumbling. Only five or six out of nearly sixty, but the rest stopped to shoot back — exactly the wrong thing to do. Bullets cracked through air, clipped leaves from the bushes, sparked and pinged off stones. Few of them were aimed in his direction anyway, and if his luck was that bad he'd better get it over with.

He looked right and left; the two companies of the 5th were advancing in staggered double line, with five meters between platoons. Thin, but he didn't have very many men with him to cover over a kilometer of front. North and south of that the ground got too rugged for easy movement, and the barbs didn't look to be in any mood for fancy flanking maneuvers; clots and dribbles of them were filtering through the narrower neck of the exit and attacking as they came without waiting to mass. Bad tactics, but they were being squeezed forward toward him like a melon-seed between two hard fingers.

"Platoon will advance with volley fire," the lieutenant of the platoon he had with him shouted, pointing with his saber. The front rank went to one knee, dipping in unison. Their rifles steadied.

"Fire!"

BAM. Greasy gray-black smoke spurted. The spent brass went flying backward as they worked the levers, and the bolts retracted and slid down; one man had a jam, the thin wrapped brass cartridge heat-welded to the walls of the chamber and the iron base torn off by the extractor.

"Scramento," the trooper muttered, snatching out his boot-knife and ignoring everything around him as he probed delicately to peel the foil away from the steel.

Braaaaaaaap. Another splatgun fired, chewing into the stationary Brigaderos as they frantically bit open cartridges and dumped the powder down the barrels of their rifles. Ramming, withdrawing the rod, fumbling at their belts for a cap . . .

The second rank of 5th troopers walked through the first, knelt, fired.

BAM.

Click. From the first rank. Rounds pushed down the grooves on top of the bolts and into the chamber with the thumb. *Clack.* Levers pulled back to lie along the stock, the same motion locking the bolts into the lugs at the rear of the chamber and cocking the internal firing pins. They rose, trotted through the reloading second rank, knelt, fired.

BAM.

Braaaaaaaap.

The lieutenant looked up and down the line, where

variations on the same scene were happening. Most of the enemy in front of him were still loading.

"Charge!" he shouted.

One of the Brigaderos fired from the hip, his ramrod still in his rifle. By a chance someone who'd never seen a battlefield wouldn't have believed it speared through the chest of the Descotter charging him. Both men wore identical expressions of surprise, until the Civil Government trooper went to his knees and then his face, the iron rod standing out behind his back. The Brigadero was still gaping when the trooper's squadmate fired with his muzzle not two feet away. The barbarian flew backward, punched away as much by gasses that had no chance to dissipate as by the bullet, his leather jacket smouldering in a circle a foot wide over his belly.

The rest clubbed their muskets or drew swords; the Brigaderos carried bayonets but evidently didn't much like to use them. The troopers fired again at point-blank range and then there was a brief flurry of butt and bayonet, the ugly butcher's-cleaver sound of steel parting flesh.

More rifle fire from ahead, from behind a boulder. Two or three men . . .

"Prone!" the lieutenant snapped; he stayed on one knee, as did Raj and his HQ group. "Somebody get —

Braaaaaaaap. The surface of the boulder sparked and spalled under the impact of another thirty-five rounds. Something hit; a rifle-barrel jerked up over the squarish boulder and stayed there.

"Forward," Raj said, and then to his trumpeter: "Sound maintain advance."

Behind them he could hear the ground crunching as the splatgun's crew manhandled it up at a trot. *That solves that problem*, he thought; he'd been wondering if the new weapon was more like close-range artillery or small arms. They were best deployed well forward, probably in the gaps between units, to shoot men onto their objectives. *Maybe an iron shield on either side of the barrel?*

"*Mi heneral?*" the lieutenant asked, hopping a step to keep up with Raj's longer stride.

The men were moving forward again, the line of bayonets glittering . . . or in some cases, dull. Nothing ahead for the moment, but the burbling echoes of the firefight in the crater were getting closer. So far they'd seen the ones the enemy had stationed here, or the quickest-witted and fastest on their feet. A serious attempt to force the gap could come any moment.

"Yes?" Raj asked, startled out of a world of lines and distances, alternatives and choices.

"Why are we attacking the enemy, sir? Not that I mind — but wouldn't it be tactically sound to make them come to us? We're across their line of retreat."

Raj looked at the painfully earnest young face. He nodded in recognition; he'd always wanted to know how to do his job better too.

"Son, if we had four or five companies, yes. As it is, we can't hold this width of front, even with those little beauties." He gestured back at the splatguns with his revolver. "There are probably still enough of them to pin us down while a lot of the rest get through and scatter into the hills.

"But. We're not really attacking them, we're hustling them, they're bouncing around like bees in a bucket and we're not going to give them *time* to sit down and organize a breakout attack. Defeat takes place in the mind of the enemy." The puppy awe in the young man's face was embarrassing. "We'll hold a bit further forward, where the chokepoint narrows."

"*Watch it!*"

They crouched slightly, instinctively, and ran forward. There had only been one Brigadero behind the boulder, and a girl loading for him. The man lay dead, slumped back against the stone with his brains leaking down the rough surface. The girl was lying curled on her side, a dagger with a gold-braid hilt and gold pommel sunk to the guard under her ribs. Her mouth was a soundless O, her eyes round and dark as her body shuddered.

Missed the kidney, Raj knew. It might take her some time to bleed out, blood leaking into her stomach cavity like water around a badly packed valve.

"Kicked t'rifle outta her hands, but t'cunt cut belly affore I could stop her, ser," the corporal said apologetically.

The girl made a small sound; the lieutenant looked at her and swallowed. The older man knew it was because he'd suddenly seen her as a *person*, not a target, not another barb; perhaps because she'd done pretty much what a Descotter woman would have in her place. Raj moved forward and put his revolver to the back of her neck, squeezing the trigger carefully; even touching was far enough away to miss, if you jerked. The body bucked once, but the sound of the shot was almost lost in the noise of battle.

He looked up. The entrance to the crater was narrowing here, and there was less in the way of large boulders for cover.

"All right," he said to his runners. "My compliments to Captains Fleyez and Morrisyn, and we'll hold here — men to take cover. Get that splatgun up here, this is a good position for it."

The trumpet sounded, and the long line of blue-coated men sank into the ground; hands shifted rocks to give good firing rests and make improvised sangars. The splatgun came bounding up under the hands of its enthusiastic crew, one wheel crunching over the Brigadero woman's legs before the weapon settled into the depression behind the boulder. That put its muzzle at waist height above the ground.

"Ah, good," the artillery corporal in charge of it said. He noticed the gold-chased dagger and pulled it out, wiping the blade on the girl's stockinged leg and checking the metal of the blade by flicking it with a thumbnail before sticking the knife into his boot-top.

Raj moved a few meters to another boulder, sat and uncorked his canteen. "The 7th and the Skinners will drive them to us," he said, half to himself. From the volume of fire, within a few minutes.

"Drive them to us, sir?" the lieutenant said. "The 7th is finally doing the 5th a favor?" His color was returning, a little.

Raj looked over at the boulder, where the gunners were piling head-sized stones in front of their weapon. They'd tossed the bodies out to have more room; the girl's long black hair hid what was left of her face.

"Nobody's doing anybody any favors here today, Lieutenant," he said. "Nobody."

"Here theyuns come, tall's storks n' thick as grass!"

Kaltin Gruder had a girl on the saddlebow before him when he rode up to the command-station at the exit to the crater. That might have been expected — although it was a bit early for an officer as conscientious as Gruder to be looting, with the odd shot still going off behind him. Except that she was about eight years old, a huge-eyed creature with braided tow-colored hair in a bloodied shift.

"Took her away from a Skinner," he said, at Raj's raised eyebrows, his voice slightly defensive.

Embarrassed at impulse of compassion, something as out of place here as a nun in a knockshop, Raj supposed. Feelings were odd things. Antin M'lewis had adopted a three-legged alley cat that spring and lugged it all the way from East Residence.

Gruder shrugged: "Well, Mitchi" — the slave-mistress Reggiri had given him last year — "can use a maidservant, or whatever. There, ah, weren't many prisoners. Most of the Brigaderos civilians killed themselves before we broke through, when they could tell nobody was getting out."

Raj nodded. That simplfed things for him . . . and for them, come to that, if they felt like that about it. He could understand that, too.

Gruder was looking around at the number of bodies lying in the five hundred meters before the final stop-line the 5th's two companies had established. A D-shape of corpses, two or three deep in spots, a thick scattering elsewhere.

"Hot work," he said.

"The splatguns," Raj said. "We put them on the flanks and had the Brigaderos in a crossfire; they were worth about another company each, in sheer firepower on the defensive."

Kaltin frowned, stroking the whimpering girl's head absently. She clung to the cloth of his uniform jacket, although the right-hand sleeve was sodden and streaking her bright hair with blood.

"This was certainly more like a battle than most of what we've seen this campaign, Messer," he said. "I've got twenty dead, and as many again badly hurt."

"Ten from the 5th," Raj confirmed. *Spirit dump Barholm's cores into the Starless Dark, I told him to give me forty thousand men. Even thirty thousand —*

He sighed and rose, swinging into Horace's saddle. "Let's see if there's some wheeled transport for our wounded."

Chief Juluk was riding up, seven-foot rifle over his shoulder. He looked as if he'd waded in blood, and quite possibly had; one of the subchiefs behind him had managed to cram his body into a ball-gown covered in ruffled lace and had a bearded head tied to his saddlebow by its long hair. That must have been a brave man, to be worth preserving.

The Skinner looked around at the carnage. "Bad like us!" he giggled. "You one big devil, sojer-man. Bad like us!"

Raj felt his head nodding in involuntary agreement.

no, raj whitehall. you fight for a world in which there will be no men like him at all.

Or like me, he thought. *Or like me.*

"Lion City next," he said aloud. "Spirit of *Man*, I hope they have sense enough to come to terms."

Kaltin had been trying to disengage the girl's hands so that he could turn her over to an aide, but she clung desperately and tried to keep him between her and the Skinners.

"What do we do if they don't accept terms?" he said with professional interest, giving up the attempt. "We've nothing that'll touch their walls."

"Do?" Raj said. He reached out and touched the girl's hair with careful tenderness; she buried her head in Gruder's shoulder. "Anything we have to. Anything at all."

CHAPTER FOURTEEN

"Excellent work, Abdullah," Raj said.

The maps were sketched, but accurate; street-lay-outs, the location of listed merchants' and landowners' mansions, the waterworks, warehouses, estimates of food-reserves, number of men in the militia and their commanders. A little of it overlapped with the Ministry of Barbarians' reports, somewhat more with Muzzaf Kerpatik's data from his merchant friends, but a good deal was new — particularly the information on the large Colonist community that controlled Lion City's grain trade. He flicked through; faster than he could read, but Center was looking out from his eyes and recording. He'd have to go over it again; Center's knowledge was not accessible to him in really useful form most of the time, not directly. Center could implant it; without the learning process it was there, but not understood.

The man bowed, touching brow and lips and chest; it looked odd, when his appearance was so thoroughly Southern Territories.

"Saayid," he said.

"Your family is still living in that house in the Ox-Crossing, isn't it?" Raj asked.

That was a suburb of East Residence, outside the walls and across the bay. Abdullah nodded.

"It's yours, and the grounds," Raj said, and waved away a pro-forma protest. "Don't deprive me of the pleasure of rewarding good service," he said.

"Thank you, saayid," Abdullah said. "And now . . . I think the merchant Peydaro Blanhko —" he touched his chest "— should vanish from the earth. Too many people will be asking for him."

Raj looked at Suzette as the Druze left the tent. "Someday I'm going to get the whole story of that one out of you," he said.

"Not with wild oxen, my love."

Raj stepped up to the map and began sketching in the extra data. "No, but I suspect that if I tickle you around that tiny mole, you'll tell all. . . . Right, that's the shipyard. Now —"

The flap of the command tent had been pinned up, leaving a large three-sided room open to the west. In full dark the camp outside the walls of Lion City was a gridwork of cooking fires and shadowed movement; Raj could hear the tramp of feet in the distance, howling from the dog-lines, and a harsh challenge from a sentry on the rampart.

They can probably see our fires from the walls, Raj thought, standing with his hands behind his back; the center of the camp was slightly higher than the edges, and he could make out the pale color of the city walls. Lantern-lights starred it. Much brighter was the tall lighthouse, even though it was on the other side of the city. The light was a carbide lamp backed by mirrors, but the lighthouse itself was Pre-Fall work, a hundred meters tall.

There were probably plenty of nervous citizens on the ramparts, besides the civic militia. Looking out at the grid of cooking fires in the besieger's camp, and thinking of what might happen in a sack.

Then they'd bloody well better give up, hadn't they?
He turned back to the trestle table. "First, gentlemen," he said to the assembled officers, "I'd like to say, well done. We've subdued a province of nearly a million people in less than two weeks, suffered only minor casualties" — every one of them unpleasantly major to the men killed and maimed, but that was part of the

cost of doing business — "and your units have performed with efficiency and dispatch.

"Colonel Menyez," he went on, "you may tell your infantry commanders that I'm also pleased with the way they've shaken down. Their men have marched, dug — and shot, on a couple of occasions — in soldierly fashion."

A flush of real pleasure reddened Menyez' fair complexion. "I've had them under arms for a full year and a half or more now," he said. "Sandoral, the Southern Territories and this campaign. I'd back the best of them against any cavalry, in a straight stand-up firefight."

Civil Government infantry usually lived on State farms assigned to them near their garrisons, and were paid cash only when on field service away from their homes, unlike the cavalry. The farms were worked by government peons, but it wasn't uncommon in out-of-the-way units for the enlisted men to be more familiar with agricultural implements than their rifles. Menyez's own 17th Kelden County Foot had been in continuous field service since the Komar operation four years ago, and many of the other infantry battalions since the Sandoral campaign on the eastern frontier. The fisc and Master of Soldiers' office had complained mightily; finding regular hard cash for the mounted units was difficult enough.

Raj went on: "I'd also like to particularly commend Major Clerett for his management of the preemptive attack over the Waladavir; a difficult operation, conducted with initiative and skill."

Cabot Clerett nodded. Suzette leaned to whisper in his ear, and he nodded again, this time letting free the boyish grin that had been twitching at his control.

"And now, Messers, we get the usual reward for doing our work."

"More work, General?" somebody asked.

"Exactly. Lion City, which we certainly can't leave in our rear while we advance. Colonel Dinnalsyn?"

The artillery commander rose and walked to the map board. "As you can see, the city's a rectangle, more or less, facing west to the sea. Here's the harbor." A carrot-shaped indentation in the middle with semicircular breakwaters reaching out into the ocean and leaving a narrow gap for ships.

"The breakwaters, the lighthouse, and the foundations of the sea walls are adamantine." Pre-Fall work; the material looked like concrete but was stronger than good steel, and did not weather. "The walls are about four hundred years old, but well-maintained — blocks up to two tons weight, height five to ten meters, towers every hundred-and-fifty meters or so. The main gate was modernized about a century ago, with two defensive towers and a dog-leg. There are heavy pieces on the sea walls, and four-and eight-kilogram fortress guns on the walls, some of them rifled muzzle-loaders firing shell. They outrange our field guns."

"Appraisal, messer?"

"The sea approaches are invulnerable. Landward, my fieldpieces could peck at those walls for a year, even with solid shot. I could run the wheels up on frames or earth ramps to get elevation and put shells over the walls . . . except that the fortress guns would outrange my boys. That goes double for the mortars. The only cheering word is that there's no moat. If you want to bring the walls down, we'll have to ship in heavy battering pieces — the ones from Fort Wager would do — and put in a full siege."

Everyone winced: that meant cross- and approach-trenches, earthworked bastions to push the guns closer and closer to the walls, artillery duels, then however long it took to knock a suitable breach. Desperate fighting to force their way through into the town.

observe, said Center.

— and powder-smoke nearly hid the tumbled rubble of the shattered wall. Men clawed their way upward, jerking and falling as the storm of bullets swept through their ranks. Another wave drove upward, meeting the Brigaderos troops at the apex of the breach. There was a brief point-blank firefight, and then the Civil Government soldiers were through.

They charged, bayonets levelled and a tattered flag at their head. But beyond the breach was a C of earthworks and barricades taller than a man, thrown up while the heavy guns wrecked the stone wall. Cannon bucked and spewed cannister into the advancing ranks —

— and Raj could see Lion City ringed by circumvallation, lines of trenches facing in and another line facing out. Beyond the outer line sprawled the camps of the Brigade's relieving armies, improvised earthworks less neat than the Civil Government's but effective enough, and stunning in their number.

A sentry leaned against the parapet of the outer trench. His face had a bony leaness, and it was tinged with yellow. His rifle slid down and lay at his feet, but the soldier ignored it; instead he hugged himself and shivered, teeth chattering in his head.

"Thank you, Colonel," Raj said, blinking away the vision. Dinnalsyn resumed his seat with the gloomy satisfaction of a man who had told everyone what they were hoping not to hear.

"The garrison," Raj went on, "consists of a civic militia organized by the guilds and cofraternities, and the household guards of merchants and town-dwelling landowners, about five thousand men of very mixed quality, and a force of Brigaderos regulars of four thousand — they were heavily reinforced shortly before we landed. Nine thousand, including gunners, behind strong fortifications. They've ample water in cisterns if we cut the aqueduct, and this city exports foodstuffs — there's probably enough in the warehouses for a year, even feeding the Brigaderos' dogs.

"I don't want to lose either time or men; but at this point, forced to chose, I'll save time and spend men. Colonel Menyez, start putting together scaling ladders of appropriate size and numbers for an assault force of six thousand men. As soon as some are ready, start the following battalions training on them —"

He listed them; about half and half cavalry and infantry. Everyone winced slightly. "Yes, I know. We'll try talking them into surrender first."

Filipe de Roors was *alcalle* of Lion City because of a talent for dealing with his peers among the merchant community. Also because he was very rich, with ships, marble quarries outside the city and the largest shipyard within, lands and workshops and sawmills; and because his paternal grandfather had been a member of the Brigade, which the other merchants thought would help when dealing with the local *brazaz* military gentry and the authorities in Carson Barracks. The post of mayor usually combined pleasure, prestige and profit with only a modicum of effort and risk.

Right now, de Roors was silently cursing the day he decided to stand for the office.

After the tunnel gloom of the main gate, even the orange-red light of a sun not yet fully over the horizon was bright, and he blinked at the dark shapes waiting. He added another curse for the easterner general, for insisting on meeting at dawn. The air was a little chill, although the days were still hot.

"Messer de Roors?"

De Roors jerked in the saddle, setting the high-bred Chow he rode to curvetting in a sidle that almost jostled one of the soldiers' dogs. The Civil Government cavalry mounts didn't even bother to growl, but the civilian's dog shrank back and whined submissively.

"Captain Foley, 5th Descott Guards," the young officer said.

Raj Whitehall's name had come west over the last

few years, and something of the men who accompanied him. The 5th's, especially, since they had been with him since the beginning; he recognized the blazon fluttering from the bannerman's staff, crossed sabers on a numeral 5, and *Hell o Zpalata* beneath — *Hell or Plunder*, in Sponglish. De Roors looked at the smiling, almost pretty face with the expressionless black eyes and then at the bright-edged hook. The dozen men behind him sat their dogs with bored assurance; they weren't tasked with talking to him, and their glances slid across him and his followers with an utter indifference more intimidating than any hostility.

"This way, if you please, Messer," the officer said.

Watching the invaders build their camp had been a combination of horror and fascination from the walls; like watching ants, but swarming with terrible mechanical precision. Closer up it was worse. The camp was *huge*, there must be twenty thousand people inside, maybe twenty-five, more than half the number in Lion City itself. A road had been laid from the main highway southeast, graded dirt with drainage ditches, better than most highways on the Crown Peninsula. Around the camp was a moat, one and a half meters deep and two across at the top; the bottom was filled with sharpened stakes. Inside the ditch was a steep-sloped earthwork of the reddish-brown soil thrown up by the digging, and it was the height of a tall man. On top of it was a palisade of logs and timbers, probably taken from the woodlots and cottages that had vanished without trace.

At each corner of the camp and at the gates was a pentagonal bastion jutting out from the main wall; the bastions were higher, and their sides were notched. Through the notches jutted the black muzzles of field guns, ready to add their firepower to the wall or take any angle in murderous crossfire. The gate bastion had a solid three-story timber observation tower as well, with the blue and silver Starburst banner flying from the peak.

All of it had been thrown up in a single afternoon.

"Ah . . . are you expecting attack, then?" he asked.

The captain looked at him, smiling slightly. "Attack? Oh, you mean the entrenchments. No, messer, we do that every time we camp. A good habit to get into, you understand."

Spirit.

The escort had shed traffic along the road to the encampment like a plough through thin soil, not even needing to shout for the way. Things were a little more crowded at the gate, although the barricades of spiked timbers were drawn aside; nobody got in or out without challenge and inspection, and the flow was dense and slow-moving. De Roors was riding at the head of the little column, with the officer and banner. A trumpet rang out behind him, loud and brassy. He started slightly in the saddle, humiliatingly conscious of the officer's polite scorn. *Puppy*, he thought. No more than twenty.

Another trumpet answered from the gate parapet; an interplay of calls brought men out at the double to line the road on either side and prompt the other travellers with ungentle haste.

A coffle was halfway through, and the officer threw up his hand to stop the escort while the long file of prisoners got out of the way. There were forty or so men, yoked neck to neck with collars and chains and their hands bound together; many of them were bandaged, and most were in the remnants of Brigade uniform. The more numerous women wore light handcuffs, and the children trudging by their stained and grimy skirts were unbound. None of them looked up as they stumbled by, pushed to haste by armed and mounted men not in uniform but dressed with rough practicality.

"Apologies, Messer Captain," said one, as the

captives stumbled into the ditch to let the troopers through. He didn't seem surprised when Foley ignored him as if he were transparent.

"Slave traders," the captain said, when they had ridden through into the camp. "They follow the armies like vultures."

Maybe that was staged for my benefit, de Roors thought. The ancient lesson: this is defeat. Avoid it. *But the Brigaderos were real.*

Inside the camp was nothing of the tumult or confusion he'd expected from experience with Brigade musters. Instead it was like a military city, a regular grid of ditched laneways, flanked by the leather eight-man tents of the soldiers. Most of them were still finishing their morning meal of gruel and lentils and thin flat wheatcakes, cooked on small wrought iron *ybatch* grills. Every occupied tent — he supposed some men were off on fatigues and so forth — had two wigwams of four rifles each before it, leaning together upright with the men's helmets nodding on them like grain in a reaped field. The men were wiry olive-skinned eastern peasants for the most part, with cropped black hair and incurious clean-shaven faces. Individually they didn't look particularly impressive. Together they had shaken the earth and beaten nations into dust.

The Captain drew closer, courteously pointing out features: De Roors was uneasily aware that the hook flashing past his face was sharpened on the inner edge.

"Each battalion has a set place, the same in every camp. There are the officer's tents —" somewhat larger than the men's "— and the shrine for the unit colors. This is the *wia erente*, the east-west road; the *wia sehcond* runs north-south, and they meet in the center of camp, at the *plaza commanante*, with the general's quarters and the Star church tent. Over there's the artillery park, the dog lines —" a thunder of belling and barking announced feeding time "— the area for the camp followers and soldiers' servants, the —"

De Roors' mind knew the Brigade's armies were vastly more numerous. His emotions told him there was no end to this hive of activity. Men marching or riding filled the streets, traffic keeping neatly to the left and directed at each crossroads by soldiers wearing armbands marked *guardia*. Wagon trains, supply convoys, officers riding by with preoccupied expressions, somewhere the sound of hundreds of men hammering wood.

The commander's tent was large but not the vast pavilion he expected; the canvas church across the open space from it was much bigger, and so was the hospital tent on the other side of the square.

His escort split and formed two lines, facing in. The guard at the door of the tent presented arms to Foley's salute, and the young officer dismounted and stood at parade rest beside the opened door flap.

"The *Heneralissimo Supremo*; Sword-Bearing Guard to the Sovereign Mighty Lord and Sole Autocrat Governor Barholm Clerett; possessor of the proconsular authority for the Western Territories; three times hailed Savior of the State, Sword of the Spirit of Man, Raj Ammenda Halgren da Luis Whitehall!" he called formally, in a crisp clear voice. Then:

"The *Alcalle* of Lion City, Messer Filipe De Roors." A murmur from within. "You may enter, Messer."

De Roors was dimly conscious of his entourage being gracefully led away. The tented room within was lit by skylights above; there was a long table and chairs, and a map-board with an overhead view of Lion City. Nothing of the splendor that a high Brigade noble would take on campaign, nothing of what was *surely* available to the conqueror of the Southern Territories. Nothing but a short forged-steel mace inlaid with platinum and electrum, resting on a crimson cushion. Symbol of the rarely granted proconsular authority, the power to act as vicegovernor in the *barbaricum*.

The man sitting at the middle of the table opposite

him seemed fairly ordinary at first; certainly his uniform was nothing spectacular, despite the eighteen-rayed silver and gold star on either shoulder, orbited by smaller silver stars and enclosed in a gold band. A tall man, broad in the shoulders and narrow-hipped, with a swordsman's thick shoulders and wrists. A hard dark face with startling gray eyes, curly bowl-cut black hair speckled with a few flecks of silver. Looking older than the young hero of legend — and less menacing than the merciless aggressor the Squadron refugees and Colonist merchants had described.

Then he saw the eyes, and the stories about Port Murchison seemed very real.

You've met hard men before, de Roors told himself. *And bargained them into the ground.* He bowed deeply. "Most Excellent General," he said.

This one could sell lice to Skinners, Raj thought a few minutes later. A digest of Lion City's internal organization, constitutional position in the Western Territories, and behavior in previous conflicts rolled on, spiced with fulsome praise, references to common religious faith, and earnest good wishes to the Civil Government of Holy Federation.

"Messer, shut up," he said quietly.

De Roors froze. He was plump, middle-aged and soft-looking and expensively dressed, a five-hundred-FedCred stickpin in his lace cravat. Raj didn't think the man was consciously afraid of death, not after coming in under a flag of truce and guarantee of safe-conduct. He knew the impact his own personality had, however, and that it was magnified in the center of so much obvious power. Yet de Roors was still bargaining hard. There were more types of courage than those required to face physical danger, and they were rather less common.

"Contrary to what you may have heard, messer, not everyone in the *Gubernio Civil* is in love with rhetoric.

I'll put it very simply: Lion City must open its gates and cooperate fully with the army of the Civil Government. If you do, I'll not only guarantee the lives and property of the civilian residents; Lion City will be freed from external tax levies for five years — and you'll get a fifty-percent reduction in harbor dues and charges at East Residence.

He leaned forward slightly. "If you *don't* . . . they call me the Sword of the Spirit, messer *alcalle*, but I'm not the Spirit Itself. If my troops have to fight their way in, they're going to get out of hand — soldiers always do, in a town taken by storm." De Roors blanched; a sack was any townsman's worst nightmare. "Furthermore, in that case I'll have to confiscate heavily for the customary donative to the men. Those aren't threats, they're analysis.

"Messer, I *want* Lion City to surrender peacefully, because I'd prefer to have a functioning port under my control in the Crown. I *will* have the city, one way or another."

De Roors mopped his face. There was a moment's silence outside as a gong tolled, and then the chanting of the morning Star Service. Raj touched his amulet but waited impassively.

"*Heneralissimo supremo*, I can't make such a decision on my own initiative." At Raj's blank lack of expression he stiffened slightly. "This isn't the east, Excellency, and I'm not an autocrat — and the General of the Brigade couldn't make a decision like that by himself.

"And there's the garrison to consider. Usually we have a few hundred regular troops here, enough to, ah —"

Raj nodded. *Keep the city from getting ideas.* Free merchant towns were common on some of the islands of the Midworld. A garrison reminded the impetuous that Lion City was on the mainland and accessible to the General's armies.

"After the news of Stern Isle came through, the General sent three regiments from Old Residence, more than thirty-five hundred men of his standing troops under High Colonel Piter Strezman. A famous commander with veteran troops. They won't surrender."

"Quite a few *Brigaderos* around here have," Raj pointed out.

"They weren't behind strong walls with a year's supplies, your Excellency," de Roors said. "Furthermore, their families weren't in Old Residence standing hostage for them."

What a splendid way to build fighting morale, Raj thought. *I'll bet it was Forker came up with that idea; he's had too much contact with us and went straight from barbarism to decadence without passing through civilization.*

"As you say, this isn't the east," he said dryly. De Roors flushed, and Raj continued: "Let's put it this way: you open the gates, and we'll take care of the garrison."

De Roors coughed into his handkerchief. Raj raised a finger; one of the HQ servants slid in, deposited a carafe of water, and departed with the same smooth silence.

"That might be possible, yes," de Roors said. He drank and wiped his mouth again. "The problem with that, Excellency, is, ummm, you understand that we're not encouraged to meddle in military matters, and — might I suggest that Lion City is of no real importance in itself? If you were to pass on, and either defeat the main Brigade armies, or take Old Residence, we'd be delighted to cooperate with you in a most positive way, most positive, you'd have no cause to complain of our loyalty then. Until then, well, it really would be imprudent of us to —"

Raj grinned. De Roors flinched slightly and averted his eyes.

"You mean," Raj said, his words hard and cold as the

forged iron of a cannon's barrel, "that if you open the gates and we lose the war later, the Brigade will slaughter you down to the babes in arms. Quite true. Look at me, messer."

Reluctantly, de Roor's eyes dragged around again. Raj went on:

"I and my men can't hedge our bets, messer *alcalle*; neither can the Brigaderos, and neither of us will let *you* hedge, either, and thereby encourage every village with a wall to try and sit this war out in safety. If you try to straddle this fence you'll end up impaled on it. No doubt that strikes you as extremely unfair, and no doubt it is; it's also the way this Fallen world is and will continue to be until Holy Federation is restored. Which, as Sword of the Spirit, it is my duty to accomplish."

"I'll certainly, ah, certainly present your views to my colleagues, Excellency —" de Roors' fear was breaking close to the surface now, not least from the realization that what might be a religious platitude in another man was deadly serious intent in this.

"Oh, you'll do better than that," Raj said.

"The man is mad!" de Roors said, as his party rode back towards the city gates. Considerably more slowly, as there was no escort to part the traffic ahead of them this time.

"What will you do, master?" his chief steward said. The iron collar had come off his neck many years ago, but some habits remained.

"Prepare to hold a town meeting," de Roors snarled. "Precisely as the *Heneralissimo supremo* demanded."

"Barholm's nephew . . ." the steward shook his head and leaned closer, putting the dogs close enough to sniff playfully at each other's ears. "What a hostage!"

De Roors cuffed the man alongside the head with the handle of his dogwhip. "Shut *up*. If we touched one hair on the Clerett's head after giving safe-conduct to address the meeting, Whitehall would sow the smoking ruins with *salt*."

He paused, thoughtful; the other man rubbed the side of his head where the tough flexible bone had raised a welt.

"And High Colonel Strezman would nail us up on crosses to look at it; you know how some of these Brigade nobles are about oaths, and he's worse than most."

"If you say so, master."

"No, our only hope is that he'll march on rather than waste time with us . . . if we *could* open the gates he'd keep his . . . no, too risky — and the others would never go along with it, they haven't met him and they don't, they don't —" de Roors shook his head. "He really believes it, he thinks he's the Sword of the Spirit."

The chief steward looked at his patron with concern, the blow forgotten. His fortunes were too closely linked to the merchant's in any case; they had been so for many years. He had never seen him so shaken in all that time. De Roors' hands were trembling where they fumbled with whip and reins.

"Maybe," he said, trying humor, "he really *is*, master. The Sword of the Spirit, that is."

De Roors looked at him silently. After a while, the steward began to shake as well.

"He's cheating me again!" Cabot Clerett broke out. "First he makes a great noise about rounding up and slaughtering some refugees in a hole, while I was fighting *real* Brigade soldiers. Now this!"

I wonder if it's hereditary? Suzette thought. Barholm Clerett never forgot a slight either, real or imagined. Men who'd wronged him when he was in his teens had discovered that with painful finality when he was enchaired as Governor thirty years later.

"Your uncle might well feel he's endangering you needlessly," she said in cautious agreement.

"Oh, it's not that!" Clerett said. He smiled. "I'm glad you care for my safety, of course, Suzette. But I can't be too cautious, or . . . It's this mission. He's going along to spoil any chance I have of a real success."

Suzette sank down beside him on the bench and took his hand. "Oh, Clerett," she said. "I thought he was going incognito?"

He took the hand in both of his. "Sometimes you seem so wise, Suzette, and sometimes so innocent, like a girl. Of course it'll come out that he went along. And since he's not covered by name in the safe-conduct, it'll look as if *he* were doing the real, the risky work. He'll be the hero, and I'll be the flunky with the walk-on part."

The young man brooded for a moment. "And that — that fellow Staenbridge."

"Cabot, you will have to learn to work with all sorts of men when you're Governor." She smiled and patted his cheek. "And women, but you'll find that *much* easier, I'm sure."

He flushed, grinned, and raised the hand to his lips. "Thank you. And," he went on, "you're right about working with all types. Although," he said thoughtfully, "the first thing I'll do is kill Tzetzas, if Uncle doesn't do it first. With all he's stolen, it'll fill the fisc nicely."

Suzette nodded. "You'll make a great Governor, Cabot," she said, her voice warm. *Paranoid ruthlessness is an asset in that job, most of the time.*

Cabot half-rose from the bench, and dropped to one knee. "Oh, Suzette," he said, his voice suddenly stumbling over itself. "You're the only one who really *understands*. Could I — could I have something of yours, to carry into battle? A pledge . . ."

A few of the oldest stories, old even before the Fall, told of such things. Suzette reached into a pocket of her campaign overalls and drew out a handkerchief. Cabot Clerett received it as if it were a holy relic, a circuit board or rolldown screen, then tucked it into an inner pocket of his uniform jacket.

"Thank you," he breathed.

I wonder, she thought, as he left, *if he minds that it's used?*

Probably not. In fact, that might make it seem more valuable. She shook her head. *They let that boy read too much old poetry,* she thought. Being so close to the Chair could restrict a child's social contacts. *Far too much.*

The final kilometer or so of the main road into Lion City was paved. The original surface had been stone blocks of uniform size set in mortar from the time the Civil Government ruled this area; that had been long before the development of coal mining made concrete cheap enough to use for surfacing. When one side wore too much under the continual pounding of hooves and paws and wheels, the blocks could be turned over, leveled on a bed of gravel and remortared into place. That had happened often enough for the remaining to be lumpy from having been turned several times. Holes in the paving had been patched, with flagstones and spots of brick and gravel set in cement.

The paws of the detachment's mounts made a thud-*scuff* sound on the hard, slightly uneven surface. Light from the setting sun cast their shadows behind them, and a blackness from the walls and gates loomed ahead. The arch of the gate glowed yellow with the coal-oil lanterns hung within the arch; that light glinted off edged metal within.

"This is extremely foolish of you, Whitehall," Gerrin Staenbridge said.

They were both riding behind the color party, dressed in ordinary troopers' uniforms with the 1st Lifeguards' *Vihtoria O Muwerti* and leaping sicklefoot on the shoulder flashes, and Senior Sergeant chevrons on the sleeves. Suzette's retainer Abdullah had given them a few tricks, a gauze bandage liberally sprinkled with chicken blood for the side of Raj's face, and two rubber pads to alter the shape of Gerrin's. Mostly they relied on the fact that few outside their own force had ever seen them closely, and more important, that few men of importance *looked* at common soldiers. They could both give a fairly convincing imitation of a pair of long-service Descotter NCO's. Which was, Raj reflected, probably what they'd both have been, if they'd been born yeoman-tenants instead of to the squirerarchy.

Raj clicked his tongue. "I need to know exactly what we're up against, and if we can find a deal acceptable to the citizens, or most of them."

From de Roors' description, Lion City was accustomed to a fair degree of autonomy in internal affairs. The ways they had of settling policy sounded odd — more like a prescription for standing in circles shouting and waving their arms and hitting each other — but that was the way most large towns were managed, here in the west.

"We need the active support of the townsmen," he went on, "if we're going to get anything done with inadequate forces. Now, *you* coming along is stupid. You're my right-hand man."

"Exactly." Gerrin's grin was white in the shadows. "Look, you're the one who'd invade Hell and fight the demons of the Starless Dark if Barholm said he needed the ice for his drinks. Damned if *I* am going to be left holding the ball if they shorten you, Whitehall. I know my limitations; we all should. I'm a better than competent commander, but I do best as a number two — when you found me, I was so bored I'd nothing better to do than diddle the battalion accounts, for the Spirit's sake. You might have some chance of pulling this campaign off; I wouldn't, and worse still, I might be expected to try. Jorg or Kaltin could hold the Crown easily enough, with the Expeditionary Force — and nobody would expect them to do more."

Raj nodded tightly. The *real* problem was that
Barholm might send someone like Klostermann out to
take over if he died . . . but he certainly couldn't win by
playing safe, in any event. They fell silent as the
embassy approached the gate.

There was an exchange of courtesies at the entrance;
then General's Dragoons fell in around the Civil
Government party. Raj looked them over, a perfectly
natural thing for his persona to do. They were well
mounted and well-equipped, with sword, two revolvers
and a percussion rifle-musket in a boot on the left side
of the saddle; they all wore similar lobster-tail helmets
and grey-and-black uniforms. The officers wore breastplates as well, and the unit had maneuvered neatly to
shake itself out beside his party. Altogether better-
ordered than the *Squadrones* had been, and just as
tough; the *Squadrones* had been down from the Base
Area only a century and a half, but they'd spent most of
that sitting on their plundered estates watching the
serfs work with no strong enemies near them. The
Brigade had an open frontier to the north, exposed to
the interior of the continent. These men all looked as if
they'd seen the titanosauroid more than once.

*If their leadership were as good as their troops, we'd
be fucked,* Raj thought.

correct, Center acknowledged. **enemy weakness
in that regard was one factor among many in my
decision to activate my plan in your time, raj
whitehall.**

The main gate of Lion City was a massive affair, four
interlinked towers in pairs either side of the passageway with a squarish platform twenty feet thick joining
them at third-story level. The main defenses were
old-style curtain walls with round towers, running
straight into the ground. Up until a couple of centuries
ago cannon had been too feeble to threaten a stout
stone wall, so defenses went high, to deter attempts at
storming. Since heavy battering guns came into use the

preferred solution was to dig a broad deep moat and sink the walls on the other side until they were barely above the outer lip. That way little of the wall was exposed to artillery, it could be backed with heavy earthworks and so support massive guns of its own, and a storming force still had to climb out of the moat and up the protected wall. Someone had done some work on the gate, though: the tower bases were sloped backward at a sharp angle to shed solid shot.

The gateway looked like a compromise, avoiding the horrendous expense of modernizing the whole city wall, which was still perfectly adequate against pirates or raiding savages. Raj looked up with professional interest as they passed in; first heavy timber gates strapped with iron and over half a meter thick, then a portcullis of welded iron bars thick as a man's arm. The arched ceiling overhead held murder-holes — gaps for shooting and dropping unpleasant things on anyone coming through — and there was a dogleg in the middle of the passageway to further hinder invaders.

Eyeballs glittered in the torchlight as the embassy came through at a walk; the gaslights common in the east were unknown here, but there were enough burning pine-knots to compensate tonight. Somebody had been busy, and piles of flimsy lath marked where the reserved area within the walls had been swept clear of sheds and shacks. The citizens crowded it, waiting to see their fates decided; there were more all along the road to the central plaza, which was not far from the gates. The usual buildings stood around it; a cathedron, here with the round planet rather than the rayed Star at its dome, a porticoed city hall, mansions. A speaker's podium had been erected in the center around the sculptured fountain, and several thousand men stood in front of it. Pretty well all men, as opposed to the crowd back along the streets, and many of them armed.

He sized up the group on the dais. A tall thin-featured man in three-quarter armor; that would be High Colonel Strezman. Blade features framed by long white hair streaked with black, penetrating blue eyes, and about a company of his dragoons on the pavement below, apart from a clump of officers. The syndics of the town had as many of their militia with *them*, and they stood on the opposite side of the podium — interesting evidence of a potential split. The heads of the guilds were there as well, each with his entourage behind him and supporters clumped on the cobblestones — merchants, artisans, and big clumps of ragged *dezpohblado* laborers ranged beside the laborers' chiefs. Many of the individual magnates had their guards with them as well, variously equipped; there was a big clump of men in robe and ha'ik, or turbans and long coats and sashes, also armed. The Colonial merchants.

Sure to be against us, Raj thought. The Colony and the Civil Government routinely used economic sanctions and outright attacks on each other's resident citizens as part of their ongoing struggle.

De Roors came to the front of the podium as soon as the greeting rituals were out of the way. He raised his hands to still the low murmurs and spoke:

"Citizens of Lion City! We are here to listen to the embassy of General Whitehall and the Civil Government army camped outside the walls of our city. To do us honor, General Whitehall has sent the noblest of his officers to treat with us; none other than the Most Excellent Cabot Clerett, nephew to the Governor of the Civil Government himself!"

Another long rustle and hum from the crowd. "As courtesy and the ancient customs of our community demand, The Most Excellent Major Clerett will speak first, listing the terms and demands of the Civil Government. The heads of the guilds, and High Colonel Strezman, will reply and the guilds will express their will to the syndics."

More ceremonies followed; blessings from Star Spirit and This Earth priests — the liturgies differed only in detail, but the Brigade cult was given pride of place — before Cabot Clerett stepped to the speaker's position.

He paused to remove his helmet and tuck it under one arm, then lifted the other palm out, slowly. It was an effective gesture, but he had the benefit of training by the best rhetoricians available in East Residence. He looked down on the sea of upturned faces, face underlit by the torches that brought out highlights in his curly black hair, face stern and sharp-boned.

"People of Lion City!" he called, in a voice pitched slightly higher than usual to carry. Training put the full power of strong young lungs behind it, and kept it from sounding shrill; his Spanjol was accented but fluent. "Hear the terms which are most generously granted to you; for wisdom lies not in rash fury, but in reasoned council and moderation. I offer —"

Gerrin stirred behind him; that was supposed to be *General Whitehall* offers. The young emissary was sticking to the agreed text, but substituting his own name or something like "the Civil Government" or "His Supremacy, my uncle" whenever Raj's name was called for. They were flanking Cabot to the left and right and a step to the rear, leaving the bannerman directly behind him to show the Civil Government's flag. Heavy silk hissed against the polished stanauro wood of the pole; the breeze was from the ocean, carrying scents of tar and stagnant water and a hint of clean seawater beyond. Out beyond the seawall to their left red lights glowed, reflected furnace-light on the smoke from the war-steamers' furnaces.

Raj kept his attention on the crowd and the leaders, checking only that the terms were as he'd specified. Cabot's voice rose in an excellent imitation of passion at the conclusion; Bartin Foley had written it, cribbing from his studies of Old Namerique classical drama.

Not much of that had survived the Fall — most of the stored data had died with the computers — but fragments had been written down from memory by the first generation, and fragments of that had survived the eleven hundred years since. He finished the promises; now on to the threats.

"Therefore, you men of Lion City, take pity on your town, and on your own people, while yet my soldiers —" Cabot's voice rolled out.

"*My* soldiers, you little *fastardo*?" Gerrin muttered. His voice was almost inaudible, but Raj was very close. Close enough to nudge the other man with his boot unnoticed.

"— are in my command; avoid deadly murder, spoil and villany, such as accompany a sack; yield peacefully. For if not, look to see the blood-drenched soldiers with foul hands defile the thighs of your shrill-shrieking daughters; your fathers taken by the silver beards, and their most reverend heads dashed to the walls; your naked infants spitted on bayonets; while the mad mothers with their howls break the clouds in anguish!"

Cabot stopped, clicked heels and stepped back. The sea of faces rippled as men turned to speak to their neighbors. A voice called out from the ranks of the laborers:

"It ain't our war! This General Raj, he's treated peaceful people right well out in the country, from what they say. What have we ever got from the Brigade but taxes and a boot up our bums? Open the gates!"

"*Open the gates! Open the gates!*" A claque took up the chant.

Out of the corner of his eye Raj could see High Colonel Strezman's tight-held jaw. He murmured an order to an aide, who hopped off the podium; seconds later a squad of Brigade soldiers was heading for the man who'd spoken. There was a moment's commotion as the laborers closed ranks, and then thrust the man scrambling backward between their legs to lose himself in the crowd. Before the rifle-butts could force a way, a squad of civic militia shifted nearer. The Brigadero officer in charge of the squad looked over his shoulder at Strezman, then turned his men around and retired, followed by jeers and catcalls, but not by rocks.

Not yet, Raj thought.

Strezman shifted, and de Roors led him to the speaker's position.

"Silence!" he shouted.

When the murmuring grew, Strezman signed to the aide and a ten-man section of dragoons threw their rifles to their shoulders and fired into the air. And immediately reloaded, Raj noted.

Silence came at last. "Civilians of Lion City," Strezman began. His Spanjol was more heavily accented than Cabot's had been, with a Namerique clang to it.

Not too tactful, Raj thought. Civilian meant "second-class citizen" at best in the Brigade lands. Only slightly more polite than *grisuh*, civvie.

"In his wisdom," Strezman continued, "His Mightiness, General Forker, Lord of Men —" that fell flat, and he ignored scattered jeers.

I imagine Strezman isn't too thrilled about Forker's little hostage play, Raj thought. The man seemed to be something of a soldier, in his way, and the intelligence report indicated he was a Brigade noble of the old school.

"— has sent a strong garrison to defend your city from the butcher Whitehall and his host." More murmurings from the crowds, and a voice called:

"Yeah, he butchered a whole *lot* of you dog-sucker barbarians down in the Southern Territories." Another, from a different section of the crowd:

"And restored Holy Federation Church, you heretic bastard!"

The crowd's growl was ugly. The militia shuffled, looking to the syndics. The armed retainers of the rich and the Colonists closed around their masters. Spots of red burned on Strezman's cheeks; this time there was a flash of armored gauntlet as he gave his orders. The Brigade troops marched out in front of the podium and brought their rifles up to face the crowd in a menacing row. Men surged away from their aiming point.

De Roors walked hastily to the High Colonel's side and waved his arms for silence. Strezman gave him a curt nod and went on, as the soldiers went to port arms.

"We have four thousand men, all veterans of the northern frontier, and plenty of powder and shot for small arms and the cannon on the walls both. Whitehall can't stay here long; the Brigade's armies are mustering, and they outnumber his pitiful force by five or ten to one. Unless he moves, he'll be caught between the relieving armies and the walls of Lion City."

Accurate enough, Raj thought. *If hostile.* He hoped there weren't too many more like Strezman in the Brigade's upper ranks.

"Whitehall will have to march away soon, if we defy him. He doesn't have heavy guns either.

"The Brigade — His Mightiness the General — have allowed you a high degree of self-government within these walls," Strezman went on; from his tone, he thought that a mistake. "In order that the walls and your civic militia could be of help in time of war. That you are even entertaining this madman Whitehall's offer is a sign that policy *may* have been mistaken. If you were so foolish as to accept it, after the war is over and the Civil Government's little force is crushed, *you* will be next. His Mightiness won't leave one stone standing on another, or one citizen alive. Furthermore, I and my command will fight regardless of your decisions, so all that treason would gain you is to transfer the battle from outside the defenses to your own hearths."

Strezman stood for a moment, the firelight breaking off his armor, then stepped back. "Carry on," he said to de Roors; gesture and voice were full of contempt for civilian sloppiness and indecision.

Speaker followed speaker; most seemed to be for holding out, although quite a few hedged so thoroughly that it was impossible to tell which course they favored. A few were so incoherent or drunk that the maundering was inadvertent. At last the representative of the Colonists took the podium; he was a plump man in a dazzling turban of torofib, clasped with a ruby and a spray of irridescent sauroid feathers. A scimitar and pistol were thrust through the sash of his long coat, but the voice that addressed the crowd was practiced and smooth.

"Fellow citizens," the Colonist began. "Let me assure you that the Jamaat-al-Islami —"

League of Islam, Raj translated mentally. That would be the local association of Colonists.

"— will fight by your side. We know this *banchut* Whitehall, our kin have told us of him — bandit, murderer, defiler of holy places! Our warehouses contain enough food to feed the whole city for a year and a day. There is nothing to fear from siege. We must defy the infi— the invader Whitehall. Were his followers within the walls, no man's goods would be safe, nor the honor of his women."

A man walked into the light below the podium; he was dressed in workman's clothes, old but not ragged, and there were bone buckles on his shoes. An artisan, not wealthy but no *dezpohblado* either.

"Your goods will be safe, you mean, Haffiz bin-Daud," he said. "I —" de Roors was making motions. "I'm one of the Sailmaker's Syndics, Filipe de Roors," the man on the pavement snapped. "I've as much right to talk as any *riche hombe*." His face went back to the Arab. "And as for the honor of our women, how safe was Therhesa Donelli from your man Khaled al'Assad?"

Another of the dignitaries on the dais pushed forward; he was an old man, richly dressed, with a nose like a beak and wattles beneath his chin. He waved his three-cornered hat angrily.

"Mind your place, Placeedo, and stick to the issues," he warned. "That case was settled and compensation awarded."

The sailmaker Placeedo crossed his arms and looked over his shoulder. Voices out of the darkness spoke for him:

"Compensation? Our daughters ain't hoors!"

"You *riche hombes* is in bed with the Spirit-deniers and the barb heretics too!"

"*Riche hombe* bastards squeeze us and use the barb soldiers if we complain; now they expect us to die to keep them in silk."

"Yes, and they bring in slaves and peons to do skilled work against the law, to break our guilds!"

Evidently that was a long-standing sore point; the bellow of the crowd filled the night, and de Roors had to wave repeatedly to reduce the noise enough that he could be heard.

"Citizens! An army is at our gates, and we must not be divided among ourselves. Syndic Placeedo Anarenz, is there anything more you wish to say?"

"Yes, *alcalle* de Roors. My question is addressed to syndic Haffiz bin-Daud of the *Jamaat-al-Islami*. He says his countrymen have enough in the warehouses. Will he give his word of honor that the grain will be dispensed free during the siege? Or even at the prices of a month ago? Will the city feed the families of men thrown out of work because the gates are closed and the *Gubernio Civil*'s fleet blockades the harbor? There are men here whose women and children go hungry tonight because trade is disturbed. Poor men have no savings, no warehouses of food and cloth and fuel. Winter is coming, and it's hard enough for us in peacetime. Well?"

Haffiz made a magnificent gesture. "Of course we —"

Before he could speak further, a rush of other men in turbans and robes surrounded him, arguing furiously and windmilling their arms. From the snatches of hissed Arabic Raj could tell that whatever politic generosity he'd had in mind was not unanimously favored by his compatriots.

The sailmaker's syndic smiled and turned, gesturing to the crowd. A chant came up:

"Open the gates! Open the gates!" Anarenz grinned broadly; that turned into a frown and frantic waving as other calls came in on the heels of the first.

"Kill the rich! Kill the rich! *Dig up their bones!*"

"*Down with the heretics!*"

This time a scattering of rocks did fly. Amid the uproar and confusion, Raj saw the old syndic go to the edge of the platform. He gave an order to a man standing there, a Stalwart mercenary in a livery uniform. The man slipped away into the night. A few seconds later, something came whirring in out of the dark and went *thuck* into Anarenz' shoulder-blade: it was a throwing axe, the same type that Captain Lodoviko had used to save his life back on Stern Isle. This one would end the sailmaker's, unless he got to a healer and soon.

Shots rang out, and the voices rose to a surf-roar of noise. Many of the dignitaries on the podium deck dove to the floorboards, and some ran around the other side of the fountain that protruded through the middle, taking shelter behind its carvings of downdraggers and sea sauroids. Cabot Clerett stayed statuesquely erect, his cloak held closed with one hand. As would have been expected of any escort, Raj and Staenbridge closed up around the bannerman and the officer.

"This may be about to come apart," Gerrin said tightly.

Raj shook his head, eyes moving over the tossing sea of motion below. The militia had — mostly — turned about and faced the crowd with their weapons. Bands of house retainers made dashes into the edge of it, arresting or clubbing men down, apparently according to some sort of plan; he saw Anarenz carried off in a cloak by a dozen men who were apparently his friends, and the crowd slowing pursuit enough for him to escape.

"I think they'll get things back under control," Raj said.

"Silence in the ranks," Cabot said distantly, his eyes fixed on something beyond the current danger.

A kettledrum beat, and there was a massed thunder of paws. A column of Brigaderos cavalry burst into the square, with men scattering back ahead of it; they spread out along one edge facing in, their dogs snarling in a long flash of white teeth and their swords bright in their hands.

Silence gradually returned, with the massed growling a distant thunder in the background. De Roors stepped up to the podium. "Let the vote be tallied!" he said.

It went swiftly; votes were by guild, with the rich merchant and manufacturer guilds casting a vote each, as many as the mechanics' organizations with their huge memberships, and the single vote of the laborers. Those whose leaders were absent were voted automatically by de Roors, as *alcalle* of the town.

He turned to Cabot and bowed. "Most Excellent, with profound regret — I must ask you to leave our city. March on, for Lion City holds its walls against all attack."

"Move it up to a trot," Raj said, as soon as they were beyond the gate.

"Sir," Cabot replied stiffly. "Our dignity —"

"— isn't worth our asses," Raj said, grinning. "Trot, and then gallop, if you please, messers."

He touched his heels to Horace. The Civil Government banner flared out above them, the gold and silver of the Starburst glowing beneath the moons.

CHAPTER FIFTEEN

Fatima cor Staenbridge twisted her hands together in the waxed-linen apron that covered the front of her body. The operating tent was silent with a deep tension, a dread that knew what it awaited. Doctors, priests and Renunciate Sisters, waited with their assistants beside the tables; beside them were laid out saws and chisels, scalpels and curiously shaped knives, catgut and curved needles and piles of boiled-linen bandages. Jars of blessed distilled water cut with carbolic acid waited beside the tables, and more in sprayers along with iodine and mold-powder. And bottles of liquid opium, with the measuring-glasses beside them. Most battalions had priest-healers attached. The ones with the Expeditionary Force had served together long enough that General Whitehall had organized them into a corps under a Sysup-Abbot.

"Will it be bad?" Mitchi asked. "Kaltin told me not to worry."

Kaltin Gruder's concubine was about nineteen, with long bright-red hair now bound up on her head; the milk complexion, freckles and bright-green eyes showed it was natural. She and Fatima waited at the head of the other helpers; Civil Government armies had fewer camp followers than most, and those led by Raj Whitehall fewer still — one servant to every eight cavalry troopers, others for officers, and the inevitable spill-over of tolerated non-regulation types. Raj insisted that everyone without assigned military duties do *something* useful, and Suzette had organized the more reliable women for hospital duty in the past two campaigns, with Fatima as her deputy.

"It will be worse than last year," Fatima said. Mitchi had been a gift from the merchant Reggiri just before the Expeditionary Force left Stern Isle for the Squadron lands. The casualties in the Southern Territories had been light. Light for the Civil Government force.

"I hope, not as bad as Sandoral," Fatima went on. Softly: "I pray, not so bad as that." The tubs at the foot of the operating tables had been full that day, full of amputated limbs.

She knew the litany now, from experience; bring the wounded in, and sort them. A dog-sized dose of opium for the hopeless, and take them to the terminal section. Bandage the lightly wounded and put them aside for later attention. For the serious ones — probe for bullets, debride all foreign matter out, suture arteries and veins, disinfect and bandage. Sew flaps of muscle back into place and hope they healed straight. Compound fractures were common, bone smashed to splinters by the heavy fat lead slugs most weapons used. For those, amputate and hope that gangrene didn't set in. Dose with opium before surgery, but there was no time to wait and sometimes it didn't work. Then strong hands must hold the body down to the table, and the surgeon cut as fast as possible, racing shock and pain-induced heart failure as well as blood loss.

A hand tugged at Mitchi's sleeve. "Is there going to be shooting?" a small voice asked in Namerique.

They both looked down in surprise. It was the girl Kaltin had brought back. She'd been very quiet and given to shivering fits and nightmares and didn't like to be alone.

"Not near here, Jaine," Fatima said gently. "We safe here."

The child blinked, looking around as if fear had woken her from a daze. "There was a lot of shooting when Mom and Da went away," she said. "We left the farm and went to a place in the woods with a lot of other people. Da said we'd be safe there, but then there was shooting and they went away. They told me to wait and hide under the bundles."

Mitchi met Fatima's eyes over the child's head, then lifted her into her lap. "Shhh, little one," she said, holding her close.

"They're not coming back, are they?" Jaine asked solemnly. Fatima shook her head. The child sighed.

"I didn't think they were, really," she said. Her face twitched. "Then the Skinner came. I thought Skinners only came and got *bad* children, but I wasn't bad. I stayed real quiet like Da said. Honest I did." Tears began to leak out of the corners of the blue eyes.

Allah — Spirit of Man — why now? Fatima thought. Or maybe it was a good time. Gerrin wasn't out of the city yet. Men were watching for the embassy to reach safety, that was the signal. Raj and Gerrin were in there in disguise, among the enemy. Anything was better than waiting with nothing else to think of.

The child went on: "He didn't skin me and eat me the way Skinners are supposed to eat bad children. He tried to get up on top of me as if I were a big grown-up lady." Her voice was still quiet, but a little shrill. "He *hurt* me."

"Nobody can hurt you here, little sparrow," Fatima said, stroking the girl's face.

"I know," Jaine nodded. "Master Gruder came in and shot him." Her face relaxed slightly. "Then he kicked him off and shot him lots more times."

The two adults exchanged another glance; nobody had told them *that*.

The noise of the camp was subdued, but the roar from the city was like distant surf. Fatima shivered again, remembering the sound when the 5th broke into El Djem like water over a crumbling dam. It had been dawn then, just the start of another day like every other. The day when everything changed.

A few minutes passed and then Jaine spoke again, smearing the half-dried tears off her face with the heels of hands: "Are you slaves?" she said, and raised her hand to touch her neck. Mitchi understood the gesture: Brigade law required chattel slaves to wear metal collars.

"Yes, I am — we don't have to wear collars in the *Gubernio Civil*," she said. "Fatima used to be a slave, but she's a freedwoman now."

The girl frowned. "Am I a slave now too?" she said. "Da — Da used to hit the slaves sometimes."

Mitchi hesitated. Fatima nodded and spoke soothingly: "You belong to Messer Gruder, but don't worry, little one. He's a very kind man. If you're a good girl and do what Mitchi and Messer Gruder tell you, you'll be fine."

Out through the entrance flap of the big tent, she could see a rocket arch into the night. It burst with a loud *pop* and a red spark.

"Mitchi, take Jaine over to the children's area," Fatima said tightly. *It has begun.*

The child began a pout; Fatima forestalled it. "I want you to help look after little Bartin and baby Suzette, all right?" she said.

Jaine nodded, and put her hand in Mitchi's.

From beyond the encampment's trench, man-made thunder boomed. Something in Fatima's stomach clenched as she recognized the sound, but her primary emotion was relief. Gerrin would be safely beyond range; that had been the signal.

"Let's go, men!" Colonel Jorg Menyez called. "Show the dog-boys what you're made of. Forward the 17th!"

The six hundred men of the 17th Kelden County Foot rose from the ground and roared, dashing forward to the bugle's call. They kept their alignment, running in a pounding lockstep; the lines wavered but didn't break up into clots as untrained men might have.

The colonel ran with them, under the flapping banner. Ahead, the southside walls of Lion City gleamed pale under the moons. Even in the dark of night, it had been a major accomplishment to get so many men so close to the defenses without attracting attention. Even militiamen, however, weren't going to overlook two battalions of men running full-tilt toward them. Not even with the surf-roar of the assembly-cum-riot still sounding through the night.

A ladder passed him, on the shoulders of the grunting, panting men who bore it. Their boots struck the ground in unison, free hands pumping in rhythm. The stolid peon faces were set in grimaces of effort, the rictus of men who are pacing themselves strictly by the task in hand. The colonel was only a little over thirty and in hard condition, but it was far from easy to keep up with his men.

Spirit, he thought. He'd seen men run less eagerly toward a barrel of free wine.

Major Haldolfo Zahpata swung his saber forward. *"Dehfenzo Lighon!"* he called. *Defend the Faith*. The motto of the 18th Komar Borderers.

"Aur! Aur!" his men screamed, as they advanced at the run. *"Despert Staahl!"* It was the ancient war-cry of the southern borders of the Civil Government: *Awake the iron!*

Zahpata grinned as he ran, feeling the chainmail neck-guard of his helmet beat on his shoulders. Jorg's idea had been a good one; he could hear officers and non-coms shouting to the men:

"Will you let infantry reach the wall ahead of you?"

The ladders they carried were ten meters long and broad enough for two men abreast to climb. Hasty training had taught the men to relieve the squads bearing the burden of the clumsy, heavy things while at full speed. That way they could be carried all the way to the wall at a running pace, despite their weight.

Zahpata grinned again, this time a baring of the teeth that had nothing to do with amusement. Two battalions of grown men were racing toward guns stuffed with grapeshot and exposing their defenseless bodies to enemies protected by a stone wall, for the honor of seeing who would put a cloth flag on top of that wall first.

Faith is a wonderful thing, he thought, legs pumping. *I have faith in you, Dinnalsyn. Do not disappoint me.*

"Now!" Grammeck Dinnalsyn said, and clapped heels to his dog.

Thirty guns sprang forward; they had approached at a slow walk, with muffled wheels and brightwork covered by rags. Now they pounded forward at a lunging gallop, the crews leaning forward in the saddle. At twelve hundred meters from the walls they halted and swung into battery. Teams wheeled, so sharply that they were just short of turning the guns over in a disasterous spin. Sparks shot out into the night as the men on the caissons pulled brake levers. Dogs squatted on their haunches to shed momentum as soon as the muzzles turned; there was a man on the last dog in each team as well as the first, and he pulled the cotter pin linking the chain traces to the caisson. The teams trotted forward another five meters, enough to be out of the way but close enough for a quick getaway, then crouched to the ground in their traces.

The gunners jumped down and flung themselves at their weapons; an iron clangor filled the air as they unlocked and pulled the locking rod and lifted each trail off its limber. This time they did not let the ends of the trails thump to the ground. The caissons each carried two iron triangles tonight, with one side curved inward. They hammered them home with stakes, one in front of each wheel, and then hauled the wheels upward and held them to the top of the curve. Others

swung hasty picks and shovels behind, digging pits for
the end of the pole trails. When the trails dropped into
the holes, the guns could not run backward down the
iron surfaces. Breachblocks clanged and rang as
the loaders shoved home rounds and levers pushed the
blocking wedges behind them.

Dinnalsyn winced as he cursed his men to speed.
This was one way to get extra range or elevation out of
field guns, whose normal job required long flat
trajectories. It also subjected the frames to wracking
stresses, because they weren't able to recoil backwards
in the usual fashion. *We ought to have more howizers,
light ones*, he thought: the stubby high-elevation
weapons were officially considered useful mainly for
siege work, and built heavy in large calibres.

Other gunners were setting up heavy carbide lamps
on tripods, with curved mirrors behind them; signal-
ling equipment in normal times, but modified for
tonight. The beams came on with a hiss and sputter
and chemical stink, bathing the ramparts in harsh
yellow-white light. It shone eerily on the backs of
hundreds of Skinners who were loping their dogs past
the artillery, then dismounting and ramming their
cross-topped shooting sticks into the dirt.

Similar floodlights were opening up on the city
walls, amid a chaotic noise of drums and horns and
hand-wound sirens. A cannon boomed with a long
white puff of smoke, and a solid iron ball ploughed into
the ground a few dozen meters in front of the foremost
troops. Dinnalsyn swept his saber downward.

"*Fire*," he shouted.

A huge *POUMPF*, thirty times repeated. Shells
ripped out over the heads of the troops — contact
fused, nobody was in a mood for accidents tonight.
Some sailed over the wall, to raise flickering crashes in
the city beyond. Others plowed short, gouting up
poplar-shapes of dirt and rock. Most hit the wall; the
explosive charges did no more than scar it, but they

would shake the men on the firing platforms above. A few struck exactly where aimed, along the row of gunports and the crenelations of the wall itself. One was uncannily lucky, and punched right through a gunport just as the cannon there was about to fire. A giant belch of yellow flame shot out through the port as the piled ammunition beside the gun went up, and chunks of stone flew skyward. Bits and pieces of the crew did as well; the cast-iron barrel probably went out backwards off the wall.

Some of the gunners cheered. "Man your fucking *guns*," Dinnalsyn screamed, trotting his dog down the gunline. "That was a fucking *miracle*."

Cottony clouds of brimstone-stinking gunsmoke drifted around the position. The first few ranging shots were critical, because after that you were often firing blind into your own smoke.

"Mark the fall of shot, it's right in front of you. Battery three — you're all *short*. Elevation, elevation, Spirit eat your eyes!"

The crews in question spun the elevating screws beneath their weapons. Their next salvo was high, screeching at head-level over the crenelations and into the city. The guns bucked wildly on the pivot-lever formed by the trail, swinging nearly upright with the muzzles pointing at the sky, then slamming back down with an earsplitting anvil chorus of iron-shod wheels on iron frames. Every time he heard it, Dinnalsyn felt his hand clench involuntarily on the hilt of his saber, waiting for the loud unmusical *twang-crunch* of a trail breaking, a wheel shattering or — Spirit forbid — a trunion cracking and sending the barrel pinwheeling off the carriage and into the crew. Every one of those rounds was taking more off the service life of the gun than fifty normal firings.

More cannon were firing from the wall. Solid shot, many of them, and aimed at *him*. That was the plan. He had a fair degree of respect for town-militia gunners; they practiced on fixed pieces with a single range of ground before their muzzles, and they could get to know both quite well. They didn't have the wide range of skills and adaptability that the full-time professionals in his crews did, but they didn't need them. Still, they were amateurs and their instinct would be to strike at the weapons that were firing at *them*, not at the far more dangerous infantry. He couldn't possibly win a counter-battery shoot with the guns on the walls: they were protected by stone, and his men were as naked as so many table-dancers in a dockside bar.

He was a sacrificial *goat*, by the Spirit.

Ahead of him the Skinners opened fire; not a volley, but the two-meter rifles were all firing at a steady four or five rounds a minute. The long muzzle flashes of the giant sauroid rifles were crimson and white spears through the night; within seconds, every searchlight on the walls and towers ahead had died. Then the nomad mercenaries shifted their aim to the firing-slits and gunports; they began drifting forward to keep out of their own gunsmoke, firing every dozen paces. The stone sparked and spalled around the targets, but not very often. Most of the shots were going through, peening off the metal of cannon, ricocheting on stone, ripping through flesh and shattering bone.

Cannon still boomed from the ramparts. Some of them were firing round shells whose crude fuses traced red lines through the night until they burst and showered the ground with splinters. A roundshot smashed into one of the Civil Government's fieldpieces with a giant *clung* sound; the noise of men screaming came a minute later, as the smashed cannon and the pieces of the roundshot scythed through the crew. Stretcher-parties were running forward . . .

"Come *on*," he whispered to himself. "Move. Damn you, *move*." Another fieldpiece was out of action, canted off the triangular braces with a cracked trail, toppling backward as the crew dove out of the way.

The first ladder went up against the wall.

"Maximum elevation," Dinnalsyn called, loud but calm. The battery commanders repeated it. "Maximum elevation, three-quarter charge." They'd made up the charges for that earlier today. Just enough to lob the shells over the wall and into the cleared space beyond.

"Come on, lads, keep it moving!" Jorg Menyez shouted.

Grapeshot plowed through the ranks near him, near enough to hear the malignant wasp-whine of the lead balls. Men flopped, shredded by dozens of hits. Others staggered at the edge, called out in pain, toppled or kept moving forward. A roundshot hit just short of a file carrying a ladder and skipped forward along the ground, knocking the men over like bowling-pins . . . except that it shattered legs and ripped them off at the knee, ten men down and their comrades on the other side of the ladder untouched except for the torque that slapped the wood out of their hands. An officer raised his sword to wave his men forward; an instant later he was staring in disbelief at the stump of his arm, the ragged humerus showing pink for an instant before the welling blood covered it.

Shit and blood and sulfur, it's always the same, Jorg thought. He stood with the saber sloped over his shoulder and the banner of the 17th beside him, watching up and down the line. There would be a first foothold, and there . . .

"Up with it, up with it!"

They were below the walls now. A ladder started to rise. Hand-thrown bombs fell sputtering, one at the foot of the ladder; it burst and the wood exploded out in splinters. Sickly yellow light mixed with the red glare of cannon to pick out eyeballs, bared teeth, the edges of the long bayonets. The cannon above fired continuously, amid the whirring crash of the Civil Government shells hammering the wall and then lifting over it. The Skinners were firing all along their support line, heedless of anything but their aiming points — heedless of the ricochets that rebounded into the Civil Government soldiers below. Men were shrieking, in pain or raw terror or a perverse exultation.

"*Volley* fire, *fire.*"

More and more ladders were going up against the wall. The men not lofting them stood and fired upward, aiming for the slits in the parapet where defenders were leaning over to fire rifles and big siege-shotguns down into the storming parties. The ladders rattled on the stone, braced far out at the base. Men in fanciful militia uniforms leaned over with hooked poles to try and push them down, and toppled from the wall as Skinner or infantry bullets struck them. The carbide searchlights played over their faces, blinding them but lightening the darkness for the attackers. More hand-bombs arched over; one exploded in midair as a Skinner struck it in flight in a miracle of marksmanship. Most landed below. An explosion on the parapet sent a dozen men somer-saulting through the air, as a grenadier was brain-shot as he drew his arm back to throw and the missile landed beneath his crumpling body.

"Come on, 17th!" a Captain called, scrambling up a ladder.

His trumpeter stood at its foot, sounding *charge* over and over. A roar, and the burly peons-in-uniform were following him, climbing with both feet and one hand and holding their rifles in the other, a wave of blue coats and bowl helmets and steel points. Up to the top, and the officer was falling backwards, time enough to twist head-over-heels before he struck the ground. The men following him were on the top rungs, shooting and then exchanging bayonet-thrusts with men on the parapet — gunners there too, swinging their rammers like giant clubs. Men in the second rank on the ladders were firing past their comrades, and he hoped to *hell* they were picking their targets. A lieutenant shouldered his way up, emptied his revolver into the press and jumped up . . . over the parapet and down onto the fighting platform, by the Spirit, and the company pennant waving over him!

Not so bad for the bloody infantry, Menyez thought, grinning like a shark.

He looked left and right. Three quarters of the ladders were up, in his sector. About the same to his right, where Zahpata's 18th Komar were making their tooth-gritting yelping screech and climbing up even as bodies fell down past them.

Menyez looked up again. Men were still climbing up the ladder beside him, the penant was still waving from the ramparts . . . and he could see shoulders and rifle-butts above the crenelations as they struggled to expand their foothold.

He took a deep breath. "We're going to plant the 17th Kelden's banner on the walls," he shouted, and drew his pistol. The bark of the rough pine logs that made up the ladder was rough and sticky under his hand. *"Follow me!"*

"Sir!"

Raj was still in his noncom's tunic, but the staff, signallers and couriers were accreting around him like coral around a shell as he pulled up Horace behind the gun-line that supported the escalade against the city wall. He stood in the stirrups and levelled his binoculars.

"That's a battalion flag on the ramparts, by the Spirit of Man!" he said exultantly. "The 17th . . . Hadolfo's got the 18th Komar up there too!"

"Shall I send in the reserve battalions?" someone asked behind him. One of Jorg's subordinates . . .

"No, of course not," Raj said, controlling his desire to turn and clout the man over the head with the glasses. "There's no room until they get a foothold over the wall." And absolutely no point in cramming men into a killing zone without room to deploy, either.

A dispatch rider reined in. "Ser. Major Gruder says sally-ports're openin' on t'main gate 'n t'north gate both, ser. Sally in battalion force from each, he says, er mebbe more."

Scramento! Raj thought. Close under the protection of the wall and its guns, the Brigaderos dragoons could mass and then try to strike at the flanks of his attack. Not successfully, but . . .

"High Colonel Strezman thinks entirely too fast," he said grimly. "Gerrin. The 5th and the 7th, and see them off."

Now it all depended on what happened on the wall. The flame-shot darkness stretched out ahead of him; there were still enemy cannon firing from the towers and from the wall to the left and right of his salient. The frustration was unbearable, the desire to get out there and *lead* . . . but if he put his banner on that wall nothing could prevent the whole army from following him. A milling mass of flesh for the enemy to shoot into. No.

no, Center agreed. **defeat followed by destruction of the expeditionary force probability of 79% +/-3 in that eventuality.**

"Get me a beachhead over the wall, Jorg," Raj said softly. "Give me room."

Jorg Menyez ducked behind the cannon on the fighting platform of the city wall. Bullets went crack-*tinng* off the scorching-hot metal, and it put him right next to the face of the dead militia gunner lying over it. He looked around the breach; another squad was trying to get the satchel charge to the iron-faced door of the tower that dominated this stretch of wall. A man fell, but another hurdled him and snatched it up. Tongues of fire licked out from the loopholes around the door, and infantrymen outside fired back from the cover of the guns or from behind bodies. The ricochets were probably as much danger to the running man as the riflemen within. He jerked, hit once, then again, went to his knees, pitched the bundle of gunpowder sacks the last two meters.

CRUMP. Most of the explosion was outward, in the line of least resistance. Enough of it hit the door to smash the sheet-iron and thick wood behind into a splintered wreck . . . that was still not enough ajar to admit a man. Hand-bombs arched down from the tower summit, and small-arms crackled from the firing slits. Civil Government infantry rushed up to the shattered door, firing through the wreckage —

"Back!" Menyez shouted. Too late, or the huge racket of battle overrode his voice.

Above them the stream of burning tallow cascaded down from the tower-top. It struck and clung like superheated glue; even in the middle of the melee, the screams of men who leaped from the wall burning were loud.

Menyez's head turned to the city. Between the wall and the houses was a clear strip fifty meters wide. Until recently it had been built over in patches, with flimsy hutments and corrals that could be passed off as temporary. Now the area *was* clear, and the rubbish and scrap lumber from the demolished shacks was piled up along the inner edge, a chest-high barricade. Beyond that were the streets; he could see mounted men there, a column of them. Shells were falling and fires burning in the cleared space, in the edge of housing beyond it. The column halted and dismounted, running forward to form up behind the barricade. The firelight shone on their helmets; General's Dragoons, not town militia.

He looked left and right. Men down, men firing at the towers, or at the approaching dragoons. The problem wasn't manpower, it was the towers and the lack of cover on the parapets from the rear — designed in for situations just like this. If he tried to send men down on ropes, they'd be vulnerable to the towers *and* the dragoons; he couldn't feed them in fast enough through this narrow lodgement. Not fast enough to do anything but die piecemeal the way they were doing now.

Tears cut runnels through the powder-smoke on his face. Of grief, and pure rage.

"Sor."

The runner from the 17th Kelden Foot was clutching his left arm with his right, to try to stop the bleeding.

"Sor, Colonel Menyez says, can't get a lodgement past the wall. Brigaderos dragoons behind barricade, too many of 'em. Can't take the towers either, not just from the parapet."

Raj sat silent for a moment, watching the flickering muzzle flashes on the parapet, like fireflies in spring.

"Go get that treated, soldier," he said. Then: "Sound retreat. Colonel Dinnalsyn, prepare to open up on the parapet again; I want their heads down while we pull our people out."

The soldier arched up off the operating table with a cry of pain that drove a spray of blood from scorched lips.

"*Hold* him, damn you," the doctor snapped.

Fatima grabbed the arm and weighed it down through the padding she clutched in both hands. Mitchi refastened the strap, her natural milk-white complexion gone to a grave-pallor that made her freckles stand out as if they were burning. The opium wasn't doing this patient much good at all; the mixture of burning pitch and tallow had caught him across most of his torso, with spatters up and down from there. One had turned his whole forehead into a blister that had burst and shed a glistening sheet of lymph across his face. The doctor was using a scalpel to separate the remains of the tunic from the skin and cooked meat to which it had been melded by the fire — this one had been a marginal, nearly triaged into the terminal section.

The doctor's hands moved with infinite deftness, swift and sure, although sweat ran down his cleric's shaven scalp into the linen of his face mask.

"More carbolic," he said.

Fatima siezed the moment and slipped a leather pad into the soldier's mouth to replace the one he'd screamed out. When the antiseptic struck the burned surfaces, the young man on the table went into an arch that left him supported only by heels and the back of his head. Muscles stood out like iron rods in his cheeks, and he might well have splintered teeth or bitten out his tongue without the pad.

He fainted. "Good," the doctor said. "More carbolic. Wet him down here. Now the scissors. *Spirit*. We'll have to cut this tissue, debride down to living flesh."

On the next table, the grating sound of a bone saw hammered at her ears. A pulsing shriek rose further down the big tent, and a sobbing that was harder to bear.

The smell was what made her swallow a rush of sick spit. Fatima had managed to make herself eat roast pork, since she'd converted to the Star faith. She didn't think she could ever do that again.

CHAPTER SIXTEEN

"Damn, *damn*," Jorg Menyez said. It might have been the pain of his shoulder, dislocated when he went back down the ladder, but Raj doubted it.

"Sit still," Raj replied.

I hate the hospitals, he thought. Visiting the wounded was about the worst chore there was; and it bewildered him a little that the men liked it — seeing the author of their pain. *Perhaps it gives them a focus.* Something to concentrate the will on.

It was a smoky dawn in the command tent; there was still a bit of noise from the hospital pavillion across the *plaza commanante*, but most of the severely wounded had either died or been doped to unconsciousness by now. The burn victims were the very worst, the pain seemed to be so bad that even opium couldn't do much.

"Damn," Menyez said again.

Hadolfo Zahpata was in the hospital tent himself, with two broken legs. Clean fractures of the femur, likely to heal well, but he was in plaster casts and suddenly primary contender for commander of Crown garrison forces when the rest of the Expeditionary Force moved on.

"I lost a hundred, hundred and twenty men — and we were so *close*, if we'd gotten up just a little sooner —"

Raj made a chopping motion with his hand, as he stood at the head of the table looking out the opening.

"*If*'s the most futile word in Sponglish," he said. "There was nothing wrong with the execution of the plan, Jorg — the plan was wrong, and that's *my* responsibility. You pulled out at the right moment; if you hadn't, you and Hadolfo would have lost your battalions."

"A broader attack —"

"— would have repeated the same failure on a larger scale." He sighed wearily. "The fact of the matter is, I was relying too much on the militia being disorganized by the town meeting. Maybe a lot of them wanted to open the gates, but they *didn't* want our men coming over the wall with blood in their eyes, not with their families behind it.

"And Strezman was waiting for us — a force ready to sally and another in central reserve to punch back anyone who got to the top of the walls. High bloody Colonel bloody Strezman is just too good to bamboozle easily — we've been fighting dumb barbs too long. I underestimated him."

He quirked a smile and lit two cigarettes, handing the other to Menyez. "If it's any consolation" — which it wasn't, he knew — "the force that sallied against our flank got cut up pretty badly before they made it back to cover. Good work, by the way, Gerrin."

Staenbridge shrugged; his eyes were red-rimmed by exhaustion as well. "Standard little affray," he said. "Incidentally, I was right back on Stern Isle. Their regular army is a different proposition from the landholders' retainers. A bit slow to deploy, though, too reluctant to get out of the saddle."

"As to what we do next —" Raj began.

observe, Center said.

This time the vision was of Lion City before the Fall. He hadn't known there was a city here back that far. Low colorful buildings, a few towers, streets of greenery with vehicles floating through on air cushions. More such advanced craft at the docks behind the same adamantine breakwaters as today, and others that had sails in bright primary shades and seemed to serve no purpose but pleasure. Yet there were so *many* of them, as if the city held hundreds of nobles wealthy enough to maintain a yacht. People strolling along the tree-shaded avenues, richly dressed in alien fashions, all healthy and well-fed and unconcerned, none bearing arms save a hunter with the head of a carnosauroid floating behind him on a robot platform. People bathing nude in the harbor itself, away from the docks, in water that was crystal clear and free of downdraggers. How could harbor water not stink and attract scavengers?

The view stabilized overhead and then flashed to a schematic of the city's hydraulic system. Water flowed in through pipes from the sea, flashed into vapor in a processing plant, flowed out through distributor pipes to every house, however humble. Even while he focused his attention on the overall view Raj marvelled at that. The lowliest peasant with hot and cold water running in any room he chose, like a great lord! With no need to send his wife to the public fountain for water or with the slops bucket to a sewer inlet — and only wealthy, civilized towns in these Fallen times had even so much. Waste water collected in a giant pipe that struck north to a mysterious factory that seemed to do nothing but sterilize the water, even though the whole ocean was nearby for dumping.

The Fall came. Most of the bright airy structures fell swiftly, to fire or hammered apart as salvage; they were uninhabitable for folk with nothing but fire to heat with, and they had been built of perishable materials. For generations only a small farming and fishing village stood on the site of Lion City. Rich land and a fine self-scouring harbor with a lighthouse brought growth. When men were numerous enough for their wastes to be a problem, a long ditch was built and connected to the storm-drains that flowed at low tide through the adamantine seawall; rainwater flushed it, now and then. A later generation covered the ditch with brick arches and built drains down individual streets connecting to it. The old sewer outlet was forgotten, deep underground. When men built the city wall, they built it over the pipe, to defend a smaller, more densely packed settlement.

A final vision: the outlet pipe ending in a gully north of the town, with a projection of Raj standing next to it.

1.5 meters in diameter, Center said.

For a moment all Raj could feel was incandescent anger. *You let my men die when there was a better way?* he thought. *Not even the Spirit —*

i am not god, Center said. **the pipe may be blocked. is probably blocked where the weight of the wall rests on it. or the inlet may not connect to the surface within lion city. in any case, "supernatural" interventions such as this increase the amount of noise in the system and reduce the reliability of my predictive function. nor did i select you to be the puppet of my tactical direction.**

"Raj?" Suzette said with concern.

He shook back to himself. The Companions were used to his moments of introspection, but not to one accompanied by the expression he could still feel twisting his face.

furthermore the attention of the garrison will now be firmly riveted on the walls.

Shut — up, he thought savagely. Perhaps that was reckless disrespect to an angel, but at the moment he didn't much care.

Raj looked up at the walls of Lion City. "They're really going to regret burning my men," he said softly.

Jorg Menyez was normally a mild and considerate man. At that moment his battered face resembled the surface of an upraised maul — also battered, but poised to smash anything in its path, stone and iron included. It matched his commander's expression quite closely.

"Oh, my oath, yes," Gerrin Staenbridge, almost

whispering. A rustle of carnivore alterness went through the circle of commanders.

"Ehwardo," Raj began. "Move the cavalry around outside the walls — make it look as if you're setting up dispersed camps." An essential step in keeping dogs healthy over a long stay in a confined spot. "Jorg, starting at dawn, give the best imitation you can of a man starting massive siege works; parallels, the whole show."

"I gather it's a ruse, Whitehall?" Gerrin Staenbridge said.

"Correct. The rest of you are to prepare for a general assault — if and only if something I . . . have in mind succeeds. Colonel Dinnalsyn, get those damned armored cars ready, too. If you'll excuse me, Messers? And Gerrin," he went on, "send me M'lewis."

Antin M'lewis usually blessed the fate that had thrown him into Raj Whitehall's path. Since then life had never been boring, and it had been lucrative — if not beyond his wildest dreams, then beyond all reasonable expectation. Particularly after he happened to be one of the two men with Raj when he put down the botched coup attempt that used Des Poplanich as its front-man. Governor Barholm had been hysterical when he promised to make the two Companions present the richest lords in the Civil Government if they saved him. He'd remembered enough afterwards to translate one Antin M'lewis, free commoner and soldier of watch-stander rank, into the Messer class and to deed him a thousand hectares of land — and not in stony, desolate Descott County, either. Good fat riverside fields, near the capital. Yes, usually he blessed the day then-Major Raj Whitehall had hauled him up on charges for stealing a shoat.

Then again, there were times when he wished he'd let the peons *keep* their damned pig.

The pipe was tall enough for him to stand in if he stooped a bit. The greasy-smooth material it was made of was like nothing he'd ever seen outside a shrine, and it led downward into the earth — into the Starless Dark, the freezing hell of the orthodox. Where the Spirit of Man of the Stars cast the unregenerate souls not worthy even of lowly rebirth, dumping their core programs into chaos.

Good thing me ma were a witch, he thought. This might be a real problem for a pious respectable yeoman, but everyone in the M'lewis family accounted themselves probably damned anyway and certainly hung if found out. So were the Forty Thieves, but even they looked queasy at the arguably supernatural and definitely menacing passageway into the earth.

They watched him silently as he stripped off his uniform jacket and boots; unlike most enlisted men, who preferred sleeveless vests of unbleached cotton beneath in summertime, he wore a shirt. Unlike most officers, his was dyed rusty black. Through the back of his belt he tucked a sheathed skinning knife, and tested that the wooden toggles of his garotte were ready to his hand for the quick snatch-and-toss. Then he tied a plain brown bandana over his hair and palmed mud over his cheeks.

"Yer nivver goin' t'leave yer gun, ser?" one of the men whispered.

It was the young recruit; M'lewis remembered him from the action on Stern Isle, where he'd wondered if he'd have a chance at the women in the refugee convoy.

"Son —" M'lewis began. Which was *just* possible; they were certainly cousins, and he'd been friendly with that branch of the family as a lad. "— whin yer sneakin', yer sneaks *quiet*. With t'gun, all I could do 'd be ter bring four thousand barbs down on me head. Jist noise an' temptation, onna sneak loik this."

Spirit. Then again, he'd probably have drunk and fucked himself into an early grave by now if he'd retired to rusticate on the new estate. Certainly the other Messers wouldn't accept him socially there, a stranger of common birth. His sons, probably, when he got around to having them, but not him. And it would be dull.

Raj stepped up and gripped forearms. "Careful and slow, M'lewis," he said. "Don't let them hear you."

The snaggled teeth showed in a grin, and he offered a fist to slap — a trifle familiar perhaps, but then, what could you do to a man on a suicide mission?

"Nao clumpin' barb'll hear this mither's chile, ser," he said.

His bare feet were noiseless on the plastic. The soft cold of it was like nothing he'd ever touched as he walked forward and down, crouching.

Raj Whitehall was motionless beside his dog. Less bound by need than the man, Horace shifted uneasily from foot to foot to foot, whining slightly. His hand soothed the animal automatically, gauntleted fingers scritching in the slight ruff at the back of the neck, just forward of the saddlbow. Other dogs shifted and murfled in the darkness, two kilometers from the main gates of Lion City. Fifteen thousand men waited, gripping their rifles or the ladders, wondering if the next hour would bring a ladle of burning pitch in the face, a limb lost, eyes, genitals, whatever their particular dread might be. The air was full of the smell of rank sweat and dog, men and animals both full of knowledgeable fear and suppressed eagerness.

Everyone thought it was payback time. Everyone, Spirit help them, thought Messer Raj would pull another miracle out of the hat.

It was full dark; neither moon would be up for another hour. Watchlights burned on the walls of Lion City, but experience had taught them that Skinners could shoot out any reflector-backed searchlight from a comfortable range . . . and the men manning it.

It was also long after he should have received word from Gerrin. When the dispatch rider reined in, he forced himself not to whirl.

"Ser," the man said.

Something's wrong.

"Spit it out," Raj said. Nightmares — the 5th destroyed in a trap, burning pitch and tallow pumped down on them in the tunnel while they died helpless —

"Ser," the rider said, his eyes fixed over the general's head. "Captain Suharez reports . . . beggin' yer pardon, ser . . . Cap'n reports the 5th has retreated from the tunnel."

Raj stalked over to the rider and slapped the muzzle of his dog. *"Down,"* he said. The animal crouched obediently. That put his eyes on a level with the man's.

"From Captain Suharez?" he said, in a calm voice. The man flinched. That was the second-ranked company commander in the unit.

"Yesser. Colonel Staenbridge an', an' some members went beyond the second dip — there was 'n other, ser, ten meters beyond t'one Lieutnant M'lewis found. The rest . . . the rest turned back, ser."

Raj pivoted on his heel, ignoring the dispatch rider. "Major Bellamy," he said. Wide eyes stared at him out of darkness as he stepped over Horace's saddle. "Up, boy . . . Major Bellamy, you will accompany me with the 2nd Cruisers. Major Gruder, you're in charge of the gate. Colonel Menyez, you're in overall command. Await the signal, then proceed as planned."

He kicked heels into his mount. Horace leaped forward, and Ludwig Bellamy and the bannerman of the 2nd fell in beside him. Behind them the massed paws of the 2nd Mounted Cruisers beat a tattoo through the night.

The ravine where the old sewer outlet surfaced was packed with men; the dogs were crouched a few hundred meters further north, together with those of the ex-*Squadrone* soldiers Raj had brought. He could see the 5th only as a shadowy presence, a sullen mass that recoiled slightly as he walked up to them.

"You retreated without orders?" he asked the Captain.

"Yes, sir," the man said. He was braced to attention and staring ahead.

At least he isn't offering excuses, Raj thought. He was moving carefully, very carefully so that he wouldn't shatter the ice surface of control that bound him.

"Ser," a voice from the dark mass said. "Ser . . . 'tis damnation there! 'T road to t'Starless —"

"Silence in the ranks," Raj said. His voice was as clear and precise as water is when it falls over a ledge of stone, before the spray and thunder. "You," he went on to the unit bannerman. "Did you turn back?"

"No ser," the man said.

He was a grizzled veteran, a thirty-year man; carrying the battalion standard was a jealously guarded privilege, open only to men three times awarded the Gold of Valor.

"Colonel Staenbridge, he ordered t'color party to remain here. Seein's t'colors wouldn't fit, ser."

"Then you may carry the colors back to the central Star shrine in camp," Raj said. "Where they will be safe from men unworthy of them."

A low moan broke from the assembled ranks of the 5th, and the bannerman sobbed, tears running down his leathery cheeks as he turned smartly and trotted for his dog. Nor was he the only one weeping.

"Tears are for women," Raj went on in the same glass-smooth tone. "Senior Captain Suharez, take this unit and report to Major Gruder, placing yourself under his orders. For whatever tasks he judges it fit for."

Suharez' face might have been carved from dark wood. "Yes, sir." He saluted and wheeled.

Raj turned toward the tunnel mouth. Behind him there was a forward surge among the ranks of the 5th Descott. He wheeled again, flinging out his hand and pointing silently back towards the main force. An officer broke his saber over his knee, and the men fell into their ranks and trotted forward behind Suharez.

Faint starlight sheened on the eyes and teeth of the 2nd Cruisers. Ludwig Bellamy stepped forward and saluted smartly.

"I'm ready to lead my men through, sir," he said.

"No, Major," Raj said. "You'll bring up the rear. Nobody is to turn back, understood?"

He raised his voice slightly, pitching it to carry in the heavy-breathing hush. "As I have kept faith with you, so you with me. Follow; quietly, and in order."

Raj turned and stooped, entering the tunnel.

The men's hobnailed boots clattered on the surface of the pipe; the sound was dulled, as if they were walking on soft wood, but the iron left no scratches on the plastic of the Ancients. The surface beneath the fingers of his left hand might have been polished marble, except for the slight trace of greasy slickness. There was old dirt and silt in the very bottom of the circular tube, and it stank of decay; floodwater must run down from the gutters of Lion City and through this pipe when the floods were very high.

Behind him the rustle and clank of equipment sounded, panting breath, an occasional low-voiced curse in Namerique. Earth Spirit cultists didn't have the same myth of a plastic-lined tube to Hell; the center of the earth — This Earth — was their paradise. This particular tunnel was intimidating as Hell to *anyone*, though. Particularly to men reared in the open air, there was a touch of the claustrophobe in most dog-and-gun men. There certainly was in *him*, because every breath seemed more difficult than the last, an iron hoop tightening around his chest.

this is not an illusion, Center said helpfully. **the oxygen content of the air is dropping because airflow is inadequate in the presence of over six hundred men. this will not be a serious problem unless the force is halted for a prolonged period.**

Oh, thank *you,* Raj thought.

Even then, he felt a grim satisfaction at what Army discipline had made of last year's barbarian horde. *Vicious children,* he thought. Vicious grown-up children whose ancestors had shattered civilization over half a continent — not so much in malice as out of simple inability to imagine doing anything different. Throwing the pretty baubles into the air and clapping their hands to see them smash, heedless of the generations of labor and effort that went into their making. *Thirteen-year-olds with adults' bodies . . . but they can learn. They can learn.*

The roof knocked on the top of his helmet. *"Halto,"* he called quietly. The column rustled to a halt behind him.

A quick flick of the lens-lid on his bullseye lantern showed the first change in the perfect regularity of the tunnel. Ahead of him the roof bent down and the sides out, precisely like a drinking straw pinched between a man's fingers.

you are under the outer edge of the town wall on the north side, Center said. **.63 of a kilometer from the entrance.**

M'lewis had come this far on his scout; he'd checked that the tunnel opened out again beyond this point, and then returned. Raj had agreed with the decision, since maximum priority was to avoid giving the entrance away. And the little Scout had been right, air *was* flowing toward him, he could feel the slightly cooler touch on his sweating face.

Of course, the air might be coming through a hole the size of a man's fist.

"Crawl through," he said to the man behind him, clicking off the light. "Turn on your backs and crawl through. There's another pinch in the tunnel beyond. Pass it down."

He dropped to the slimy mud in the bottom of the tunnel and began working his way further in. The plastic dipped down toward his face, touched the brim of his helmet. Still smooth, still untorn. The weight of the city wall was on it here, had been for five hundred years. Mud squished beneath his shoulderblades, running easily on the low-friction surface of the pipe.

The weight of a wall fifteen meters high and ten thick at the base, two courses of three-by-three meter stones on either side, flanking a rubble-concrete core.

Do not *tell me how much it weighs*, he thought/said to Center.

Now he was past the lowest point, and suddenly conscious of his own panting. Something bumped his boots; the head of the man following. One man following, at least. At least two or three more, from the noise behind. No way of telling what was further back, how many were still coming, whether the last five hundred or five hundred and fifty had turned and trampled Ludwig in a terror-filled rush out of this deathtrap, this anteroom to hell. The plastic drank sound, leaving even his breath muffled. Sweat dripped down his forehead, running into his eyes as he came to hands and knees. He clicked the bullseye open for a look when the surface began to twist beneath his feet. Another ten meters of normal pipe, and then —

Spirit, he thought. What could have produced *this?*

the pipe crosses under the wall at an angle of forty degrees from the perpendicular. this section is under the edge of a tower, Center said with dispassionate accuracy.

The towers were much heavier than the walls. The sideways thrust of one tower's foundations had shoved the pipe a little sideways . . . and squeezed it down so that only a triangular hole in the lower right-hand corner remained. This time the fabric *had* ruptured, a long narrow split to the upper left. Dirt had come through, hard lumpy yellow clay, and someone recent had dug it out with hands and knife and spread it backwards.

Raj waited until the man following him came up behind. "No problem," he said, while the eyes in the bearded face were still blinking at the *impossible* hole. "Come through one at a time; take off your rifle, helmet and webbing belt, then have the man behind you hand them through. Pass it on."

He kept moving, because if he didn't, he might not start again. One man panicking here and the whole column would be stalled all night.

He took off the helmet and his swordbelt, snapped the strap down over the butt of his revolver and dropped the bundle to the floor.

"Keep the lantern on," he said to the soldier behind him.

Right arm forward. Turn sideways. Down and forward, the sides gripping him like the clamps of a grab used to lift heavy shells. Light vanishing beyond his feet; they kicked without purchase, and then the broad hands of the trooper were under them, giving him something to push against. Bronze jacket buttons digging into his ribs hard enough to leave bruises. Breathe in, *push*. Buried in hell, buried in hell . . .

His right hand came free. It groped about, there was little leverage on the smooth flaring sides of the pipe, but his shoulders came out, and that was the broadest part of him.

For an instant he lay panting, then turned. "Through," he called softly. "Pass my gear, soldier." A fading echo down the pipe, as the man turned and murmured the news to the one behind *him*.

It had only been a little more than his body length. Difficult, but not as difficult as concrete would have been, or cast iron, anything that gripped at skin and clothing. The light cast a glow around the slightly curved path of the narrow passage.

Again he waited until the first man had followed, grabbing his jacket between the shoulderblades and hauling him free.

"Second birth," he said.

The *Squadrone* trooper shook his head. "The first was tighter, lord," he said. His face was corpse-palid in the faint light, but he managed a grin. Then he turned and called softly down the narrow way:

"*Min gonne, Herman.*"

Not much further, Raj thought, looking ahead. Darkness lay on his eyes like thick velvet.

.21 kilometers.

"I'll have them *decimated,*" Gerrin Staenbridge hissed.

Raj didn't doubt that the other man meant exactly what he said; that he'd line up his battalion and have one man in ten taken out of the ranks and the others forced to beat him to death with rods. It was the traditional penalty for mass cowardice in the face of the enemy.

"I don't think that will be necessary," he said, his voice remote.

Gerrin turned and began a motion that would have slammed his fist into the concrete wall.

"Neither will that," Raj said, catching the thick wrist. "We have a job to do, Major."

"Yes, sir," Staenbridge said, straightening and running a hand under the neck-guard of his helmet. His hand kneaded brutally at the muscles at the base of his skull. "We've improvised, as you can see."

There were a little over a hundred men of the 5th Descott in the huge underground chamber, most of Company A and the twenty men of the Scouts who'd gone in first. It was large enough that they didn't crowd it, even with more and more of the 2nd Cruisers coming out of the pipe, jumping down the two-meter drop to the floor or lowering themselves by their hands. Not quite jet-black, the risk of a covered lantern was worth the lessened noise when men could see what they were doing.

The chamber was nearly twenty meters across and about three high. Originally it had been domed, but the roof had buckled at some unknown time. Bent and twisted rods of metal protruded from the concrete, and the huge writhing shape of a large tree's taproot. Staenbridge had been busy; the men must have made a human pyramid to lift one up, and he had hitched a rope made from buckling rifle slings together to one of the steel rods. Beyond that a darkness gaped.

"That connects to an old storm drain," the Major said, pointing. "Beyond that, an exit onto a street. M'lewis is there with a couple of his scouts, keeping it warm. Fairly deserted."

"It should be, it's past midnight," Raj said.

He walked over to the dangling slings; they were of tough sauroid hide, supple and very strong — the Armory tested them by hanging a hundred-kilo weight to one end and rejecting any that stretched or cracked.

"Send everyone on up, and then follow," he said.

He bent his legs and jumped, his sword-hand clamping down on a buckle hard enough to bend it. Arm over arm, he pulled himself smoothly upward toward the light.

The streets of Lion City had been laid out by cows. Quite literally, back in the days when it had been a little farming village where the odd ship called. When stone buildings went up, they stood by the sides of laneways worn by herdsmen driving their beasts back to their paddocks at night, and once the pattern was set it was too difficult to change. Too difficult for the people who'd run Lion City; back in the Civil Government a town this size would have had at least some semblance of a gridwork imposed at one time or another. If nothing else, a spiderweb of narrow streets flanked by three to five-story buildings was simply too easy for rioters to hold against troops, throwing up barricades and dropping roof-tiles down on stalled columns.

I've got something of the same problem, Raj thought. Maxiluna was up, but it was still dark in the alleyway; Lion City didn't run to gaslights, either, and even in East Residence a neighborhood like this wouldn't have been lit. Dark and very quiet, only the squall of an alley-cat breaking the silence. With the militia standing watch-and-watch on the walls and their families laboring to carry them food and water and do whatever else a city under siege needed, most folk would be well and truly asleep when they could find the time. Probably a few eyes were peering at him from behind shuttered windows, but men — and women — see what they expect. It would take a while for anyone to realize that this was not another unit of Brigade troops going out to relieve a section of wall.

He had just that long, and enough more for the damnably alert High Colonel Strezman to receive the report and get his garrison moving. If that happened before he was where he had to be, then he and everyone with him was dead.

Center's street-map of Lion City was eleven hundred years out of date, but the machine intelligence had seen everything he had. With his own eyes, and through reports — Muzzaf's, Abdullah's, the Ministry's. A glowing hologram opened before his private vision, and a green thread showed him the closest route to the gates. Not so good, they had to jink around the easternmost tip of the harbor.

"Gerrin, Ludwig," he said.

The two men were at his side; one dark, one fair, but otherwise much of a size.

"We're going to form up in column of fours —" all that could get through many of these streets, with the sleeves of the outer men brushing the brick and half-timber buildings on either side "— and head straight for the main gates at a run; I'll lead."

The two battalion commanders glanced at each other. How *anyone* could lead through this blacked-out maze was a question, but they'd learned that this man didn't claim what he could not do.

"Gerrin, you take the right-hand tower complex. Ludwig, give me your Company A; I'll take the left. You deploy in the main plaza just inside the gates and keep the reaction force off our backs — because they *will* hit, soon and hard. Understood?"

Two sharp nods, and they turned away to pass the orders to their subordinates.

Raj raised his voice slightly. "Keep it quiet, men, and keep it fast, and don't stop for anything at all."

Pavement racketed beneath their feet, echoing as they pounded into a run. Raj held his saber-sheath in his left hand to keep it from slapping him as he loped. This wasn't all that subtle a way to manage the movement, but at present subtle mattered a lot less than quick; seven hundred foreign soldiers were a big conspicuous object in any town, much less one under siege. Streets went by, narrowing or widening, cobbles or brick or occasionally hard-pounded dirt underfoot. Now and then a ragged beggar woke in a doorway and fled squalling; the normal Watch would be on the walls with everyone else. Buildings looming on either side, mostly dark, once a yellow blaze as a window was thrown open above. He caught a moment's glimpse of a woman holding a candlestick in one hand, catching her nightgown at the throat with the other, her face a study in shocked surprise.

"Faster!" he called.

He was breathing deeply; it had been a long hard day already, but a run of a klick or so didn't bother a man in good condition. It had *better* not bother any of his troopers, dog-soldiers or no.

"Halt!"

A bit of jostling as some of the rear didn't get the word. The plaza stretched ahead of him, the wooden platform still around the fountain; that was dry, with the city's outside water supply cut. For a moment he wondered what had happened to the Syndic of the Sailmakers, the man who'd wanted to open the gates. Only a single street of houses on the other side before the cleared space that ringed the wall, and a broad street through them from plaza to gates.

"At a quick walk," he said to Staenbridge. "Try out your Namerique, Gerrin. Captain Hortez —" one of the Descotter officers he'd posted to the 2nd Cruisers as company commanders "— tell the men to fix bayonets, load and shoulder arms. Sling their helmets." That would show their barbarian haircuts and coloring. "Follow me."

The towers bulked ahead, squat pairs on either side of the gate joined by a bridge over the arch itself, making the gateway into a huge block of masonry twenty meters high. There were lights there, one above the gate itself, another over each tower door on the rear. Not many lights inside, because the troops would be peering out at the encircling army and wouldn't want to destroy their night vision. The door to each tower was half a story up, with a staircase leading to an arched door wide enough for two men. Those were open, with soldiers lounging on the stairs.

Gerrin's company peeled off to the right. *Ignore them*, Raj told himself. Nothing he could do, and if he couldn't count on Gerrin Staenbridge he didn't have a single competent man with him and might as well die anyway....

Closer. The soldiers were in General's Dragoon uniforms. *Damn*. He'd been hoping for city militia, but High Colonel Strezman had done the sensible thing. Certainly what Raj would have done, were he holding a city whose leaders had publicly considered surrender. He was willing to bet the other three gates were in the hands of Brigaderos regulars as well.

His mouth was dry with the running. He worked it to moisten it, concentrating on marching. Not stiff, just a company of soldiers going where they were told to, with the easy swing of men who'd done the same thing a thousand times before and would again. Really not much light, only a single kerosene lamp over the doorway, far too little to see details. The civic militia wore dozens of different outfits or their street-clothes according to whim and the depth of their pockets, so the distinctive Civil Government uniform might pass, *would* pass until it was too late.

"Whir dere ko?" a man challenged in Namerique. *Who goes there?* A young man's voice, probably a noncom. Strezman would be stretched thin, watching his putative allies along kilometers of city wall and keeping a big enough reaction force ready as a reserve.

The men at the gate scooped up their dice and stood, buttoning their jackets. They reached for their weapons, not concerned, just veterans' reflexes.

"Captain of Guards Willi Kirkin," Raj said.

His Namerique had something of a Squadron accent, and he let the harsh syllables roll across his tongue. There were quite a few Squadron refugees serving as mercenaries among the household troops of the magnates of Lion City.

The other man's reply sounded nervous, which was to be expected after the riot of the previous evening.

"What're you doing here, then, southron? Halt. Halt, I said!"

"Ni futz, greunt," Raj went on in a bored voice. *Don't get upset, trooper.* "The Colonel thinks the *grisuh* may try something tonight, and we've been sent to reinforce the gate. Better us than those chicken-hearted civvies."

Raj was at the foot of the stairs. He pulled a piece of folded paper from his pocket. Time slowed as the corporal reached for the note, then got his first good look at Raj's face. His beardless, brown-tanned Descotter face, with the cold gray eyes like slitted ice under the brim of the bowl helmet.

The young Brigadero had only a ginger fuzz on his own cheeks. His eyes were green and very wide. They bulged as Hortenz' pistol bullet took him under the angle of the jaw and snapped him around like the kick of a plow-ox.

"*Go!*" Raj screamed.

His shoulder hit the door to the tower as his hand came clear of the holster with his revolver. Raj was no gunman, no pistol-artist, just a fair to middling shot.

The sword had always been his personal weapon of choice, and with that he was very good.

There was a ready room beyond the door, with five men in it — three sitting around a plank table playing cards, another two lying on benches. A grid flashed over Raj's vision, and the outline of one man glowed. The man with the pistols already nearly out of the holsters strapped to his thighs as he surged backward from the table. *The one good enough to fill the doorway with bodies while his comrades rushed to swing the iron-strapped teak closed again.*

A green dot settled on the man's chest as Raj swung the pistol toward him. The weapon bucked and roared, and the gunman's chest blossomed with a red flower exactly where the dot had rested. Dust puffed from the grey-green cloth around the impact point, the man was falling and Raj wheeled. The dot slid across a face. *Crack*, echoing within the stone walls. An eye erupted. On a neck. *Crack*. Arterial blood spouted against the whitewashed wall and ceiling as the brigadero spun. Against ribs. *Crack*. Another man had rolled behind a bench, fumbling with the hammer of his rifle. *Crack* through his pelvis.

The hammer clicked twice more by reflex. Raj staggered for a moment, wheezing in the fetid air through his mouth: he had ample strength and speed for that three-second burst of gunplay, but the skill was as much beyond him as a circus juggler's talents. The first kill's body was still twitching in a great pool of spreading blood. The men on his heels hesitated for a second, awe on their faces.

"Go, *go*," Raj ordered, over the moaning of a dying Brigadero.

His hands clicked open the revolver, dumped the spent brass, reloaded. Hortenz dashed by, through the ground-level door to secure the first floor of the towers and the exterior gunslits. Another squad of 2nd Cruiser riflemen went past to the staircase in a bristle of bayonets, behind a lieutenant. Raj tossed his revolver into his left hand and drew his sword with his right. One part of his mind was still shuddering with the icy feeling of . . . otherness, of being a weapon, pointed like a rifle by a directing hand. He'd use the trick again if he had to, as he'd use anything that came to hand. That didn't mean he had to like it.

The stairs were a narrow spiral, almost pitch-black. Iron hobnails and heel-plates gritted and clanged on the stone, from the squad ahead and the men following close behind. It would be a great pity if he slipped and toppled back onto their bayonets. The thought twitched at the set grin that rippled his lips back from his teeth. Gunfire crashed ahead of him, red muzzle flashes blinding in the dimness. Men shouted; he kept going past the door, past the tumbled bodies of Brigaderos and a trooper of the 2nd. All the enemy bodies had multiple bayonet wounds; the 2nd had learned to make very sure of things.

"Get those charges up here," he shouted down.

Men came back into the stairs, their rifles slung and their arms full of linen powder-bags for the light swivel guns on the second level of the tower; one of them had a coil of matchcord around his neck. *Remember that face. That's a sergeant, if he lives.* More gunfire slapped at his ears, echoes bouncing through the narrow corridors, screams, shrieks of fury and fear and raw killing-lust.

"GITTEM, GITTEM!" That was his ex-*Squadrones* forgetting themselves, giving the Admiral's war shout.

The stair gave out at the third-story landing. Only a ladder led above to the top of the tower; he snapshot, and a man tumbled down it and halted halfway, his legs tangled in the rungs. Blood spattered across Raj's face. He stepped aside, swearing mildly to himself, and let the next dozen or so behind him take the ladder without pausing, ripping the corpse free and bursting out onto the tower roof. More followed, including an officer; he could hear orders up there, and then a staccato volley.

"Quick," he said to the man with the charges.

The door opening right into the rooms above the arch of the gateway was barred. Raj thrust his pistol into the eyeslot and pulled the trigger; there was a scream, and somebody slammed an iron plate across it. The cloth bundles of gunpowder tumbled at his feet.

"Good man," Raj said. "Now, pack them along the foot of the door, in between the stone sill and the door. Cut them with your knife and stick the matchcord — right." He raised his voice; more men were crowding up the stairs, some to take the ladder and others filling the space about him. *"Everyone down the corridor, around the corner here. Now!"*

The quick-witted trooper and he and another lieutenant — Wate Samzon, a *Squadrone* himself — played out the cord and plastered themselves to the wall just around from the door. The matchcord sputtered as it took the flame. Raj put his hand before his eyes. White noise, too loud for sound. He tensed to drive back around to the door —

— and strong arms siezed him, body and legs and arms.

"Ni, ni," a deep rumbling voice said in his ear. "You are our lord, by steel and salt. Our blood for yours."

Lieutenant Samzon led the charge. A second later he was flung back, hands clapped to the bleeding ruin of his face, stumbled into the wall and fell flat. The men who followed him fired into the ruins of the door and thrust after the bullets, bayonets against swords, as their comrades reloaded and fired past their bodies close enough for the blasts to scorch their uniforms. When they forced through the shattered planks the men holding Raj released him and followed them, with only their broad backs to hold him behind them.

The only Brigaderos left in the big rectangular room were dead, but the troopers of the 2nd Cruisers were still looking terrified — of the winches and gear-trains that filled the chamber. A year ago, anything more complicated than a windmill had seemed like sorcery to them, and some had screamed with fear at their first sight of a steam engine. They'd gotten over that, but they had to *do* something with these machines, these complex toothed shapes of black iron and brass.

Raj knew fortifications and their ancillary equipment from years of study. "You, you, you," he said crisply. "Take that maul and knock those wedges loose. Pull those lockbars out — those long iron rods through the wheels with the loops on the end. The rest of your squad, grab that crank and get ready to put your backs into it. Those winches too."

The inner gates were not held by a bar across the leaves. Instead, thick iron posts ran down from this chamber through loops on their inner surfaces into deep sockets set in the stone beneath, covered with wooden plugs when the gates were open. Toothed gearwheels raised and lowered the massive posts, driving on notches cut into their sides. Metal clanked and groaned as the troopers heaved at the crank-handles. Winches running iron chains lifted the portcullis into a slot just in from the channels for the bars. The chain clacked over the drums, making a dull ringing as the great iron gridwork rose over the tunnel way.

"Ser!" A panting trooper with the 5th's shoulder flashes. "Colonel says they've got the outer gateway."

Which was controlled from the right-hand towers, as this inner one was from the left. Raj nodded curtly and stepped out of the chamber, calling up the ladder to the top of the tower:

"Two white rockets!"

General assault, all around the circuit of the walls. Back inside the lifting room, gunfire blasted, needles of pain in the ears in such a confined space. A duller explosion followed.

"Shot through the door," the sergeant of the platoon said, as Raj returned. "It started to open."

He nodded to the door at the outer side of the room; that would give to the middle section of the arch over the gate, a series of rooms above the roadway where the murder-holes gave onto the space below. It was wood and iron; there were lead splashes on the planks and frame where the soft hollowpoint bullets had struck — they had terrible wounding power but no penetration. The brass-tipped hardpoints had punched through, and then an explosion from the other side had buckled the whole portal.

"Thought they was goin' to chuck a handbomb through," the sergeant said. A few of his men were down, wounded by ricochets from their own weapons. "Must've gone off in their hands," he went on with satisfaction.

Raj nodded. "Get those prybars and open the door," he said. "Quickly, now."

They'd have to clear out the men there, or the troops coming through the tunnel would get a nasty surprise. Gerrin would be working his way in as the men under Raj's command worked out through the line of rooms over the tunnel.

And it was time he checked on Ludwig. Now that the focus of concentration was relaxing a little, he could hear a slamming firefight going on out in the plaza. No point to the whole thing if the Brigaderos broke through to the towers before his men got here.

"Prepare to receive cavalry!"

The company commander was down with a sucking chest wound, and Ludwig Bellamy was doing his job as well as trying to oversee the battle.

The Brigaderos cavalry were charging again, straight down the street. It was wide, by Lion City standards, which meant they were coming in six abreast and three ranks deep. The front rank of 2nd Cruisers knelt with their rifles braced against the cobbles and the points of their long bayonets at chest height. Two more ranks stood behind them with rifles levelled. It seemed a frail thing to oppose to the big men on tall dogs that raced toward them, the shouting and the long swords

gleaming in the pale moonlight — but the pile in front
of the position gave the lie to that: dead men and dogs
lying across one another in a slithering heap.

Once Ludwig Bellamy had believed that nothing on
foot could stand before brave men charging with steel
in hand. Messer Raj had disabused him of that notion,
him and what was left of the Squadron.

The charge slowed at the last instant. War-dogs were
willing to face steel, but their instincts told them to crouch
and leap, not impale themselves in a straight gallop.

"Fire!"

The sound crashed out, like one giant shot impossibly
long and loud. The muzzle flashes lit the dim street with
a light as bright as a red day for an instant. It lit the edges
of the Brigaderos swords and the fangs of their dogs like
light flickering from hell. A hundred heavy 11mm bullets
drove into the leading rank of the charge. All of the first
mounts were struck, most of them several times, and the
muscular grace of the wardogs turned to flailing chaos in
a fraction of an instant. Half-ton bodies cartwheeled into
the barricade of flesh, or dove head-first into it if they
had been brainshot, as several had. The sounds of impact
were loud but muffled. Few of the men had been shot,
but they parted from their tumbling animals, arcing to
the pavement or disappearing under thousands of
pounds of writhing flesh.

Their screams were lost in the sounds of the
wounded dogs. One came over the bodies, its hind legs
limp and with an empty saddle, dragging itself up to
the soldiers. It was still snarling when two bayonets
punched through its throat.

"Reload!"

The Brigaderos in rear ranks had managed to halt
their dogs in time. They tried to come forward at a
walk, levelling their revolvers. Men fell in the front
rank of the Cruiser line as the pistols spat. Behind him
a shout rose, and rockets soared from the gate towers.

"Fire!"

The Brigaderos turned and spurred their dogs, turning aside into alleys as soon as they could. Behind them was a solid block of dismounted dragoons, filling the roadway from side to side and coming on at the quickstep. The 2nd Cruiser lieutenants shouted:

"Prone, kneeling, standing ranks." The first line of men propped their rifles over dead Brigaderos and dead wardogs. "*By* platoon sections, *volley* fire, *fire*."

BAM. BAM. BAM. BAM.

The enemy raised a shout and charged, rifles at the port, leaning forward as if against rain. Men from the rear ranks pushed forward to fill the gaps each volley blasted, and they came on. Not pausing to fire until they were close, not when they loaded so much more slowly.

"This is it, boys — they're going to run over us or die trying. Make it count, aim low. *Fire!*"

BAM. BAM. BAM. BAM.

Bellamy skipped back to view the rest of the action. Holding the roadways into the plaza wasn't too much trouble, no — but it tied down too many of his men. Even with all five hundred, minus Company A, he wouldn't have enough to hold the whole perimeter of the plaza, and Strezman was sending in everything he had. More than three thousand men, coming through the houses and mansions around the square, firing from windows and rooftops. Ignoring everything else to retake the main gate before the assault force reached the wall.

Just what Messer Raj told me he'd do.

Any second now he'd have to pull back to prevent his men being overrun in detail. How long a battalion line would last in the open against five times its numbers the Spirit alone knew.

They'd last as long as they lived.

"Damnation to Darkness," Raj swore softly.

Cannon were going off all along the walls of Lion City, shaking the stone beneath his boots. But raggedly, and fewer than he would have thought. A lot of them could see the open gates, and more could see the glare of fire shining from the gate-tower windows, or hear the firing from within the walls.

The room with the winching material was full of smoke; powder-smoke, and from the barricade of burning furniture the holdouts were defending one room in. Wounded men were coming out of the door, and more troopers of the 2nd Cruisers forced their way toward the action. His eyes watered and he coughed as he leaned out the slit window, but the breath of air on his sweat-sodden skin was like a shock of cold. So was what he could see. The bulk of the 2nd Cruisers were withdrawing across the plaza toward him, backing three steps and volley-firing, backing again; the stuttering crash of their rifles carried even over the cannonade from the walls. Their line had bent back into a C-shape as Brigaderos swarmed after them, thrown into confusion by their passage through house and alley, but attacking relentlessly despite gruesome casualties.

The light was bad and his eyes were watering, but he could see the battalion flag of the 2nd Cruisers in the center of the bowing line. The enemy were pressing in, a reckless close-range exchange of slamming volleys that no troops could stand for long. The ex-*Squadrones'* rate of fire was much higher, but there were so *many* of the enemy. Their firepower was diffuse, but it was enormous in relation to the target, and they were swarming around the flanks. In minutes the 2nd would be forced to form square, and hundreds of enemy troops would pour past them to hold the gate. And the gatehouse was *still* not clear.

A solid pulse of noise bounced through the gate towers: men and dogs howling. Raj stiffened, gripping the stone sill and craning to see. He could just make out the opened inner gate. Red flashes came through it, and then a sudden sullen wash of fire — handbombs and burning pitch being poured into the roadway. Not as much as there would have been if the gate towers were fully manned, but too much, too much. Some of the first men through were reeling with wounds, and others rode dogs with burning fur that streaked off across the plaza or rolled whether their riders jumped free in time or not.

Yet the troops were in hand, not panicking. Those hale enough spilled through and then formed on either side of the gate in three-deep lines, then trotted-cantered-galloped into the plaza in response to trumpet calls. Split into two rectangles of men and dogs and bright swords, and charged for the flanks of the 2nd Cruisers, where the Brigaderos lapped around them like waves eroding sand at high tide. The enemy were unformed, focused on the single task of driving toward the gates. They had no chance of forming to receive a mounted charge; and when they saw the line of saber-points and snarling wardogs coming out of the darkness and firelight their will broke. Screaming, they turned and ran back for the shelter of the buildings, running across the hundreds of their dead.

"The 5th, by the Spirit," Raj said softly. His voice was hoarse from the smoke. Mostly from the smoke.

More men were riding through the gate-mouth, in pulses like water pouring through a hole in the hull of a sinking ship. They dismounted, the dogs peeling off as the handlers led them, the men fixing bayonets. Trumpet calls and shouted orders sent them forward at the double, with a long ripple down their line as the files closed around the places of absent men. An armored car followed with a mechanical pig-grunt from its engines that racketed back off the stone; a splatgun jutted from the bow, in place of the usual light cannon. The brass hubs of the tall wire-spoked wheels shone as it rattled off across the uneven pavement in the gap between two companies of the 5th Descott. Seconds later the rolling crash of a full battalion's platoon volley-firing echoed back from the plaza, and the savage *braaaaaaap* of the new weapon.

The cannonade from the walls had stopped. A moment later an explosion somewhere deep in the gate towers punished his eardrums and made the stonework shudder under his feet. The flash of handbombs from the murder holes stopped; to either side of the towers, he could see pennants waving as the assault force gained the walls, and some were already sliding down ropes to the inner side. A column of men on foot broke out of the gate below him, and then a pair of guns rumbling along behind their dog-teams.

The firing was dying away, but lights were going on all across the town amid a bee-hum of civilian panic; down by the harbor, ships were casting loose from the docks to try their chances with the steam rams outside the breakwater — they must have been ready and waiting for the signs. With a roar like heavy surf collapsing a breakwater in a storm, the army of the Civil Government broke over the walls and flowed in to the helpless city behind.

"This's as far as it's safe," Gruder said.

All the other towers had surrendered quickly enough, when Civil Government troops came calling at the back entrance with field guns for doorknockers. Some of them were empty even before the soldiers arrived, their militia defenders tearing off their uniforms and running back towards their homes. All except those here on the northeast quadrant, where the men holding them had hauled down the Lion City banner of a rampant cat and left their own flag of white crescent on a green field flying defiantly.

"Hate to waste men on the rag-heads," Gruder said, scratching at a half-formed scab on his neck.

Raj's smile was bleak as the dawn still six hours away. "I don't think that will be necessary," he said quietly. "I've sent — ah."

Juluk rode up, his pipe between his teeth. His men ambled behind him, their dogs wuffing with interest at the smells on the night air.

"Hey, sojer-man, you do *wheetigo* trick, fly over walls, eh?"

"I didn't want to stay home scratching my fleas with you sluggards," Raj replied. Horace and the Skinner chief's dog eyed each other.

He pointed at the towers ahead. "Know who's there?" he said.

Juluk stretched and belched, knocking the dottle out of his pipe against one bare horn-callused heel. "Wear-breechclout-on-heads," he replied.

The Skinners' home range touched on the Colony's northeast border. That was their name for the Arabs; they called the people of the Civil Government the *sneaks*, and the western barbarians *long-hairs*. Or they just used their generic term of contempt, farmer.

"They think they're heroes," Raj said. "I say that if any of them are alive when the sun comes up, your women will laugh you out of the camps when you go home. They'll offer you skirts and birthing-stools."

Juluk's giggle broke into a hoot. He turned to his followers: *"L'gran wheetigo konai nus! Eel doni l'bun mut!"*

The big devil knows us! He's given us the good word!

"And that," Raj said as the nomad mercenaries pounded by, screeching like powered saws in stone, "takes care of that."

"Further resistance is hopeless," Raj called up toward the second-story window. "Colonel Strezman, don't sacrifice brave men without need." *Not least because the Civil Government can use them*, he thought. Whatever happened here in the west, there would be war with the Colony again within two years.

His skin prickled. He was quiet sure High Colonel Strezman wouldn't order him shot down under a flag of truce. He wasn't at all sure that one of his men might not do it anyway.

The last of the Brigaderos regulars had holed up in

several mansions not far from the plaza. Like most rich men's homes throughout the Midworld basin they were courtyard-centered dwellings with few openings out to the world; their lives were bent inward, away from noise, dust, thieves and tax-assessors. Their thick stone walls would turn rifle bullets, and the iron grills over the windows might make them forts in time of riot. How little they resembled real forts was shown by the smashed courtyard gate and the rubble beside it, where a single shell from the field-gun back down the road had landed. Most of the windows were dark, but there was enough moonlight for the riflemen crouching there to see the street quite well; also a building was burning not too far away.

A long silence followed. The street-door of the central house creaked open, and Strezman walked out surrounded by a knot of his senior officers.

"My congratulations on a brilliant ruse of war," he called, stopping ten meters away. "Your reputation preceeded you, Messer Whitehall, and now I see that it is justified."

He spoke loudly, a little more loudly than the distance called for. There was blood on the armor covering his right arm, and on the blade of his single-edged broadsword. He wore no helmet, and his long white hair fluttered around an eagle's face in the hot wind from the fire. Torchlight painted it red, despite his pallor.

"My congratulations, High Colonel, on a most skillful and resolute defense," Raj said sincerely.

Given the cards he was dealt, Strezman had played them about as well as he could — as well as anyone could without Center whispering in their ear.

"Will you surrender your remaining men?" Raj asked formally. "Your wounded will be cared for, and the troopers and junior officers given honorable terms of enlistment in the Civil Government forces on another front. Senior officers will be detained pending the conclusion of the war, but in a manner fitting to their rank and breeding."

Strezman swallowed, and spoke again. Still louder, as if for a larger audience.

"My orders from His Mightiness are to resist to the last man," he declaimed. "Therefore I must decline your gracious offer, Messer Whitehall, although no further *military* purpose is served by resistance. To honor the truce, I hereby warn you of my intention to attack."

Their eyes met. *The hostages*, Raj knew. The lives of these mens' families were forfeit, if they surrendered . . . or if they were *known* to have surrendered. Even though a stand to the death here accomplished nothing, not even much delay.

The officers with Strezman drew their swords and threw away the scabbards. They raised the blades and began to walk forward, heads up and eyes staring over the massed rifles facing them.

Raj chopped his hand down. Smoke covered the scene for an instant as a hundred rifles barked; when it cleared every man in the Brigaderos party was down, hit half a dozen times. The High Colonel was on his knees; blood pulsed through teeth clenched in a rictus of effort and he collapsed forward. The tip of his sword struck sparks as it left his hand and spun on the cobbles, a red and silver circle on the stones.

Raj flung up his hand to halt the fire. In a voice as loud as the Brigadero colonel's a moment before, he called:

"Let the bodies of High Colonel Strezman and his officers be returned to their households —" the servants who followed their masters to war "— to be delivered to their prince, in recognition of how their men — how *all* their men — died with them in obedience to General Forker's orders."

The vicious little sod, he added silently. He hoped the Brigade didn't depose Forker any time soon; the

man was worth five battalions of cavalry to the Civil
Government all by himself. If shame didn't keep him
from harming the garrison's families, fear of his other
commanders probably would, after Strezman's final
gesture. Although if there was any justice in this Fallen
world, the Brigade would chop him, and soon.

"Gerrin," he went on in a normal voice. The other
man's torso was bound with bandages over ribs that
might only be cracked, but he was still mobile.

"Get the rest of them out; there must be eight
hundred or so. Down to the docks before daylight,
suitable guards, and onto those two merchantmen
Grammeck commandeered. Have someone reliable,
Bartin say, handle it. The ships can pick up pilots and a
deck officer apiece from the rams, they've come into the
harbor. I want them sailing east by dawn, understood?"

No need for a decimation, Raj thought grimly. The
5th Descott had lost more than that, running the
gauntlet of the murder-holes of the gatehouse and in
the headlong charge that cleared the plaza for the men
behind them.

He looked down once more from the podium around
the fountain; only a day and a night since the town
meeting gathered here . . . now the square was filled with
soldiers. The 5th and the 2nd Cruisers still in neat ranks
before him; many of the others mixed by the surge over
the walls and the brief street-fighting that followed. Many
missing, already off among the houses. The only firing
came from the sector of wall still held by the Colonial
merchants, the burbling of their repeater carbines and
jezails as an undertone to the savage hammering of
Skinner long rifles. He didn't think that would take long;
he could see one of the towers from here, and squat
figures made stick-tiny by distance capered and danced
on its summit, firing their monstrous weapons into the air.
Every once and a while, a figure in Colonist robes
would be launched off the parapet to flutter in a brief

arc through the air. Some of the screams were audible this far away.

"Fellow soldiers," Raj said. "Well done." A cheer rippled across the plaza, tired but good-natured. "A donative of six months' pay will be issued." The next cheer had plenty of energy. "I won't keep you, lads; just remember we need this place standing tomorrow, not burnt to the ground. You've done your jobs, now the city — and all in it — is yours until an hour past dawn. All units dismissed!"

Behind them the gate-tower he'd stormed was fully involved, a pillar of flame within the round stone chimney of the building. With luck it wouldn't go beyond that . . .

The 5th Descott still stood in ranks before him, immobile as stone. Certain things had to be done by the forms. He nodded, and spoke again:

"Colonel Staenbridge."

"Sir."

"I have need of trustworthy men to guard key locations and apprehend certain persons tonight."

Thus missing the sack, one of the rare pleasures of a common soldiers' hard, meagre and usually boring life. Most of the troopers would think of it as a far worse punishment than being the lead element through the gate — which Kaltin Gruder had assigned the 5th on the unanimous insistence of officers and men.

"Are the 5th Descott Guards ready to undertake this duty?"

"*Mi heneral*, the 5th is always ready to do its duty." The sound that came from the ranks was not a cheer; more like a short crashing bark.

"Excellent, Colonel." He paused. "I see that the 5th's banner is absent. Please see that it is returned to its proper place immediately."

"*Mi heneral!*"

Mitchi sat and held up the hand-mirror and

preened, throwing a hand behind her tousled mass of red hair and arching her back. The necklace of gold and emeralds glittered in the lamplight between her full pink-tipped breasts. The tent was a warm cave in the night, light strong panels of tanned and dyed titanosauroid gut on a framework of skeelwood and bronze. All the furniture was similar, including the bed she and Kaltin Gruder shared, expensive and tough and very portable.

"You're vain as a cat," Gruder said, running a hand up her back. He was lying with one arm beneath his head. She shivered slightly at the callused, rock-hard touch. "Aren't you ever going to take the damned thing off?" There were red pressure-marks beneath it.

"I may be vain, but you stink of dog and gunpowder, Kaltin," she said tartly. "Mmmmm." He began kneading the base of her slender neck between thumb and forefinger.

"Well," he said reasonably, "I fought a murthering great assault action last night, did some hard looting, then worked my arse off all day keeping the city from burning down and getting the men back in hand. A busy man doesn't smell like a rose."

"Not too busy to find this," she said, turning and lying on his chest. She propped her chin on her elbows, and the jewels swung between them. "Or that little dog you found for Jaine."

"Or a good deal else," he agreed, chuckling. "Professional soldier's instincts. She'll need a riding dog on the march . . . How's she settling?"

"Jaine? Very well; she's got neat hands with my hair and clothes, she's clean and biddable. Sweet little thing, too, everyone likes her." She moved a leg over his hips and giggled. "*You're* not settled at all. I'd have thought you'd be worn out on the town matrons."

"I like my women smiling and running toward me, not screaming and running away," he said, putting his hands around her narrow waist and lifting her astride him. Her breath caught as she sank back on her heels and began to move.

"Besides," he went on, running his hands up and gripping her breasts, "as the wog saying goes: *Stolen goods are never sold at a loss.* Hard loot looked like a better way to spend the time, with fifteen thousand men inside the walls and running loose. Lineups."

Mitchi gave a complex shudder and threw back her head, stroking the hands that caressed her. "What's that sound?" she asked.

"That?" Gruder said.

A roar like angry surf was coming from Lion City. Louder than the town meeting had been, since all the gates were open. "That's a rarity, wench — some people getting what they deserve. Now shut up."

Syndic Placeedo Anarenz looked as if he was going to survive the wound the throwing-axe had put in his back, although the left arm might never be as strong again. Right now it was strapped to his chest by the Army priest-doctor's bandages. He stood as straight as that allowed, meeting Raj's eyes. The general's face might have been a Base Area idol rough-carved out of old wood, his eyes rimmed and red with fatigue.

"Your tame prince certainly predicted our fate accurately, *heneralissimo supremo*," Anarenz said bitterly.

Raj rubbed his chin; sword-callous rasped on blue-black stubble. "I don't think many infants were tossed on bayonets," he said mildly.

Or that many silver-haired elders got their brains beaten out, he thought. Not unless they were foolish enough to get between a soldier and something he fancied.

Lion City was orderly now, with infantry in *guardia* armbands on every corner seeing that their comrades went nowhere but to authorized taverns and knocking shops. Little remained from the previous night of rape, pillage and slaughter but the occasional gutted building, and not many of those. Guards had kept the major warehouses from damage, and the shipyards and other critical facilities; the rest of the town was missing most of its liquid wealth and small valuables, and several hundred young women smuggled out to the camp. They would probably be sold in a few days, at knock-down prices along with the households of the Colonial merchants and the magnates he'd put under proscription.

"Also," he went on, "I saw how your own guild reacted to my warning."

Placeedo Anarenz started slightly, and stared for a moment. "You," he breathed. "You were one of the guards?"

Raj nodded. "This —" he indicated the podium and the plaza "— is something of a reunion. Even the syndics are here."

They were standing under guard in front of the assembled citizens. It was a larger crowd than the town meeting, most of the adult population of Lion City. Much quieter as well, ringed with troops holding their bayonetted rifles as barricades; battered-looking men, many in remnants of militia uniform. Equally battered-looking women, in ripped and stained clothing hastily repaired or still gaping. Torches on poles lit their upturned faces, staring at him with dread.

Another building-block in the reputation of Raj Whitehall, he thought bitterly.

"I was a syndic," Anarez said. "Why aren't I down there with them?"

"Because you argued for opening the gates," Raj pointed out. "Also you're the next Mayor."

Anarenz grunted in shock, staggering until the two burly sailmakers at his side steadied him. Pain-sweat glistened on his forehead from the jostling that gave his wound.

"Why *me?*" he said. "I thought you'd have some bureaucrat ready . . . or one of our local arse-lickers who'd buy his way into your favor the way he did with the Brigade. De Roors is good at that."

Anarenz was a brave man. He still shivered slightly at Raj's smile.

"You actually care about the welfare of the citizens," the general said. "That makes you more predictable; men like de Roors don't stay bought. I'm going to need stability here. I'll be leaving plenty of the Administrative Service to oversee you, don't worry. Messer Historiomo to begin with, but he'll be taking over all occupied territory, and I've advised him to consult you."

Raj turned to face the wounded man. "There's a saying, Goodman — Messer *Alcalle* — Anarenz, back in the east. That the Governor's Chair rests on four pillars of support: a *standing* army of soldiers, a *sitting* army of bureaucrats, a *kneeling* army of priests, and a *creeping* army of informers. It's a settled way of doing things, and it functions . . . but here I need the active support of the people I'm liberating from the Brigade."

He nodded to the huddle of Syndics below the podium. "After this, I don't think the magnates of other cities will try to sit things out."

Aloud, he went on: "Citizens of Lion City!"

A signal, and the soldiers ripped the rich clothing from the former oligarchs of the town, leaving a group of potbellied or scrawny older men edging away from the bright levelled menace of the bayonets, and a few others trying hard to look brave — a difficult task, naked and helpless. There were a hundred or so of them, all the adult males of the ruling families.

"Here are the men," Raj went on, pointing, "who are the true authors of your misfortunes. Here are the men who refused to open the gates peacefully and exposed your city to storm and sack."

An animal noise rose from the crowd. Oligarchs were not popular anywhere, and right now the commons of Lion City needed a target for their fear and fury, a target that wasn't armed. De Roors turned and knelt toward the podium, bawling a plea for mercy that was lost in the gathering mob-snarl. A rock hit the back of his head and he slumped forward. The old Syndic who'd had his guard try to assassinate Anarenz spat at the mob, lashing out with his fists as work-hardened hands cuffed him into the thick of it. A knot of women closed around him, pried-up cobblestones flailing in two-handed grips. The others disappeared in a surge of bodies and stamping feet, dying and pulping and spreading as greasy stains on the plaza pavement.

"Spirit of *Man*," Anarenz shouted, pushing forward. "Stop this, you butcher! *Hang* them if you want to, that'll terrify the syndics of the other cities."

"No," Raj replied.

His voice cut through the noise much better than the sailmaker's did, and the mob were recoiling now — from themselves, as much as from what remained of the city's former rulers.

"No, doing it this way is better. The magnates elsewhere will know I've a much more terrible weapon to use against them than my army." He nodded to the crowd. "And *they* will know there's no going back; if the Brigade wins, it'll make an example of Lion City."

Anarenz looked at him with an expression more suitable for a man who'd stumbled across a pack of carnosauroids devouring an infant.

"For the *Spirit's* sake, is there *anything* you won't do to win your bloody war?" he shouted. "Anything?"

Raj's head turned like a cannon moving with a hand on its aiming-wheel. "No, Messer *Alcalle*," he said. "There's *nothing* I won't do to unite civilization on Bellevue, and end things like this forever. For the Spirit's sake."

Suzette sank down beside Raj and leaned her head against his shoulder. "You did what you had to do, my love," she said softly.

His hands knotted on the table, and the empty

bottle of *slyowtz* rolled away. The spray of plumb-
blossom on the label curled about a stylized H; it was
the Hillchapel proprietary brand. How long was it
since he'd been home?

"Only what you had to do."

Raj's arms groped blindly for his wife. She drew his
head down to rest on her bosom, rocking it in her arms.

lady whitehall is correct, Center said. **observe —**

I know! Raj cut in. Lion City rising behind him,
other cities closing their gates. Costing him men,
costing him time, neither of which he had to spare.

"I know," he said aloud.

"Shhhh, my love." The commandeered room was
quiet, only the light hissing of the lantern breaking the
silence. "You're with me now. No need to be the
General. Peace, my love. Peace."

For a moment the hard brilliance of another image
gleamed before Raj: the Old Residence seen in the
near distance, its wall towers and walls silent but
threatening simply for their enormous extent.

The vision faded. **yes,** said Center. **peace. for now.**

THE END

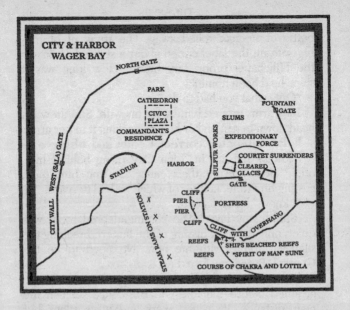

CITY & HARBOR WAGER BAY

- NORTH GATE
- PARK
- CATHEDRON
- CIVIC PLAZA
- FOUNTAIN GATE
- SLUMS
- COMMANDANT'S RESIDENCE
- EXPEDITIONARY FORCE
- COURTET SURRENDERS
- CLEARED GLACIS
- SULFUR WORKS
- STADIUM
- HARBOR
- GATE
- CLIFF
- PIER
- PIER
- FORTRESS
- CLIFF
- CLIFF WITH OVERHANG
- CITY WALL
- WEST (SALA) GATE
- STEAM RAMS ON STATION
- REEFS
- SHIPS BEACHED REEFS
- REEFS
- "SPIRIT OF MAN" SUNK
- COURSE OF CHAKRA AND LOTTILA

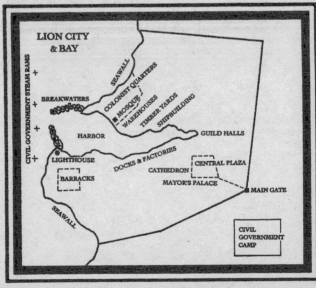

LION CITY & BAY

- CIVIL GOVERNMENT STEAM RAMS
- SEAWALL
- COLONIST QUARTERS
- BREAKWATERS
- MOSQUE
- WAREHOUSES
- TIMBER YARDS
- SHIPBUILDING
- HARBOR
- GUILD HALLS
- LIGHTHOUSE
- DOCKS & FACTORIES
- CENTRAL PLAZA
- CATHEDRON
- MAYOR'S PALACE
- MAIN GATE
- BARRACKS
- SEAWALL
- CIVIL GOVERNMENT CAMP

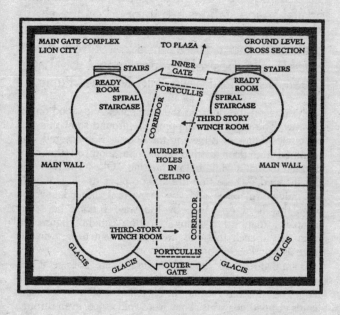

FALLEN ANGELS

Two refugees from one of the last remaining
orbital space stations are trapped on the North
American icecap, and only science fiction fans
can rescue them! Here's an excerpt from *Fallen
Angels*, the bestselling new novel by Larry
Niven, Jerry Pournelle, and Michael Flynn.

*   *   *

She opened the door on the first knock and stood out of
the way. The wind was whipping the ground snow in swirling circles. Some of it blew in the door as Bob entered. She
slammed the door behind him. The snow on the floor
decided to wait a while before melting. "Okay. You're here,"
she snapped. "There's no fire and no place to sit. The bed's
the only warm place and you know it. I didn't know you
were this hard up. And, by the way, I don't have any
company, thanks for asking." If Bob couldn't figure out
from that speech that she was pissed, he'd never win the
prize as Mr. Perception.

"I am that hard up," he said, moving closer. "Let's get it on."

"Say what?" Bob had never been one for subtle tech-
nique, but this was pushing it. She tried to step back but his
hands gripped her arms. They were cold as ice, even through
the housecoat. "Bob!" He pulled her to him and buried his
face in her hair.

"It's not what you think," he whispered. "We don't have
time for this, worse luck."

"Bob!"

"No, just bear with me. Let's go to your bedroom. I don't
want you to freeze."

He led her to the back of the house and she slid under
the covers without inviting him in. He lay on top, still
wearing his thick leather coat. Whatever he had in mind,

she realized, it wasn't sex. Not with her housecoat, the comforter and his greatcoat playing chaperone.

He kissed her hard and was whispering hoarsely in her ear before she had a chance to react. "Angels down. A scoopship. It crashed."

"Angels?" Was he crazy?

He kissed her neck. "Not so loud. I don't think the 'danes are listening, but why take chances? Angels. Spacemen. *Peace* and *Freedom.*"

She'd been away too long. She'd never heard spacemen called *Angels.* And— "Crashed?" She kept it to a whisper. "Where?"

"Just over the border in North Dakota. Near Mapleton."

"Great Ghu, Bob. That's on the Ice!"

He whispered, "Yeah. But they're not too far in."

"How do you know about it?"

He snuggled closer and kissed her on the neck again. Maybe sex made a great cover for his visit, but she didn't think he had to lay it on so thick. "We know."

"We?"

"The Worldcon's in Minneapolis-St. Paul this year—"

The World Science Fiction Convention. "I got the invitation, but I didn't dare go. If anyone saw me—"

"—And it was just getting started when the call came down from *Freedom.* Sherrine, they couldn't have picked a better time or place to crash their scoopship. That's why I came to you. Your grandparents live near the crash site."

She wondered if there was a good time for crashing scoopships. "So?"

"We're going to rescue them."

"We? Who's we?"

"The Con Committee, some of the fans—"

"But why tell me, Bob? I'm fafiated. It's been years since I've dared associate with fen."

Too many years, she thought. She had discovered science fiction in childhood, at her neighborhood branch library. She still remembered that first book: *Star Man's Son,* by Andre Norton. Fors had been persecuted because he was different; but he nurtured a secret, a mutant power. Just the sort of hero to appeal to an ugly-duckling little girl who would not act like other little girls.

SF had opened a whole new world to her. A galaxy, a

universe of new worlds. While the other little girls had played with Barbie dolls, Sherrine played with Lummox and Poddy and Arkady and Susan Calvin. While they went to the malls, she went to Trantor and the Witch World. While they wondered what Look was In, she wondered about resource depletion and nuclear war and genetic engineering. Escape literature, they called it. She missed it terribly.

"There is always one moment in childhood," Graham Greene had written in *The Power and the Glory*, "when the door opens and lets the future in." For some people, that door never closed. She thought that Peter Pan had had the right idea all along.

"Why tell *you*? Sherrine, we want you with us. Your grandparents live near the crash site. They've got all sorts of gear we can borrow for the rescue."

"Me?" A tiny trickle of electric current ran up her spine. But . . . *Nah*. "Bob, I don't dare. If my bosses thought I was associating with fen, I'd lose my job."

He grinned. "Yeah. Me, too." And she saw that he had never considered that she might not go.

'Tis a Proud and Lonely Thing to Be a Fan, they used to say, laughing. It had become a *very* lonely thing. The Establishment had always been hard on science fiction. The government-funded Arts Councils would pass out tax money to write obscure poetry for "little" magazines, but not to write speculative fiction. "Sci-fi isn't literature." *That* wasn't censorship.

Perversely, people went on buying science fiction without grants. Writers even got rich without government funding. *They couldn't kill us that way!*

Then the Luddites and the Greens had come to power. She had watched science fiction books slowly disappear from the library shelves, beginning with the children's departments. (That wasn't censorship either. Libraries couldn't buy *every* book, now could they? So they bought "realistic" children's books funded by the National Endowment for the Arts, books about death and divorce, and really important things like being overweight or fitting in with the right school crowd.)

Then came paper shortages, and paper allocations. The science fiction sections in the chain stores grew smaller. ("You can't expect us to stock books that aren't selling." And they can't sell if you don't stock them.)

Fantasy wasn't hurt so bad. Fantasy was about wizards

and elves, and being kind to the Earth, and harmony with nature, all things the Greens loved. But science fiction was about science.

Science fiction wasn't exactly outlawed. There was still Freedom of Speech; still a Bill of Rights, even if it wasn't taught much in the schools—even if most kids graduated unable to read well enough to understand it. But a person could get into a lot of unofficial trouble for reading SF or for associating with known fen. She could lose her job, say. Not through government persecution—of course not—but because of "reduction in work force" or "poor job performance" or "uncooperative attitude" or "politically incorrect" or a hundred other phrases. And if the neighbors shunned her, and tradesmen wouldn't deal with her, and stores wouldn't give her credit, who could blame them? Science fiction involved science; and science was a conspiracy to pollute the environment, "to bring back technology."

Damn right! she thought savagely. We do conspire to bring back technology. Some of us are crazy enough to think that there are alternatives to freezing in the dark. *And some of us are even crazy enough to try to rescue marooned spacemen before they freeze, or disappear into protective custody.*

Which could be dangerous. The government might declare you mentally ill, and help you.

She shuddered at that thought. She pushed and rolled Bob aside. She sat up and pulled the comforter up tight around herself. "Do you know what it was that attracted me to science fiction?"

He raised himself on one elbow, blinked at her change of subject, and looked quickly around the room, as if suspecting bugs. "No, what?"

"Not Fandom. I was reading the true quill long before I knew about Fandom and cons and such. No, it was the feeling of hope."

"Hope?"

"Even in the most depressing dystopia, there's still the notion that the future is something we build. It doesn't just happen. You can't predict the future, but you can invent it. Build it. That is a hopeful idea, even when the building collapses."

Bob was silent for a moment. Then he nodded. "Yeah. Nobody's building the future anymore. 'We live in an Age of Limited Choices.'" He quoted the government line without cracking a smile. "Hell, you don't *take* choices off a list. You *make* choices and *add* them to the list. Speaking of which, have you made your choice?"

That electric tickle . . . "Are they even alive?"

"So far. I understand it was some kind of miracle that they landed at all. They're unconscious, but not hurt bad. They're hooked up to some sort of magical medical widgets and the Angels overhead are monitoring. But if we don't get them out soon, they'll freeze to death."

She bit her lip. "And you think we can reach them in time?"

Bob shrugged.

"You want me to risk my life on the Ice, defy the government and probably lose my job in a crazy, amateur effort to rescue two spacemen who might easily be dead by the time we reach them."

He scratched his beard. "Is that quixotic, or what?"

"Quixotic. Give me four minutes."

WARNING: THIS SERIES TAKES NO PRISONERS

Introducing

CRISIS OF EMPIRE

David Drake has conceived a future history that is unparalleled in scope and detail. Its venue is the Universe. Its domain is the future of humankind. Its name? *CRISIS OF EMPIRE*.

An Honorable Defense
The first crisis of empire—the death of the Emperor leaving an infant heir. If even one Sector Governor or Fleet Admiral decides to grab for the Purple, a thousand planets will be consigned to nuclear fire.
David Drake & Thomas T. Thomas, 69789-7, $4.99 ____

Cluster Command
The imperial mystique is but a fading memory: nobody believes in empire anymore. There are exceptions, of course, and to those few falls the self-appointed duty of maintaining a military-civil order that is corrupt, despotic—and infinitely preferable to the barbarous chaos that will accompany its fall. One such is Anson Merikur. This is his story.
David Drake & W. C. Dietz, 69817-6, $3.50 ____

The War Machine
What's worse than a corrupt, decadent, despotic, oppressive regime? An empire ruled over by corrupt, decadent, despotic, oppressive *aliens* . . . In a story of personal heroism, and individual boldness, Drake & Allen bring The Crisis of Empire to a rousing climax.
David Drake & Roger MacBride Allen, 69845-1, $3.95 ____

Available at your local bookstore, or send your name and address and the cover price(s) to: Baen Books, P.O. Box 1403, Riverdale, NY 10471.

S.M. STIRLING
and
THE DOMINATION OF THE DRAKA

In 1782 the Loyalists fled the American Revolution to settle in a new land: South Africa, Drake's Land. They found a new home, and built a new nation: The Domination of the Draka, an empire of cruelty and beauty, a warrior people, possessed by a wolfish will to power. This is alternate history at its best.

"A tour de force."   —David Drake

"It's an exciting, evocative, thought-provoking—but of course horrifying—read."
—Poul Anderson

MARCHING THROUGH GEORGIA
Six generations of his family had made war for the Domination of the Draka. Eric von Shrakenberg wanted to make peace—but to succeed he would have to be a better killer than any of them.

UNDER THE YOKE
In *Marching Through Georgia* we saw the Draka's "good" side, as they fought and beat that more obvious horror, the Nazis. Now, with a conquered Europe supine beneath them, we see them as they truly are; for conquest is only the *beginning* of their plans . . . All races are created equal—as slaves of the Draka.

THE STONE DOGS
The cold war between the Alliance of North America and the Domination is heating up. The Alliance, using its superiority in computer technologies, is preparing a master stroke of electronic warfare. But the Draka, supreme in the ruthless manipulation of life's genetic code, have a secret weapon of their own. . . .

"This is a potent, unflinching look at a might-have-been world whose evil both contrasts with and reflects that in our own." —*Publishers Weekly*

"Detailed, fast-moving military science fiction . . ."
—Roland Green, *Chicago Sun-Times*

"*Marching Through Georgia* is more than a thrilling war story, more than an entertaining alternate history. . . . I shall anxiously await a sequel."
—Fred Lerner, *VOYA*

"The glimpses of a society at once fascinating and repelling are unforgettable, and the people who make up the society are real, disturbing, and very much alive. Canadian author Stirling has done a marvelous job with *Marching Through Georgia*."
—Marlene Satter, *The News* of Salem, Arkansas

"Stirling is rapidly emerging as a writer to watch."
—Don D'Ammassa, *SF Chronicle*

LARRY NIVEN'S KNOWN SPACE IS AFLAME WITH WAR!

Once upon a time, in the very earliest days of interplanetary exploration, an unarmed human vessel was set upon by a warship from the planet Kzin—home of the fiercest warriors in Known Space. This was a fatal mistake for the Kzinti of course; they learned the hard way that the reason humanity had decided to study war no more was that humans were so very, very good at it.

And thus began The Man-Kzin Wars. Now, several centuries later, the Kzinti are about to get yet another lesson in why it pays to be polite to those hairless monkeys from planet Earth.

The Man-Kzin Wars: Featuring the Niven story that started it all, and new Known Space stories by Poul Anderson and Dean Ing. • 72076-7 • $4.95 ⎯⎯⎯

Man-Kzin Wars II: Jerry Pournelle and S.M. Stirling weigh in with a tale of Kzinti homelife; and another adventure from Dean Ing. • 72036-8 • $4.99 ⎯⎯⎯

Man-Kzin Wars III: Larry Niven's first new Known Space story in a decade as well as new novellas from Poul Anderson and Pournelle & Stirling. • 72008-2 • $4.99 ⎯⎯⎯

Man-Kzin Wars IV: Donald Kingsbury on just why we fight the Kzin and a story by S.M. Stirling and Greg Bear on the Man Who Would Be Kzin. • 72079-1 • $4.95 ⎯⎯⎯

Man-Kzin Wars V: An all new Jerry Pournelle and S.M. Stirling short novel plus aliens a la Thomas T. Thomas. • 72137-2 • $5.99 ⎯⎯⎯

All featuring fantastic series covers by Stephen Hickman!

Available at your local bookstore. Or you can order any or all of these books with this order form. Just mark your choices above and send the combined cover price(s) to: Baen Books, Dept. BA, P.O. Box 1403, Riverdale, NY 10471.

Name: _____

Address: _____

_____